BETTER LATE THAN NEVER

L.A. WITT

Copyright Information

This is a work of fiction. Names, characters, places, and incidents are either the product of the author's imagination or are used fictitiously. Any resemblance to actual persons living or dead, business establishments, events, or locales is entirely coincidental.

Better Late Than Never

First edition

Copyright © 2025 L.A. Witt

Edited by Cecily Green & Mackenzie Walton

Cover Art by Lori Witt

All rights reserved. No part of this book may be reproduced or transmitted in any form or by any means, electronic or mechanical, including photocopying, recording, or by any information storage and retrieval system without the written permission of the publisher, and where permitted by law. Reviewers may quote brief passages in a review. To request permission and all other inquiries, contact L.A. Witt at gallagherwitt@gmail.com

Ebook ISBN - 978-1-64230-399-5

Paperback ISBN - 978-1-64230-360-5

Hardcover ISBN - 978-1-64230-361-2

HUMAN POWERED CREATOR

No artificial intelligence was used in the making of this book or any of my books. This includes writing, co-writing, cover artwork, translation, and audiobook narration.

I do not consent to any Artificial Intelligence (AI), generative AI, large language model, machine learning, chatbot, or other automated analysis, generative process, or replication program to reproduce, mimic, remix, summarize, train from, or otherwise replicate any part of this creative work, via any means: print, graphic, sculpture, multimedia, audio, or other medium. This applies to all existing AI technology and any that comes into existence in the future.

I support the right of humans to control their artistic works.

ABOUT BETTER LATE THAN NEVER

Lieutenant Commander Connor Marks is starting over. His kids are grown up. His divorce is final. He's settled into his new command and a beautiful house in Spain. Nothing left to do but move forward.

And maybe explore his bisexuality after all this time.

Unfortunately, his options are limited. He doesn't speak enough Spanish to connect with the locals, and getting involved with other service members can get... complicated.

When HM1 Alex Barlow stumbles across a hot guy on a hookup app, of course it's that gorgeous new physician Alex sees all the time at the hospital. Of course he's looking to hook up with a guy. Of course he's exactly Alex's type.

The only problem is that Connor is an officer while Alex is enlisted. The fraternization regs are crystal clear—they can't even be friends, never mind hook up.

Never mind be *more* than hookups.

But the Navy's regs can't cool the chemistry sizzling between Alex and Connor.

And nothing—not even their own stubbornness or

Alex's toxic, persistent ex—can stop them from falling in love.

CW: Discussion of past abuse, brief on-page violence; combat-related PTSD.

CHAPTER 1

CONNOR

Judgment of Absolute Divorce.

A Decree of Divorce is hereby granted to Aimee Lynn Marks and Connor Daniel Marks. The marriage existing between the parties is hereby terminated, effective the date signed below.

The document on my screen went on for a few more paragraphs of dense legalese, but I didn't need to read the whole thing. The important part was... it was over. Our marriage. All the legal steps. Everything. We'd been separated for almost three years, and as of today, our divorce was final.

My lawyer had sent me a PDF to read and submit to Navy Legal and personnel since the hard copy would take a week or so to reach me here in Spain. I'd forwarded it to those departments, and really, I hadn't even needed to read the document itself; my lawyer's email had said it all:

Connor,

The divorce decree is attached. Congratulations—you're a free man!

Jennifer

I was a free man.

In my silent office, I sat back in my chair, closing my eyes as I released a long breath. Relief settled over me as profoundly as it had when I'd received word that I was heading home from each of my two boots-on-the-ground combat deployments a lifetime ago. It was a different kind of relief, though—as volatile as my marriage had been at times, there'd never been the fear or the threat of IEDs and rocket attacks. No blood. No violence.

Still, this relief brought with it a deep calm. A sense that life was going back to something like normal. No more fighting. No more worrying what the next day would bring.

Aimee and I wouldn't be staying in regular contact after this. She had her own career, and we'd split the money from the sale of our house last year. She was fine financially and hadn't wanted alimony even after I'd offered. What she wanted more than anything was a clean break. Apart from things like the kids' college tuition or eventual weddings, we had no reason to continue communicating. Both boys were adults, and while she and I were reasonably civil, there was too much animosity for us to stay friends. Honestly, that was fine with me. I also wanted a clean break.

Still, I hoped she'd be happy going forward; she was a good person and a great mom to our sons, and even if we'd been a mismatch, we'd had good times together. I genuinely wished her the best.

I wished *myself* the best, too. My life was mine again. I was single. I'd jumped on these overseas orders to kick off the solo life, and now, three months after arriving in Spain... I was *free*.

I opened my eyes and stared up at my office ceiling. I'd been married since I was nineteen. A father since I was eighteen.

Now I was forty. Single. Living on another continent for at least four years.

So... now what?

I let my gaze drift down to my desk where my phone lay dormant beside my keyboard. I'd perused a few hookup apps since I'd arrived in Rota, but I hadn't made a profile. I was admittedly nervous about using them for a few reasons, not the least of which was that the people on said apps were either locals or part of the military community.

It was risky, casting a line within the military community, especially in places like this where that community was quite small. Far too many opportunities to create an awkward and potentially rank-threatening situation with the wrong person. I'd worked too damn hard to get where I was only to derail my career by inadvertently swiping right on someone in my chain of command, someone who was married, or someone who was enlisted. Or all three.

So... yeah. Getting involved with people in the military on a base like this was risky at best.

The locals presented a different challenge. I'd swiftly discovered after arriving here that this area's population generally spoke limited English if they spoke it at all, which many didn't. A few did, but it wasn't as common as I'd naively expected. And why should they? This was Spain, not England. The problem was that my limited Spanish—which I was working on!—didn't really lend itself to the kinds of conversations I'd want to have with a potential hookup.

See, I wasn't just looking to get laid. I wanted to meet a *man*. After all these years, I finally had the freedom to explore the side of myself I hadn't noticed until long after I'd had a ring on my hand. It was going to be awkward enough getting physical with another guy for the first time in my life; a language barrier would only make that worse.

I scratched my neck and sighed into the silence of my office. Maybe coming here had been a bad idea after all. Maybe I should've taken orders in the States.

A knock at my door startled me, but I recovered. "Come in."

The door opened and one of my corpsman, HM3 McCoy, poked her head in. "Sir, your 1100 appointment is here."

Right. Right, I still had patients to see.

"I'll be right there. Thank you, HM3."

She nodded, slipped out, and shut the door.

I gave the divorce decree on my screen another glance. Then I closed the document, pocketed my phone, and headed out to see my next patient.

The single life could wait a little longer.

An hour after I left work, I was more optimistic that I had, in fact, made the right choice in taking orders to Spain. The dating/hookup pool was still discouraging, but the pool I was sitting beside? The one in the walled villa I was renting for a song out by the ocean in Sanlúcar de Barrameda? It was perfect.

I'd enjoyed a quick swim to unwind from a long day,

and now I was relaxing in the shaded cabana with an ice-cold beer in my hand. The beautiful house, manicured garden, and turquoise swimming pool didn't solve the issue of how to put myself out there in this country, but I really couldn't complain.

Thumbing through one of the dating apps I'd found, I hemmed and hawed about how to do this. The only non-military profiles I'd found so far that indicated they spoke English were students at the nearby university in Cádiz. *Way* too young. Once I filtered out anyone under thirty, the well dried up substantially.

I sighed and put my phone down beside me on the table. Gazing out at the sparkling cerulean water, I took a pull from my beer. Maybe I needed to work a little harder on learning Spanish. The base had a few classes. The one I'd taken had been helpful for day-to-day life, but it hadn't taught me much about connecting with men for sex or dating.

¿Cómo se dice, I want to try sucking dick?

The thought made me snort.

But then my gaze drifted back to my phone. Maybe I was going about this the wrong way. Maybe instead of figuring out how to approach guys, I should put myself out there and see if anyone came to me. Then I could follow their lead. Hell, I could come right out and say I was new to this, had never been with a man, and really wanted to find out what it was like.

In my job—both the military and as a physician—I'd always had the attitude of "take charge and get it done," but maybe in this situation, I needed to fall back into the mindset I'd had as a medical student: when in doubt, defer to someone with more experience.

Fuck it. Why not?

I put my beer down and snatched up the phone again. I pulled up the app that had seemed the most promising. Or, well, the one that had seemed most intuitive to navigate, anyway. After a couple more second thoughts, I finally bit the bullet and made an account.

I was a free man.

And now, for the first time in my adult life, I was putting myself out there.

Please don't let this blow up in my stupid face...

CHAPTER 2
ALEX

God, these apps were trash.

Okay, that wasn't entirely fair. They were great when I lived someplace where I was fluent in the common language, and where the people who spoke the same language as me weren't all military or military-adjacent.

Rota... did not qualify as *either* of those things.

There were fewer than 10,000 Americans here, and a pretty good portion of those were dependents. Of the actual service members and civilian contractors, a whole lot *less* than 10,000 were both single *and* gay or bi men. Of those vanishingly rare unicorns who *were*, an irritating number were off limits because the Navy was a goddamned buzzkill sometimes.

Take, for example, the commanding officer of one of the airwings. He was jaw-droppingly hot—all the swagger and sexiness of a fighter pilot, and well into his silver fox era. Like me, he wasn't out. The only reason I knew he was queer at all was because I'd run into him in, of all places, a club in Barcelona. That had been one of the hottest nights of my life, after which we'd sworn each other to secrecy, gone our separate ways, and never even let ourselves make eye contact in the produce aisle at the commissary. If anyone ever found out about that, our careers would be *done*.

Fuck's sake. Maybe I should've been an officer after all. At least then I could hook up with another officer.

Not that I made a habit of hooking up with anyone who wore a uniform. Though Don't Ask Don't Tell was a distant memory, it had been firmly in place when I'd first enlisted, and I was still spooked by the experiences of some friends who'd had bad experiences coming out in the post-DADT military. Most had been fine—I knew several who were quite openly married to same-sex partners without any fuss, including the CO of the hospital where I worked—but it had only taken a few to commit me to staying in the closet until I retired.

That commitment to keeping my sexuality and my personal life private had been galvanized last year. I'd had an ill-advised fuck-buddy-turned-boyfriend-I-guess arrangement with a civilian contractor for a little over a year before it had gone tits up. The less said about *that* shitshow, the better, but it had definitely spooked me away from getting involved with guys on-base. Americans, anyway; the Spaniards all seemed happy to keep things discreet, and the American and Spanish forces—for all we shared a base—didn't interact as much as people thought. So I could fuck my way through the Spanish Marines and no one in my chain of command would ever know.

Fine by me. Those guys were *hot*.

I glanced up from my phone to make sure no one had slipped into the waiting area while I'd had my nose buried in the app. Nope. Slow day in Radiology, which was never a bad thing. I'd spent enough time in combat zones to eagerly embrace the boredom of a lull, considering I knew all too well what the alternative was. Sitting here with my boots on my desk and a hookup app on my screen was not the worst way I could spend my day.

I could've done without the sexual frustration, though. At least when I was busy, I wasn't thinking (much) about how empty my bed was these days. Some of that was my own fault; lately I hadn't been putting a lot of effort into fishing in my very, very limited puddle. Some of it was... Well, that very limited puddle.

Eighteen more months, I reminded myself as I pointlessly scrolled the stupid app. Eighteen more months, and then I'd be retired. I'd be a civilian, and I'd be stateside, and I'd be—

Whoa, wait, what the fuck?

I sat up so fast my phone almost tumbled out of my hands. I steadied it, and for a panicked second, I was terrified I'd accidentally swiped the profile. The last thing I needed was to alert the guy that I'd found him on the app.

Because that photo...

No, that's not...

Is it?

Something about him was familiar, though. That wasn't uncommon here, of course—I'd found a lot of guys on the app who I also recognized from the base. It was almost a game sometimes to find an American and see if I knew who he was.

But this photo pinged me differently than *"oh, hey, that's the redhead at the post office"* or *"ah, I had a feeling that one cop was into dudes."*

I pulled my phone closer, peering intently at the image. It was the typical shirtless bathroom selfie, and he had a sexy body, that was for sure. A few tattoos. Smooth abs.

Narrow waist. This wasn't someone who'd have any trouble passing the Physical Readiness Test, that was for sure.

Nothing about his physique tipped me off about who he was, though.

No, it was the hint of his jaw. Most of his face and head were cut off, but he'd left enough to show his sharp jawline, and that tickled something in my brain. Hit some synapse that recognized him as more than a generic rando who I'd seen around base.

I tapped the profile and, very carefully avoiding an accidental swipe, thumbed through the photos. Still nothing of his face, which—no shit. Most guys were discreet on this app until they'd at least made a connection. There were a couple more angles of his jaw, though, and the familiarity held fast.

One shot of his arm showed a tattoo that tripped another synapse. I covered part of the screen with my hand so that only the bottom of the design showed—sort of like how his cropping of his face only showed his jaw—and my heart jumped into my throat.

"You have got to be shitting me," I whispered. I knew that ink. I fucking knew it because I'd seen it peeking out from beneath a short sleeve.

A short *camouflage* sleeve.

But...

No. *No*, that wasn't him. No way.

I moved away from the photos and read the profile.

Connor. Age: 40.

Distance: Less than 1 km away.

My heart was absolutely slamming into my ribs now.

No. Fucking. Way.

Recently divorced, the intro read, *and recently arrived in Rota. Never been with a man before but I'd like to give it a try. Casual and discreet for now. Open to more later with the right guy.*

I put my phone down and covered my face with both hands, almost muffling my groaned, "Are you *serious?*"

Because between the jaw, the tattoo, the location, and the description, if that wasn't Lieutenant Commander Marks...

Oh my *God*. Just passing him in the hallway almost made me trip over my own feet. Like that airwing CO, he was unreasonably sexy. Built like someone who actually enjoyed going to the gym. A charming smile that made any male-attracted person in the vicinity lose their train of thought. Brown eyes so dark they were almost black. Hair that was nearly as dark except for the dusting of gray around the edges. There was a rumor that his female patients—including the married ones—always put a little extra effort into their appearance when they were going to be seeing him. He'd only been here about three months, and I was pretty sure half the base was buzzing with, *"Have you seen the hot new doc at the hospital?"*

So, yeah. Dude was fucking gorgeous.

And he was *queer*, too? Queer, and looking to hook up with a guy?

I usually preferred men who had experience, but if Marks wanted someone to guide him through the motions of sex with a man—holy fuck yeah, I volunteered as tribute. Especially since, being divorced, it was highly unlikely that he was a blushing virgin. He probably knew his way around having sex. This would just be sex with a few adaptations.

Sex with the gorgeous doctor with gray-sprinkled dark hair and tattoos and that smile that turned me completely stupid.

The gorgeous doctor... who was an officer.

"Fucking hell," I grumbled.

Why couldn't I find an *enlisted* guy who was this attractive? I mean, okay, there were plenty, but they were always straight, married, in my chain of command, or became deeply *un*attractive the instant they opened their mouths (looking at you, MA1 Weyland).

"I'm so stupid," I told myself, and I shoved my phone into my pocket before raking my hand through my short hair. "So fucking stupid."

Maybe I needed to ping Isidoro again. He was a Spanish Marine who I'd hooked up with quite a few times; his English was about as good as my Spanish, but we managed well enough for some scorching hot nights together. He was still stationed here, wasn't he?

I didn't know for sure. Mostly because we hadn't texted or fucked in…

In three months.

Since I'd zeroed in on that hot ass doctor who'd made me forget that other men even existed.

Yeah. I was stupid.

And I wasn't going to get any less stupid any time soon because *Lieutenant Commander Marks wanted to find out what it was like to bang a dude.*

Fuck. My life.

It was bad enough being a grown-ass man on the cusp of forty and having a crush like teenager. Seeing him on that app, seeing him as everything I would ordinarily swipe right on so fast I'd break my damn phone—that was just mean.

Ugh. I'd already known I needed to distract myself from him, but now I needed to step that up. Text Isidoro again. Maybe hop a train to Sevilla and hit up the clubs there. Or take a trip to Madrid or Barcelona. Could my liver handle another weekend on Ibiza? Kinda seemed like it was worth a try.

Yeah. That was what I'd do. Book a ticket to—

The waiting area door opened, and a Marine who looked about fourteen stepped in.

Well, it wasn't the distraction I wanted, but it was a distraction.

I'd take it.

"Guess I should watch where I'm going next time," the Marine said with a laugh as he gingerly pulled his blouse back on. "How long do you think I'll be on light duty?"

"That's up to your primary care manager," I said blandly. "All I do is take the pictures."

He held my gaze, then chuckled, and a moment later, he was on his way back downstairs to his PCM. I hadn't told him that he had slightly-worse-than-hairline fractures to his radius and ulna—that kind of diagnosis was above my paygrade, even if the fractures were clear as day on the X-rays I'd just taken.

The kid didn't seem all that surprised when I'd pulled the images up on the screen to make sure they'd come out all right. He'd come to medical because his wrist was sore and swollen after a fall yesterday, and both he and his PCM had been concerned he'd fractured it. Now he was on his way back to her with confirmation that, yep, he'd fractured it.

I didn't think he'd need surgery, but he would be in a cast for the next six to twelve weeks. Been there, done that.

I shuddered at the memory. At least he'd just taken a fall at work. It probably hadn't been the best day of his life, but he'd been joking about it and didn't seem overly bothered apart from the pain. If I had to guess, the injury was less a result of tripping over a toolbox and more that he and some of his buddies had been bored and horsing around. Marines—what can you do?

Sailors did shit like that, too, which was how I'd wound up on light duty a few enlistments ago after a sprained ankle. The two times I'd broken bones? Well, those had been years ago, but I relived the incidents in my nightmares more often than I cared to think about.

I absently flexed my long-healed left hand and tried not to think about the past. I rolled my shoulders beneath my utilities, which were suddenly a little too hot in this office that had suddenly become way too stuffy.

Fuck.

I sat down at my desk again and fanned my face with a file folder. I still had like five hours left before I could bust out of here; time to pull my focus away from bad memories.

It wasn't even that broken bones triggered me. I wouldn't have lasted as a radiologic technologist—or even a corpsman at all—if I couldn't cope with broken bones. That memory was just tender today thanks to a rough night.

Stupid nightmares.

I tossed the folder aside and wiped a hand over my face. Maybe it was time to see a therapist about this. They had civilian therapists who could do televisits now, right? I could probably find one back in the States who'd help me sort all this shit out. I'd pay for it out of pocket, too; even after the Brandon Act, I wasn't taking the chance of my insurance telling my chain of command about it.

What can I say? After eighteen-plus years on active duty, I had trust issues.

That was something to look into after work, though. Today, I had to get my head together enough to concentrate.

But of course, the universe wasn't done fucking with me today.

When I'd stumbled across Lieutenant Commander Marks's profile earlier, I'd been too off-balance to think of much beyond *"goddammit, that hot guy I can't have is queer and available."*

The problem with a pool of men this small, though, was that if I saw him on the app, that meant other guys would too. Which, in and of itself, was fine. The issue was that I personally knew of at least one other man who really, really didn't need to know that Marks was queer and available. I should've known it wouldn't take him long to find out.

And I definitely should've known he'd be sauntering into Radiology to rub it in my face.

Sure enough, about the time I was finally calming down from my brief mental short-circuit, Tobias Miller walked in. As he always did, because fuck him, he didn't bother knocking and swung my office door open hard enough for it to bang against the wall, startling me out of my damn skin. He knew I was jumpy about shit like that, which was exactly why he did it.

As I peeled myself off the ceiling, he dropped into the empty chair across from my desk, phone in hand and a familiar shit-eating grin on his face. God. Just what I needed. He was in jeans and a black golf shirt, and I hated that he looked good in them. I hated that his longish and neatly arranged salt-and-pepper hair was still sexy, and that his graying beard accentuated his sharp jaw and high cheekbones. I hated that when he eventually turned around and walked out, his jeans would be clinging to that ass the way they always did, because he was clearly still going to the gym as religiously as he always had.

He was such a gorgeous man. Shame it was only skin-deep.

Still grinning like the asshole he was, he jiggled his phone at me. "You been on the app today?"

I gritted my teeth, irritated with the intrusion, and I played casually stupid. "No, I haven't. Why?"

He smirked, because of course he did, and tapped his screen. When he showed it to me, I wasn't at all surprised to see Marks's profile. About the only thing Tobias did at work these days besides bother me was prowl around online for his next piece of ass.

I sat back, trying to affect nonchalance. "Okay?"

Tobias snickered. Then he very pointedly swiped right, winked at me, and pocketed his phone. "Seems like your type. I'm surprised you haven't—*ooh*, right. You *can't*, can you?"

It took so damn much work not to roll my eyes. That would only egg him on. "No, I can't. He's all yours." I half-shrugged, then nodded toward my computer screen. "And I've got work to do, so…"

He huffed a laugh. "Yeah. Looks like you're really busy here today." But, mercifully, he got up. "You know, *our* paygrades are still allowed to hook up."

"Yep. They sure are." I stood and gestured toward the door. "Goodbye, Tobias."

He scowled, shoulders dropping as he apparently realized his attempt to make me jealous hadn't worked, and neither had the thinly veiled suggestion that we fuck again. I knew him. Whether he was interested in Marks or not, he knew Marks was my type. In his mind, him connecting with Marks would get under my skin, either because I'd be jealous that Tobias could have him and I couldn't, or because I'd be jealous that Tobias was sleeping with someone else. It had been almost a year, and he was still deluding himself into thinking I'd eventually get desperate and want him back.

Not a fucking chance, slimeball.

At least he left after that, which meant he was probably on his way to a meeting or something. As soon as I was alone, I shuddered at the memories of our "relationship." The sex with him had always been consensual, but it had also left me feeling... uncomfortable in ways that were hard to describe. I'd had some incredibly casual and even anonymous hookups over the years, but only Tobias had ever left me feeling like I was just a hole to put his dick in. And that was before we'd started kind-of-dating, and he'd started fucking with my head as much as he'd fucked my body.

I chafed my arms. God, I couldn't believe I'd wasted so much time and energy on that asshole. Never again. Not with him, and not with anyone else attached to the base, because the worst part about Tobias was that we worked in the same building. I couldn't get away from him any more than I could get away from—

Alarm straightened my spine in the same moment cold dread started wrapping around it.

Lieutenant Commander Marks.

I was frustrated as all hell because I couldn't get away from him. I couldn't touch him, but I also couldn't avoid seeing him around the hospital.

The same hospital where Tobias worked.

Tobias, who'd swiped right on Marks.

"Oh, *fuck*," I murmured into my empty office.

The thing was, Tobias wasn't a bad-looking guy at all, and he could be charming as hell when he wanted to be.

Hell, he'd gotten me to date him even when I'd sworn off relationships until I was out of the military. The love-bombing was easy to see in hindsight, but at the time, not so much.

And I was experienced with men. Marks wasn't a clueless virgin, but he was new to the queer scene, and even older guys could get bamboozled by someone who said the right things and played the right games.

Tobias knew how to say the right things and play the right games.

I rubbed the back of my neck and exhaled as that cold dread wound tighter around my spine. I knew it wasn't just me. Isidoro had experienced Tobias's bullshit. My buddy Crawford had been with the asshole a couple of months ago; he hadn't realized until afterward that Tobias was the guy who'd fucked with me, and he'd been with him one time and one time only. We'd both had the same experience with him—namely, that Tobias knew how to toe that line before being gently pushy turned into coercion. He *would* take no for an answer, but he was just manipulative enough that he wasn't easy to say no *to*. I'd gotten the impression he saw limits and boundaries as goals. I'd found it annoying, as had Crawford and Isidoro, but none of us had left the experiences feeling like any boundaries had been violated, per se —just brushed up against and pushed.

There wasn't much we could do in terms of getting his chain of command involved. He hadn't technically done anything wrong, and anyway, he was a civilian contractor, so he'd have to step a lot farther out of line than that to even get a talking to. All we could do was pass his name around to anyone we knew and, whenever we saw new guys pop up on the apps, extend that information to them.

And now I knew for a fact that Tobias had right-swiped

on Marks. That didn't mean Marks had reciprocated, but he might. Hell, most guys would.

So what the fuck was I supposed to do?

I could reach out to Crawford and have him private message Marks. That felt like outing Marks, though. Even though he had a public profile, he didn't have his full name or face on it. Would he appreciate me letting someone else on base know he was queer?

"Shit," I whispered into the silent office. I couldn't just... *not* give Marks a heads up about Tobias. He didn't seem like the kind of guy who was easily manipulated, but he was new to being with men. An unscrupulous guy telling him, *"No, no, this is* totally *what gay men do"* could easily persuade him to do things he normally wouldn't.

Shame I couldn't get to Marks first and help him figure out his boundaries *before* someone like Tobias got his hands on him.

Which... it occurred to me how ironic it was that if Marks and I hooked up, we could both be severely disciplined just because of our ranks. Meanwhile Tobias could operate like a predator who knew exactly where all the lines were, and no one could touch him.

Fuck it. One way or another, I needed to talk to Marks. I'd probably die of embarrassment, and he probably would too, but at least he'd know about who Tobias really was. What he did with that information was up to him.

My chance came about an hour later when I was on my way back from doing an ultrasound in the emergency department. I was halfway from the ER to the elevators when Lieutenant Commander Marks came around the corner, brow furrowed as he read something on a chart.

I stopped so suddenly my boot squeaked on the floor. "Uh, Lieutenant Commander—do you have a minute, sir?"

He halted, his head snapping up, and he blinked. "Um…" He glanced down at the chart in his hand. "I've got a patient." Furrowing his brow, he asked, "Is it urgent?"

"No. No, sir, it's—" I cleared my throat. "It can wait."

He eyed me uncertainly. "Uh…"

"I just need to—" Why was it so damn hard to access the thoughts I'd neatly arranged for this conversation? Probably because I hadn't expected it to be happening right fucking now. And because while the overhead fluorescents weren't flattering for anyone, they picked out his high cheekbones and the sparkle of silver throughout his short, dark hair. And I—

"HM1?" he prodded, sounding curious and maybe a little nervous himself.

Fuck. What was I—oh, right.

I shook myself. "It's not urgent, sir. Just—I'll be in Radiology for the rest of the day unless I get called back to…" I gestured over my shoulder at the ER. "If you have a minute…"

He still seemed off balance and even a little suspicious, but then he glanced at his watch. "Like I said, I've got a patient. I'll, uh, I'll come by Radiology afterward."

I nodded sharply. "Thank you, sir."

Then we continued in opposite directions, and I just hoped we could do this without both of us dying of embarrassment.

CHAPTER 3

CONNOR

It was a genuine miracle I'd remembered how to speak during that conversation with HM1 Barlow. His initial words had barely registered at all because my mind went blank the second we made eye contact.

He was one of the first people I'd noticed when I'd checked into this duty station, and given how attractive I found military uniforms, that said a lot. There were some seriously hot men and women stationed here, but HM1 Barlow—oh hell. Camouflage utilities were sexy on most people, but they had no business looking as good as they did on him. And those blue eyes should *not* have screwed with my balance or my ability to speak.

Especially not when he actually needed to speak with me and I needed to have my military bearing. Maybe some dignity too. Those were both in severe short supply whenever I saw him.

Thank God, I'd managed to catch up and not make an ass of myself.

But now he wanted to talk with me? Alone?

I mean, people in this hospital had to talk to each other. That wasn't unusual. I'd probably had conversations with everyone in this building already and I hadn't even been here that long. Nature of the beast.

It was the part where he wanted to speak privately that unnerved me, and for the next hour, every spare second I had was spent trying to suss out what was on his mind.

Was this some confidential situation with a patient? Except that wouldn't have been an *"at your earliest convenience"* type of thing. And he wouldn't have been flustered like that.

A conflict with someone else in the hospital, maybe? One of my subordinates? But that wouldn't make sense. Though I outranked him, we weren't in each other's direct chain of command. I'd send patients to him for imaging, and he'd send results back to me. His department was about as attached to mine as the pharmacy or obstetrics; we communicated and sent patients back and forth, but we didn't answer to each other. Unless it *was* about one of my subordinates? Or one of his, if he had any?

Utterly delusional wishful thinking had me wondering if this was something personal. The way he'd blushed and stammered, I mean…

Yeah, right. He was probably straight. I wasn't out. He had no reason to think I'd be receptive to anything.

And, oh yeah, there was that whole rank thing.

What a shame, I thought as I headed upstairs to Radiology. Because I'd had a thing for him ever since I'd checked into this command.

He was close to my age, that much I knew. I'd seen him in his dress whites at a recent change of command ceremony, and his service stripes indicated he'd been in for at least sixteen years. Plus he'd lost the baby face that a lot of the junior enlisted and even some of the senior enlisted guys still had.

Keyword, Connor: Enlisted.

He's enlisted. Off fucking limits.

I rolled my eyes. Yeah, he was off limits, but that hadn't stopped me from getting tongue-tied over his gorgeous blue eyes. It definitely hadn't stopped me from wishing the Navy would change the uniform policy and require us to wear covers indoors because then I wouldn't have to notice his sandy blond high-and-tight.

I shook myself. I was almost to Radiology, and I needed to get my head together. At the very least, not get an untimely and unprofessional hard-on.

Outside the door, I paused for a deep breath, then laughed at myself for being such a dumbass. We were adults. Well past the ages of awkward crushes and ridiculous shit like that. This was probably a professional conversation that he just wanted to have away from prying ears. They happened all the goddamned time.

Steeling myself, I went inside.

HM1 Barlow was nowhere to be seen, but there was a woman in civvies fidgeting in a chair. She gnawed her thumbnail and kept glancing toward the door that led back to the X-rays and other imaging equipment.

She glanced at me, and her eyes widened a little. I flashed her a quick smile, but it didn't seem to help. Gesturing at the door, she asked, "Did they call you up to...?"

I cocked my head, but then my brain caught up. "No, no." I shook my head. "I just need to get some paperwork for someone's reenlistment package."

The lie worked, and she relaxed, though not completely. I didn't blame her; her child was probably in the back being X-rayed. Must not have been terribly young if they'd gone in without her, but I knew that anxiety. I'd seen it in my patients, and I'd been there myself as the worried dad at the doctor's office or hospital. *Many* times.

"You two realize this is your fault, right?" I'd said to my sons last year, pointing at the gray coming in at my temples.

"Don't blame us." Landon had shrugged with all the flippancy he'd absolutely inherited from me. *"Blame physics."*

The memory almost drew a laugh out of me, but I kept it back so I wouldn't upset the nervous mother.

A moment later, the door opened, and a boy who was probably nine or ten stepped out. Not super young, but right about the age of *"Mom, I can do it—I don't need you to come with me."* And I knew the instant I saw him that he'd been sent up for a chest X-ray; the puffy eyes and miserable expression spoke of some kind of bug. Then he coughed into his elbow—a painful, rattling cough. Yeah, he had something going on in his lungs. Poor kid.

HM1 Barlow was right on his heels, his expression full of empathy. "I sent the images down to his pediatrician. As soon as he has a look at them, he'll let you know."

The woman nodded, trying to both smile at him and grimace sympathetically for her son. "Thank you." Then she herded the boy out into the hallway. He coughed again, the sound almost making my chest hurt too.

HM1 Barlow cleared his throat, sounding quite a bit healthier than the son but almost as nervous as the mother had looked. When I turned to him, his expression backed it up.

Fuck. This wasn't going to be a comfortable conversation, was it?

I shifted my weight. Despite the uniform regs forbidding us from putting our hands in our pockets, I almost did just because I was so damn nervous. "You, uh... You wanted to see me?"

"Yes, sir." He swallowed. "Let's, um..." He tipped his head toward the small office beside the waiting area, and we went in there.

From here, he'd be able to see through the window if anyone came into the waiting area, but we'd have privacy, especially after he'd shut the door.

Barlow leaned against his desk. He started to fold his arms across his chest, but then dropped his hands to the desk's chipped laminate edge, where he started drumming his fingers rapidly. "Listen, um..." He cleared his throat again. "This is more personal than professional, sir, but..."

I shifted a little and leaned against the door. "Okay. So... off the record?"

He studied me, then nodded, and he seemed to struggle to look me in the eye. "Yeah. Off the record." He took a deep breath. "I want to preface this by saying I don't want to cause any embarrassment or awkwardness, but I feel it's necessary to bring it up because there are some things you should be aware of."

Well, this definitely wasn't a direction I anticipated. I had no idea what to say, so I just silently waited for him to continue.

His jaw worked, and he stared at the floor between us. Then he sighed, took his phone out of his pocket, found something on it, and handed it to me. "I really, really don't want to make anything weird, but I found this."

I took the phone but almost dropped it because I

instantly recognized my profile on the screen. Heat flashed through me, especially into my face, and I handed the phone back. "Right. Yeah. I..." I gulped. "There's other service members on there, though." I shrugged as casually as I could. "Is it... Is there a reason I shouldn't be on it?"

"No. No." He put the phone aside and scratched the back of his head. "No, it's... There's a lot of us on it. It's— *I'm* on it, too. I'm not judging."

He was on it?

No shit, he's on it—how do you think he found your profile, idiot?

But still. He was on it. Which meant he was—

Oh for fuck's sake. Of course the guy I'd jerked off to more times than I wanted to admit to was actually queer. And he was on that app, which meant he was on the prowl, which meant...

I had to fight back a groan that was equal parts embarrassment and frustration.

"Listen, there's..." He hesitated, then picked up his phone again. "I wasn't even going to say anything." He was thumbing through something on the app, I thought. "The reason I asked to talk to you was that I wanted to give you a heads up to steer clear of him."

Barlow again handed me the phone, this time with someone else's profile on the screen. As I took it, confusion pushed its way past everything else. I peered at the screen, skimming over the bio and a couple of the photos. The guy in the profile was probably attractive, but I was too busy mentally short-circuiting to notice. He had about five years on me, and according to the app, he was less than one kilometer away. On-base, then. Big surprise.

Passing back the phone again, I asked, "So... what's his deal?"

Barlow suddenly looked uncomfortable in a very different way. Not from this conversation, but from the topic. My neck prickled—oh, shit. What *was* this guy's deal?

Barlow rested his hands on the edge of the desk again, and he met my gaze through long lashes. "To be perfectly blunt, Tobias is not a man I would trust with someone who doesn't have experience."

I wanted to bristle and snap back that I was hardly a virgin. I just hadn't been with a man. On the other hand... I mean, fuck. There was a reason I'd been nervous about experimenting with other guys for a while, even while Aimee and I had been separated. I'd told myself I was just playing it safe and not taking chances with the Navy deciding it was adultery, but I'd been legally separated, so... not adultery. I'd just been nervous.

I shifted my weight against the door. "He's not safe?"

"He's not..." Barlow looked almost pained as he considered his answer. "I don't know that I'd call him dangerous, but I wouldn't call him safe, either, if that makes sense."

My stomach curdled. "Seems like his chain of command should hear about it."

Barlow scoffed. "He's a civilian contractor."

"Oh." I rolled my eyes. "Of course he is."

"Right? And I mean, he hasn't done anything... actionable, I guess? He's a dick—enough of one that I felt the need to warn you about him—but he's not..." He trailed off as if he wasn't sure how to finish that.

"I get it," I said quietly. "And, um... I appreciate the heads up." I hesitated. "And the discretion?"

He locked eyes with me. "I wouldn't out you. I assume I can trust you not to do the same?"

"Absolutely." I tried not to think too hard about why I was suddenly out of breath. "I won't say a word to anyone."

"Thanks."

"Of course," I rasped. "And, um… Thanks for the heads up, HM1."

"Don't mention it, sir."

Then I left his office, and spent the rest of the day trying to remember how to concentrate.

CHAPTER 4

ALEX

Through a series of clumsily translated WhatsApp messages, Isidoro and I reconnected, and yes, he was still in the area. Apparently he'd been gone for a few weeks to visit family in the Basque region, and after he'd come back, he'd started seeing someone. That had lasted all of a month, though, and he was now as single as I was.

Perfect.

And it was perfect. That Friday night, we shook the walls of his apartment in El Puerto de Santa Maria, the next town over from Rota. All the tension and frustration I'd been carrying all week long went down his throat, then an hour or so later, into his ass. By the time I collapsed beside him, shaking all over and drenched in sweat, I was exactly as wrung out as I'd desperately needed to be.

He sank onto his stomach, and his beard scuffed on the pillow, almost muffling the slurred Spanish profanity rolling off his talented tongue.

I gave a quiet, breathless laugh, but his words and the brush of his beard on the pillowcase jolted me uncomfortably back into reality.

You're not him.

What the hell, Alex? Who did you think you were fucking?

Oh, I knew who I'd been fucking. I'd just... gone somewhere else in my mind for a moment, and that was where I'd been when I'd come in Isidoro. *Both* times.

Fucking hell.

I murmured to Isidoro that I'd be right back, kissed him on the shoulder, and then levered myself up out of bed. I stepped into the small bathroom and got rid of the condom, and as I washed my hands, I met my own gaze in the mirror.

What is wrong with me?

Isidoro was one of those passionate, attentive lovers who could usually keep my focus like no other. When his hands or mouth were on me, or when one of us was balls deep in the other, there was no thinking about anything except him and the things he did to my body. If he was kissing me, I was right there in the moment until he was good and done with me.

But tonight...

For fuck's sake, Alex. Stop pining after what you can't have.

I rolled my eyes, dried my hands, and schooled my expression before returning to the bedroom.

Isidoro had rolled over and cleaned himself up, and now he was lying there on his back, gazing at me with hooded eyes.

God, he was sexy. His olive skin was tanned and his near-black hair was cut short. That toned, tattooed body—oh, fuck me, I could lick every inch of it. I had, in fact. I had tonight.

Except tonight, I'd spent the whole time imagining I was exploring someone else's body with my lips and tongue.

Something must've registered on my face, because Isidoro's sultry expression shifted to one of concern. "¿Hay algo mal?"

Though my Spanish was limited, I'd picked up enough to know that one—*Is something wrong?*

Fuck. Not the time to be wearing my frustration over Lieutenant Commander Marks on my sleeve. Especially because, knowing Isidoro, he'd immediately worry that Tobias was the problem. He had firsthand experience with the asshole, though he'd been smarter than me and only hooked up with him twice, and I could tell when he was worried Tobias was sinking his claws into me again. We may have just been casual hookups, but that didn't mean we didn't care about each other.

I forced a smile and rejoined Isidoro in bed. "Nothing's wrong." I stroked his short hair and claimed a kiss before he could ask any further. He relaxed, and we just lay like that, kissing lazily and sliding our hands all over each other.

At least when we were making out like this, I couldn't mistake him for anyone else. Not Marks, anyway. While American service members had to be cleanshaven, Spanish Marines were allowed to have neatly trimmed beards, and oh, fuck, they rocked that look. The highlight of my commute each morning was coming through the gate and being greeted by a sexy, uniformed man with a beard. Too bad Isidoro wasn't on sentry duty anymore; those winks and grins we'd exchange while he "checked my ID" could carry me through the most awful shift.

He was here right now, though, and the coarseness of his beard kept me from forgetting whose tongue was teasing mine.

The problem was that it didn't keep me from thinking about whose tongue *wasn't* exploring my mouth. Whose hands *weren't* drifting all over my skin. Whose body *wasn't* pressed up against mine.

Seriously, what was *wrong* with me? I'd been attracted to men I couldn't have before. It was frustrating, but not like this. And this was hardly the first time I'd thought about a guy I wanted while I was with someone else. I'd come, and I'd be satisfied, and the man I was with wouldn't be any the wiser.

This time, I wasn't satisfied, and Isidoro had caught on that I wasn't entirely here. Yeah, I had him distracted for now, but sooner or later, he was going to ask again.

He didn't keep me waiting long.

He drew back and met my gaze, his lips slightly swollen and his eyes very concerned. "¿Hay algo mal?" he asked again.

I shook my head, trailing my fingertips along his collarbone. "No. Estoy bien."

His eyebrow arched. Maybe we didn't share a language—his English and my Spanish were equally limited—but body language was hard to misinterpret. Then he sighed and let go of me. I had a second to worry I'd pissed him off and he was about to get up and boot me out, but then he grabbed his phone off his nightstand and came back.

The screen added a cool glow to his face and lit up his eyes and his furrowed brow as he typed something. I didn't mind; this was the only way we could communicate beyond the most basic phrases we both understood. Most of the conversations we'd had went like this.

After a moment, he showed me the screen. Beneath where he'd typed out something in Spanish, the app had translated it to:

> You are distracted. Have I done something wrong?

Guilt twisted beneath my ribs. I felt bad enough about not being completely here; that he was blaming himself hit hard.

I gently took his phone, tapped out a message in English, then handed it back so he could read the translation.

> Work is distracting. I'm sorry. It's not you.

He frowned as he read. When he flicked his eyes up to meet mine, I honestly couldn't tell if he believed the lie or not. I hoped he did; I didn't feel good about lying to him, but I was too ashamed of the truth. Too embarrassed that I was wrapped up in someone like a teenager with a crush on a rock star who didn't know he was alive. And honestly, it would've been cruel, telling him that this whole time we'd been in his bed, I'd been thinking about Lieutenant Commander Marks. Sometimes lying really was the kindest approach, and this was one of those times.

Isidoro took the phone back and typed again. When he showed me the screen:

> Is it only work?

Was I wearing my guilt on my face or something? Fuck. I typed back:

> Problems with someone else at the hospital. It will be fine. Just frustrating.

That was technically the truth, though I still hated being this cagey.

Fortunately, it seemed to be enough, and Isidoro put the phone aside. Pulling me back into his arms, he murmured something that I thought roughly translated to, *"I can make you forget."*

And for the most part, he did. I was too close to forty for three orgasms in a night, but Isidoro was barely thirty, and he definitely had a third one left in him. A third one that I made sure to wring out of him slowly and decadently until *he* forgot that my mind had ever been anywhere but here.

When I finally left for the night around 0200, I was satisfied that he thought he'd distracted me from everything.

But the whole way back to my apartment in Chipiona, all I could think about was Lieutenant Commander Marks.

CHAPTER 5

CONNOR

The air in my cabana was thick with the lingering heat of the afternoon. The sweetness of the flowers in my yard and the smell of my freshly cut grass mingled with the sharpness of the weed my neighbors were smoking on the other side of the high wall.

It was almost 2200 and the sun was still up, though it was easing toward the horizon and turning the sky warm shades of red and purple. I still wasn't used to that—the sun setting so late in the evening. That was harder to adapt to than things like siesta and when restaurants were and weren't open. They didn't affect how things ran on-base, but it had been eye-opening the first time I'd tried to go to a Spanish supermarket during siesta or find something to eat at what I normally thought of as dinnertime. Culture shock was a strange thing, that was for sure.

I'd get used to it all. Every place had its own rhythm and its own sounds, and I'd adapt to Spain just like I had all my other duty stations. Probably just in time to move, but better late than never, I guess. And definitely better than trying to adapt to a combat zone again.

I sat back in the cabana chair and enjoyed the warmth, though I tempered it with a cold beer. I gazed out at the gorgeous yard surrounding the pool. It was perfectly manicured, and the only credit I could take for that was paying for it; my rent included pool maintenance and garden service. Both workers had been here earlier today, and they did amazing work. Everything was beautiful.

Beautiful, and... empty.

Outside the walls of the villa, the world was alive with the soft sounds of people enjoying their evenings. My neighbors talking and—from the sound of it—playing some of kind of game. The café half a block away was hitting its dinner rush, and the scrape of chairs on pavement, the clatter of silverware, and the chatter of people filtered through the peaceful night to me.

Inside these walls, though, everything was silent. Even the pool was glass smooth, not sloshing against the sides like it sometimes did. All the gentle noise outside emphasized how utterly quiet and still everything was in here.

It made me fantasize for a hot minute about what it would've been like to be stationed here when the boys had been younger. They'd no doubt be splashing in the pool, loving that there was still daylight—even if it was fading—this late at night. It was a Saturday night in July, so it wasn't like they'd need to go to school the next morning. They could enjoy the pool without burning to a crisp like they would in the afternoon; their mother and I had cursed them both with the fair skin of my Irish and her Swedish ancestry.

The thought of them swimming here right now made me smile, but then it tugged at my heart. They weren't little boys anymore. Quinn was twenty-two and living with his girlfriend. Landon had turned twenty just before I'd left for Spain. He was living with his mom while he went to a community college, and then he'd probably transfer to a university. Quinn would be graduating from college next year, and I doubted he'd wait that long before proposing to Savannah.

I took a deep pull from my beer. I was proud of my sons, and I was close to both of them, but I still regretted how much of their lives I'd missed, especially early on. I'd been in Iraq when Landon was born. In Afghanistan when Quinn had spent a week in the hospital with a respiratory bug. After that, I'd shifted gears and gone to medical school, so at least I wouldn't be deploying for a while, least of all to combat zones. Didn't mean I was the most present father, though, especially when I started my rotations.

I'd done my level best to make up for lost time. During my two shipboard deployments later on, I'd been in constant contact with them, and I'd even managed to have Aimee fly out with the boys to meet me in port a couple of times.

But I'd still missed so much.

And now I was missing them. As kids, as adults; I just missed having my sons nearby and being able to talk to them without working around time zones.

I even caught myself missing Aimee. Not the fighting, just... having her here. Having *someone* here.

Closing my eyes, I pushed out a long breath. I was just lonely. Of course I missed my kids, but when I found myself truly longing for my ex-wife to be with me—that was when I knew there was more going on here. For the last three years before we'd separated, Aimee and I couldn't even be in the same room without my hackles going up. In the three years since, the anger had mostly died away, and if anything, I was mildly annoyed or totally neutral about her. The animosity was gone, but so was the affection.

So yeah, when I started wishing she could be here, that meant I was getting desperate.

I looked at my phone, which was lying on the table beside my beer bottle.

The app I'd downloaded was still on it, though I hadn't looked at it since my conversation with HM1 Barlow. Admittedly, what he'd said had spooked me. And all the reasons I'd been reluctant to make a profile still existed. The language barrier with the locals. The political and disciplinary risks with the military community.

I was curious, though. And lonely as hell.

It had also occurred to me several times that Barlow had a profile on that app. It meant he was queer and single too. It meant that, had we not been what we were in the Navy, I *might* actually have had a snowball's chance in hell with him.

Curiosity had been tugging me toward the app ever since we'd talked, but I hadn't indulged. My profile was still active, but I hadn't been back on. It wasn't a good idea. Why torture myself with seeing his photos and reading his preferences when I couldn't have him? Also, it felt kind of intrusive. It was a public profile, but if I knew it was him…

Then again, he'd found my profile, so if he didn't want me to see his, he'd likely have blocked me. Right?

Either way, the siren's call of his profile was tough to ignore.

And maybe I was just a little too lonely and masochistic tonight, but I finally caved. I picked up my phone and opened the app for the first time in days.

Before I could hunt down the hot corpsman, though, I

realized I had some notifications. I'd turned off push notifications—I hated those on *any* app—so I hadn't noticed them until now.

Three were private messages. Unsurprisingly, two were very obviously spam. Delete. Delete.

The third, though...

I sat up a little as I peered at my screen. I recognized that profile photo. And the username.

Tobias.

Holy shit. That was the guy Barlow had been warning me about. And he'd messaged me already?

I tapped the message, more curious than anything.

> Hey, saw your profile! I remember stepping out into the gay scene. Isn't easy! Happy to help you find your footing. Or we can just have a good time. (wink emoji)

I couldn't decide if my skin was crawling because of the message itself—if there was some creepy subtext—or if it was Barlow's warning that had me regarding him warily. Both, maybe? Because Barlow had seemed really uneasy about Tobias. Enough that he'd felt compelled to approach me and warn me about him. That wasn't something he'd just pull out of his ass, was it? Stirring up drama? Keeping me from connecting with Tobias? It wasn't like he even knew me—why would he care if I hooked up with someone?

Everything about our conversation had struck me as genuine, from his warnings about Tobias to his discomfort with talking to me about it. So he probably wasn't full of—

An instant messenger window popped up. I jumped, nearly dropping my phone.

When I recovered, I realized the message was from Tobias.

My heart pounded as if he'd just materialized here in my backyard even though his location showed as twenty-six kilometers away in Jerez de la Frontera. I could ignore him. Block him. Pretend I'd never seen the message.

Curiosity prodded me. More than anything, though, my gut said to listen to Barlow.

So, I closed the messenger without reading it and I blocked Tobias's profile. I felt weird about that, but also like it was the right decision. Barlow didn't know me, but something about Tobias had rattled him enough to come say something, and listening to him felt like erring on the side of caution.

I was still curious about Barlow himself, though, so I pulled up the search function.

He wasn't hard to find. Filtering out profiles to just English-speaking trimmed the results by about eighty-five percent, leaving just a handful of locals and a smattering of Americans. Narrowing it further by age—eliminating the twenty-somethings and over fifty—left only two pages of results.

And *that* profile, I was pretty sure, was Barlow's.

The photo showed a shirtless white man with broad shoulders and tattooed biceps. I'd never seen Barlow's upper arms, so I had no idea if he had ink, but something told me that was him.

The location showed him as being nine kilometers away in Chipiona. I hadn't been to that town, but I drove by the exit for it every day on my way to work. It was close. Too damn close.

Still, I tapped the profile and thumbed through the photos. Like me, he hadn't included any face pics, but as I looked at what he had provided, recognition definitely grew. Especially once I got to some of the fully clothed shots.

There was one where he had on a T-shirt with an open button-up over it, and something about the way that shirt sat hit the same note as how his camouflage blouse fit him.

He wasn't ripped like some of the guys on this app. Slim enough to meet the military's requirements, but no six-pack or anything like that. Same as me. That made him even more attractive, if I was honest; the thought of getting naked with a man who'd be right at home in a men's fitness magazine intimidated the hell out of me.

I switched back to the text part of his profile and started reading, telling myself I was just looking for ideas for my own profile.

I'm in my late 30s. Single and looking to stay that way, but I'm always down for a good time. One-time hookups, fuck buddies, or someone to take off with for a weekend in Barcelona or Ibiza—I'm your man. I'm not out in my day-to-day life, so discretion is a must. I'll be discreet for you too, but don't come looking for someone to cheat with.

My mouth had gone dry for some reason, and I took another swallow of beer. I'd never been much for partying and clubs, but the thought of hitting up the gay club scene had intrigued me ever since I'd found myself a single man. Were there clubs near here? Except that probably wasn't safe, given the proximity to the base. Some of the other cities nearby? Or maybe up in Madrid? Or... Barcelona? Ibiza?

With HM1 Barlow?

I laughed aloud at that. Yeah, right. The best I could

hope for was to bump into him in a club and get to watch him with other men.

That... oh, fuck. Goose bumps sprang up all over me, and I shivered despite the heat of the evening. God, I wished...

I shook myself and kept reading.

The next section made me gulp—*What I'm Like in the Bedroom*.

I caught one word—switch—before I closed the profile, then the app, and sat back in my chair as I drained what was left of my beer. I really, *really* shouldn't read that part. I'd only drive myself even more insane, and it *would* cross the line into intrusive.

Closing my eyes, I pressed the empty but cold bottle against my forehead. I needed to stop doing this to myself. HM1 Barlow was about as off limits as a person could be without being my direct superior or subordinate. The military strictly forbade even the slightest fraternization between officers and enlisted, and it didn't matter why.

What I needed to do was get my ass to another city, hit up a club, and find my footing there. Connect with someone who wasn't military. Weren't there some areas in Málaga with a lot of British expats? They wouldn't be attached to the military and they'd speak English. Seemed like a good place to start. All I had to do was get over there, get to a gay bar, and...

And...

Then what?

I deflated a bit. Tipping my head back against the chair, I looked around. The sun had set, and darkness settled over my yard, broken up only by the porch light and the glow of various neighbors' houses. The evening was still full of the sounds of people dining nearby, but that was mostly muffled by my pounding heart.

What would I *do* in a club? I'd been a married father well before I'd turned twenty-one, so even when I'd gone to clubs after basic training or during A-school, it had just been to drink and have a good time with my friends. Same when I was deployed on a ship. There'd been plenty of married officers *and* enlisted who cheated their way through every port call, but I'd never done more than drink and get loud. While I may not have been the best husband in the world, I'd been absolutely faithful to my wife.

So here I was, forty goddamned years old, thinking about stepping on to the gay club scene where I'd be surrounded by experienced men half my age. I was going to make an ass of myself, wasn't I?

I closed my eyes again and swore into the humid silence.

What I really needed was someone to go with me, like when I'd gone to bars with the guys during A-school. Someone I could trust to point me in the right direction, give me a primer on what to do and what not to do, and hell, even tell my dumb ass what to wear.

"Someone to take off for a weekend in Barcelona or Ibiza"—the words echoed in my head in HM1 Barlow's voice—*"I'm your man."*

I stared up at the night sky. That wasn't against the rules, was it? Officers and enlisted weren't allowed to fraternize, but if we just *happened* to be at the same club and we just *happened* to started talking to each other...

Squirming in my chair, I knew this was a terrible idea. It would be a professional risk, and it would probably break my stupid brain that already wouldn't stop record-scratching every time HM1 Barlow crossed my mind.

There were two big reasons, however, why I knew I'd broach the subject with him anyway.

One, because I had no idea what else to do and I was getting desperate.

And two…

Because fuck me, I *wanted* to.

CHAPTER 6

ALEX

Friday night's roll in the hay with Isidoro had been a hot one, but it felt like a distant memory on Monday morning. Every bit of distraction he'd wrung out of me before I'd gone home wasn't doing me a damn bit of good anymore, and it had nothing to do with him or Lieutenant Commander Marks.

I never spent the night with hookups, and nights like last night were the main reason why. Horrific but familiar nightmares had shaken me out of a restless sleep at least three or four times before my alarm had gone off. Halfway to work, I'd had to pull over and calm myself down, calling on every coping mechanism I had to push away the tentacles of an impending panic attack.

An hour after I'd mustered for work, I'd had to drag out all those coping mechanisms once again, and I could only be grateful no one had been in Radiology right then. Luckily, I'd pulled myself together before any patients had come in, but it had been a close call. I'd even managed to slip away to change out of my sweaty utilities; good thing we all kept extra clothes on site in case someone puked or bled on us.

A few hours later, I was still jittery and off-balance, but I doubted anyone noticed but me. After years of dealing with this bullshit—not to mention fighting to keep it out of anyone's sight—I was a seasoned veteran (so to speak) at pretending I was fine. And by this point, I *was* more or less fine. If anything, I felt a little like I was trying to function after a sleepless night and skipping a couple of meals—lightheaded, struggling to concentrate, kind of shaky. PTSD was a constant companion, and I was as used to it as anyone could get, but it wasn't fun.

I'd be all right, though. Especially once I got home and didn't have to *pretend* to be all right anymore.

For now, I had patients.

"If these are actually safe," the young Sailor said suspiciously, "why do you leave the room every time you turn it on?"

I offered what I hoped was a reassuring smile. "Because you're only getting three images taken. I use it on a couple dozen people per day every day."

He didn't look reassured. "But if it's safe..."

"It's safe in small doses. The exposure I would get if I stayed in the room for every image I took over weeks and months would definitely be dangerous." I paused. "You take Motrin, right?"

He snorted. "Good ol' Vitamin M." He wasn't wrong—the military issued Motrin for every goddamned thing from an acute injury to recovery from major surgery. Vitamin M, indeed.

"And you only take what you're prescribed, right?"

The Sailor nodded.

"Right. But if you took the whole bottle at once, it would be toxic, wouldn't it?"

He pursed his lips, clearly seeing where I was going

with this but not liking that he'd been wrong. "Maybe that means Motrin is toxic, then."

It took a lot of work to not roll my eyes. Calling on every ounce of professionalism and military bearing I possessed, I blandly said, "Anything is toxic in a high enough dose." Then I stepped back. "All right, hold still. One more image, and we're done."

I went into the next room, and as I pushed the button for the X-ray to do its thing, I finally indulged in that eyeroll. For the millionth time, I was glad this hospital didn't have an MRI machine. Instead, we sent patients out in town to Spanish hospitals for MRIs, which meant *they* could deal with the concerned conspiracy theorists worried about radiation (there was none), carcinogenic contrast dye (it wasn't), and the magnets rearranging DNA strands (they didn't). Oh, the stories their translators told after some of those appointments...

With the Sailor's X-rays finished, I took the lead apron from him and sent him on his way. I transmitted the images to his doctor along with my notes, and that was that. Then I headed out into the waiting area to see if anyone was waiting.

There was, and I did *not* expect the person in question to be Lieutenant Commander Marks.

Fuck. Because I wasn't already wildly off-balance.

"Oh. Uh..." I stammered, then remembered myself. "Good morning, sir." Sometimes I hated the formality of rank, but it did keep some distance between us that I desperately needed right now.

"Good morning, HM1." He held my gaze, but then flicked his eyes away. "I, uh... I wanted to ask about something." He gulped. "Related to our last conversation."

Aww, fuck. So much for professional distance.

And did we have to do this now? While I was still reeling from last night and this morning's fuckery?

Apparently so.

I cleared my throat and gestured for my office. "Sure. Yeah. Let's, um... Let's sit in there." It was more cramped than the waiting area, but offered a modicum of privacy.

With the door shut, we settled in. Though I was far too restless to sit, I needed the desk as a buffer and to hide my shaking legs, so I took a seat behind it. Marks took the guest chair, and he looked about as nervous as I felt.

"Okay." I folded my hands on the desk to keep them still. "What do you need, sir?"

"I, um..." He lowered his gaze and scratched the back of his neck. Then he dropped his hand into his lap and looked right at me. "Listen, I'm pretty sure I found *your* profile."

The heat that rushed through me was not helping this situation. The last thing I needed was to know that Lieutenant Marks knew all about what I liked in bed. Or that he'd seen some of those photos; they weren't revealing per se because I valued my career and privacy, but they were suggestive too. Isidoro had straight up told me he'd jacked off to one of them. *Several* times.

"I don't want to make you uncomfortable," Marks said quickly. "I, uh..." His face turned red and he couldn't hold my gaze anymore. "I'm sorry—that was not the smoothest way to start this conversation."

Smoothest? Why would he care about being smooth with me? It wasn't like we could—

Oh. Oh, fuck. He wasn't... was he?

Before I could go too far down that steamy rabbit hole, he blurted out, "I really want to try the whole club scene. The, uh... The gay club scene." His blush deepened and he raked a hand through his short, dark hair. "I'm just so fucking clueless about all of it."

I blinked, both because I couldn't believe the direction this was going, and because I wasn't sure what to make of Marks being this flustered. He always seemed so cool and composed, but right now? Not so much.

"Where, um..." I cleared my throat again. "Where do I come in, sir?" The formality helped to remind me where we stood, but it didn't help *much*.

He pressed his lips together, then finally met my gaze. "There was a line in your profile. About... About going to places like Barcelona and Ibiza. I, um... I got the impression that isn't to check out the architecture."

I coughed a laugh as some warmth rose in my own face. "I mean, some people probably *do* go to Ibiza for the architecture."

"But something tells me you don't." Though he was still flustered, he seemed to look right into me. All the way past my professional façade and military bearing to those booze-blurred memories of Ibiza that had nothing to do with architecture.

"No," I rasped. "I don't."

"Right. And I... I want to try places like that."

"Not for the architecture?"

"Not for the architecture." He shifted a little, still clearly nervous. "I know where the lines are. With..." He tapped the insignia on his camouflage blouse. "Ranks. We can't fraternize."

I reached for my water bottle. My tongue was suddenly sticking to the roof of my mouth. Some of that was lingering from my earlier panic attack and the stubborn jitteriness, but some of it? *Not* from earlier. Oh, what I wouldn't have given to fraternize with this man. Given half the chance and

I'd have locked the door, dropped the blinds, and fraternized with him right over my damn desk.

After a sip of water, I croaked, "So, what? You want some guidance? Which clubs to go to?"

"I... Kind of?" He chewed his lip, a gesture that had no business being that sexy. "I mean, we can't go places together. But if we were in another city and we happened to cross paths in a club, there's nothing that says we can't talk to each other. Or that you can't give me a few pointers about what the fuck I'm supposed to do in a place like that."

Ooh, hell.

"I, uh... I guess..." I needed some more water, not that it helped much. "That's true. I don't think anyone would be surprised if we ran into each other and started talking." I drummed my nails rapidly on my desk. "And if someone saw us in a place like that, I doubt they'd have any inclination to rat us out."

He eyed me quizzically, then seemed to catch on. "Because they'd have to admit they were there too."

I nodded. "In my experience, the people most likely to out someone or get them into trouble are also the ones most afraid to out themselves." I gave a quiet, caustic laugh. "Self-loathing is a hell of a drug."

"That's true," Marks said. "So, if we *did* just... *happen* to run into each other in a place like that..." He inclined his head and raised his eyebrows.

Why did I feel like there wasn't enough air in this room? But not in the same way there wasn't enough when I was having a panic attack? Enough to make me dizzy, but not enough to send me spiraling.

"I don't see why not." I shrugged, hoping I looked more chill about this than I was. "If we, uh... If we happen to be in the same place at the same time." The word "sir" lodged in my throat. I wasn't sure why. Or maybe I was, because... fuck. Marks looked at me. I looked at him. Was his heart thumping as hard as mine was? Were we on the same wavelength? And did he have any idea how absolutely insane it would drive me to watch him bumping and grinding with men who weren't me? To be the one helping him get in that close to those men?

Goddammit.

On the other hand, getting to watch him in that environment would be hot as hell, and it was the closest I'd ever get to him, so why not?

I swept my tongue across my dry lips and pretended not to notice that *he'd* noticed. "I... was thinking I might go up to Sevilla this weekend. There's a club there. Castillo de Danza." I shifted nervously, grateful for the desk between us because, yeah, just thinking about this was making me feel some kind of way. "Maybe I'll hit it up on Saturday night."

Surprise sketched across his face, but it was quickly replaced by understanding. And interest. "Castillo de Danza, huh? And Sevilla?" He tilted his head. "You don't go to Málaga?"

"Oh, I do. But Sevilla's closer."

He frowned. "Closer means a bigger risk of running into..." He circled his finger in the air as if to encompass the hospital where we worked.

I laughed softly. "You haven't traveled much outside of this area yet, have you?" I paused. "And this is your first overseas duty station, isn't it?"

Marks blinked. "How do you know that?"

"Because rule number one of living overseas? Go off-base and drive more than twenty klicks in any direction, and suddenly there isn't an American in sight."

"I've heard that. Kind of figured it was an exaggeration, though. Like how they say Norfolk is full of signs that say *'no dogs or sailors on the grass'*?"

I barked a laugh. "It's no exaggeration, trust me. Especially in a place like this where the language barrier is such an issue."

He cocked a brow. "Even with translator apps?"

"Pfft. Okay, obviously you're new here because you haven't been using them long enough to develop trust issues."

"You don't use them?"

"Oh, I do. Sometimes they're a necessity. But when they're wrong..." I whistled and shook my head.

His curious little grin was too damn cute. "I feel like there's a story there."

"Mmhmm. Two weeks after I got here, I saw chocos fritos on a menu. My stupid app told me it meant 'fried chocolate.'"

Alarm raised his eyebrows. "What did it mean?"

I rolled my eyes. "Fried cuttlefish."

"No shit?" He made a face even as he laughed. "Oh my God. That sounds..."

"I mean, it wasn't bad? But it definitely wasn't what I was expecting." I waved a hand. "So yeah, even those of us who are adventurous enough to go off-base don't completely trust the apps. The people who are too scared to go through the gate?" I shook my head.

Marks pursed his lips thoughtfully. "So... the odds of running into someone we know in Sevilla..."

"In a *gay bar* in Sevilla."

"Right. Point taken." He met my gaze. "And you said the place is called Castillo de Danza?"

I nodded, my pulse ticking up as I realized we were doing this. Then I remembered how he said he hadn't done this before at all, and my stupid mouth moved before my brain could tell it not to: "Do you need advice on what to wear?"

He froze. "Oh. Uh. Yeah? Probably?" He grimaced. "I have a decent fashion sense, but I have no idea what people wear to a place like that."

Chewing the inside of my cheek, I weighed the options. Finally, I offered, "If you want to send me pics of what you have, I can yay or nay them."

"That could work. Or—" He hesitated.

I raised my eyebrows.

Marks fidgeted with renewed nerves. "You, uh... You could come by and tell me what works. Probably more efficient that way."

Oh, fuck me.

Then he cringed. "That's a bad idea, isn't it?"

"I mean, it depends."

"On?"

"Where do you live?"

"Out in Sanlúcar."

"Do you have a lot of American neighbors?" I couldn't remember if many service members lived out there.

Marks shook his head. "My whole street is locals." He paused, and he seemed to be warming up to the idea. "I have an enclosed driveway, too. Not a garage, but someone would have to really look through the slats of the gate to see your car."

God, I loved Spanish houses. "Okay. Okay, sure. That's probably safe enough."

Right then, the door to the waiting area opened, and a woman walked in with a child.

"Shit." I got up. "I need to—listen, I'm free tonight. If you text me your address and a time, I can be there."

He glanced toward the window as he too got up. "I need your number."

I scratched it out on a sticky note and handed it to him.

"Okay." He flashed me a smile as he pocketed the note. "I'll see you then."

This was a bad idea.

A stupid, career-threatening, recklessly *terrible* bad idea.

I told myself that all the way home, and then all the way to Sanlúcar. We weren't getting into the territory that would get him disciplined for conduct unbecoming a gentleman and me for... well, I'd never actually looked up what the formal name was for *"you're banging an officer and now you're in trouble."* And I wasn't going to look it up now because I wasn't banging—and wouldn't *be* banging—an officer.

Also, I was driving.

To that officer's house.

Which wasn't as serious as banging him, but it *was* well into fraternization territory. The military had a massive bug up its butt about officers and enlisted service members even being friendly with each other. I'd never really understood why. If we were in the same chain of command, fine, but if not, then who the fuck cared?

Big Navy, that was who, and I was too close to retirement to get my ass kicked out.

And yet, there I was, taking the third exit off that roundabout in the middle of Sanlúcar and following the GPS's directions down a narrow one-way street and up a hill and...

Why am I even arguing with myself? It isn't like I'm going to turn around.

I didn't, either. A minute or so later, I pulled up to the house indicated on my GPS. Back at my apartment, I'd grabbed a shower and used that time to talk myself the rest of the way down from this morning's panic. Now I was still shakier than I would've liked, but the nervousness now was decidedly more pleasant. I was here to see a man I had no business seeing, thinking about things we had no business doing, and that was a welcome distraction from everything that had happened earlier.

There was a car parked on the street that I suspected was his, and I parked behind it. Engine idling, I texted him to let him know I was here, and a moment later, the wide black gate started to rattle open. After I'd pulled into the driveway, the gate shut behind me.

And holy shit, Marks's place was *huge*. It was brilliant white stucco like so many other houses around here, with a red tile roof and dark hardwood trim. Potted flowers encircled a palm tree beside his front porch, and a wrought iron fence with an ornate gate spanned the front of the villa. Judging by the pale blue reflections rippling on the underside of the eaves, there was a pool in the backyard.

Then the front door opened, and I forgot all about the palatial house.

How dare you look that good in shorts and a T-shirt?

I'd never seen him out of uniform aside from in his pictures on the app, and those pictures hadn't done him justice. He wasn't a meathead like some of the guys on base, but he was built and sculpted. Outside of work, his hair was a bit less styled—more finger-combed and even a touch messy, which was so damn sexy.

And without the military bearing that was so ingrained in all of us, he had a relaxed air about him that made my pulse go nuts.

"Hey." He smiled with a hint of nerves. Or was that shyness? Either way, it was cute. "Come on in."

Heart thumping hard against my ribs, I came up the steps and followed him into the house. Of course it was equally impressive inside, and it was also *cool*. Like, literally cool, probably because of the marble floors at our feet.

"Nice place, sir," I said.

He turned a look on me that was definitely laced with shyness. "We're out of uniform and off duty. You don't have to call me 'sir.'"

I was hesitant. Keeping that in place would remind us both where we stood and what lines we couldn't cross. On the other hand, I hadn't come here because I was being careful or smart, so why not drop the formalities while I was at it?

"Oh. Okay. Uh." I cleared my throat. "What... what *do* I call you? Because I don't even know your first name." I mean, I did—I'd seen it on the app, of course—but I felt weird and presumptuous about just using it.

He laughed softly. "Connor. Yours?"

"Alex." And damn, now we were even less separated by professionalism and military bearing. In his house. Yeah, this was a bad idea, but whatever—I was here. I shifted my weight. "So, um... Clothes?"

"Right. Yeah." He gestured for me to follow him. "In the bedroom."

With his back safely to me, I mouthed a curse, then a prayer for help keeping my hands to myself.

Walking into this man's bedroom with him, I was going to need it.

CHAPTER 7

CONNOR

I didn't think this through, did I?

No, I had not. Because if I had, I'd have vetoed it before the suggestion even came out of my mouth. Long before HM1 Barlow—*Alex*—set foot in my house, never mind my *bedroom*.

But I hadn't. And now he was here. In civvies. With his tattoos and his powerful arms and legs on full display thanks to that snug T-shirt and those faded shorts. And somehow, I had to operate like a functional adult human being while he was standing beside the bed where I'd thought about him last night with my dick in my hand.

I was pretty sure I'd once been a sane, functional adult human being who didn't do stupid shit, but good Lord, did that go out the window whenever I was around Alex. What the hell? I was a grown-ass adult, but all he had to do was smile and I—

"Okay, let's see what we have to work with." Alex folded his arms and peered into my closet.

"Probably nothing too exciting," I said with a laugh. "I don't have any leather pants or anything like that."

He snorted. "Good, because I don't know if you noticed, but Spain is fucking *hot*. Especially in July."

"I had picked up on that, yeah."

"Right, so leather pants in this kind of heat..." He wrinkled his nose and shook his head. "That smell is not attractive."

I laughed. "Duly noted."

He flashed me a grin, but then turned serious and looked right at me. "I guess... well, what do *you* think looks hot on a man?"

Whatever you happen to be wearing.

By the grace of God—or maybe years of self-censoring so I didn't fuck myself professionally—I kept those words to myself, though my face was probably turning red. "Uh... I mean..." I shrugged. "Nothing too crazy? I've never quite understood the whole leather and harness thing." I gestured across my chest to imply one of those black leather harnesses I'd seen guys wearing in porn and in videos of clubs.

Alex chuckled. Not unkindly or like he was making fun of me, though. "That's kind of its own scene. Sometimes it's the guys who are into kink and leather. Sometimes... I mean, some guys just like it, you know? But you don't have to wear one."

"That's a relief," I said with total honesty. "Don't get me wrong—it looks hot on some guys. I just, uh... I don't think it's my thing. For myself." Christ, could I ramble a bit more?

"You're good." He looked at the various shirts and pants I had hanging in the closet. "You don't wear a lot of color, do you?"

"A lot of—" I furrowed my brow and studied my own wardrobe. And okay, he might've had a point. I had a lot of black, white, and gray, plus some blue, though nothing very loud. A pair of newish jeans were probably the most brightly colored thing I owned. With a self-conscious laugh, I leaned against the footboard and shook my head. "I guess I don't, do I? I never really noticed."

He shrugged. "Eh, everyone has their own tastes." He turned to me, curiosity in his blue eyes. "You don't like dressing to be noticed?"

That...

That was an interesting question.

I squirmed under his scrutiny. "I don't think I've ever considered whether what I'm wearing will make someone notice me or not. Just... not big into wild colors, I guess?"

"So I won't talk you into a Hawaiian shirt?"

I scoffed. "You first."

His eyebrow rose. "Don't threaten me with a good time."

"You wear Hawaiian shirts?"

Grinning, he gave a little half-shrug. "I spend all goddamned day in camouflage. When I go out, I don't like to blend into the background, you know?"

"So... you do wear Hawaiian shirts."

"I've been known to, yes."

I tilted my head. "Maybe it's because I've only seen you in camos and..." I gestured at him. "But I'm struggling to picture you in a Hawaiian shirt."

Grin still firmly in place, he whipped out his phone. He tapped the screen a few times, then turned it for me to see.

And sure enough, there he was—sunglasses, a backwards baseball cap, and the loudest red-and-yellow Hawaiian shirt I'd ever seen.

Though if I was honest, that only vaguely registered because I zeroed right in on the white T-shirt he was wearing under it. On how it sat snugly across his chest and abs, the shadow of some ink just starting to peer through the thin fabric, and—

I laughed to get my breath moving as I tore my gaze away from the photo. "Okay, so you do like bright and loud."

Alex chuckled and shrugged as he pocketed his phone. "Guilty. Like I said—I'm wearing camo all day."

"So am I. Maybe I need to start brightening things up." I shifted my weight. "So, um, is there anything in here that would be passable for a club, though? Or do I need to go shopping?"

"Sure, we can work with this. Easily." He skimmed over the clothing on display. "There isn't a super-strict dress code anywhere. It's mostly wear what you like and what you like to see on other guys." He paused. "If we were hitting up someplace on Ibiza or something, then I'd say to wear as little as possible."

I blinked. "Are you serious?"

"Mmhmm." He met my gaze and must've seen my incredulity. "It's *hot*, amigo, and it only gets hotter when you've got fifty guys dancing with no sense of personal space."

"Oh." I swallowed. "Right. I, uh... That makes sense." And now was definitely not the time for me to be thinking about what Alex might or might not wear in a situation like that. Or just how close he'd get to those other guys or—

"I guess the question is, do you want to blend in or stand out?"

It took me a moment to land on an answer, and that was only in part because I'd been momentarily distracted by thoughts of Alex on Ibiza. I chewed my lip and considered it. "I... Well, I don't really want to blend in." I laughed nervously. "Kind of defeats the purpose in a place like that, doesn't it?"

"Depends on what you're hoping to get out of it."

"What do you mean?"

"I you're just there to get a feel for it—figure out the vibe, figure out of it's your scene—then maybe you don't want to be noticed. There's nothing wrong with being a wallflower while you're trying to get your feet wet."

"I guess?" I swallowed. "What would you do in my shoes?"

Alex rocked his head from side to side as if he were thinking about how to answer. "I... honestly think I'd be intimidated as all hell."

I straightened. "You would?"

"Well, yeah. I started going to clubs when I was like sixteen. Back when I was young, stupid, and fearless." He met my eyes, and his were filled with a startling amount of sincerity. "I won't lie—I can't imagine venturing out into that in my thirties."

"Or forties," I muttered.

"Yeah." He exhaled. "I'm not trying to talk you out of it or scare you away from it. I just—I get it, you know? It's a new scene. New world. Stepping out into that without the immortality of being young and stupid..."

The candor seemed like it should make me nervous, but it actually settled something in me. Yeah, I was still intimidated as all hell by this whole idea, but knowing Alex understood—that being uneasy about stepping into that scene was a normal, natural response—made me feel less like I was doing this wrong. Whatever this was. Because Jesus fuck, it was all so alien to me.

"It might've helped if I'd done much clubbing in my twenties," I said. "Not gay bars, but clubs in general."

Alex's eyebrows flew up. "You didn't?"

"I mean, I did a little? But I was married with a kid before I even went to basic training."

His lips parted. "Really?"

I nodded. "I did some partying during A-school and in between deployments, but I was never, you know, looking for anything. Just drinking and being stupid."

"Well. Shit. So this is all *really* new territory for you."

"You could say that, yeah." I rolled my shoulders, wondering when they'd started getting so damn tense. "So, I don't know if I want to be a wallflower or not. I kind of want to dive right in, but I also kind of hope no one sees me." I sighed. "I don't know. Am I overthinking it?"

He shook his head. "No. You're not." He looked at my wardrobe again. "Maybe something simple. Not necessarily enough to stand out, but you won't blend into the woodwork either." He started to reach for a shirt, but hesitated. "May I?"

"Yeah, of course. Please do."

He gave a sharp nod, then started thumbing through the various clothes I'd hung up. "All right. Let's see what we can put together..."

CHAPTER 8

ALEX

In the days leading up to our jaunt to Sevilla, I wondered more than once if I was making a mistake. Just standing in Connor's bedroom and talking about clubs and all that shit had scrambled my damn brain. Knowing I was going to be in a club with him, watching him dip his toes into the scene, had overheated more than a few synapses this week.

And now here I was, standing in front of the hotel across the street from mine—we didn't dare stay in the same place—realizing I had severely miscalculated.

The glass doors had opened, and Connor had stepped out, and... oh God. My dumb ass had put together something for him to wear that wouldn't make him stand out too much and wouldn't make him blend into the woodwork... not once considering that I was making him look like *exactly* the kind of man who'd yank my attention away from *anything*.

Okay, that already described him, but I'd gone and made it worse.

The black button-up shirt was open and loose over that skintight pale gray T-shirt. The jeans weren't tight enough to reveal if he dressed to the right or left, but they weren't baggy either. They sat perfectly on his hips, and maybe the untucked shirt was a good thing; I didn't need an unobstructed view of how his jeans clung to his ass.

It was a simple outfit. There was nothing flashy about it. Nothing that should've made me forget how to breathe.

Except it also happened to be a look that I'd always loved. There was a reason I'd gone with a similar ensemble myself—the only difference was the button-up was bright red and the tee was white.

Good one, Alex. Take the hottest man you've ever seen and dress him in a way that would turn your *head.*

The streetlights above us picked out some highlights in his hair as he came down the steps. Like a lot of officers, he didn't have the severe high-and-tight like I did, so his dark hair was long enough to style. Instead of being neatly arranged the way it always was at work, it was closer to how he'd had it when I'd come to his house—finger-combed and artfully mussed. Not what I'd call messy, not deliberate bedhead—I suspected he was too used to keeping it neat in uniform to go too wild with it in civvies—but definitely a more relaxed style than usual.

Somehow, I managed to keep my expression neutral and friendly as he approached.

Connor stopped in front of me and gestured at himself as he gave me an uncertain look. "Are you sure about this?"

"You don't like it?"

"No, no, I do. But it's—" He looked around us. "Well, I guess it's cooled off, hasn't it? I was sweltering in shorts earlier."

"Funny how that happens when the sun goes down."

He rolled his eyes and flipped me off.

I laughed. "Nah, you'll be fine. Especially since Castillo

de Danza actually has A/C, and they *use* it." In fact, I hoped they had it cranked to max tonight, because I was already getting a little warm just standing out here with Connor. God help me if it turned out he knew how to dance.

I suppressed a shiver and motioned for him to come with me. As we started down the sidewalk, I said, "So when did you get into town?"

"Last night." He slid his hands into his pockets. "I wanted to spend today checking out the city since I'd never been here."

"Yeah? Where'd you go?"

"Pretty much everywhere TripAdvisor said to go. Plaza de España. The Alcazar. The cathedral."

"No wonder you were sweltering. That's a lot of walking."

He chuckled. "No kidding. At least the cathedral was cool on the inside. I thought I was going to melt at Plaza de España."

"Ugh, tell me about it. The first time I went there, I thought it would be smart to go during siesta. You know, since there's nobody out and about."

Connor glanced at me. "Yeah? How'd that go?"

I groaned and rolled my eyes. "That was the day I realized *why* siesta is at two in the afternoon—because it's the *hottest fucking time of day*."

"Ooh. Okay, yeah. That makes sense. I think that's when I was in the cathedral. It was hot as fuck outside, and everything was closed when I came out."

I nodded. "Yep, that sounds like siesta."

"I'll get used to that one of these days."

"Good luck with that."

We turned a corner a block or so down from our hotels

and followed a narrower street. Restaurants were still open and crowded, which made sense—it was 2230 on a Saturday night, so people were still eating dinner.

"What did you think of the cathedral?"

"It was big," he said. "Like, I knew that, but holy shit..."

"Right? I made the mistake of going to that one before I went to the one in Cádiz. The one there was kind of a letdown after the big one here."

"I could see that. I went to Cádiz a couple of weeks after I got to Rota, but I didn't get to the cathedral because it was a Sunday. Nice city, though."

"It is. I go there a lot. Some great restaurants."

Connor nodded. "I ate at one of the cafés in the plaza outside the cathedral. I need to go back and try some others." He glanced at me. "Any chance I can hit you up for some recommendations?"

"Of course." I paused. "And fair warning? As you're traveling around Spain, now that you've seen the cathedral here, a lot of the others will be kind of anticlimactic. Not just the one in Cádiz."

"Yeah?"

"Yeah. I mean, they're all cool, but once you've seen one, you've kind of seen them all, except for the ones that have something *really* unique going for them."

"Like the big one they're still building in Barcelona?"

"Sagrada Familia, yeah."

"You been to that one?"

I nodded. "Several times." I chuckled as I added, "Even though I don't usually go to Barcelona for the architecture, I do still check it out once in a while."

Connor laughed, and I almost tripped over my own stupid feet.

You are not going to have any trouble turning heads tonight, Lieutenant Commander. Holy shit.

Thankfully oblivious to my near stumble, he said, "During orientation when I got to Rota, they said something about this one cathedral somewhere that I want to check out. I can't remember the name, but it's like an old mosque that was turned into a cathedral?" He cocked his head. "Is that real, or did I hallucinate it because I was so jetlagged?"

I laughed. "It's real. That's the Mezquita in Córdoba."

His eyes lit up. "Have you been there?"

"Couple of times. It's really cool; definitely worth visiting." I glanced at him. "If you look closely, a lot of the cathedrals are converted mosques. That one's just the most obvious."

"They are?"

"Mmhmm." I grinned. "Next time you go to the one here, check out the belltower."

Connor shot me a look. "Are you fucking with me?"

"Nope."

He pursed his lips. Then he halted and took out his phone, and I realized he was pulling up the photos he'd taken today. He paused on one and peered at it. "Okay, what am I looking at?"

I stepped in close to him so I could see too. On the screen was the belltower in question. "Right, so you see the top part where the bells are?" I covered them with my thumb. "Now look at the rest."

He pulled the phone a little closer. "Okay, so it's—wait, no shit. Is that... Wait, what the hell?"

I chuckled. "It's the minaret from the mosque that used to be there."

"Wow. How did I not notice that?"

"Because you just got here. Give it some time, and you'll

start seeing the Moorish architecture in a lot of the historical spots."

"And here I thought you weren't into—" He stopped abruptly when he turned to me. So did my breath.

Because oh, hell—we were *really* close.

I quickly broke eye contact and sidestepped to put some space between us. "I'll have you know, I do pay attention to historical stuff and architecture." I motioned for us to start walking again, and as we did, I added, "Just not when I'm trying to get laid."

Connor coughed a laugh as he put his phone in his pocket. "Hey, at least you've got your priorities straight."

"That's about the only thing straight about me."

He snorted. "Oh my God. And I thought *my* dad jokes were bad."

I just laughed, and we continued down the block to where a brightly colored neon sign glowed above tinted glass doors. "That's the place."

Connor tensed a little, and he pushed out a nervous breath.

The temptation to put a reassuring hand on his back was almost overwhelming. "Relax. It's just a club."

"Uh-huh. Says the guy who's been going to clubs since he was a teenager." He swallowed. "Didn't you say you'd be intimidated in my shoes?"

Damn, maybe that hadn't been the best thing to tell him, even if it was true. "I did. And I would be. But I'd also hope I had someone there to tell me, 'dude, it's just a club—let's go have a couple of drinks and dance.'"

He seemed to consider that. "Okay, that... doesn't sound *too* terrifying."

"Exactly. Oh, and just so you know, they pour the drinks *strong* in there. Pace yourself."

I'd gone into Spanish clubs with younger guys from the base before, and they'd invariably puff out their chests and insist they could handle it. After all, they were a Sailor! Or a Marine!

But Connor—either because he was a doctor who knew better or a seasoned officer who'd learned the hard way—was apparently wise enough not to play chicken with his own liver. "Duly noted. I'll probably just stick with beer anyway."

"Good call." I dug into my pocket. "Also, you'll want to wear these." I held out a pair of bright orange earplugs.

Connor eyed them, then me. "Really?"

"Trust me. You'll still be able to hear just fine, but it'll cut through the noise enough that you can actually hear someone talking."

He shrugged and plucked the earplugs off my palm. "Eh, I won't argue with not damaging my hearing."

"Hasn't the military done that enough?"

"What?"

"Oh, fuck you."

God, I loved the way this man laughed. His smile made me dizzy, and I loved it, even though it frustrated the hell out of me because I wanted to—

Focus, Alex. Focus.

We didn't have to wait long to get in the front door. It was only 2300, so the Spanish club scene hadn't begun to kick up yet. Any club in town would be almost deserted at this hour; normally, I wouldn't bother showing up until midnight, since that was when the locals usually materialized. This time of night, it was just a smattering of expats and tourists, the bartenders, and the deejay.

I'd done that on purpose tonight. This was Connor's

first foray into this scene, and I didn't want to overwhelm him.

That wasn't true. I'd have sawed off a limb for the chance to overwhelm him. Strip off that carefully curated outfit, mess up that perfectly styled hair, and—

No, Alex. No. Don't even fantasize about it.

What I *didn't* want to do was turn him loose in a night club that was in full swing. Too much noise. Too many people. Too easy to get disoriented.

Right now, Castillo de Danza was about as lively as a strip club on a Tuesday afternoon. The music was loud and there were people on the dancefloor, but it wasn't utter chaos and sensory overload. Yet.

I watched Connor surveying the scene, his nerves on full display. Then I shouted over the music, "Why don't we get something to drink?"

He shook himself and turned to me. "Uh. Okay. Yeah. A drink sounds good." At the bar, he looked over the various beers on tap and seemed to get even more lost. I had no idea if he'd tried any Spanish beers yet, but he eyed the brands like none of them were familiar. Finally he leaned toward me. "What do you suggest?"

The words *"depends on what you like"* almost flew off my tongue, but I hesitated. Even a simple decision like that could pile on to that fish-out-of-water feeling that was probably setting in hard.

I gestured at the options. "Cruzcampo is good. It's kind of on the fruity side if you're into that."

"Sounds good to me."

I turned to the bartender and ordered us a pair.

Beside me, Connor chuckled. "You know, it's funny—everyone who found out I was going to Spain said I'd only need to know three Spanish phrases."

I rolled my eyes. "Let me guess." I ticked them off on my fingers. "¿Donde esta el baños? Dos cervezas, por favor. Dos *más* cervezas, por favor."

He laughed, oblivious to what that did to my head and my balance. "Yes, those. You heard them too?"

"Everyone does. Trust me. And then you get here and find out that not only are those grammatically incorrect, but people in Spain don't call the restrooms 'baños.' And the bartender will want to know what *brand* of cerveza." I rolled my eyes again.

Right then, the bartender handed over our dos cervezas, and I paid him.

As we stepped away to find a table, Connor said, "I could've paid. You don't have to pay my way."

I waved dismissively. "You can buy the next round."

"Eh, fair enough."

This early in the evening, there were plenty of unoccupied tables, and we found one with a good view of the sparsely crowded dancefloor. Connor rested his forearm on the table and sipped his beer. "Oh, you're right—this *is* good."

"Isn't it?" I sipped my own, grateful for the cold and the bittersweet flavor. "It's not my favorite of the Spanish brands, but I like it a lot."

"Yeah?" He met my gaze, unaware of the disco lights sparkling in his dark eyes. "What do you like?"

What... What do I like? What are we—oh. Right. Spanish beers.

I took another sip and put the glass down. "Alhambra makes a lot of good beers."

"Alhambra?" He tilted his head. "Isn't that—I thought that was the old fort or whatever in Granada?"

"Oh, it is. But there's a beer brand that uses the same name. Good shit. And the palace is worth visiting, too."

"So I've heard. At least I'll remember the name of the beer."

"I know, right?" I laughed. "Do you like wine? Sherry?"

"Not sherry." He wrinkled his nose. "Too fucking dry. I'll cook with it, but..." He shook his head.

"Same. If you do like cooking with it, though, you're in the right place—we basically live in the heart of Spanish wine country and the sherry capital of the universe."

"Good to know. One of the doctors in my department keeps telling me I need to visit some of the bodegas." He made a face and shrugged. "I like wine, but I'm not big on the whole wine tasting thing, you know? Just let me buy a bottle, damn it."

"Ugh." I groaned. "I got dragged on a bodega tour last year. I appreciate a good wine, don't get me wrong; I just *do not care* how it's made."

"Right?" Connor raised his beer. "Or like the breweries that want to tell you all about every fucking step of the process." He paused. "Though I think my issues with that are partly my brother's fault."

"How so? Home brewer?"

"God, yeah. And thanks to him, I know more than I ever care to know about yeast, hops, and..." He flailed a hand. "I swear, if I hear one more monologue about beermaking, I will drown myself in a fermenter."

I almost choked on my own beer. He was always so mellow and calm at work—well, when he wasn't nervous and stammering about us crossing paths on a hookup app. Watching him rant and rave was way funnier than it should've been. "He's really driven you nuts with it, hasn't he?"

"Ugh. *Yes*." Connor took a deep swallow of his beer. "I just want to drink it and enjoy it. I don't give a fuck about the rest."

"Same." I clinked my glass against his, and we both chuckled as our eyes locked.

And for the hundredth time tonight, I wondered if this was a good idea.

How the hell was I going to stay sane once every man in this building started to notice him?

CHAPTER 9

CONNOR

When Alex and I had first walked into Castillo de Danza, I'd immediately thought, *okay, this isn't so bad.* Loud and full of flashing lights, sure, but it wasn't packed with people and didn't seem like too much.

An hour or so later...

Holy fuck.

The dancefloor was absolutely packed with squirming bodies. The line at every bar was five or six people deep. The music had been cranked up so loud, the earplugs weren't even helping all that much.

I was secretly relieved he'd brought us here early, before the real noise and chaos started up. I'd had a chance to adapt to the environment, scope out all the exits, and get used to the cacophony before it had all ticked up to this point. My combat PTSD was relatively mild compared to other people I'd served with, and places like this weren't a massive trigger for me. Still, they did tug at some of the memories I'd made in warzones. Had I walked into the club while it was like this, I might've had to walk right back out. Taking some time to get acclimated made a big difference, though, and by the time it had reached this level, I was okay. My demons were tucked into the deepest recesses of my consciousness where they belonged, and I didn't have that *"oh shit"* feeling I could get when something plucked at the threads of my past trauma.

I'd be fine.

The alcohol had helped, too. I wasn't one for self-medicating and never had been, but even I could acknowledge there were times when it helped take the edge off.

Now if it could take the edge off my nerves about being here—being in a gay nightclub and maybe stumbling my stupid ass onto an attractive man's radar—that would be great. No such luck so far.

Especially since, at the moment, I was alone.

Well, "alone," seeing as there had to be five hundred people in this room. But I was standing by myself beside the table Alex and I had commandeered earlier. I felt a little like I was standing in the middle of a school of fish—they all whipped around me in a vortex of color and activity, but I doubted any of them even noticed me.

Was that a good thing? A bad thing? I couldn't quite decide. I also hadn't ventured far from this table since we'd gotten here, except to get a second round of beers for Alex and me.

Now my glass was empty, Alex was nowhere in sight, and this table felt like a buoy in the middle of a choppy sea—the only thing I could use to orient myself, and I was afraid to get too far away from it.

Which kind of defeats the purpose of being in a club, idiot.

Yeah, it did. I knew it did. But I hadn't had high hopes tonight. I was going to venture into a club and see what it was like. That was it. Mission accomplished. Actually meeting someone and hooking up with them? Not likely.

It was especially not likely now when every face in the room blurred together in a single colorful mass of *not Alex*. When a face did come into focus, they were...

God, so many of the guys in here were way too young. There were plenty who were my age and older—I'd definitely seen some gray and some lines in this crowd—but most of the men in here were in their twenties. *Maybe* early thirties. Some were probably close to my sons' ages, which... no. Just, no.

Was it too early to call it a night? I'd done what I came here to do, and I was pretty sure that was as good as it was going to get this time. That was fine. As eager as I was to land in bed with a man, it didn't have to be tonight. I'd known I was bi for almost fifteen years; waiting a little longer to actually experience a man wouldn't kill me.

Especially since there weren't a lot of men here who spoke English, and so many of them were so young, and only one of them was Alex Barlow, and...

I closed my eyes and pushed out a breath. The bass thumped alongside my pounding heart, vibrating up through the floor and along my bones.

Coming here with Alex probably hadn't been a good idea. How the hell was I supposed to pay any attention to other men when the one I'd spent last night fantasizing about was right there and out of my reach? Couldn't I have just brought my own ass to a club and fumbled my way through without asking him to guide me into—

"Oh my God." Alex's voice broke through all the noise in the club and in my head, and when I opened my eyes, he'd appeared beside the table. "Sorry about that." He gestured over his shoulder as he placed two bottles of water between us. "Line was a mile long."

I'm so glad you're back.

"It's okay." I picked up one of the bottles. "Thanks."

He flashed a smile that almost broke my brain, and I concentrated on downing a good half the water in one go. Air conditioning or not, this place was hot as hell now that it was full of people.

I realized a second too late that Alex had asked me something. My own distraction had kept me from hearing part of it, and the noise of the club swallowed the rest. "Sorry, what?"

He leaned closer and shouted over the noise, "I asked if you were going to hit the dancefloor."

Heat surged through me, and I held the cold bottle tighter. "I, uh... I haven't..." With a self-conscious laugh, I gestured at the floor. "I haven't danced in a club in *years*."

Oh, fuck me—that smile.

"Well. What are you waiting for?" He gestured in the same direction I had. "Now's as good a time as any."

I gulped. "I don't want to make an ass of myself."

Alex shrugged. "Most people in here will be too drunk to notice. The rest will either be checking someone else out, or checking you out and not giving a damn how you dance."

"Yeah, right." I sipped my water again. "I doubt too many people in here"—I circled my finger in the air—"are paying much attention to the forty-year-old guy."

"Ooh, I wouldn't bet money on that."

I shot him a skeptical look.

Alex studied me. Then he laughed, shook his head, and clapped my arm. "My friend. You really are new to the queer scene, aren't you?"

"Um. Yes?"

He sighed with exasperation, though there was still humor in his eyes. "Do you think I—a guy looking down the barrel of forty myself—would come to a place like this if no one paid attention to older men?"

Okay. That was a fair question.

Before I could respond, he leaned over the table, and though he still had to shout over the noise and through my earplugs, his voice came across like a conspiratorial whisper. I could hear him just fine, but the words took a second to actually register, mostly because he was suddenly close enough to me that I caught a hint of a subtle and intriguing cologne.

Then my brain caught up to what he'd said:

"Trust me—get out on the dancefloor, and you won't have any trouble finding someone to dance with."

I straightened a little. "You don't think so?"

He smirked. "Tell you what." Nodding toward the crowded floor, he said, "Go out there for three songs. If no one wants to dance with you, I'll cover your train ticket and your hotel for this trip."

Well, I wasn't one to turn down a deal, and I liked the challenging gleam in his eyes a lot more than I probably should have.

"All right." I shrugged and brought up my water bottle for another swig. "You're on."

His grin was toothy and wide. "That's what I thought."

"Yeah, yeah." I started to step away from the table, but hesitated. "I, uh…" I scanned the crowd. "Don't… really know how to dance."

He waved that away and took me by the elbow. "No one does. Just move to the beat. Start with your hips, then do whatever feels right." He gestured at the crowd as he tugged me toward it. "That's what everyone else is doing."

I was dubious of that. I'd seen too many videos of people showing off their dance moves. I'd even treated a kid in the ER who'd sprained his knee on a dancefloor, insisting "I've been doing those moves forever."

I didn't have "moves." I didn't buy that everyone else out there was just going with the flow and faking it till they made it.

But could I say no to that glint in Alex's eyes? To that tug at my elbow?

No, I could not.

So I let him lead me away from the safety of our table into the dense mass of people.

When he released my arm, I had that momentary panic like a lifeline had just snapped, leaving me in rough waters with nothing to cling to. But he was still close by. Still in sight.

He gave me a reassuring wink, and then he started doing exactly what he'd told me to do—move to the music. Start with the hips and go from there.

And... forget dancing. I wasn't sure I could remember how to walk now that I was watching him move.

The momentum of the crowd kept me from being completely still; I moved a little to keep people from crashing into me, and out of necessity, that meant moving with the music. So at least I wasn't just standing here like a dipshit.

But for the most part, all I did was stare at Alex.

At the way his hips moved like they had a mind of their own.

At the way he put up his arms and closed his eyes and just seemed to get lost in the music.

Fuck. Hadn't he said this place used air conditioning?

Because it was suddenly way too damn hot, and I didn't think it had to do with all these bodies around me.

Right then, someone emerged from the crowd, and I lost my own rhythm for a couple of beats when his hands slid over Alex's waist. Alex's eyes fluttered open, and oh, God, if I'd thought his earlier grin was sexy...

Someone bumped into me, and I remembered I wasn't supposed to be just standing here. I tore my gaze away from Alex so I could concentrate on moving. That helped. Checking out some of the other men helped, too.

And oh, hell, there were some hot men in this room. I'd been afraid walking into a gay club that it would be like I'd seen on TV or in photos—perfect bodies and six-packs as far as the eye could see. Yeah, there were men here who wouldn't be out of place in underwear ads, but there were also normal guys. Some who were way too young, but not all.

If I'd had any lingering doubts that I was bi—and I didn't—they would've evaporated in the heat of this dancefloor. So many attractive men. So many broad shoulders and gorgeous asses. So many disarming eyes and perfect lips; I'd been curious for a long, long time about what it would feel like to kiss a man, and my pulse raced at the thought that it might happen tonight. That before the sun rose, I might know what another man's mouth tasted like.

Christ, was I getting hard?

I was. How could I not? I hadn't been touched in four years. Tonight, I might break that dry spell. With a man. With one of the men in this room right now.

Fuck, yes. Bring it on.

Without thinking, I gave a quick glance around to make sure my lifeline was still here. I found that red shirt in the crowd and—

My breath stuttered.

He wasn't just dancing close to that other guy—he was dancing *close* to him. A hand firmly on the other guy's ass. I couldn't see much of Alex's face, but I could see enough of the other guy's to know he *wanted* Alex. He wanted him bad. His dark eyes were absolutely gleaming with need. Their faces *almost* touching, and all he or Alex would need to do was inhale deeply and they'd be kissing.

Alex said something. The guy laughed. Even at this angle, Alex's smile fucked with my balance. So did the way he used the hand on the guy's ass to pull them even closer together. God, was his thigh between the other man's legs? And was that—

Jesus. Alex's untucked shirt had mostly hidden it, but when they moved just so, I realized the guy's hand was in Alex's back pocket.

Oh, fuck, I did not need to watch this.

I turned away and again tried to concentrate on what I was doing. Not what *they* were doing behind me. Not on how much I wished it was my hand in Alex's pocket or my ass under his palm. Not on how badly I wanted to be the one hovering less than an inch away from knowing how Alex kissed.

Someone appeared beside me, and a hand slid around my waist. I missed a step, the combat-trained side of me momentarily thinking someone was getting the drop on me, but I relaxed as I realized he was moving with me. I leaned back into his heat, and he slid his arm all the way around me, flattening his hand on my stomach. Hot breath rushed past my neck, and I decided then and there I loved the way it felt when a man's hips pressed against my ass.

I covered his hand with mine. Then I decided to get a little braver and reach back to find his hip. Oh, hell. That was sexy. So was the way he growled in my ear. I had no idea what he was saying—my Spanish definitely wasn't *that* good—but it sounded hot and dirty.

He ground against my ass, and I realized he was aroused, too. I turned around in his arms and found myself gazing into a pair of utterly stunning eyes. It was hard to tell in the flickering disco lights, but I was pretty sure they were hazel. Maybe even green. His near-black hair was longer than mine, and he wore it well; this was definitely not a man subject to uniform regulations.

His smile was a little asymmetrical, and it made the floor beneath my feet feel a little uneven. Oh my God, he was sexy.

When he ran the tip of his tongue along the inside of his bottom lip… fuuuck.

I didn't have to think at all about how I moved with him. My body fell into sync with his, and he was so close to me now, he had to have felt the way my heart was thundering. Even if he didn't feel that, well, there were other dead giveaways that I was into this, and he grinned as he ground against my hard-on.

He said something I didn't catch. A question, that much I understood; again it was Spanish, and from the way he was grinning, it was filthy and suggestive. Maybe even a little cocky. I realized it could've been anything from "are you having a good time?" to "your place or mine?"

And that…

That sent a panicked shiver down my spine, cracking through the heat and the arousal and the alcohol.

I leaned in slightly to the side so he knew I was trying to speak, not kiss him, and he tilted his head to offer his ear.

"Do you speak English?"

He drew back again and shook his head. "¿Hablas español?"

I shook my head.

He frowned, then shrugged as his grin came back to life. Whatever he said next was fast and flirty, and he punctuated it by sliding his hands up my waist and pulling me in closer. It was probably something to the effect of, *"We don't need to talk—just dance."*

And maybe do more than dance.

Yeah, we could dance. We could even make out a bit, maybe.

But how did we take things further? Because I was still nervous about getting intimate with a man. With anyone, honestly, since I'd only ever been with one person in my entire life.

How were we supposed to communicate? How was I supposed to ask if he'd been tested for STIs or assure him that my own tests were clear? How was I supposed to insist that, no, really—condoms were non-negotiable? Or that I'd never done this before and needed him to take things slow?

Okay, this wasn't a good idea.

Dancing? Sure. Venturing out into the club scene? Definitely.

Hooking up with this guy or anyone else here who didn't speak English? Yeah, no. That wasn't going to fly.

Just dancing, then. I could live with that.

My partner apparently could, too. Either that, or he sensed me subtly backing off, as if I'd unconsciously telegraphed that this wasn't going anywhere beyond the dancefloor. We danced for another song and a half or so, and then he gave me a little grin and a nod before drifting back into the crowd. No hard feelings.

Not long after him, another man found me. He was

probably in his early thirties, same as the other, and he also didn't speak English. Fine. I wasn't here to talk.

And apparently Alex was right that I wouldn't have to dance alone.

As this new guy pressed his back against me and his ass against my hips, I glanced around, sure I was going to find Alex with *I told you so* across his smug face.

If he'd noticed anyone dancing with me, it probably wasn't even registering on his radar now. He was with someone else. Someone who had him flush against his chest the way my dance partner was against mine. The man's hand was partway under Alex's shirt, pressed against his abs, and Alex tilted his head back and bit his lip as the man's mouth explored the side of his neck.

Holy. *Fuck.*

Nothing the man in my arms was doing ignited my senses like watching Alex getting felt up and *tasted* by someone else.

My dance partner leaned back against me, rubbing his ass over my dick, which was getting hard again. He glanced over his shoulder, grinning hungrily.

He thought that was for him, didn't he?

He had no idea I was distracted by that gorgeous sandy blond in the red shirt with the other man's lips on his neck and his jeans tented by an obvious—

Oh, fuck me.

Alex was hard. He wasn't obscenely on display, but that bulge drew my gaze and made my mouth water.

Christ. Forget worrying about the language barrier. I wasn't going to get anywhere with anyone tonight because there was only one man in this place I wanted. And of course, he was the one man in this building I absolutely could not have.

Fuck my life.

It was almost 0500 when I finally dropped onto my hotel bed. Still dressed, though I had managed to kick off my shoes, I lay there and just… breathed.

My ears still rang from the music and my muscles still ached from dancing, but more than that, my skin still tingled everywhere the men in the club had touched me.

Everywhere I wished *Alex* had touched me.

Especially outside our hotels where we'd parted ways.

"You had fun tonight, right?" he'd asked, looking almost shy.

"Yeah! Yeah. I had a blast." I'd exhaled and raked a hand through my sweaty hair. "Fucking tired, though."

"You and me both." He'd held my gaze a moment, an unspoken thought pinching his brow, but then he gestured at his hotel. "We should get some sleep."

"Definitely. Uh. Thanks for bringing me here." I paused. "Or, well, for 'running into me at the same club in Sevilla.'"

His tired laugh had lit up the whole street. "Any time. I'll see you on Monday."

Monday. Right. Because we'd be heading back separately tomorrow so we didn't rouse any suspicion if someone we knew saw us.

But no one could see us right then. Had I read too much into the way he held my gaze a beat or two longer than necessary? Or the fact that when I'd told him I was calling it a night, he'd decided to do the same instead of taking his pick of men who clearly wanted him?

Would anyone see us if we stayed in the same room tonight?

Cowardice kicked in, though, and I just murmured, "See you Monday." Then we'd gone our separate ways, and here I was—alone in my hotel room, still sure I could smell his subtle cologne even over the sweat and booze of the club.

I felt weird that he'd gone back to his room alone. He'd engaged in some seriously hot dancing with some incredibly hot men, but he hadn't hooked up with anyone?

I closed my eyes and wiped my hand over my face. Just as well, maybe. I wanted him to have a good time, but I wasn't sure I could stay sane knowing that right this minute, he was getting naked and sweaty with another man. I was already losing my mind from those images of him dancing, every one of which was seared into my brain like a porno.

"Fuck," I whispered into the stillness.

I wanted that man so damn bad, and now I was hard as a goddamned rock. I'd practically been at half-mast all night, and though I was exhausted, the horniness was not going to relent on its own. Especially now that I was alone and could really let my mind drift back to the club, back to the dance-floor, back to Alex getting felt up and touched and—

God, why couldn't it have been my *mouth on his neck like that?*

The bed creaked as I squirmed, and my dick rubbed uncomfortably against my zipper.

What the hell was I waiting for? I was alone. Alex wouldn't know. None of our superiors would know. It wouldn't be the first time I'd jerked off thinking about him.

And it wasn't like I was going to get any sleep until I did something about this hard-on.

I undid my belt and jeans, and I was almost embarrassed by the groan I released when I closed my fingers around my dick. I doubted anyone heard me—the hotel was dead silent, so everyone was probably asleep—and anyway, whatever, I was too horny to care about anything.

Anything except that mental image of hands sliding all over Alex's lean body.

Of his lips parting as someone else's lips skated up the side of his neck.

Of his hips gyrating in time with another man's, the bulge in his jeans giving away how into it he was, and oh, fuck, the other guy *had* to be hard in that moment, too. Who wouldn't be with that ass pressed up against him? I'd have been on the verge of coming if I'd been in his place—hands all over Alex, lips exploring his neck, dick thrusting up against his ass like we were a few layers of clothing away from screwing, and—

I shouted as my hips bucked off the bed and cum erupted on my hand and stomach. I kept pumping, kept gasping, until there was nothing left and I was this close to too sensitive.

Then I sank back to the bed. Fingers still around my cock. Cum everywhere. Breath coming in deep, sharp gulps.

And Alex Barlow still firmly on my mind.

CHAPTER 10
ALEX

Eyes still shut, legs still shaking, I just stood there in the shower for a moment, letting the hot water rush over me while the last few aftershocks of my orgasm rippled through me.

Oh my God. Wow.

It was a genuine miracle I'd even made it into the shower before I'd had to get myself off. The whole evening, the whole walk back to the hotel and up to my room, the whole time I'd been stripping off my clothes—I'd been so horny I was lucky I could walk.

At least the night had cooled down considerably; it wasn't cold by any stretch of the imagination, but stepping out of that stuffy club, it hadn't been unreasonable to partially button my thin shirt. Connor hadn't questioned me, anyway, and he hadn't noticed the hard-on I'd sported for half a block.

The walk had calmed me down a bit.

Standing between our hotels? Locking eyes with him? Remembering how fucking sexy he'd been with those men on the dancefloor? Wondering if I should just say fuck it and ask him to come up to my room with me?

Yeah, the buttoned shirt had come in handy.

And now *I'd* come, and I was surprised my orgasm hadn't dropped me to my knees right here in the shower. Every time I came while I was thinking about Connor, it was earthshaking. On the heels of a night spent watching him in a club? *Holy* fuck.

Which probably meant that sex with him would be a serious letdown.

I opened my eyes and turned around to rinse off the cum. That was the way things like this always worked, and I knew it. Every time I'd been into someone for a while before I finally slept with them, I built them up so much in my mind, the real thing ended up being... meh. Nobody could live up to the person they were in a fantasy.

So... fine. I'd keep this to fantasies. Really fucking hot fantasies about loud, bed-breaking sex with the man who made me stupid just by existing. Eventually, I'd get used to that, and I could think about him with my hand on my dick at night and coexist with him in the hospital during the day. Same as I had with that captain who'd been in charge of the emergency department when I'd first transferred to Rota. He'd eagerly and vocally bottomed for me in my mind, and we'd interacted like consummate professionals at work.

No reason I couldn't do the same with Connor.

Though, I'd never seen Captain Pickering at a club. I'd never witnessed him biting his lip as someone ground against him, or sliding his hands up some lucky bastard's back.

I shook myself, then hung my head to let the water rush over it.

I was stupid. That was all there was to it. I had a hot

colleague who might as well have had DO NOT TOUCH tattooed all over him, and I wanted that forbidden fruit.

When I got back to Rota tomorrow, I'd text Isidoro. Even the other night when I'd been distracted, the sex had still been good. If we hooked up a few more times, I'd shift gears from wanting what I couldn't have to lusting after the man who happily jumped on every opportunity to suck my brains out my dick.

Yes. That was what I'd do.

Tonight, sleep.

Tomorrow, back to Rota.

Tomorrow night?

Isidoro.

I was way too tired to make one of the early trains, but whatever. The ride from here to El Puerto was only an hour and some change, so even if I left later in the afternoon, I'd still be home well before dinnertime.

The only downside was that the Sevilla Santa Justa train station was *crawling* with people. My very slightly hungover head was less than thrilled, but I intended to appease it with some coffee from that one café inside the station. And one of their pastries, because those were amazing.

I got a ticket for the 1440 train, which gave me a solid hour and a half before I needed to head for the platform. Plenty of time to wade through the line and get something to eat.

The line crawled forward, and I caught up on my socials while I waited. Nothing too exciting going on. My family back home was posting vacation photos since it was that time of year. My brother and sister-in-law had taken their huge family to his in-laws' cabin near Lake Chelan in Eastern Washington, and the kids were clearly having a good time. My parents were there, as were the in-laws, so it looked like my brother and his wife were getting a break, too. With six kids—they'd each brought two kids into their marriage, and they'd had two more together—neither of them got a lot of downtime these days.

I smiled to myself as I thumbed through the photos. I'd joked with my parents that between him and my sister, who had three kids, I was off the hook for grandkids. At the time, I'd been kind of relieved that there was no pressure on me. These days, especially as I watched everyone grow up through photos while I was stationed on the other side of the world, regret sometimes crept in. On my rare visits home, it was just me. No partner. No kids. I still didn't even know if I wanted kids, mostly because I was still eschewing relationships.

"Alex, honey," Mom had gently said the last time I was home. "I understand not wanting to settle down in your twenties, but you're almost forty."

"I know. And I'll be retired in a couple of years." I'd shrugged it away like it was nothing. "Once I'm out of the Navy and figure out what comes next, then I can think about settling down with someone."

She hadn't been happy about that, though she'd let it go.

These days, I wondered if *I* was happy with it. Was that why I'd been such a tangled mess of frustration? Was I lonely? Itching to finally connect with someone and have a partner instead of banging my way through my active duty years? Hell, maybe I was hungry for some *real* intimacy after that miserable year with Tobias.

I sighed and pocketed my phone as the café line moved

forward. I was just hungover. That was all it was. Hungover, and a little frustrated because I'd spent last night alone.

Alone, Alex? Or not with Connor?

Ugh. Fuck that thought. I couldn't have spent last night with Connor. I couldn't spend *any* night with Connor. And even if we did hook up, that wasn't going to do anything about this melancholy feeling I got when I watched my family vacationing a few thousand miles away.

Eighteen more months. Then I'd be a civilian, and I'd be stateside, and I could think about—

"Fancy meeting you here."

I whipped around, and even though I recognized his voice, I was still startled to see Connor standing there. And when had he started wearing *glasses?* "Oh. Hey." Why was my heart suddenly racing? "Uh... Great timing." Really? That was all I could think to say?

He chuckled. "Something like that." Gesturing at the end of the line, he said, "I'm going to get something myself. Mind if I join you?"

The correct answer was, *"We should probably stay separated as much as possible, sir, not eat our pastries together, and definitely not sit together on the train. Sir."*

What came out was, "Sure. Yeah. No problem. I'll wait for you after I get mine." There weren't any tables available in here, so we'd have to take our food to go.

He flashed me a smile that brought back way too many memories of last night—especially the one in the shower—and then he continued toward the back of the line.

Fuck me. We were going to have a late breakfast together and then ride the train back to El Puerto together, weren't we?

From the excited flutter in my stomach... yeah. We were.

I was sorely tempted to text Isidoro then and there to lock down something for tonight. At least then I'd know there was relief on the horizon.

In fact, that was a damn good idea.

I took out my phone and sent him a message through WhatsApp, hoping the translator didn't mangle it too much:

> Are you free this evening?

I was next in line when he responded:

> Duty tonight. (sad emoji)

Gah. Duty rotations could be the biggest cockblock on the planet.

> No worries. We'll get together soon. (winking emoji)

Then I put my phone away again, and it was my turn to order. I was tired enough that my Spanish was clumsier than usual, but the lady was patient as I stumbled through ordering a coffee. I pointed out the pastry I wanted, which was a decadent, chocolate-filled monstrosity that meant an extra half hour at the gym tomorrow. I had no idea what they were called, only that they were *divine*.

Once I had my food and coffee, I caught Connor's eye and gestured out into the flow of traffic through the train station so he knew I'd be out there. He nodded, and I stepped out of the café.

Just my luck, a family was getting up from a small table, and I commandeered it. I put my backpack under it and slipped my foot through the strap so no one swiped it. I knew a few too many people who'd learned *that* lesson the hard way.

The coffee was exactly what I needed—dark and rich with just a touch of cream. A couple of sips seemed to make my headache abate slightly; a placebo effect, sure, but I embraced it wholeheartedly. If the hospital's cafeteria ever started serving good Spanish coffee, I'd be a happy man. As it was, there were a couple of places near my apartment in Chipiona that had the good shit, so I usually stopped at one or the other before I headed for work.

Work, which I'd go back to tomorrow. Where I'd inevitably cross paths with one Lieutenant Commander Marks on a regular goddamned basis.

Sighing, I lowered my coffee and watched him through the café's front window. He was looking at something on his phone, and I didn't think it was fair how attractive he was with glasses on.

C'mon, dude. Don't you know I'm trying to not *drool over you?*

Fortunately, no, he didn't. By some miracle, I'd managed to keep that under the surface and carry myself like a normal person around him. Or at least give the impression that was what I was doing.

I pulled my gaze away and took a bite of the pastry, concentrating on that instead of him. I'd always heard people rave about French pastries, but Spain made some damn good ones, too. They were never dry, never too sweet, and they only set me back a euro or two. It was probably a good thing that my favorite bakery in Chipiona wasn't the one across the street from my apartment and there was almost no parking nearby. I basically had to walk to it, which was just as well, considering how much I'd stuff my face if they were more convenient. If that one place in Cádiz ever opened a location near me, I'd never fit into my uniforms again.

A set of footsteps broke away from the hurried foot traffic in the train station, and I looked up to see Connor striding toward me, a small paper bag in one hand and a coffee cup in the other. And the glasses. Still had on the glasses.

Fuck. You are so hot...

Unaware of my stupid mind, Connor took the chair opposite me. He also put his foot through the strap on his backpack—smart man—and then opened the small paper bag from the café. "Popular place," he mused.

I pointed at the fruit tart he was pulling out; that was what I would've ordered had they run out of the chocolate ones I liked. "Take a bite of that, and you'll understand why."

An eyebrow quirked up. Then he shrugged, picked up the tart, and took a bite.

God. Was there *anything* this man did that wasn't attractive as all hell? That look on his face...

Can't I make you make that face? Just one time?

No, I couldn't, and I needed to get off that train of thought immediately.

I sipped my own coffee. "So, what did you think of Castillo de Danza?"

Good one, Alex. Bring up last night. That'll keep you focused on not wanting to lick him.

Unaware of me being a complete dumbass, Connor said, "It was... I mean, it was fun, I guess?"

I studied him. "You guess?"

"It's... I don't know." He sat back. "I think I shorted out a little because I was already nervous about venturing out into that scene, and then I realized half the guys there are the same age as my kids."

Right. Right, he had kids. I kept forgetting that. I fidgeted in my chair, tapping my fingers on my coffee cup. "How many kids you have, anyway?"

"Two boys." A fond smile formed on his lips. "They're both adults—twenty and twenty-two. But like, that's the demographic in clubs, so..." He wrinkled his nose.

I laughed. "I never thought of that. Some of them are half my age, but if I had kids and they were that age... Yeah, that might fuck with my head."

Connor chuckled almost soundlessly. "Just a bit. Otherwise, it was fun. I don't know if it's my scene, though."

"Because of the ages?"

"No. I'm a little uncomfortable with the language barrier. It's fun to dance with people, but going any further than that?" He grimaced.

"Yeah, I get it." I pulled a piece off my pastry. "I've got a guy I hook up with sometimes who doesn't speak much English. It's a challenge."

Something flickered across Connor's expression, and I refused to consider that it might be jealousy.

"How does that work?" He brought up his coffee for a sip. "Just use a translator app for everything?"

"Pretty much."

He almost spat out his coffee. "Wait, what? I was joking!"

"I'm not. Hey, you do what you gotta do."

"Okay, sure, but like—*while* you're hooking up with someone?"

Laughing, I popped the bite of pastry into my mouth. "I mean, we're not passing a phone back and forth when we're right in the middle of things. But it's how we figured things out ahead of time, and how we talk after."

I could not for the life of me figure out why he looked flustered. Or why he was blushing.

"That seems..." He cleared his throat before trying again. "That seems, I don't know, awkward? I can't imagine whipping out a phone in bed."

"Eh, it's not bad. Not what I'd call ideal—I wouldn't do it if we both spoke the same language—but it gets the job done in a pinch."

"Huh." Connor stared into his coffee cup. "I didn't think of doing that, but... maybe." He still didn't seem comfortable with the idea.

"You don't have to go that route," I said. "Hit up one of the clubs in Málaga; there's always some British expats and tourists there. They're safer than Americans."

He lifted his gaze. "How so?" But then he answered his own question: "Because they're definitely not military."

I nodded. "Exactly."

"Maybe I'll give that a try. But, um..." He held my gaze, suddenly looking far too adorably shy. "Thanks. For, you know, bumping into me in the same club and showing me the ropes."

I laughed softly. "Don't mention it. It was fun for me, too."

He... oh God, he really blushed. "Yeah, it... It looked like you were having a good time."

Oh, hell. How much had he seen? Not that I'd exactly been hiding in the shadows or anything, but the thought of Connor seeing me—maybe even *watching* me—getting handsy with those guys?

Why was *that* so hot?

Because I was stupid, that was why. Fucking stupid.

I shifted in my seat and drummed my fingers on the table. "It was a pretty fun night."

"But nobody you wanted to take back to the hotel?" There was teasing in his voice, but genuine curiosity too.

I locked eyes with him. Oh, there'd been someone I wanted to take back to the hotel, but he didn't need to know that.

I went for my coffee, and just before I took a sip, I rasped, "Just... didn't connect with anyone."

His eyebrow flicked up ever so slightly.

Before he could ask any further, though, an announcement came over the loudspeaker. I tilted my head to listen.

Connor straightened. "Is that us?"

I nodded, listened for another few seconds, then got up. "Platform nine."

He pulled on his backpack as I did the same, and we collected our remaining coffee and pastries. We stepped into the flow of traffic, found the right escalator, and took it down to our platform. The train was idling beside it, and we stepped onto one of the cars.

The train filled up quickly. Usually did on the weekends. Still, we found a pair of seats facing each other.

"Do you have any preference?" I gestured at the seats. "Moving forward or backward?"

He shrugged. "Nah. You?"

"Nope." I took one of the seats, and though there was room on the overhead rack for both our backpacks, I kept mine at my feet. Connor did the same; couldn't be too careful.

He settled into his seat, and we both played on our phones for a little while until the train started pulling out of the station.

Connor pocketed his phone and pressed back against

his seat with a sigh. "This was a fun weekend, but I'm ready to head home."

"Tired?"

He exhaled. "Just a bit. I'm getting too old for this."

Laughing, I nodded. "I feel that. I usually go do tourist shit on the weekends instead of clubbing. It's still tiring, but it doesn't fuck up my sleep pattern quite as much."

"Maybe I should try that." Connor gave a soft, self-deprecating laugh. "Who knows? I could get lucky and meet some random English-speaking tourist on a guided tour."

Jealousy flared hot in my chest. I wasn't even surprised this time, and I didn't have any trouble schooling my expression or my tone; practice makes perfect, apparently. "Stranger things have happened, right?"

"I mean..." He half-shrugged. "I have zero experience with meeting people as an adult, so it's as good a place to start as any."

"Right, you said you got married young."

He laughed dryly, gazing out the window as the train picked up speed. "I got married young even by military standards."

I straightened. "Oh yeah?"

"Uh-huh. We started dating when we were fifteen, had our first son during our senior year, and got married six months after we graduated." He paused, then murmured, almost more to himself, "*Way* too fucking young."

I whistled. "Jesus. But we all think we're adults at that age. I look back at the version of myself who thought he was all badass on the way to boot camp, and I just think, *you dumbass.*"

Connor laughed with some more feeling, meeting my

gaze again. "Yeah, I remember that from boot camp. All the guys in my company were exactly like that."

"Not you?" I furrowed my brow. "And wait—boot camp? Were you prior enlisted?"

He nodded. "I was a teenager with a wife and a kid. I needed job security with health insurance, so... I enlisted. And no, I wasn't one of the guys who thought I was hot shit and all grown up because they handed me a gun. I was still fucking terrified from when a hospital sent me home with a baby two days after I took a history midterm." He huffed out a laugh. "*That* was a humbling experience, let me tell you."

"Oh my God." I actually shuddered. "I panicked enough over those tests. A baby? When I still couldn't parallel park to save my life? Fuck no."

Connor's laugh this time made my spine tingle. He was just gorgeous when he smiled. "I mean, I still can't parallel park to save my life? But I survived the kid thing." His expression turned a little sheepish. "Though... I was gone for some of it. Boot camp, then A-school. I, uh... I don't think my wife ever forgave me for being gone when our second son was born."

"It isn't something you can control, though."

"No, but I get it. She was stressed out just taking care of our almost-two-year-old. Then things got a little scary in the delivery room with Landon, and she was shaken up from that for a while, and..." He sighed. "She knew it wasn't my fault that I was gone, but I think she still resented me for it."

"That seems to happen a lot," I said quietly. "I know people who tried to time their babies around deployments, but if the Navy changes its mind about something..."

"Right?" He pressed back against the seat and let his gaze drift out the window again, watching the scenery pass by as the train took us out of Sevilla. "When I enlisted, we figured it would be a six-month deployment every couple of years, you know? So maybe once during my whole four-year enlistment? But I ended up doing two twelve-month tours downrange during that time."

I stared at him. "No shit?"

"No shit. I don't know if it was just bad luck or what. The Navy needed corpsmen really badly in both Iraq and Afghanistan, so..."

"Wait, you were a corpsman?"

He turned a slight smile on me. "Well, yeah. Did you think I went from being an aircraft maintainer to a physician?"

"Hey, it's the military—would you really be surprised if you found out a doctor used to be an aircraft maintainer?"

"Okay, good point. But—yes, I was a corpsman. At the end of my enlistment, I wanted to go to medical school, and after my wife and I talked it over, we figured going the ROTC route was the best bet. The G.I. Bill would cover some of it, but not all; having the Navy cover it and then serving a few years?" Connor half-shrugged. "At least then I wouldn't be deploying again until the boys were older, and we'd still have housing, health insurance—all of that."

"Ah, yeah. That makes sense. And then, what? You just decided to stick with it?"

Another shrug. "By the time I was coming to the end of my contract, I was just sort of... used to it, I guess. Being in the military, I mean. And I'd already put in enough years that it just made sense to stay in until I could retire."

I nodded. "Yeah. Same. When I got to the end of my second enlistment, it was like, well—I'm already halfway to twenty. Might as well just stick it out and get a pension." I absently trailed a finger along the edge of the armrest as I studied him. "This is your first overseas duty station, right?"

"Yep. I've been CONUS my whole career aside from Sandbox and shipboard deployments. You?"

"I spent a few years in Yokosuka. Otherwise, same—just Sandbox and shipboard."

He grimaced sympathetically. "You went downrange, too?"

I nodded, pretending not to notice the spiders creeping up my spine. "Three tours."

"Shit," he whispered. "Two was almost too much for me."

"I think *one* was too much for me." I shifted a little, trying to chase away those spiders. "I liked Yokosuka, though. I got to see a lot of Japan, so that was great."

"Oh, man, I was hoping for orders to Japan. I love it here, don't get me wrong, but Japan is a dream."

"You've still got time. And you can always hop a military flight and visit after you retire."

"Ooh, that's true. Well, someday, then." He watched me, the passing scenery flickering across the edges of his glasses. "So what was the best part about living there?"

I thought about it. "I mean, for one thing, there's the food..."

CHAPTER 11

CONNOR

The train ride from Sevilla flew by. We weren't even on a bullet train—well, we were, but it wasn't running at full speed. We just cruised along at a moderate clip through small towns, farmland, and scrubby open space that reminded me a lot of Southern California.

The hour and fifteen minutes or so just went by fast because I spent the whole time talking with Alex.

We talked about the Navy. About the places we'd been. About some of the crazy shit we'd experienced from boot camp to our current command, though we both steered well clear of combat. I was grateful for that; a lot of people loved telling war stories, and it was even therapeutic for some. That wasn't the case for me. Maybe it wasn't healthy, and maybe I needed to talk about it, but that was what professionals were for.

Not the smoking hot corpsman who had no idea how much I wanted him. And definitely not out in public. If I was going to pick apart my worst memories, it was going to be in the privacy of my own home with access to alcohol and a place to heave in peace.

Whether it was because he didn't like talking about it either, or he just didn't bring it up, I appreciated that Alex didn't delve into the subject. I was enjoying myself way too much to revisit that part of my past.

All too soon, the speaker above our heads announced that we would be pulling into El Puerto de Santa Maria. Most of the people in our train car got up, including Alex, so I followed suit. We put on our backpacks and headed toward one end of the car where several people were waiting by the door.

My stomach somersaulted as we stood there. I stole a glance at Alex, and though I felt like an idiot for it, I wished this wasn't about to be over. As much as this weekend had been an exercise in more restraint than I'd ever realized I had, I'd enjoyed it. I enjoyed being with him. Lusting after him and checking him out when he wasn't looking, yes, but also shooting the shit and just... being with him.

It pissed me off that the Navy would even frown on this much "fraternization" just because of our ranks. Even if they really wanted to die on the hill that officers and enlisted shouldn't fuck, was it honestly so bad for us to be *friends*?

The Navy didn't give a shit about my opinion on the matter, though, and whether I liked it or not, the station we were rapidly approaching would be where we parted ways. We'd be back to passing in the halls of the hospital and interacting on a professional level while I spent every damn night giving myself tennis elbow.

I surreptitiously gazed at Alex, who was checking something on his phone.

Does this have to be over now?

Of course the answer was yes, but that didn't stop me from mentally pushing back against it.

The train pulled up to the platform and stopped, and we followed the other passengers out. As we headed into the station, I peered up at the signs over our heads. "Okay, so..." I looked around. "Which way is the taxi stand?"

Alex glanced at me. "You took a cab?"

I shrugged. "I wasn't sure what the parking situation would be."

He nodded. "Makes sense. I, uh..." He hesitated, chewing his lip. Then he quietly ventured, "We're, um, kind of heading in the same direction. I could drive you so you don't have to spend the cab fare."

Bad idea. Bad idea!

We needed to go our separate ways sooner than later, because every minute I spent in his company made me care a whole lot less about what the UCMJ had to say.

But I still asked, "Are you sure?"

"Why not?" He flashed me a smile that erased any lingering ability I had to turn down his offer. "Like I said, I'm going that way, too."

I swallowed. Could my sanity really handle twenty minutes in the car with him?

Probably not.

Was that going to stop me?

Not a chance.

"Uh. Sure," I said. "If, um... If it's not too far out of your way."

I was imagining the way his face lit up when he smiled. I had to be.

"All right." He jerked his head toward the parking lot. "Let's roll."

Blood pounded in my ears as I followed him through the small station and out into the packed parking lot. He led me to a dusty red sedan, and as he popped the trunk, he said, "It's not exactly a Rolls Royce, but it'll get us there."

I laughed and put my backpack in the trunk beside his. "Have you seen mine? I'm amazed the quarter panel hasn't fallen off."

Alex laughed, and I ignored the way that made my heart flutter. "We probably bought them from the same lemon lot."

"Probably, yeah." Almost everyone on base drove some kind of beater they'd picked up for next to nothing from a lemon lot; they were ugly, they sputtered, and the parts had probably been discontinued since 1982, but they could usually limp through a three- or four-year assignment. All part of the overseas duty station experience.

We got in, and Alex started the car, blasting the air conditioner. The car was hot as hell from sitting out in the sun for two days, but his A/C actually worked, and it quickly cooled things down.

He pulled on a pair of sunglasses, put the car in gear, and headed out of the parking lot. The conversation continued much like it had on the train—all things military—which was good, because I wouldn't have been able to contribute to any deeper or more complex subject. Sitting this close to him, knowing this brief time together was dwindling down to mere minutes, had me restless, mentally flailing for some way to draw it out a little longer.

Futile and stupid, sure, but I couldn't help it. I couldn't get last night out of my mind, and everything about this weekend was making me reckless. I wanted him. The consequences of indulging felt about as real and tangible as the distant hills that were barely visible in the haze. No one would know, so who the fuck cared?

That was just the frustration from last night talking, and

I knew it. I'd been on the dancefloor with a lot of *very* attractive men getting *very* physical with me, and now I just needed an outlet.

Do you believe that, Dr. Marks? Do you? Do you really?

No, but I kept feeding myself that line of bullshit as the highway took us closer to Sanlúcar. There was frustratingly little traffic on this infuriatingly straight stretch between El Puerto and Sanlúcar; Alex wasn't even speeding, but we flew past the fields and tiny clusters of buildings. The only hinderance we encountered was a wagon being pulled by two plodding mules, but even they were off to the side so Alex could—and did—easily get around them.

As we passed the sign indicating the Sanlúcar city limits, I fidgeted in the passenger seat and cleared my throat. "So what made you pick Chipiona?"

Alex shrugged. "Cheaper than Rota or El Puerto. And I'm right on the beach." He glanced at me, his grin making my pulse race. "Can't really argue with that, am I right?"

"Yeah, that's fair. I haven't been out there yet. I drive by the exit for it all the time, but I've never stopped."

"It's a nice little town. Turns into a ghost town during siesta, but if you're there when everything's open..."

"Don't they all turn into ghost towns during siesta?"

He wobbled his hand in the air. "Some more than others. I mean, they all button up pretty tight during that time, but sometimes you can at least find a fast food place or something if you're desperate. Chipiona?" He shook his head. "I'm surprised I haven't seen any tumbleweeds roll through."

I snorted. "Same in Sanlúcar, at least down by the beach. I haven't ventured into any of the fast food joints."

"They're not half bad, honestly. Kind of put the ones in the States to shame sometimes."

"Do they?"

"Mmhmm. I try not to eat much fast food, but I mean, once in a while, a Big Mac hits the spot, you know?"

"Don't tell any of my patients, but..." I nodded. "Same."

He chuckled. "Secret's safe with me."

We exchanged glances over the center console, and my pulse ticked up another notch. I wanted a lot of secrets to be safe with him. I didn't want to ask him to risk his career to fool around with me, but goddamn, if he wanted to risk it? I'd take him up on it and my lips would be *sealed*.

Say the word, Alex.

All too fucking soon, he pulled down my street. Easing to a stop behind my car in front of my house, he said, "Well. We're here." He turned to me, and was that... disappointment? It was hard to say, especially since he had on sunglasses, but his expression did seem to take a subtle downturn.

"Yeah. Yeah, we are." I unbuckled my seat belt but didn't reach for the door. I could barely hear the idling engine over my pounding heart, and when I met Alex's gaze, he was chewing his bottom lip.

God, I want you so damn bad.

By some miracle, I kept those words from tumbling off my tongue. Because I did want him. And he was here. And I was here. And who the hell was going to know?

Maybe I still had some liquid courage left in me from last night, though, or maybe I was just too far beyond caring about consequences, because I finally said, "Do you, uh, want to come in?"

Alex took off his sunglasses, and he swallowed so hard, I heard it. Meeting my gaze without the dark lenses hiding his eyes anymore, he asked, "Do you *want* me to come in?"

My voice came out raspy: "You can park in the

driveway again." I gestured at the closed gate. "Don't think anyone will see."

He flicked his gaze toward the gate. Swallowed again. Looked at me again. "That... That wasn't my question."

If my heart beat any faster, he was going to need to drive me to the place we both worked.

To hell with it. I'd already put the offer out there—might as well own it.

"Yeah." I moistened my lips. "I do."

He studied me again, long enough I was sure he was trying to figure out how to politely remind me of all the reasons he needed to just drop me off and get the hell out of here.

I wasn't ready when he said, "Open the gate."

Oh, fuck yes.

I reached for the door. "I need to unlock it from inside the house. Give me a minute?"

He nodded, and I got out of the car. I fumbled with my keys on the smaller gate, but got it open. I was halfway up the steps when I realized I'd left my bag in his trunk. Oh fucking well. I had to fumble a bit with the keys on the door, too. As soon as the lock gave and the door opened, I hit the button for the gate, and it started to rumble open.

When Alex's engine revved, I had a heartbeat to think he might've come to his senses and taken off.

He hadn't. He turned into the driveway. As he shut off the car, I hit the button again, and the gate rattled closed behind him.

Then he was on his way up the walk.

Up the steps.

Across the porch.

Into the house.

And he didn't stop once he was through the door. He

kicked it shut behind him, and suddenly his hands were on my neck and his mouth was against mine.

Oh.

Holy.

Fuck.

Wrapping my arms around him, I stumbled back across the foyer until I hit the wall. Alex pushed me up against it, pinning me there with his hips as his fingers slid up into my hair. I had my hands on his back, gripping handfuls of his shirt as he stole my breath and my senses and every thought from my head.

Whatever I'd been imagining it would be like to kiss a man—to kiss this man in particular—turned to dust next to the reality. His lips were soft and assertive, and when he deepened the kiss, his tongue explored my mouth like he wanted to savor every taste of me. His fingers trembled against my scalp, and with his hips pressed so tightly against mine, I could feel every inch of his cock, thick and hard against mine. Some of the guys I'd danced with last night had been aroused, same as I had, but something about the way he ground against me—something about knowing this was *Alex* getting turned on by *me*—made it so much sexier this time.

I slid my hands up his back, loving the way he shivered in my arms. Watching him dance with other men had been hot. Feeling him—his heat, his reactions, his amazing body—was *incredible.*

Alex broke the kiss and touched his forehead to mine, panting hard into the narrow sliver between our lips. "Was this—" He paused for a gulp of air. "Was this why you wanted me to come in?"

"What do you think?" I growled, and this time I was the one to claim his mouth.

Oh, fuck me, that little moan? Easily the sexiest thing I'd ever heard. And felt. Because he was kissing me, and he was touching me, and his voice vibrated against my lips, and... how was this real?

I decided to get braver and slid my hands down. I hesitated when I reached his lower back, and he whimpered into my kiss as he ground his dick harder against mine. Dizzy with need, I ventured lower, and just like that I had two handfuls of the most perfect ass I'd ever seen.

"Goddammit," he murmured. "Fuck. I want... I want you so fucking bad."

It was a legitimate miracle that I didn't come in my pants then and there.

"Yeah?" I squeezed his ass. "Same."

He made a sound somewhere between a purr and growl, then came back in for another kiss. He kissed me deeper and harder this time, leaving gentle and assertive behind in favor of greedy and aggressive. I'd never been kissed like this in my life, and I *loved* it.

Suddenly his lips left mine, but before I could make sense of anything, he went for my neck, and I arched off the wall as he kissed up and down the side of my throat.

"Oh my God," I breathed. "That is... Oh fuck..."

His lips curved against my skin. "Like it?"

"There is nothing you've done that I haven't liked."

"Good." Then he was doing it again, his soft lips and coarse stubble on my neck driving my senses absolutely wild.

"Ungh. Alex..."

Another low growl as he kissed up from my collarbone.

"You know I've... I've never been with a man, right?"

"Mmhmm." He kissed beneath my jaw. "I'm aware."

I struggled to find my breath, never mind my voice. "So

I might need... need you to guide me, but... God, Alex, I want to do *everything* with you."

The groan he released had me grateful for the wall holding me up. I was already turned on to the point of delirious; realizing he was, too? That liquefied my knees and my spine.

He came up to meet my gaze. "Everything?"

I nodded. "Everything."

He bit his lip. Then he slid a hand between us, and when he cupped my dick through my shorts, my knees actually shook.

"Oh, God," I murmured, gripping his shoulders just to keep me upright. I couldn't help pushing back, rutting into his palm as he teased me.

Alex made some sound low in his throat—something primal and hot and full of need. "You know this can only be a one-time thing, right?"

"Uh-huh." I licked my lips and looked right into the fire in his eyes. "Guess we should make it count."

Oh, that grin was too sexy for words. Drawing me back in, he murmured, "We'll definitely make it count."

His kiss wasn't as aggressive this time. Instead, it was languid and all-consuming, just like the way he rubbed me through my shorts; it was like a promise to take his sweet fucking time with me until I was a wrung-out mess.

Please, please, yes, please.

"Not gonna lie," he murmured between kisses, "I have fantasized more than once about fucking you."

I couldn't help the whimper that escaped. "Oh God..."

"Might be a bit too much this soon, though. If you've never—"

"I've bottomed before."

He drew back and met me with a quizzical look. "I thought you hadn't been..."

Heat rushed into my face. "I, uh... My ex-wife and I. She wanted to give pegging a try."

"Ooh." His eyebrows rose, interest sparking in those stunning blue eyes. "And did you like it?"

I ran the tip of my tongue across my lip. "I've done a lot of fantasizing about you fucking me, if that tells you anything."

A shiver ran through him, and he closed his eyes as he squeezed my dick through my clothes and groaned, "Oh, fuck..."

"You want to fuck me?"

His eyes fluttered open, and they were full of even more fire now. "*Yes.* I absolutely do." He licked his lips. "I want to turn you around and plow you right up against this wall."

I almost choked on my own breath.

He wasn't done, though. "But if I only get to be with you one time, you better believe we're not going to rush anything." He ran his thumb over the head of my dick, then lifted his hand away. "By the time we get to me fucking you, I want you *begging* for it."

Oh, hell. Did he not understand that I was already at that point?

I swallowed. "Do you, um... Do you have condoms?"

He tensed, then nodded. "Yeah. In my bag." He drew back. "Maybe I should get them before we get too carried away?"

Though I was sure we were well past carried away, I said, "Good idea."

Alex kissed me once more, then let me go and gestured at the door. "Be right back."

He slipped out, leaving the door open a crack so it

wouldn't lock behind him, and I closed my eyes as I listened to both my thundering heart and his quiet footsteps.

This was real. Alex wanted me as much as I wanted him. And he wanted to make this count.

I might die before this afternoon was over.

As Alex came back up the walk, I decided I was okay with that.

He stepped back into the house with his backpack on his shoulder and mine in his hand. He left mine by the door and raised his eyebrows. "Bedroom?"

I led him down the hall and into the same room where we'd picked out my clothes for the club. Why did that feel like it had happened months ago?

He put his bag on the mattress, rifled through it, and produced a pack of condoms and a bottle of lube. Then he put the bag aside, put the necessities on the nightstand, and faced me with a devilish grin on his lips. He hooked a finger in my belt loop and drew me in, not that he met any resistance.

"You came prepared," I said.

His blush was adorable, and he shrugged. "Going clubbing, you never know..." He ran his hands down my back to my ass, and just before he kissed me, he purred, "Only one guy in that place interested me, though."

"Funny," I murmured against his lips. "I had the same problem."

"Is that right?" He kneaded my ass, pulling me in tight against his hard dick. "Looked like you were enjoying some of the other guys."

"So did you."

"Mmm, I don't mind dancing and getting felt up." He turned me a little so I was leaning against the bed, and then he was going at my neck again. "But the whole time, I just wanted to take you back to the hotel and..." He trailed off into a moan.

Jesus Christ. Last night was suddenly a million times hotter, knowing Alex had been stealing glances at me. That while he'd been dancing and touching other men, he'd wanted to have his hands and body and talented mouth all over me.

And that was exactly what I wanted right now.

I tugged at his shirt. He got the message, stepped back, and peeled it off. I seized the opportunity and did the same, and then he was in my arms again, hot skin against hot skin as he kissed me like his life depended on it. The slide of his palms up my back was even more of a turn-on than him fondling me through my shorts; once he had unencumbered access to my dick, I was going to lose my damn mind.

I couldn't wait.

I started undoing his belt, and he sucked in a sharp breath. For a split second, I thought I'd misread the situation and I was going too fast.

But before I could back off, he was fumbling with my belt, too. We undid them, and while we were at it, took off our shoes since we'd both completely neglected to do that in the foyer. Finally, everything came off, and when we came back together this time...

Oh fuck yes. Especially when he nudged me back and lowered me onto the mattress. I parted my thighs, and he settled between them, still standing beside the bed but bending down to kiss me as our cocks—with nothing at all between them now—rubbed together.

He kissed my neck. My collarbone. Then he teased my nipple with his lips and tongue and even his teeth.

I arched off the mattress just like I had the wall. "Fuck, Alex..."

He laughed, his breath rushing across my skin and giving me goose bumps. "I haven't even done anything yet."

"Oh, you have."

"Just wait."

"I've been waiting my whole fucking life to—holy shit!" I pushed myself up on my elbow and stared down as he ran his tongue around the head of my cock again.

He looked up through his lashes. "You were saying?"

"I..." Was I? I shook my head. "Nothing important."

He grinned, and then that amazing mouth was around my cock. I kept myself propped up so I could watch. I could barely breathe. This was hardly the first time someone had given me head, but it was the first time in over four years, and it was definitely the first time someone had done it this *well*. This *enthusiastically*. God, this man sucked dick like it was his favorite thing in the entire world, and the whole damn room spun around me as he licked his way from head to base and back again. He didn't neglect my balls, either— he teased them with featherlight fingertips and sometimes even his tongue, and I was surprised I could still *breathe*.

"I love what you're doing," I slurred. "It's... oh, Jesus. But..."

He lifted his head, some alarm in his eyes. "What?"

I exhaled. "If you keep doing it, I'm gonna come."

Relief took over his expression. "Well. We can't have that yet, can we?" He pushed himself all the way up, dusted a kiss across my lips, and nodded toward the pillows. "Lie back over there."

I shifted around, and he joined me, settling beside me and draping an arm over me as he met my lips in a long, sexy kiss. Having him like this was almost better than having his mouth on my cock; the latter would've made me come, but this was just... perfect. Tracing my hands all over him. Basking in the heat of his body against mine. Kissing someone who actually liked kissing and didn't seem to be in any hurry to do something else.

Ever since I'd caught that first inkling that I was bisexual, I'd wondered if I would ever really know until I had sex with a man. But I'd been so turned on just fantasizing about Alex that I'd been pretty sure that ship had sailed.

If there *did* happen to be a lingering thread of doubt somewhere in my consciousness, though, it vanished. I loved everything about this. I loved the broadness of his body, the coarseness of his stubble, the low sounds he made —everything that said I was getting intimate with a man had me dizzy with hunger and heat.

That fact that it was *this* man?

Oh, God. In that moment I had no idea if any other person on the planet would ever turn my head again. No one existed except Alex and his artful, masterful kiss and his fucking amazing body. Nothing mattered at all except how much he overwhelmed me, how damn good it felt to be touched like this—intimately and hungrily by someone who actually wanted me—for the first time in *years*. I hadn't even realized how touch-starved I'd been until now, and I couldn't get enough of him. I was overwhelmed, and I wanted *more*.

I moved my hand from his hip into the space between us, and when I closed my fingers around his cock, we both whimpered. Alex shuddered as he pushed himself into my hand, rocking as if he wanted to fuck my fist. Then he was stroking me, too, and we fell into the most mind-blowing rhythm, pumping each other and kissing until we were both breathing too hard to keep making out.

"Jesus fuck," he slurred against my lips.

"Uh-huh," I murmured. "So damn good."

He squeezed his eyes shut and tilted his head back, and I couldn't resist—I went for his neck like he'd gone for mine. That was even hotter than I expected. His groan vibrated beneath his faintly stubbled skin, and he thrust harder into my hand. This was something I'd somehow missed in my fantasies—how hot it would be when he responded to the things I did. The little shivers. The lip bites. The moaned curses.

What would he look like and sound like when he came?

I was the one to groan that time, pushing hard into Alex's tight fist as I imagined him falling apart. Could I make him forget how to speak? Because I was pretty sure he had me close to that point.

I lifted my head and whispered, "Roll on your back?"

His eyelids fluttered, and then he focused on me, the blue of his eyes almost lost to his blown pupils. It seemed to take him a second to process what I'd said, but he caught up and did as I'd asked.

I moved over the top of him, and my plans to go south were waylaid when he wrapped his arms around me and pull me down into a kiss. He parted his thighs for me like I'd done for him earlier, and oh hell, I hadn't realized how hot it would be, getting on top of him like this. When I slowly rocked my hips, our cocks rubbed together, and Alex whimpered and arched under me.

"Fuck, I am so turned on," he breathed.

"Yeah?" I grinned down at him, marveling at the sight of him this overcome with lust. "So you wouldn't say no if I wanted to go down on you?"

His eyes flew open this time, and he swept his tongue across his swollen lips. "Don't let me stop you."

I laughed softly and kissed him again, but hesitated. "I, uh... I've never done this, so..."

Alex's grin made my spine tingle. "You've gotten head before, right?"

"Of course. Yeah."

"So you know what you like." He carded his fingers through my hair. "Just do that—long as you don't use your teeth, you'll be fine."

I snapped my teeth at him, and reveled in his burst of laughter.

"Smartass," he muttered before claiming my mouth again.

I grinned against his lips, then indulged in a longer kiss.

I was still a little nervous about sucking dick for the first time, but I'd also wanted to for *years*. And he was right—I did know what I liked. How complicated could it be?

Before I lost my nerve, I broke the kiss, crawled down his beautiful body, and gave the underside of his cock a long, slow lick. Exhilaration ran through me like a surge of electricity, both from the realization that I was finally living out the fantasy of giving a guy head and from the strangled moan that escaped Alex's lips. As I tentatively teased him with my lips and tongue, his legs trembled and his back arched, but he kept his hips almost completely still, which I appreciated. It was hot, watching a guy get his mouth fucked in a porno, but I wasn't sure I was or ever would be ready for that.

This, though? Licking up and down the shaft and around the head? Taking him partway into my mouth while I stroked him with my hand? Driving those sharp, whispered curses out of him with little flutters of my tongue? Oh, yeah. Oh, fuck, yeah, I was ready for this.

"Connor..." He gripped the sheet beside his hip, clawing at it like he needed something to hold on to. "Oh my God, that's good..."

I couldn't describe the thrill. Not just sucking dick for the first time, but making Alex lose his mind like this. That was even hotter than the feeling of his thick, hard shaft sliding between my lips and against my tongue, and that said something. I'd always wondered how I'd actually like this, and it turned out I liked it *a lot*. I'd wondered what it would be like to have a cock in my mouth, and that part was great, but mostly I should've known how utterly fucking hot it would be to drive someone this wild. I'd always loved giving oral. Loved making a partner shake and gasp and swear. That part hadn't changed in the least just because he had different equipment than my mouth was used to.

Holy fuck, this is so much better than I thought it would be.

Alex's trembling voice just made it even much hotter. "You don't... You don't have to finish me." He sounded like he was struggling to form words. "If you're not... not ready for... Christ, Connor..."

I *might've* been ready for that. I was a little hesitant—it was new, after all—but right now, I was up for just about anything. Hell, if this was going to be the one and only time I ever got naked with Alex—and God only knew when I'd get near any other guy any time soon—then I wasn't holding back.

I lifted my head, still stroking his spit-slick cock with one hand. "I kind of do want you to come. But I also want you to fuck me."

He squeezed his eyes shut as he made a choked sound. Then he pushed himself up on his elbow so he could look at me. "I can come twice in a day."

Ooh. Well, now that was an interesting idea.

"So can I," I said with a grin.

He bit his lip, looking in that moment like he wanted to eat me alive. "We have all day. We can always fuck later."

It was my turn to bite my lip as a shiver of anticipation went through me. "In that case..." I started stroking him again. "Just, uh, tell me when you're gonna come?"

He nodded vigorously. "Of course. Always."

We exchanged grins, and then...

Then I went down on him again, this time with a goal in mind. I pumped him harder. I focused my mouth on the head of his dick. I still wasn't entirely sure what I was doing, so I kept doing what I knew I liked—what would take me over the edge—and that seemed to work. Alex whined softly and trembled, and this time, he let his hips move just enough to gently push into my mouth. Not so much that he'd challenge my gag reflex, but enough to signal he was getting into this—that he wanted more. He was even thicker and harder now, sliding back and forth on my tongue, and the salt of pre-cum made the room sway; holy fuck, I was really going to do this.

A flash of doubt hit me—*was* I sure I wanted this? *Did* I really want him to come in my mouth?

"God, Connor," he moaned. "I'm... I'm getting there."

Yes. *Yes*, I absolutely wanted every drop of his cum.

I had the briefest worry that I might choke, but I quickly came to my senses and remembered that high-volume, high-velocity projectile cum was more of a porno thing than a reality thing. He wasn't exactly going to blow out the back of my skull.

Sure I could handle whatever came—so to speak—I gave him everything I had. He got even thicker and harder, and exhilaration and anticipation crackled through me as his balls pulled up and his breathing got faster and sharper.

Finally, he rewarded me with the hottest, sexiest moan

I'd ever heard, followed by, "Fuck, I'm gonna come. I'm gonna come. Oh, *fuck!*"

His hips jerked, and then, with a wordless cry of abandon that my neighbors back in Norfolk probably heard, he came. The rush of hot, salty liquid across my tongue was a new sensation, that was for sure, but I liked it. I swallowed without thinking twice, and I kept teasing him until he mumbled for me to stop.

When I pushed myself up again, I was treated to something even hotter—the sight of Alex lying there, flushed and sweaty with a hand over his face as he trembled all over and tried to catch his breath.

He lowered his hand and met my gaze, and a drunken little grin spread across his lips. I came up to him, and he pulled me down, and I didn't have to ask if he minded kissing me after he'd come in my mouth. We made out lazily for the longest time as he held me against his feverishly hot body.

After a while, he touched his forehead to mine. "I want to return the favor, but I also want to top you. And I don't want you to be too sensitive." He carded his fingers through my hair. "Don't worry, though—before I leave today, you're coming down my throat."

I almost came on him right then and there, but somehow, I held back. Sliding a hand up his chest, I whispered, "I'm not in any hurry if you're not."

He grinned, and then he kissed me again.

And no, neither of us was in any hurry for anything.

CHAPTER 12

ALEX

I was still tingling all over from that orgasm. Thank God Connor was willing to chill for a bit before we got going again; I had no doubt he was still turned on as all hell, but I needed a few minutes. Everything was way too sensitive to do more than hold him against me and kiss.

Fortunately, he didn't seem to mind that. Connor *loved* kissing, and he was so fucking good at it. Maybe he didn't have experience with men, but this part? Oh, he knew his way around a long, languid kiss, and I couldn't get enough.

After hell if I knew how long, we came up for air. Breathing hard against his talented lips, I whispered, "Are you sure you've never been with a man?"

Connor's laugh was breathless and near silent. "I think I'd know if I had, righ?"

"True." I kissed him lightly. "But for your first time sucking dick..." I couldn't help shivering. "That was amazing."

He grinned, running his hand up my back. "Well, that's good to hear. I've wanted to try it for a long, long time, and I was always afraid I wouldn't know what to do."

I couldn't help laughing myself. "I get that. We're all nervous the first time we try anything. But your oral skills..." I whistled, shaking my head. "Take it from someone who's experienced a bad blowjob—you're *fine*."

He raised his eyebrows. "A bad blowjob? Is that even possible?" He paused. "Okay, I've had some that weren't great—back when my ex and I were both completely inexperienced and clueless—but *bad?*"

"Oh, my sweet summer child..." I settled onto the pillow beside him because my arm was going to sleep, and he shifted onto his side, draping his arm over my stomach. Trailing my fingers along his forearm, I said, "Trust me, there is such thing as a bad blowjob. Usually one that involves teeth."

Connor shuddered. "Ow. That... doesn't sound pleasant."

"It wasn't. Not *either* time." I rolled my eyes. "I don't do three strikes and you're out—I gave him *two* chances, and I thought that was *more* than generous."

"You're a better man than me," he said dryly. "I wouldn't have let those teeth anywhere near my dick again, thank you very much."

"I don't blame you. I was much younger and more of a people pleaser back then."

"You're not a people pleaser anymore?"

The time I'd spent with Tobias flashed through my mind—what little people pleasing had still lingered in me was dead and gone by the time I'd rid myself of him. But I wasn't going to bring him up and kill the mood, so I just chuckled and said, "You think I'd last as a people pleaser? Pfft. I'm a corpsman."

He laughed. "Okay, point taken."

That... actually sobered me. Only someone who was or

worked with corpsmen would truly understand how much the job, as much or even more than a lot of military jobs, chewed up and spit out people pleasers.

Connor understood.

Because not only had he been a corpsman himself, he *did* work with corpsmen.

As a physician.

As an officer.

As someone way the fuck above my paygrade, and someone whose bed was not a place I should be if I still wanted to retire with my veteran benefits.

He must've seen the sudden shift in my mood, because he touched my face and whispered, "Hey. You still with me?"

"Yeah. Yeah. Just..." I sighed, clasping his hand in mine. "Reminded myself why we shouldn't be doing this."

His shoulders fell as he released a breath. "Fuck."

"I'm... God, I'm sorry. I didn't mean to kill the mood."

Connor shook his head. "You didn't. It's just a reminder that we have to make this count, I guess."

"There is that." I let go of his hand and carded my fingers through his hair, reveling in the cool softness and the way he closed his eyes and pressed into my touch. "It sucks. Because under any other circumstances, I'd already be looking forward to doing this again."

"Me too." He opened his eyes. "I know it has to be a one-time thing. As much as I want to do it again..." He shook his head. "But... that doesn't mean I'm in a hurry for it to be over."

"Neither am I."

"Good. Because I've been dying to be touched, and everything we've done..." He exhaled hard. "It's just so damn good."

"Yeah, it is. And... dying to be touched? Does that mean it's been a while?"

He laughed quietly. "That would be an understatement."

"Yeah?"

Connor nodded. "This is the first time I've been touched since before my ex-wife and I separated. It's..." He exhaled. "I didn't realize how much I was missing that until now."

"Yeah?" I smoothed his hair. "How long has that been?"

"We were separated for three years. It was probably..." He rocked his head from side to side. "Close to a year before that, maybe? And that was after a year or two of really sporadically doing anything."

"Jesus," I whispered. "I can't imagine going that long."

"Eh, I think I was just so focused on moving on, being a dad, doing my job..." Connor sighed. "Didn't really spend much time thinking about what I needed or wanted. But now that I'm here and I'm alone, and my boys are off on their own..." He trailed off.

"Time to think about yourself?"

"Long past time, yeah." He looked right in my eyes. "To be clear, that's not why I wanted this. With you." Pulling me a little closer, he softly added, "Yeah, I've been dying to be touched, but this? This is because I haven't been able to get you out of my head."

"Me too." I brushed my lips across his. "I, well—it hasn't been *that* long since I've been laid. But I've been wanting you like crazy ever since I saw your profile." Longer than that, but he didn't need to know I'd had a crush on him since the day he'd reported for duty in Rota.

"It hasn't been that long?" An eyebrow arched and some

mischievous curiosity sparked in his eyes. "How long has it been?"

"Uh..." The heat in my face killed any thought I might've had about playing this cool. "Well..." I cleared my throat. "I've got an occasional booty call out in El Puerto."

"Do you?" There'd been a hint of jealousy the first time I'd mentioned Isidoro, but now there was just curiosity and maybe a little mischief.

"Yeah," I said. "He's a Spanish local. The guy I told you about who I talk to using the translator app."

"Mmhmm. And when was the last time you were with him?" He was fighting a grin.

"Why?" I laughed. "You really want to know how long it's been since I was in another guy's bed?"

"Just curious." Connor half-shrugged as he let that grin come to life. "Call it living vicariously through someone who actually has a handle on his sexuality and navigating the scene in this area."

"You don't seem to be struggling too hard with your sexuality."

"Eh." He wobbled his hand in the air. "I've known for a long time that I'm bisexual, but it's been intimidating, putting myself out there and getting into bed with someone. I envy people like you who had the freedom and the confidence long before I ever did."

"We all come to things in our own time," I said. "You're not the first queer guy to dip his toes in as an adult and you won't be the last."

"Well, that's a relief," he said with a dry laugh.

"I'm serious. Back in Yokosuka, there was this civilian contractor who was—I want to say late forties? I think he was almost fifty. I was the first man he ever touched."

Connor's eyebrows rose. "Really?"

"Mmhmm. He came from a seriously repressed background, and he'd had a nasty divorce for a lot of reasons that had nothing to do with his sexuality. None of us had a clue he was gay until I ran into him in this really tiny gay bar in Nagasaki. It was one of those places you had to know someone to even find, so God only knows how he heard about it, but there he was, and there I was, and... do the math."

"Wow. So you've done this before, then? Helped some older guy get the hang of sex with a man?"

I smiled and trailed my fingertips down his arm. "You make it sound like I'm running a charity."

He laughed, unaware of what that did to my pulse. "That's not what I meant. Just... that you've got the patience for it, I guess?"

"Patience?" I slid closer to him and kissed him. "I don't know if you've noticed, but I've been enjoying the hell out of being in bed with you. Patience, my ass."

He laughed softly as he ran his hands up my back. "Fair enough. And I hope you weren't kidding about topping me."

Excitement zipped through me. "If you want me to top you, you better believe I will."

Connor bit his lip, eyes gleaming with renewed hunger. "Yes, please?"

Oh, fuck yeah...

"Have you, um..." I hesitated. "You said you bottomed with your ex-wife, right?"

"Yeah. Like I said, she wanted to try pegging." He blushed as he added, "Turned out we both liked it."

"Okay, so you know how much prep you need, and you know how much you can take."

"Mmhmm. And I, uh... I didn't stop just because she and I did, if that makes sense. So it hasn't been four-plus years since I've been penetrated, if that's what you're wondering."

"Oh yeah?" I cocked a brow. "So it's something you enjoy doing on your own?"

The blush deepened, and he nodded again. "I enjoy it a *lot*."

"Good," I said. "I'm always worried about hurting someone the first time. I use a ton of lube and go really slow, but if someone is nervous enough…" I grimaced.

"Yeah, I was afraid that would happen when we tried it. We started with something small, though, and worked up to bigger over time." He glanced down, then met my gaze with a wicked grin. "I actually have a toy that's almost exactly as thick as you, so I know I can handle it."

"Oh, really?" I returned the grin. "And do you like that toy?"

"Mmhmm." He slid his hand over my dick, which was rapidly hardening, and I gasped at the contact. "I have several, and that one is my favorite." He teased my balls with his fingertips, and I lost the ability to come back with something witty. He kissed me lightly, then murmured, "Please fuck me. I want to come with your dick in my ass."

I had to catch my breath. "Has anyone ever told you that you have a filthy mouth?"

"I've heard that accusation from time to time." Connor's eyebrow flicked up. "Is that a complaint?"

"Not in the least. I love dirty talk."

"Mmm, good to know. So is that a yes on fucking me until I come?"

"Absolutely."

"Good," he whispered, and then we sank into a longer, lazier kiss. The hypersensitivity from earlier was gone, and though I wasn't fully hard yet, that probably wasn't far off.

Not when I had Connor's hot body against mine, his erection pressed to my hip as he absolutely devoured my mouth.

Maybe it was just as well this was a one-time thing—making a habit of sex with this man would probably kill me.

Still, I couldn't help but agree when he whispered, "God, I wish we could do this again." He dipped his head and started on my neck, and his voice was a low growl as he murmured, "I want you so fucking bad, and I know that's not going to stop after tonight."

I bit my lip, tilting my head back so he could access as much of my throat as possible.

In between sizzling hot kisses on my skin, he asked, "Any chance you bottom, too?"

"I'm about as switchy as they get." I arched under him, pressing my hard dick against him. "But you want to get topped today, so..."

He shivered, then whispered, "Well, if I have to choose between the two—I definitely want to get topped."

I almost groaned with frustration. We did have to choose, didn't we? Because while we were both reasonably fit, we were also long past twenty-five. There was only so much we were going to be able to do in one day.

"Well, lucky for you," I slurred, "you've already made me come once. So we won't have to worry about me going off too fast once I'm in you."

Though... hell. Just thinking about pushing into his gorgeous ass had my toes curling, so maybe I wouldn't last as long as I thought?

Connor lifted himself up over me and kissed me again as he settled his hips and his hard-on against mine. I traced every inch of him I could reach with my hands, memorizing every plane and angle of his body. If I could only have this one time with him, I was going to commit it *all* to memory.

Every last detail, from his weight over me to that soft moan when I teased his lips with my tongue.

He was *shaking* when he broke away and whispered, "Fuck me? Please?"

"Hell yes." I cupped his face and kissed him softly. "Grab the lube."

"Condom too?"

"Not yet. I need to get you ready first."

He nodded, and he pulled away to get the bottle from the nightstand. The sudden absence of his skin touching mine left me breathless; I *needed* his body against me.

He came back to the middle of the bed and held up the lube. "So, um... How do you want to do this?"

I took the bottle and gestured for him to roll over. "On your side. It'll be more comfortable for you."

Connor stole a quick kiss, and then as I opened the lube bottle, he did as he was told. I put a little on my fingers, trying to ignore how hard my hard was pounding with the sheer anticipation of being inside him. In my mind, I was already rocking in and out of him, driving curses and groans from both of us until we were coming and shaking and melting into a satisfied heap on the mattress.

First things first, though.

I molded myself to his back and kissed the side of his neck. "I'll go slow. I promise."

"You don't have to. I've done this."

"Oh, I know." I traced the curve of his ass cheek with the back of his hand. "But going slow means I can tease you."

I might've liked that frustrated groan a little too much. I didn't apologize for it, though.

I wasn't kidding about teasing him, either. I teased his hole far longer than I needed to, until he was whimpering and swearing, and only then did I gently slip in a fingertip. By the time I'd worked up to two fingers, he was touching himself and rocking back against me, every sound he made full of lust and need.

"You like that, don't you?" I murmured.

"Yeah," he breathed. "I... God, I want your dick. Like now."

"Mmm, I know you do." I kissed the back of his shoulder as I crooked my fingers inside him. "But it's so much fun to make you beg."

He started to say something else, but I added a third finger, and his voice fell to a near sob. He pumped himself faster, probably desperate for friction both inside and out.

"Don't go too fast," I teased. "Can't have you coming before I fuck you."

"Then fuck me, damn it," he growled.

"I will. But first I want to—"

"Alex," he panted. "Please. Just... put on a damn condom and *fuck me already*."

"Mmm, I could do that," I purred in his ear, still sliding my fingers in and out so slowly it was almost frustrating for *me*. "Or I could keep making you squirm."

"Alex." He shivered hard, clenching almost painfully tight around my fingers. "Just. Fuck me."

It was tempting to make him go even further out of his mind, but I was getting close to going out of mine. So, I slipped my fingers free and kissed the back of his shoulder again. "Give me a second to put on the condom."

He exhaled. "Oh thank God..."

"Hey. He had nothing to do with it."

Connor just laughed and shook his head.

I made quick work of putting on the condom, then added a generous amount of lube.

"How do you want me?" he asked.

"Move to the edge of the bed." I got up onto my feet. "Like when I was blowing you earlier."

He did, and I stood between his thighs. I fingered him a little more, just to make sure there was plenty of lube, and then...

Then I gave him what he'd been begging for.

There were few things I loved more than watching it register on a man's face as I eased into him. Something about that look that was overwhelmed, relieved, and needy all at once. He closed his eyes and arched, stroking his own dick lazily as I carefully worked myself in.

"Like that?" Holy fuck, I was out of breath.

"Y-yeah." He squeezed his eyes shut and bit his lip. "God, Alex, you feel so..." He moaned, and I wondered for a moment if standing had been a good idea after all. I was so turned on, my knees were shaking, and I wasn't entirely sure I could hold myself up.

I'd damn sure try, though, especially as Connor swore and gasped as he took me deeper. I'd always gotten off on getting another man off, but Connor's pleasure was straight up addictive. I could get drunk on the sexy sounds he made and the sight of him laid out in front of me like a pornographic gift, taking every inch of my dick while he jerked himself off and writhed with pure bliss.

Somehow, I found my breath and my voice, and I whispered, "Do you like it like this? Slow and..." I closed my eyes as I buried myself all the way inside him. Pulling out slowly, I slurred, "Or do you want it harder?"

He exhaled sharply. "I... Fuck. I love it like this. But I also want... I also want you to *rail* me."

The whimper that escaped this time was mine—my head full of images of him crying out as I pounded him deep and hard while in reality, I was still slowly, languidly sliding my dick in and out of his tight, slicked hole. I didn't know which I wanted more either, only that I couldn't get enough and I couldn't take any more, and...

"You're so damn hot," I breathed. "I want to fuck you into the mattress, but I love it like this too." I took a few more slow strokes before I shakily whispered, "Jesus Christ, Connor. Tell... Tell me what you want. Anything you want."

I meant it to. In that moment, I'd have done anything to give him more of the pleasure that was already written all over his gorgeous face.

Connor rocked his hips in time with mine. Then he gazed up at me with fire in his eyes, and he pushed himself up on his elbow, curved his other hand behind my neck, and whispered, "C'mere."

I did, letting him draw me down into a kiss that was as slow and sexy as the way our bodies moved together. This was perfect. Just... just perfect. A man who could kiss the soul right out of my body. My dick moving in him just right to have me almost on the edge of coming. His fingers twitching against my neck as he moaned against my lips.

I started to slide out again, and right then—right as I was pulling almost all the way out, Connor broke the kiss and looked right in my eyes.

"Alex," he whispered. "Fuck me. *Hard.*"

Without warning or even thought, I thrust back in, and he fell back onto the mattress with a sexy, helpless cry.

"Like that?" I started withdrawing again, slowly like before.

"Yes!" He started pumping himself fast and hard now, and his eyes were still squeezed shut as he demanded, *"More."*

What could I do but give this beautiful, vocal, responsive man exactly what he wanted?

I pushed my hands under his ass and lifted his hips, and we both gasped as the angle went from amazing to *oh my fucking God*, and I slammed into him deep and hard. His cries drove me on, and my thrusts made him cry out even more, and we fell into this perfect, dizzying feedback loop. Moving inside him felt incredible, and watching him and hearing him had me so damn close to the edge, I had to fight back my orgasm. I wanted him to come first—wanted his orgasm to set mine off. I wanted the sight and sound and sensation of Connor coming unraveled to be what sent me into oblivion.

"Oh my God," I moaned, sounding to my own ears like I was close to sobbing. Maybe I was. "You feel so... Fuck, baby, I want you to come."

Connor made a choked sound, and he pumped himself faster, his skin flushed as he drove us both on. "God, yeah..."

"Is that good? Is that—"

"Just like that." His eyes flew open and met mine. "Holy fuck, Alex, that is so..." He dug his teeth into his bottom lip as he rocked his hips just right to nearly catapult me over the edge.

And then, with a breathless cry of release, he jerked under me, and jets of cum landed on his flat stomach.

Hottest thing I'd ever seen. Hands down.

I thrust as hard as I could, trying to get as deep as Connor could take me, and then I let go, and my legs almost dropped out from under me as my orgasm crashed through me and into him.

With one last shudder, I slumped over him, holding myself up on shaking arms.

"Oh my God," Connor moaned. "That was…" He trailed off, closing his eyes as he shivered beneath me.

I arched an eyebrow, still trembling and panting over him. "I hope whatever you were going to say wasn't bad."

He rolled his eyes, then gestured down at the cum all over his abs and chest. "Yes, Alex. Worst. Orgasm. Ever." Another eyeroll as he reached for my neck. "Get down here."

I laughed as he pulled me down to him, and we were both grinning when our lips met.

My back, unfortunately, didn't like that position, so we didn't stay that way for long. I pulled out and got rid of the condom, then dropped onto the bed beside him by the pillows where he had moved while I was up. We'd need to do a bit more cleanup thanks to all the lube and cum, but that could wait while we kissed and caught our breath.

After a while, he met my gaze, and he grinned. "Well, I've been sexually frustrated for a long time, but this was definitely worth the wait."

I laughed, running my knuckles along his jaw. "Glad I didn't disappoint."

"Mmm, no, definitely not." He kissed me again, letting it linger for a moment or two. Then, "Should we grab a shower?"

"Probably. Depends on if you think we're done."

Interest and heat both sparked in his eyes. "You don't think we are?"

"We don't have to be. I can't promise I've got another orgasm in me, but I'm pretty sure I can get another one out of you."

Ooh, he liked that idea, that was for damn sure. "So you're not bored of me yet?"

"Hardly. And like I said, I'm not in any hurry for this to

be over." I paused, then grinned. "Plus, I mean, if I stick around until after dark, I'm even less likely to be seen leaving."

Connor laughed. "I like the way you think. Especially since the sun doesn't go down until late."

"So you don't mind being stuck with me until like 2300 or so?"

He coasted his palm up my chest. "Do I look like I want to chase you out?"

"Well, no, but I don't want to overstay my welcome."

"Mmm, I don't think that's going to be an issue." He curved his hand behind my neck and leaned in close. "Especially not if you make good on sucking me off later."

I shivered as I kissed him softly. "I am nothing if not a man of my word."

CHAPTER 13

CONNOR

Coming to Spain had been an exercise in more culture shock than I'd anticipated. The buildings were different—more stucco walls and tile roofs than I'd ever seen in my life. The signs were different, from their shapes and colors to the words printed on them. Even having a meal in a restaurant wasn't what I was used to thanks to the language barrier, knowing when a place would even be open, and when they were serving tapas versus dinner. The first couple of weeks had been overwhelming to say the least.

Returning to the now familiar world outside my house after the day I'd spent in bed with Alex felt a lot like those early days of fumbling and stumbling through an alien new world. It was like I'd been here before, but many years ago, and everything seemed just slightly different now. It reminded me of when I'd been down with the flu for a solid week during the last year of my marriage; re-emerging into the world had been almost as disorienting as the fever that had knocked me on my ass.

The drive from Sanlúcar to Rota had become as ordinary as the one I'd taken from my home in Virginia Beach to the base in Norfolk a million times. Today, it was like something out of a dream.

I knew why. Yesterday had been one of the hottest things I'd ever experienced, and coming back to earth after something like that left me off-balance and struggling to focus. I knew how and why I felt like this. The question was just... what now? Where did I go from here? Back on that hookup app? To another club? Just... stock up on lube and hope I didn't actually develop tennis elbow? Ugh, I was a mess. An absolute—

"Lieutenant Commander?"

I shook myself and looked up from the keyboard I'd been staring at. "Hmm?"

Leaning into my open doorway, HM2 Anderson studied me, a quizzical look on her face. "I just asked if you wanted some coffee." She gestured over her shoulder. "I was heading to the breakroom to get some for myself."

"Oh. Uh." I blinked, then looked at the cup on my desk, which was not only empty—the dregs at the bottom were bone dry. "Coffee would be great, thanks." I smiled sheepishly up at her as I handed over my cup. "I probably need it."

"You said it, not me."

I just rolled my eyes.

She laughed. "I'll be right back."

"Thanks, HM2."

"Don't mention it, sir."

She left my office, and I covered my face with both hands. For fuck's sake, I *needed* to get my head together.

Yesterday was a one-time thing. It shouldn't have even been that much, but I'd never been that attracted to someone in my life—especially not someone who was also apparently that attracted to me.

I want you again.

Every time Alex crossed my mind—which he did *constantly*—that thought followed.

And every time, I'd run myself through all the very real and very non-negotiable reasons why yesterday *was* and *had to be* a one-time thing. Even that much had been a risk.

Worth it, though. So damn worth it. I could still feel everything we'd done, from my ass (which was a little sore, but not unpleasantly so) to that spot on my collarbone where his stubble had scraped just slightly.

Absolutely worth it, but not worth doing again. Not with what we'd both be risking. And hey, now I knew what it was like to sleep with a man, so at least I wouldn't feel completely clueless with the next guy.

I don't want the next guy. I want—

I pushed myself up from my chair and headed out of my office. HM2 was just coming back with my coffee, which I thanked her for profusely. Then I headed down the hall to get my stupid ass to work, both because it was my goddamned job, and because I couldn't think of any other way to get Alex off my mind.

Yeah.

About that last part.

Every other patient, it seemed, needed to go up to Radiology, and every time I submitted an order, my mind went back to that gorgeous corpsman. He might not have even been there today—there were two radiology techs, plus their supervisor—but the department may as well have been renamed *"Where That Guy With the Miraculous Mouth Works."*

I closed my eyes and exhaled as I paused outside my next patient's door.

I want you again.

I did. I definitely did. But I couldn't have him, and I needed to move past him.

This *would* pass. It had to. I'd had a relentless crush on my neighbor after I'd moved into an apartment when Aimee and I separated, and I'd gotten over that eventually. Yeah, I'd jerked off thinking about him, and I'd forgotten how to speak a few times in his presence, but eventually, I'd gotten it through my stupid skull that it wasn't going to happen.

I'd get there with Alex, too.

Except Orlando and I had never hooked up. To my knowledge, he was straight, and he'd never reciprocated. It was a lot easier to move on from someone who I had absolutely zero chance with, especially when I knew they weren't interested in me.

Alex...

I had the marks on my hips and the dull ache in my muscles to remind me just how much he reciprocated my desire.

I also had a job to do, and I pulled my head together enough to school my expression and step into the patient's room. All through the appointment, I was attentive and did my job, which in this case meant referring a young Sailor for physical therapy on his knee.

"The MRI looks good," I told him after reviewing the images he'd had done at a nearby Spanish hospital. "No tearing or anything like that." I flashed him a quick smile. "A few weeks of physical therapy should resolve the pain."

The kid sighed. "I've got the PRT coming up. And I need to pass it with flying colors because I *need* this promotion."

"You'll be able to make it up once you're cleared for full duty."

His shoulders sank, but he didn't protest. I understood. The Physical Readiness Test was an important part of a service member's score when they were up for a promotion. While being unable to participate due to medical reasons wasn't *supposed* to affect their rating, I'd been around long enough to know that it absolutely could. If a command had two equally excellent Sailors, but one had to sit out the PRT due to illness or injury, the healthy one was going to get the higher rating. Guaranteed.

I studied the kid. "When is your command doing the PRT?"

He thought about it. "I think six weeks?"

Pursing my lips, I peered at the chart notes and MRIs again. "Are you allowed to use the stationary bike instead of running?"

He nodded.

"All right. Go straight to the physical therapy department after this to get your appointments set up. Give it a couple of weeks, then start *carefully* conditioning on the bike. Follow up with me weekly, stick to your physical therapy, and we'll reassess a week or two before the PRT." I inclined my head. "*Do not* push yourself too hard, or you *will* hurt yourself enough to be on light duty with a PRT waiver for this PRT *and* the next one. Got it?"

Brightening, he nodded again. "Yes, sir. Thank you."

"Don't mention it. And if it starts to hurt more, come back in."

"Okay. Okay, I will. Thank you again, sir."

I made a few more notes in his chart, sent the referral through to physical therapy, and signed off on his light duty chit before sending him on his way. I was confident he'd be all right by the PRT. He'd sprained his knee, but it was relatively minor, and the stationary bike would be a good way for him to rehab it *and* be ready for the PRT. Well, as long as he didn't overdo it, and I'd been a military physician long enough to know that was a distinct possibility. Twenty-something kids were immortal, and being in the military only made that worse.

Not that I'd learned any of that the hard way or anything, and I totally didn't have the irritable knee and bitchy shoulder to show for it.

Though… my years of youthful immortality had very little to do with the aches and stiffness I was feeling today.

Annnd there went my brain, right back to the place it had been all fucking day.

"Get a grip," I muttered to myself as I continued to the room where my next patient was waiting.

Throughout the day, I was such a mental trainwreck that I seriously considered seeing if Alex wanted to hook up again, consequences be damned. We could be discreet. We could be smart about it. As long as we didn't get caught, who cared?

It also occurred to me around the time I was sitting down to lunch that we wouldn't automatically get busted if we were seen together. If we were making out or getting handsy or something, sure. But if we were just talking in the hall or even out in public—the Navy couldn't prove that was an "overly familiar" relationship.

The UCMJ was clear about fraternization between officers and enlisted, but the water could get a little murky when it came time to prove the fraternization was actually a problem. A violation of the custom of officers and enlisted staying apart? Yes. Knowingly disobeying a lawful order? Yes.

There was also, however, a part of the statute that required the prosecution to prove that the fraternization brought discredit on the Navy or was not prejudicial to good order and discipline. Alex and I weren't in the same chain of command. We were under the same commanding officer, yes, and part of the same command, but we were in different departments. He wasn't my subordinate. We could fuck each other senseless during our off time, and it would never have any impact on our jobs.

And if we weren't doing anything out in public or at work, then there was nothing to bring discredit on the Navy.

But I was just gaslighting myself if I thought any of that would keep us from losing our careers and benefits. There was no way in hell our courts-martial would land in front of judges who would decide, *"Nah, these two banging when they're off the clock isn't hurting anyone or making the Navy look bad. We'll let it slide."* Never in a million years. It wouldn't happen with a straight couple, and it sure as shit wouldn't with a same-sex one.

Absolute best-case scenario? The Navy would force me to retire with my full benefits because that was less headache than prosecuting me when I was already eligible for retirement. I'd seen plenty of people force-retired for offenses that would've had them hemmed up to hell and back if they'd still had a few years left.

Alex wouldn't be so lucky. He could go to Captain's Mast, get stripped down to E-5, and then booted out because of high-year tenure; an E-5 had to make E-6 by a certain point in their career, and though I didn't know all the particulars of Alex's career, I was pretty sure he was past that point. They could kick him out as an E-5, and while he *might* keep his VA benefits if the CO was feeling generous, he'd lose his pension.

If we got caught, I *might* get lucky and escape somewhat unscathed, but no matter what, Alex would be fucked.

And that was the *best*-case scenario.

The thought sobered me right up. Yes, I wanted him, but the last thing in the world I wanted was to be the reason he lost everything he'd worked so hard for.

Footsteps jarred me out of my thoughts, and I looked up just as HM2 Anderson came into my office, a stack of folders in her hand. She paused and tilted her head. "You all right, sir?"

No, I wasn't, but the "sir" at the end of her question was a stark reminder of why I couldn't confide in her or even admit that I was struggling today.

Officer. Enlisted. Couldn't be too familiar. Couldn't be too friendly.

Couldn't fraternize.

"I'm fine, HM2." I smiled despite my somersaulting stomach. "Just tired from the weekend."

"I know that feeling." She handed over the stack of charts. "I just need you to sign off on some things when you have a chance."

I glanced at them; mostly prescription renewals, which required more brainpower than I currently possessed, but I'd find a way. "Thanks, HM2. I'll get them done by EOD."

She nodded and left my office again. As soon as I was alone, I dropped my military bearing. I slouched back in my chair and swore into the silence.

I should've felt a million times better after finally getting laid.

But all I could think about was the man I couldn't have, and I was a goddamned mess.

CHAPTER 14

ALEX

Real life *never* lived up to fantasy. The real thing was *always* a letdown from the fantasy. *Always*.

When I'd accepted Connor's invitation to come inside after driving him home, I'd reminded myself of that. I'd told myself that hooking up with him was exactly what I needed to get my mind back on the rails. Give in to that attraction, indulge in the sex I'd been fantasizing about, and then walk away and move on. Once I broke through what I'd imagined it would be like and experienced the real thing, I wouldn't be so hung up on that unrealistic mental porno I hadn't been able to shut off.

Yeah.

About that.

Three solid days after I'd slept with Connor, I wanted him even more than I had before I'd ever laid a hand on him.

I kept asking myself, was the sex really that good?

And... yeah. Yeah, it *had* been that good. He'd been generous and responsive and vocal, and oh my God, I wanted *more*.

Several times, I'd considered hitting up Isidoro, but each time, that thought hadn't lasted. He'd always been fun in bed, but I knew to my core that sex with him would just leave me aching for more of Connor.

What the fuck? Since when did I get *this* hung up on anyone? Especially after I'd gotten it out of my damn system? There'd been times I'd left so satisfied that I was looking forward to the next time, but not like this. Never like this.

Maybe it was because I *couldn't* have him again?

Except... no.

The whole forbidden fruit thing had never really been my thing, mostly because the consequences were usually more of a headache than they were worth. This time, the consequences would derail my whole damn life. Connor's, too. If our CO really wanted to be a dick and make an example of us, she could slap us with an Article 92 and boot us out of the Navy. It probably wouldn't be a dishonorable discharge; a Sailor had to fuck up way harder than blowing an officer to score one of those. No, we'd likely get administratively separated, which did not look good on a résumé *and* could cost us our veteran benefits. Connor *might* be able to just retire since he was past twenty years, or the powers that be could decide to fuck us both equally.

Either way—not ideal.

A pile of potential consequences like that was usually more than enough to deter me from pursuing something I shouldn't. While I had done plenty of clubbing and partying in high school, I hadn't done any with my military peers until the fourth year of my first enlistment because I'd been too afraid of getting hemmed up for underage drinking. I'd curtailed my speeding while I was stationed in Japan because tickets and fender benders were international incidents that I hadn't wanted to deal with (my lead foot still existed in Spain, mostly because I could just pay the cop right then and there and be done with it).

And as it happened, today I was treated to a reminder of yet another forbidden thing I wasn't the least bit tempted to do.

My patient was on crutches, miserably favoring his right leg, and he looked like he'd taken a beating, too. There was a big scrape on his cheek, a bandage on his forehead, and another peeking out from beneath the sleeve of his blouse.

I took the order from him and skimmed over it.

X-ray. Right hip. Puncture wound on right buttock, possible bone chip or fracture to pelvis.

What the—

Oh. *Ooh*.

I fought hard to keep my military bearing and not let a chuckle slip through. "Let me guess—just got back from Pamplona?"

His eyes went huge. Then he groaned. "Oh God. Did my doctor put that in the notes?"

"No. But it's that time of year." I grimaced and tried to sound playful as I asked, "You know you're supposed to run *ahead* of the bulls, right?" I didn't bother mentioning we weren't supposed to run with them at all; if he hadn't already gotten an earful from a superior, it was coming when he handed over his light duty chit.

Rolling his eyes, he nodded. "Yeah. I know. I was doing good until I tripped. Fucking uneven streets..."

"I'm sure. Well, let's take you back and see what's going on in there."

Running with the bulls was definitely one of those situations where the consequences outweighed the thrill. I'd entertained the idea for a hot minute when I'd taken the orders to Spain, but quickly decided against it when I realized all the ways it could go spectacularly wrong. Plus I'd realized they were fighting bulls, and I was vehemently against bullfighting, so... no.

And that was all before I'd gone to orientation upon arrival, and the base CO had made it very clear that, "If you run with the bulls, I will find out." He'd held up a Spanish magazine with a photo on the cover from the annual running of the bulls ... with three Sailors' faces clearly front and center.

Message received, Captain.

Not everyone got that message, though, and once in a while, somebody got hurt, as was the case with the kid I was X-raying. A lot of people did fly under the radar. They ran with the bulls, came away unscathed, and didn't get caught.

This was my third year in Rota and the second service member I'd seen with injuries from that event. There were probably plenty of others. Those who hadn't had so much as a scratch, and those who hadn't been caught by anyone who cared.

If they *were* caught, though, whether by a bull or their superiors, they were pretty well fucked. The military did not take kindly to people damaging government property, and getting your dumb ass hurt doing something stupid was an express ticket to Captain's Mast or even court-martial.

Not worth it in my book.

But getting your dick sucked by a lieutenant commander before plowing him into his mattress is *worth it?*

I shook that thought away and focused on my patient.

It was a challenge, getting him reasonably comfortable for the X-ray. He was sore all over, and naturally, the area I was X-raying was tender thanks to the sutured wound. I managed to get three good, clear images, though, and I sent him on his way.

From the looks of the X-rays, he'd been lucky. His doctor had been concerned that the horn and the resulting fall might've fractured or chipped a bone, but everything was intact as far as I could see. If there were any concerns about soft tissue damage (beyond the obvious), he'd have to go off-base to one of the Spanish hospitals.

Something told me his sore ass wouldn't be his biggest problem in the coming weeks. There was no hiding an injury like that from his chain of command, and I'd seen people go to Captain's Mast for less. A corpsman I used to work with had spent two months on restriction and had her pay docked because she'd let herself get excessively sunburned. Another had been disciplined hard for getting alcohol poisoning, both because it compromised his readiness for a few days and because he'd been underage. On my first combat deployment, another corpsman and I had helped a Marine hide the fact that he'd sliced his hand open playing with a knife; we'd seen it happen, stitched him up, and solemnly told his superiors that we'd watched him trip and accidentally grab on to some razor wire.

Taking a horn through the butt cheek and getting knocked around during the running of the bulls? There was no hiding that, and God help him if the base CO found out about it, which he probably would.

This patient was going to be regretting his life choices for a little while. His ass needed to heal, and he'd probably be on restriction and lose some pay. He wouldn't get a Good Conduct Medal, and it would take several years longer for the stripes on his dress uniform to turn from red to gold. If he didn't have a pattern of bad behavior, that would probably be the end of it. I'd seen plenty of careers come back from a hell of a lot worse.

If I got caught fraternizing with Connor—with Lieutenant Commander Marks—the fallout would be far more dire. It would've been anyway, but I knew for a fact we had a CO who liked to be a hardass about doing things by the book.

I dropped into my chair at my desk and swore into the silence of my office. I needed to get the hell over him. It was just sex. It was just a one-time thing, and we'd both known it. We'd wanted to make it count, and we had, and there was nothing left to do but move on like adults who valued the careers we'd worked for all this time.

I couldn't have him. End of story.

The sooner I accepted that and forgot about him, the better.

As much as I was struggling to concentrate on anything that wasn't Connor, I did at least have something to look forward to that evening. About once a month—or, well, usually less often than that—I FaceTimed with my parents back home. Not as often as I would've liked, but they were the West Coast was nine hours behind Spain and they traveled a lot, so it was challenging to schedule calls.

After a light dinner, I settled on my balcony with a glass of wine. From here, I had a gorgeous view of the ocean and Playa de Cruz del Mar, a popular Chipiona beach. The pale sand was crowded with people soaking up the sun and playing in the water; they still had a lot of daylight left, and the most brutal heat of the afternoon had eased considerably. I loved the view, and I loved that my balcony was situated just right to be in the shade during the hottest hours. It was a great spot for my calls with my parents, too, especially since my mom always enjoyed seeing the gorgeous view.

And they should be calling soon, shouldn't they?

I checked my phone. It was a few minutes past 1900, which was our agreed upon time. I put the phone back on the table and sipped my wine as I gazed out at the beach. They were busy these days; I joked that retirement had them running around more than they ever had while working and raising three kids. For all I knew, they were on their way home right now after visiting with friends or attending one of a million classes they took at the local art center, senior center, and any other place that could keep them busy.

So... I could wait. It wasn't like this was a terrible imposition, sitting out here on the balcony with some good wine.

I was kind of twitchy, though, and it took a while to put my finger on why. Though I usually enjoyed the peaceful solitude of my balcony, it was bugging me tonight. For reasons I couldn't quite pin down, it felt less like solitude and more like... solitary confinement? Was that it?

No, that was a bit dramatic. I wasn't confined or being kept away from anyone. If anything...

I sat up as the piece clicked into place.

I wasn't being kept away from anyone, but no one was exactly volunteering to be here.

I didn't have a boyfriend. I didn't have a lot of friends. My family was on the other side of the world. My neighbors didn't speak English.

And I'd recently had a taste of intimacy, even if it had just been sex and conversation, with someone I absolutely couldn't have. Connor's absence made perfect sense, but it sat like a grain of sand in my shoe—irritating and unavoidable.

Deflating against my chair, I sighed and reached for my wineglass again. It was empty already, so I went back inside to refill it. As I settled back into my chair and took a sip, I reminded myself that I could still go out tonight. I could hit a nearby club, or connect with a local on the app. Once I was done chatting with my parents, I could go out and do something about this obnoxiously lonely feeling.

Speaking of chatting with my parents...

I checked my phone again. 1932.

Okay, that was odd. They could be late sometimes, but not usually half an hour late. Not unless...

My heart sank again, adding to this funk I was in. The only time they'd been more than ten or fifteen minutes late was when they'd forgotten.

With my good mood draining away, I opened my text app and sent my folks a message.

Hey, are we still on to FaceTime?

Then I let my phone clatter onto the table, picked up my glass again, and drained it. I knew the answer already. I could feel it to my core. I honestly hoped they didn't try to make any excuses this time, because those hurt a lot worse than when they just forgot. It was usually something about being out with the grandkids, or one of my siblings dropping by or... something. Something that they thought was a perfectly reasonable explanation for missing my call. And the explanations *were* perfectly reasonable.

I just wished they understood how much it hurt to hear all the different things that could pull them away from our rare phone calls.

I was halfway through my third glass of wine when my phone pinged. For a second, I let myself fantasize that

Connor was hitting me up to screw around. Or that Isidoro wanted a booty call. Hell, I knew my mood was in the toilet when the thought of getting a message from Tobias didn't sound half bad.

But I knew it wasn't any of those men.

> Oh, honey! I'm so sorry! We planned a day at the zoo with the grandbabies and won't be home for a few hours.

Yeah. That tracked.

I sent back a bland message about how it was fine, we'd reschedule, and I hoped everyone had fun at the zoo. Two of those were true. We would reschedule, and I did hope everyone enjoyed the day. It was fine? I didn't know about that. Being this far away from my family was hard enough without always being the last priority.

But was I really surprised? No. No, I was not. Because this wasn't the first time, and it sure as shit wouldn't be the last time.

I went into the kitchen for more wine. This time, I brought the bottle out with me, and I had every intention of finishing it before the sun sank into the Atlantic.

I wasn't worried about being too drunk for a hookup. I felt too much like shit to even think about being with someone tonight.

My thoughts drifted to Connor again, because of course they did. Probably because he was the last man I'd touched. The last person to make me feel like I was worth any kind of effort.

Of course I couldn't have him. Of course he was off-limits. On the other hand, maybe that saved us both the awkwardness of him explaining that he wasn't interested in me now that the novelty had worn off screwing dudes. God,

I should've just left instead of going into his house. I never should've gone to Sevilla. I never should've...

Well. Whatever. Every choice I'd made to spend time with him, I shouldn't have, and I shouldn't again. In the military, there were certain non-negotiable truths: bored Sailors shouldn't run with the bulls, and lonely ones definitely shouldn't hook up with officers.

Sitting here on this beautiful balcony overlooking that gorgeous beach, with a bottle of good Spanish wine, my silent phone, and a conspicuously empty chair beside me, I swore into the breeze before taking a deep gulp from my glass.

And all the way to the bottom of that bottle, I wondered if the kid with the punctured butt cheek was regretting his life choices tonight as much as I was regretting mine.

CHAPTER 15

CONNOR

After a swim in my pool, I lounged in one of the cabana's sun-warmed wooden chairs. My phone was beside my beer bottle on the table, and I just chilled while I waited for the FaceTime request. The sun was still high but getting lower, dimming the blinding brightness of the day by a degree or two, though dusk was still another two hours away. The air was thick with heat and humidity, which felt good on my wet skin.

I took a pull from my beer and gazed out at the pool. I'd made it through the work day. It hadn't been easy, and I'd been a distracted mess, but I'd made it. Nothing left to do with the day except chat with one of my sons.

And speak of the devil, the familiar FaceTime ping came through. I smiled as I grabbed the phone off the table.

My younger son, Landon, appeared on the screen. "Hey, Dad!"

"Hey. How are things?"

"Eh." He shrugged, then brushed a couple of curls out of his eyes. "Things are fine. I've mostly been working lately. It's nice to have a break from classes, but that just means working more."

I laughed. "Welcome to adulthood."

He made a face, which made me chuckle. I missed my kids like crazy, and seeing Landon on the phone just made that hit even harder. As we caught up and I told him about Spain, my chest ached. I wanted him and his brother to come visit sooner than later, but I also kind of wanted to push the trip back; it was easier to deal with missing them when I knew they'd be coming to see me soon. Once they'd left...

Well. That wasn't something I wanted to dwell on tonight.

We did land on the subject of their visit, though. He and Quinn figured they had about a ten-day window, plus a day or two on either end for travel. They were just waiting on Quinn's girlfriend to confirm their chosen dates would work, and then they'd book their flights while I put in my leave request.

"Just let me know as soon as you can," I said. "And you have your passport and everything?"

"Yes, Dad," he said, rolling his eyes. "It doesn't expire for like seven years."

"Okay, okay. Do you guys want to fly commercial, or chance it with Space A?"

Landon quirked his lips. "I think commercial? We've only got so much time, and we'll all be cutting it close to get back before classes start."

I nodded. "Yeah, good call." The space-available military flights were a great perk for service members and dependents, but they were risky. There was no guarantee there'd be space available on a given flight, or that the flight would happen at all, and those decisions were often made at the very last second. It was entirely possible that my boys could be waiting a solid week or more before they were finally able to board a plane, and with college starting up soon, I didn't blame them for not taking the chance.

"Well," I said. "Give me the dates you guys want to travel, and I can book your tickets. Or book them yourselves and let me know how much to send you."

"Okay, will do. Where do we fly in, anyway? Like Madrid or something?"

"You can, but then it's a four-hour train ride. Alternatively, there's Jerez de la Frontera, which is close to me."

He blinked. "Hairy what now?"

I laughed. "Jerez de la Frontera. I'll text it to you so you can see how it's spelled."

"Thanks. And that's close by?"

"About a half hour, forty-five minutes away. It's about an hour flight from Madrid, or you can take the train from Madrid."

Landon pursed his lips. "I'll talk to Quinn and Savannah. See what they want to do."

"No hurry. It's a nice train ride, but it's also a short flight. So... six of this, half dozen of the other. And remember, this isn't the Norfolk airport," I told him. "Madrid is *huge*, and you do not want to have to sprint through it because half of your forty-minute layover got chewed up by customs."

He made a face. "But I hate sitting around in airports."

"Your call, kid." I shrugged. "Sit around and be bored, or try to Usain Bolt across one of those terminals."

Landon scowled. "Okay, okay. We'll book a long layover."

We talked for a while longer, and then he had to get ready for work, so we ended the call.

I set my phone face down on the table beside my beer bottle. I let the quiet settle over me like the chill after the sun had set, taking the summer heat with it.

We hadn't talked about anything earthshattering. It was mostly about travel and their upcoming visit, as well as the classes he'd be taking soon; exactly the kind of conversation we'd have had over the kitchen table or in the living room.

It left me unsettled, though. As if we *should've* been talking about bigger and more important things, not just having a normal everyday chat. It felt anticlimactic, leaving me happy that I'd spoken with my son but still feeling like *"that's it?"*

I knew that feeling well from deployments and combat tours. And I also knew their mother had asked them to be upbeat whenever they talked to me. Don't tell me about bad things, whether they were struggling in school or a good friend had moved away. Don't burden Dad with things that'll make him worry.

Some of the biggest fights I'd ever had with Aimee had been about that. She insisted she was trying not to add to my stress while I was deployed. I insisted that I wanted to know how my family was really doing, and once I'd found out she was hiding things—and asking the boys to hide things—I worried even more.

Now, every time I talked to the boys and everything was fine, I was afraid there was more going on.

On top of that, there was that same familiar feeling that when the call ended, he was gone. A world away from me in his mother's apartment while I drank my beer in the muggy silence.

When I'd been in warzones or on ships, their absence had been painful but as close to normal as anything ever was in those places. Here, in a rental house that was big enough for my whole family, I felt like he or his brother should come wandering outside at any moment, swim trunks on and drinks in hand. Like I should've been just waiting for them to come trooping down the back porch stairs so we could all cool off in the pool before grilling burgers or steaks.

That wasn't going to happen, though. Even if I still lived in the States, the boys were adults now. They had lives that didn't involve me or their mom on a daily basis. All those years kids spent at home? All the family time and soccer games and dinners at the kitchen table? They were over, and I'd missed a lot of them because of my career.

Now I was missing even more. And I wouldn't even be spending the years after the kids moved out making up for lost time with their mom, because...

Well, because that was gone too.

I sat back against the deck chair and closed my eyes.

I missed my kids. I missed having a partner.

I missed...

Fuck.

I missed not being alone.

Lying in the darkness, drenched in cold sweat, I stared up at the ceiling and tried to catch my breath.

The dream felt fragmented now, coming in flashes of color and fear rather than as vividly as when I'd been asleep. I couldn't taste sand or blood anymore. A swig of water from the bottle I kept beside the bed helped ground me in the here and now; both the taste and the cold, not to mention the familiar motions of reaching for it, uncapping it, and taking a drink.

I was still jittery. Fucking hated that feeling. Some part of me—probably one saturated in toxic masculinity—thought it was childish to be so shaken up by a bad dream. It made sense for one of my kids to wake up terrified back when they were little. I was a grown man.

A grown man, I reminded myself, with a head full of trauma that the military wouldn't let me get therapy to treat. Nightmares weren't weak or infantile; they were par for the goddamned course.

As I steadily came back down to earth, I caught myself missing my ex-wife. Our relationship had lasted long past the end of its shelf life, and I wouldn't have gone back for anything. In moments like this, though, I was all too aware that our marriage hadn't been *all* bad. On nights when my combat demons dropped in for a visit, Aimee had always known how to bring me back into the present and calm me down. She'd never given me grief for waking her up, and she'd never looked at me differently after she'd seen me cry after an especially bad nightmare. Regardless of the fact that we'd ultimately divorced, I was grateful for a lot of reasons that she'd been in my life. One of those reasons was nights like that.

Nights like *this*.

Sighing into the silence, I wiped a hand over my face. After being separated for this long and after my deployments, I should've been able to handle this alone. And I supposed I could. Wasn't like I had much choice.

Was I handling it *well*? Hard to say.

Getting back to sleep after a nightmare like that was

always hard. It had been easier when I'd had Aimee curled against me, her warm presence and gentle touch keeping me anchored in reality as I tried to slip off to sleep. Alone, it was easy to get lost in the darkness again. To start losing track of what was real, what was a dream, and what *had* been real at one time while the lines blurred between consciousness and sleep. With or without her, more nightmares almost always came, but she'd feel me jerking or shaking, and she'd wake me up. Sometimes it happened several times in a night. Sometimes I didn't remember it, but I'd know when I saw her the next morning, heavy circles under her eyes as she clung to her coffee cup.

Maybe it was just as well I was sleeping alone these days. At least then my nightmares only fucked up *my* sleep.

I did manage to grab a few hours of sleep. The nightmares still came, and I remembered waking up shaking at least two more times before my alarm went off. I was groggy as all hell, even after a shower and a mule-kick-strong cup of coffee, but there wasn't much I could do about that. At least my ex-wife hadn't lost any sleep over it.

I made it to work on autopilot, sucking down coffee all the way, and I refilled my travel mug as soon as I got to the hospital. There was a corpsman in the breakroom nursing a gigantic energy drink, and while I would've sold my soul for that kind of stimulant, it wasn't going to happen. I couldn't even look at the logo of an energy drink brand without feeling the phantom twinge that heralded a kidney stone beginning its southbound journey.

The coffee would just have to do. Good thing I'd long

ago learned how to function at a hundred percent—okay, seventy-two percent—when I hadn't slept well.

After a briefing from some of the hospital's higher ups almost put me into a coma, and then a meeting with my department nearly finished me off, I was seriously considering indulging in that energy drink after all. *One* can wouldn't give me another kidney stone, right?

"Either give me something strong or fucking shoot me," I remembered gritting out to an emergency room doctor. *"But do it fucking now."*

Coffee it was.

I thankfully made it through an uneventful sick call. Nobody had anything out of the ordinary—the odd injury from overdoing it at the gym, a handful of people who definitely needed to be home in bed no matter what their supervisors had to say about it, and a young Marine following up after being treated for a badly sprained ankle.

I had a feeling there would be a basewide safety briefing in the next week or so about ATVs thanks to a pair of Sailors who came to see me. They'd sheepishly admitted that their scrapes, bruises, one's sprained wrist, and the other's concussion had happened on an ATV tour where they'd "totally listened to everything the guide told us!" Yeah, right. I had two sons who'd been teenage daredevils. These two weren't fooling me.

I sent them off with light duty chits, prescriptions for high-octane Motrin, and a list of symptoms that were "get your ass to the emergency room" serious.

After sick call was over, I ducked into my office for a quick bite to eat and some more coffee. And while I was at it, I took out my phone and perused the gay club scene in a few cities. Sevilla again, but also places like Granada, Málaga, and Madrid. Someplace I could go hook up with someone and forget about the man who kept elbowing his way into my thoughts. I mean, at least that was a more pleasant place for my focus to drift than to my combat days, but it was still distracting and frustrating. I couldn't have him, so I needed to look elsewhere.

Just browsing the options of clubs in various places actually gave my tired brain a welcome boost. It was something to look forward to, and it admittedly revved up my libido. Even though it was hard to imagine being this attracted to any other human being than Alex, I knew I could be. And this weekend, so help me God, I *would* be.

But for right now, I had patients to see, so I headed back downstairs.

I was halfway down the hall with my nose in a chart when bootsteps started coming from the opposite direction. Out of sheer habit, I looked up, and I stopped sharply enough that my own boot squeaked on the gray linoleum.

Alex halted too, eyes wide.

Oh, hell. I was awake now. Like me, he was in uniform —green camouflage with the sleeves crisply rolled to partway up his strong biceps. I thought about the snug T-shirt he was wearing underneath, and how much I'd love to see it stretched across his abs if he'd just unbutton that blouse and—

Alex found his military bearing before I did. "Uh. Good morning, sir."

I cleared my throat. "Good morning, HM1."

We exchanged nods, then continued in opposite directions, Alex completely oblivious to the way my heart was slamming against my ribs.

God help me if we ever crossed paths outside. He was already hot in uniform, but if we were outdoors, we'd both have our covers on. Which meant he'd have to salute me.

Why that struck me as hot, I had no idea. Only that I simultaneously hoped it happened and prayed it never did. I didn't really care much about rank, and things like submission or subservience had never done it for me. But the thought of Alex snapping to attention and saluting me—why did that make my pulse race?

Probably because I was tired as hell and nothing really made sense.

And maybe a little because I could imagine him doing it perfectly professionally, oozing military bearing from head to toe, but with a glint in his eyes for me and me alone. Something mischievous and sly, visible only to me in the shade of his cover.

Yeah. I was an idiot.

I was also suddenly overwhelmed with the desire to reprise our weekend in Sevilla. In particular, everything that happened *after* that trip.

All the risks I'd run through still existed. All the potential fallout was still there, waiting to come crashing down on us if we dared push our luck again.

But that intense attraction was still there too.

As much as I'd never been the reckless risk-taking type, I wanted to be this time. Not for the thrill or the rebelliousness, but for another chance to feel all the things I had when we'd been behind closed doors.

Was what why I was imagining him saluting me with a spicy little glint in his eye? Probably.

And it was just that—something I was imagining. Something I needed to forget about and move on from so I could do my job and keep my career. It was that simple.

It was also just my goddamned luck that I crossed paths with him again an hour later. He was heading out of the emergency department with one of the portable ultrasounds, and apparently we were on our way in the same direction.

Neither of us spoke. We didn't look at each other.

But then the hallway came to an intersection. Left would take me to the elevators to go down to my department. Straight would take him to Radiology.

By all rights, I should've turned and he should've continued.

But... we both stopped.

I gnawed my lip and chanced a look at him. He did the same. Neither of us bothered with military bearing this time; there was no one else around, and if he was anything like me, he'd forgotten all about it.

When I locked eyes with him, it was suddenly hard to breathe. Maybe I was seeing things, but I swore, behind all the caution and nerves in his expression, there was that glint of hunger. As if he too wanted a rematch, but this wasn't the time or place.

There was never a time or a place for two guys like us, but that didn't stop me from wanting it, and I was pretty sure it wasn't stopping him either.

Fuck it. We hadn't been caught in Sevilla. We could do it again.

Thinking fast, I glanced around us. Then, keeping my tone casual and conversational, I said, "I'll, um... I'm going to check out Paraíso in Madrid on Saturday night." I smiled. "Maybe I'll see you there."

Alex's lips parted and his eyes widened.

I turned to go before I lost my nerve, but he called after me, "Lieutenant Commander?"

I faced him again, heart pounding.

He swallowed hard. "You said Paraíso, right?"

My mouth had gone dry, so I just nodded.

"Okay." He flashed me a quick smile. "Have a good time."

"I will. Thanks."

And then I left.

And I had no idea what I hoped he'd do with the information I'd given him.

CHAPTER 16
ALEX

To say Connor's offer was tempting would be a massive understatement. The moment he'd put it out there, I'd wanted to take him up on it. More than once since I'd come back to Radiology, I'd seriously considered it.

And then, the day after Connor had made that offer, Tobias came strutting into my office like he owned the place. Before dropping into my guest chair, he "accidentally" clipped the metal file cabinet with his shoe, the metal *clang* making me jump just like it always did.

Gritting my teeth, I didn't even try to hide my annoyance as I asked, "What?"

"What?" He blinked stupidly, acting completely innocent as if he was welcome here and that he hadn't just deliberately poked at my PTSD.

"I've got work to do." I gestured at a stack of file folders that he didn't need to know were for my chief to deal with. "I'm pretty sure you have to do things, too. At least once in a while."

That barb hit its mark, and he glared at me. Tobias hated when people joked about civilian contractors getting paid out the ass to do basically nothing. Probably because he knew that was exactly what he was doing, no matter how much he wanted everyone to believe he did important shit.

He crossed his arms. "Someone switch your coffee to decaf? Or are you just being a bitch for no reason?"

I gritted my teeth, determined not to let him under my skin, and I repeated, "I have work to do."

"Of course you do." He didn't move. "So where'd you go last weekend?"

My blood turned cold. Oh fuck. He didn't see me, did he? "What makes you think I went anywhere?"

"You weren't home."

"I wasn't—" I inclined my head. "Were you at my place?"

Tobias shrugged. "I was in Chipiona and stopped by to see if you wanted to grab a drink." He huffed an ugly laugh. "Since your car was gone, I figured you must've actually gone out of town instead of to your fuck buddy's place."

That made my damn skin crawl, but I affected annoyance. "For the record, I don't want to go grab a drink. Ever. I also don't want you coming by my apartment. Is that clear?" I gestured toward the door. "And would you mind getting out of here? I really do have work to do."

He chuckled as if he'd gotten some reaction he wanted, and he made a big show of getting to his feet. "I'll get out of your hair. But hey, if you're not busy this weekend, let me know and we can—"

"I could be bored off my ass with a parade keeping me awake outside my window," I growled, "and I still wouldn't reach out to you."

He just laughed dismissively and left.

Alone in the office again, I leaned back against my chair and ground out a "fuuuck." I hated that he was this persistent. I hated how many times it had worked in the past—I was as lonely as he'd carefully made me, and he knew exactly how to take advantage of that. He was just biding his time until I finally got desperate enough that his company sounded better than my own.

Not this time. No fucking way.

Not after I'd finally had a taste of something good, even if I couldn't have it again.

It was kind of mind-boggling how much a single brief trip with Connor had further soured my feelings for Tobias. Just seeing the asshole's face had already filled me with disgust and resentment. Now that I knew Connor's gentle touch, playful laugh, and sweet personality, the mere sound of Tobias's voice nauseated me.

How the fuck did I waste so much time on you?

Because he love-bombed me and isolated me from what few friends I had at the time, so...

Ugh. Wasn't that the truth. And most of those friends had since transferred out of Spain and into the realms of occasional social media contact. I hadn't made any new friends during that year with Tobias, so once I'd come out of his chokehold, I'd been isolated and alone. Exactly the way he'd undoubtedly planned it, and exactly right so that I'd come crawling back now and then for some intimacy, no matter how much I'd hate myself afterward. I'd done exactly that more times than I cared to think about, and if I felt much lower than I did now, I'd probably give in again. Fucking fabulous.

I rubbed my eyes with my thumb and forefinger. I *had* to stop giving in. No amount of loneliness was worth the self-loathing after a night like him.

Maybe I needed to spend more time in Isidoro's bed. At least that would chase away the craving for human contact.

He didn't want anything serious, and there was too much of a language barrier for much of a relationship anyway. Plus it was only a matter of time before one or both of us were transferred someplace else.

And it wasn't just intimacy that was hard to find. The long-term active duty life didn't lend itself to relationships, and it didn't lend itself to friendships either, especially overseas. As soon as I started to really connect with someone, one of us would be sent elsewhere. I did make friends at work and around the base, but we'd inevitably end up on opposite sides of the planet, keeping up via social media and nothing else.

And it didn't help being an unmarried senior enlisted guy with no kids. Most of the people my age had families and hung out with other families. I couldn't make friends with the younger service members or even the chiefs above me for the same reason I couldn't screw Connor—fraternization.

I wondered sometimes how I'd let Tobias get so close to me and stick around for so long, but what could I say? I got as lonely as the next person, and that made it really fucking hard to say no to the unicorn—the queer guy who spoke English, wasn't off-limits, and wanted me, even if all he really wanted was a hole to fuck and a head to fuck with.

Why did the man I actually clicked with—both in and out of bed—have to be someone I couldn't even be *friends* with?

Sitting back in my chair, I rubbed my eyes and sighed.

I couldn't stand being with Tobias.

I couldn't be more than fuck buddies with Isidoro.

And I wasn't allowed to be with Connor.

I hadn't thought it was possible, but today, I was lonelier than I'd been in a long, long time.

CHAPTER 17

CONNOR

An hour and a half after I walked into Paraíso, I couldn't ignore the mix of disappointment and relief. Alex wasn't here. We weren't going to do something stupid and reckless that could derail our careers and lives.

But also... he wasn't here. We weren't going to have a rematch and relive that ridiculously hot night that was seared into my memory.

Which was a good thing for two men who wanted to keep their careers and their VA benefits. We'd both given up way too much and worked way too hard to toss it all away now in exchange for some good dick.

It was a bad idea. I should've known it was, really. And why did I pick *Madrid*, for fuck's sake? Couldn't I have gone for a city closer to home? I mean, I didn't want to be so close that we might bump into someone we knew. Still, there were plenty of cities between Rota and Madrid that were far enough away that we weren't likely to happen across anyone from our base, least of all our hospital.

You picked Madrid because you knew this was a terrible idea and he wasn't likely to show up.

That was possible. Like I'd extended an invitation that I'd subconsciously known he wouldn't accept. Taken the risk without *actually* taking the risk.

Damn. I was disappointed, but I supposed I was relieved, too. My career was safe from my stupidity for another day.

Well, just because I wouldn't be dancing (or more) with Alex didn't mean I had to waste this trip. I was here in this club, and I'd caught a couple of men glancing my way. The way that beautiful Spanish guy near the bar had raked his eyes up and down my body had done wonders for my confidence; it was hard to be afraid I was unattractive when someone that hot was openly checking me out.

Someone emerged from the crowd and quite clearly wanted to dance with me. He was a little shorter than me with long black hair, mischievous dark eyes, and a devilish smile.

Even as I stepped in to dance with him, I'd already decided we wouldn't be hooking up—he was *way* too young. Early twenties, if I had to guess. *Maybe* twenty-five. I'd feel too weird getting intimate with someone this close to my sons' ages.

He was cute, though, and he was fun to dance with. I liked the way he smiled and the way he moved, and this seemed harmless enough—dance for a few songs, have a good time, go our separate ways.

That was exactly what we did, too, and it was fun. I was starting to be less self-conscious on the dancefloor; everyone was here to have a good time, and nobody cared what anyone else was doing unless they wanted to be doing it with them.

The young guy and I drifted away from each other after a handful of songs, and I danced by myself for a little while.

I paused to get a drink—just water, since I didn't want to get too fucked up in a place like this—then returned to the floor.

Someone else found me in the crowd, and though he didn't hold a candle to Alex—did anyone?—he was definitely attractive. In fact, as I moved in closer, I decided *this* was a guy I could see myself leaving the building with. He was older than the last one, though I definitely still had several years on him.

Potential for a hookup, maybe?

Eh, we'd see. Right now, we'd try dancing. If that went well, we could move toward the bar or a table, talk, and go from there. I didn't even know his name yet, so no need to start double-checking I still had those condoms in my back pocket.

It wasn't that I was opposed to anonymous sex. Even working in healthcare hadn't scared me away from the idea.

The language barrier, though... that still made me nervous. What if he didn't understand a boundary I tried to communicate? What if *I* didn't understand one of *his?* God, that thought made my stomach knot up.

So... no hooking up unless we could understand each other. He didn't even need to be fluent; just enough that we could clumsily communicate and not do something one or both of us regretted.

There *had* to be *someone* in here who spoke some English. Everyone said it was a little more common in Madrid than in Andalusia, and I'd already encountered a few English speakers in my hotel and at the train station. I could find someone in this place who spoke it too, right? Or was I hunting for a unicorn?

Trying to find something you know isn't here so you can leave empty-handed without feeling like a failure?

Now you listen here, subconscious...

After the guy and I finished dancing, I decided I needed to cool off a bit and catch my breath, so I went to the bar again. I had just gotten a bottle of water when someone appeared beside me. I thought he wanted my spot at the bar, so I stepped aside to make room, but then I realized he was looking right at me.

Oh, he was hot, too. Wavy black hair. A gorgeous grin. Sexy eyes that might've been blue or green; it was hard to tell in this light.

He said something to me in rapid-fire Spanish, and I blinked. I'd barely caught any of the words, and the few I had, I didn't understand.

He smiled. "British?"

I shook my head. "American."

"Ah. You speak English, then?" His accent was thick, but I understood him, thank God.

"I do. And you do too, apparently?"

"Ah, some." He wobbled his hand in the air. "Not, uh, not like..." He gestured at me.

I shrugged. I could work with that.

"Your name?" he asked.

"Connor," I shouted over the music. "Yours?"

"Emiliano." He took my hand. "Come on. Let's dance."

I smiled and let Emiliano lead me back out onto the floor.

He could dance, too. Goddamn. I had to wonder what else he could do with those hips. Maybe before tonight was over, I'd find out.

I liked the way his hand felt on the small of my back. I liked the closeness of our bodies, and the way his eyes sparkled in the disco lights. I liked being out in the open with a man, touching him in ways that were obviously *not* platonic.

How the fuck did I go my whole damn life without ever even dancing with a man?

Ooh, right. Married.

Well, no time like the present to make up for lost time.

By the end of the second song, though, I had a feeling he wasn't interested. He wasn't being rude or looking at me with disgust, but he was looking around a bit more, as if searching for someone else. Eh, it stung a bit—rejection was never fun—but he wasn't a dick about it and there were still plenty of men in this club.

We danced for a few more songs before going our separate ways. It had been a little disappointing the first couple of times that happened, but some guys might've been here just to dance, not hook up. And some of them might have decided after a little dancing that I wasn't someone they wanted to hook up with.

I could live with that. I was having a better time than I'd expected. Finding my groove on the dancefloor. Feeling less like a fish out of water and more like I might actually belong here.

Someone else appeared behind me, sliding a hand around my waist to my stomach and pulling me back against his firm, hot body. Oh, hell yeah.

Then his lips brushed my ear, and over the thumping music and through my earplug came the words, "One more song, and I was going to have to cut in."

I spun around in his grasp, and... oh, fuck.

Alex grinned, his eyes absolutely on fire.

"You..." I stammered. "You came."

"Of course I did." He tugged me in closer, and his voice barely carried over the music as he growled, "It's all I've been able to think about."

My knees almost melted out from under me. "You and me both."

He bit his lip, then leaned past me to speak in my ear. "If I could kiss you out in the open like this..."

I was kind of grateful for the music, since it swallowed up my very manly and dignified whimper. "We probably shouldn't even be doing this much."

"Probably not. But we are." He slid his hands up my back. "If this shows up in a video online somewhere, we were drunk, it was dark, and we didn't recognize each other on the dancefloor."

I bit my lip and drew him in closer. "Think they'd buy it?" It *was* pretty dark apart from the disco lights.

His laugh was almost soundless, but I could feel the huff of breath, both in the rush across my skin and the way his chest moved. "Long as no one sees us leave the club together or doing more than dancing."

He was probably right. And I'd been as straitlaced as they came throughout my career; I could get away with one drunken *whoops* in the dark.

I drew back enough to meet his gaze, and that didn't help me keep a handle on my self-control. The temptation to kiss those lips was almost overwhelming. I'd been craving him like I'd never craved a damn thing in my life, and I wanted to taste his mouth again. "Christ, Alex..."

His eyebrows rose, as did the corners of his lips. "Hmm?"

"I don't care who you are," I rasped. "I don't care what rank we are. I want you so damn bad I can't think about anything else."

He stared at me, gaze full of both lust and surprise. "You do?"

"The invitation to meet me in Madrid wasn't a clue?"

Alex bit his lip as need smoldered in his eyes.

I wanted him. His mouth. His hands. His body. Every inch of him.

We could get away with what we were doing. It was dark. It was just dancing. We could tell anyone who saw us that we were drunk.

Crossing the line into getting physically intimate—well, that wasn't a chance I was willing to take. Judging by the sliver of distance Alex was keeping between us—and the fact that he kept looking longingly at my mouth but never moved in for a kiss—told me we were probably on the same page.

"Swear to God," he said, "I'm going to end up fucking you in the alley behind this building."

In that moment, that didn't sound half bad. Not the most comfortable or sanitary location, but I'd have Alex's dick in my ass, so—

"Wait two minutes," he growled, jostling me out of my thoughts, "then meet me in the men's room."

And with that, he released me and disappeared into the crowd like a mirage, leaving my skin cool with his absence.

I... hadn't imagined that, had I? I hadn't hallucinated the sexiest dance and the filthiest promise of my life?

I was pretty sure I hadn't. And if I was dreaming, well, I was going to follow this dream for as long as I stayed asleep. My nightmare-battered psyche owed me one, damn it.

After the longest two minutes of my life, I made my way through the crowd toward the back hallway, and I found the door to the men's room. There were a few guys in here using it for its intended purpose. One stall was quite obviously occupied—at least two men were moaning and murmuring in Spanish, punctuated by skin slapping skin. Nobody in the room seemed to notice or care.

They also didn't look when Alex grabbed the front of my shirt and hauled me back out into the hallway, which was crowded and *very* dark, and—

Fuck, yes. I had him up against the wall, kissing him hard as he cupped my ass and pulled me harder against him. His kiss was even more frantic than it had been in my foyer a lifetime ago, and that said something. He was needy and vocal, moaning softly as he explored my mouth like he'd never tasted me in his life.

When I drew back, we were both panting and shaking all over. My hard-on strained against the front of my pants, rubbing his equally hard cock through our clothes.

"I've worked in healthcare too long to fuck in a bathroom stall," he panted, "but I just couldn't wait another minute."

"Same," I said, and claimed a longer, deeper kiss.

No, we wouldn't fuck in there. The other guys in that stall were welcome to it, but... no.

"Goddammit," I panted. "We *need* to go somewhere else."

Alex shivered and rutted against me. "Yeah, we do."

I thought fast. "Where are you staying?"

He blinked a few times as if he had to think about it. "The Regente Oeste."

I nodded. "Okay. We're going to go back out there," I whispered, gesturing vaguely toward the rest of the club. "And we're going to dance. With other people. If anyone from the base is here..." I shook my head. "They won't think anything of it."

Alex licked his lips. "And after we leave?"

"I'm staying at the Casa Chueca. Room 53." I slipped a card key into his back pocket as I whispered, "Please come fuck me."

The moan that escaped his lips was full of more wanton hunger than I'd ever heard before. "Did you bring condoms?"

"And lube."

Alex squirmed. "Goddammit, I want to go now."

"Me too."

Our eyes locked.

"Do we really have to go out and pretend we want to be with other people?" he asked. "I mean, what do you think the odds are of someone from the base being here?"

I chewed my lip. "Probably pretty fucking slim."

"Uh-huh. Exactly." He slid his hand down over the front of my pants, making me groan with need. "How about you get your ass back to your hotel, get naked, and I'll be there in half an hour?"

"You think I can wait half an hour to get fucked?"

He grinned, though his own desperation gleamed in his eyes. "I can wait if you can."

I was pretty sure that half hour was going to make me go up in flames.

But Alex would definitely be worth the wait.

CHAPTER 18

ALEX

Telling him I'd be there in thirty minutes had been a mistake. If I'd said fifteen minutes, I'd be balls deep in him by now. One of us might have even come already.

But no, I was milling around on the sidewalk in front of his hotel, glaring at my phone and willing the last seven minutes to go by.

Connor was in there. Right now. In his room, probably on his bed, naked and ready for me to dick him down like I'd been *dying* to do. And what was I doing? Standing out here like an idiot.

Fuck it. I had five minutes now—somehow I didn't think Connor would mind if I showed up a little early. Not if the absolute *"get your pants off and your dick in me"* in his eyes had been anything to do by.

I jogged up the hotel's front steps and strode across the lobby. The elevator crawled down, because of course it did, and as soon as the doors were open, I jumped inside and jabbed the button for the fifth floor. I didn't think I'd ever been more aware of all the grinding and groaning of an elevator's mechanisms; it was just impossible to ignore this time how fucking slowly they were doing their thing. Or maybe time had just slowed down because I needed to get into that man's room *right the fuck now*.

Mercifully, it got me to the right floor before the sun burned out, and I squeezed out through the slowly separating doors. I followed the numbered doors until I reached Connor's. Once there, I double-checked I'd come to the right room, tapped the keycard against the reader, and when the light turned green, I pushed open the door.

Oh. *Hell.*

Connor lay back on the bed, completely naked with his hard cock in his hand. He watched me with hooded eyes as he stroked himself slowly, and I barely remembered how to shut and deadbolt the door behind me.

"Oh my God," I whispered.

"Come here," he ordered. "Doesn't do either of us any good if you're all the way over there."

"No," I murmured as I started unbuttoning my shirt, "but I gotta say—the view is—"

"*Alex.*" He squirmed on the bed. "Please."

I didn't need to be told a third time. Shirt half-unbuttoned, I crawled onto the bed and on top of him. With his free hand, Connor grabbed my shirt and dragged me down to him, meeting me in a deep, needy kiss. It had only been half an hour since we'd been making out beside the men's room, but I swore it felt like we hadn't touched in years. Every nerve ending in my body lit up with desire as we kissed and pawed at each other. When was the last time I'd been with a man who could kiss me right into oblivion like this?

Last weekend, I believe.

Between us, we fumbled with my clothes, and we managed to get my shirt untucked and my pants undone.

He'd barely wrapped his fingers around my hard-on before he pleaded, "Fuck me." He sounded like he was on the verge of tears. "God, Alex. Please. I want... I want..."

"Absolutely," I growled. "Let me get you ready."

"Already there," he panted. "Just... Just need your dick."

I couldn't help groaning with pure need. He'd gotten himself ready for me, too? Fucking hell. "Lube? Condom?"

He motioned toward the nightstand, and sure enough, everything we needed was there.

Just rolling on the condom almost had me losing it. I was hardly a minuteman, but the sheer anticipation of burying myself in Connor had me right on the edge. As I put some lube on the condom, I raked my eyes over him, then met his gaze.

"Put a pillow under your ass," I ordered.

Connor grabbed one, lifted his hips, and put the pillow under him. As soon as he'd settled onto it, I moved between his legs, pushed his thighs farther apart and pressed against his hole.

I hadn't even pushed in yet when he breathed, "Oh, God..."

Grinning down at him, I purred, "You really want it, don't you?"

"*Yes.* God, I—ooh, fuck, yeah..." The bliss rolling across his face as I eased myself in was too sexy for words. I loved being with someone so responsive; just one careful stroke inside him, and he was already trembling and biting his lip like I had him on the edge.

I withdrew, then eased in a little deeper. Even though his face said it all, I couldn't resist asking, "You like that?"

"Uh-huh." He arched under me, and his eyelids fluttered before he fixed his gaze on me. "You feel so damn good."

"So do you," I murmured with complete honesty. I was no stranger to sex, definitely no stranger to topping, but being in bed with Connor made me high in ways I'd never experienced before. Maybe because this was all so new to him. Maybe because he was just so fucking gorgeous. Either way, I couldn't get enough of him, and he moaned and gasped like he couldn't get enough of me.

Fucking perfect.

"Been thinking about this ever since last time," he said. "Just... so good."

"Mmm, me too." I leaned my hands on the bed beside his arms and picked up the pace a little. I wasn't going fast or hard—not as fast or hard as I absolutely could if he asked—but it was enough to knock more moans and curses from his parted, kiss-swollen lips. "Like that? Or... more?"

"This is perfect," he slurred. "Want to try it harder one of these days, but... this is perfect."

My head spun, both at the arousal in his voice and the thought of doing this again. I didn't know how we could make that happen, but in that moment, I'd have done anything to wind up like this with Connor again and again and again.

"I *so* want to switch sometime," he murmured breathlessly, still furiously pumping himself. "But I just... I needed your... oh, God, yeah..."

I almost lost my rhythm. The hunger in his voice, along with the desire to fuck me like I was fucking him, had me dizzy with pleasure and anticipation. I wanted to come. I wanted to pull out, turn around, and beg him to top me before I burst into flames. I wanted to cry. *Fuck*, I just felt so damn *good*.

"Don't stop," he moaned, arching under me. "I'm gonna come."

"Yeah?" I gazed down at him, absolutely mesmerized by the sight of this gorgeous man unraveling as I rode him. I couldn't believe he was here. That *we* were here. That I was fucking him. That his beautiful body was laid out in front of me as he jerked himself off. I'd been so convinced I'd never have him like this again, and now I did have him, and it was perfect, and I was so damn close to losing it and—

"Fuck!" I shouted, forcing myself as deep as I could as I came so hard the room turned white. "Oh my God..."

"Oh, that's so hot," he whispered, and he rocked his hips a little, which drove my orgasm out for another second or two before I collapsed over him.

"Jesus..." I pressed my forehead to his shoulder. "I... That caught me by surprise."

He laughed and he didn't sound at all put off that I'd come, even though he'd been close himself.

I kissed the side of his neck, which made him shiver. Then I pushed myself up on shaking arms and met his beautiful eyes. "Let me get take care of the condom. Then I'm going to finish you off."

"Yes, please," he growled, eyes afire with need.

I got rid of the condom and washed my hands in record time, then returned to the room where Connor was just like I'd found him before: lying back, naked, stroking his hard dick. Only now he was flushed and sweaty, and oh my God, that man needed to come *right now*.

I climbed back on the bed and settled between his thighs again.

"Oh, *fuck*," he groaned as I pushed two fingers into him.

"That good?"

"Yes. Oh my God. I've never... No one's ever..."

"You've never been fingered before?"

"Not while I was getting jacked off, no."

I licked my lips. "What about while you were getting blown?"

A harsh breath rushed out of his parted lips, and he whispered, "Never."

"Well. High time we fix that, huh?"

I didn't give him a chance to respond before I nudged his hand out of the way and went down on him. I licked and teased him for all I was worth, still finger-fucking him as he egged me on with whimpers and curses.

"Keep doing that," he begged. "Keep—all of it. God, that's so perfect. Oh my fucking—yeah, that's so good." He writhed and arched, fucking himself on my fingers while I sucked him off in earnest. I'd always loved giving head, but with Connor it was turned up to an eleven. I couldn't get enough, and I wanted his orgasm like I'd wanted my own.

His cock thickened between my lips, and his words turned into slurs and moans, and then he growled, "Fuck. Fuck! Oh yeah, I'm—I'm coming."

And a second later, his cum shot across my tongue, and I reveled in his helpless cries as I kept him going until he shuddered and sank back to the bed in a shaking, cursing heap.

I slipped my fingers free and lifted myself up on my arms, and I'd barely moved over the top of him before he hauled me down into his trembling arms. For a moment, we just lay there, shaking all over and breathing hard.

Then he kissed me softly. "Really... Really glad we bumped into each other in that club."

I grinned. "What were the odds?"

As I sank into another kiss... yeah. I was seriously glad we'd "bumped into each other" in that club.

And even more blown away that it had been his idea.

Since when does anyone want me this much?

CHAPTER 19

CONNOR

The relief of being in bed with Alex, wrung out and satisfied as we lazily kissed, was even more profound than it had been the first time. I'd wondered more than once if I was just remembering the sex being a lot hotter than it actually was, but no, round two absolutely lived up to my memory.

And... he was *here*. When I'd thrown out that reckless suggestion about running into each other at Paraíso, I didn't think I'd actually expected it to happen. Or for this to happen. Or for us to still be here, tangled up in a languid kiss after we'd shared a brief shower. With our hard-ons taken care of and now that we'd caught our breath, one of us should've come to our senses by now, but... no. Alex knew as well as I did that we shouldn't be here, and yet he was still holding me close and exploring my mouth like he had every intention of staying.

Eventually, we came up for air. Trailing a fingertip along my jaw, he said, "So much for a one-time thing, I guess."

I laughed as I slid my palm up his chest. "Yeah. I guess we kinda blew that one."

"You could say that." He brushed his lips across mine again, but when he drew back this time, he'd sobered a little. "I, um... I won't lie—I wish we could do this again. But the risk..." He shook his head.

My heart sank. Though I knew he was right, I wanted to argue anyway. There were plenty of men in that club who probably could've rocked my world tonight, but I didn't believe for a second that any of them would've left me as blissed out and satisfied as Alex had. That, and beyond the sex, I liked him. We barely knew each other, but what little time we'd spent together made me want more, and I didn't just mean between the sheets. I could even be happy just being friends with him; sure, I'd still be painfully attracted to him, but having him as a friend beat not having him at all.

Except the Navy forbade us from being friends, too, so fuck it—we might as well break the rule instead of bending it.

"We *can* do this going forward," I said.

Alex tensed. "We... We can?"

"Sure." I clasped his hand gently between us. "As long as we're discreet and we're not stupid about it—there's no reason we can't do it without getting caught."

Alex searched my eyes uncertainly. "Do you think we *should*?"

"No. But somehow I don't think that's going to change anything."

Chewing his lip, he studied me, the uncertainty still etched all over his face.

"Being here like this is the stupidest thing I've ever done." I traced my fingertips along the shaved side of his head. "But I just can't convince myself it's wrong. Or that I don't want to do it again"

He exhaled. "Yeah, I... I can list every reason why this is a supremely bad idea. And I thought about all of them on the train ride up here." He shook his head. "But I couldn't talk myself out of it."

"Same." I laughed softly. "And that's a long train ride for second thoughts."

Alex nodded. "I know, right? I figured if I hadn't convinced myself not to go through with it after four hours on a train, then..." He half-shrugged. "Does that make me stupid?"

"Well, if it does, then I'm not really in any position to judge. I did the same four-hour second-thoughts train ride, and I'm the one who suggested this in the first place, so..." I half-shrugged. "Yeah, not going to throw stones."

He grinned, but it faded a little. "Okay, so we can skip the part where we try to talk ourselves out of this because it's a lost cause."

"You want to do this, then? Going forward?"

"Yes," he said without hesitation. "I know why it's a bad idea. I know why it's a fucking terrible idea. But I just..." He trailed off, shaking his head.

I wasn't sure what to say.

Before I could think of something, he whispered, "When we were in bed the first time, you asked how long it had been since I'd slept with someone else."

I winced. "I was just curious. I don't mean to pry into—"

"No, no, it's okay." He looked in my eyes. "The truth is that I was with someone the weekend before." He swallowed. "And the whole reason I was with him that night was because I couldn't get *you* out of my mind."

My lips parted. "Really?"

"Yeah. I... I have no idea what's going on here. Or why my professional self-preservation goes out the window whenever I consider what we should do or what I want us to do. I just know I can't stop thinking about you, and it's only gotten worse since we hooked up the first time." Alex pushed out a breath. "And it's not just because you're someone I shouldn't be with. That's not how I roll."

Fuck. And I thought I'd been speechless before.

Somehow, I found my voice. "It's... That's not how I roll either. When I was a kid, maybe, but as an adult..."

I squeezed his hand between us. "I think we can both trust each other to keep this discreet."

"Definitely. I mean, I don't think mutually assured destruction is the healthiest way to—"

I barked a laugh. "Oh, fuck. No, that's not what I meant. I meant that we're both motivated to keep it out of anyone else's sight, so we can trust each other not to let something slip."

"True. True. I'm a steel trap with stuff like this." He snorted. "Comes with the territory of being in the closet this long."

"Wait, you're not out?"

Alex shook his head. "Not really, no. I haven't had a—" He hesitated. "Well, I did get involved with someone for a while. Longer than I should have, really. And it was ugly and awful and—" He waved his hand. "Anyway, even that wasn't what I'd call a real relationship."

Curiosity burned hot in me, but this seemed like a card I should let him lay down on his own time, so I let it go. "And there hasn't been anyone else?"

"No. I haven't been in anything I'd consider an actual relationship the whole time I've been enlisted, so I never bring guys to the Navy Ball or command functions or anything. I've never come out." He gave a small shrug. "I know it's accepted now, but I still remember the DADT days."

"Shit," I breathed. "That's a long time to be on your own."

"It is. But I've also seen what the Navy does to relationships. Deployments, money being tight, moving around every couple of years. I figured I'd just have booty calls until I retired, and then maybe think about finding a partner."

"Wow. Damn. I mean, I get it—I know firsthand what you're talking about. Not that my marriage would've lasted either way, but the military life definitely put a strain on things."

"I don't doubt that," he said softly. "I've watched a lot of marriages and long-term relationships fall apart, and even when the military isn't *the* problem, it's almost always *a* problem."

I grunted in agreement.

"What about you?" He held my gaze. "Are you out?"

"Not at work, no. My sons and my parents know I'm bi. A few friends back home do. But I've never really come out or anything."

"So chances are, if anyone saw us together, they wouldn't suspect we're screwing."

That brought me up short. "Oh. Yeah, good point." Being friendly would still be frowned upon, and it could still get us disciplined, but despite my earlier *"we might as well fuck since we can't be friends,"* I knew damn well that wasn't the case. I'd just been trying to find a reason to say *"let's do this anyway."*

If the Navy found out we were friends, they'd warn us about being too familiar, spending time together outside of work, and all that bullshit. As likely as not, we'd get a stern talking to, and that would be the end of it.

If they found out I knew what Alex's dick tasted like? Well, that could get messy, and not in a fun way.

But if no one had any reason to think we were any more than friends?

"I guess we won't register on anyone's radars, then," I said. "Assuming we even work with anyone with enough time on their hands to care."

He laughed. "In our command? Pfft. On a busy day, I've got enough plates spinning, I could find out my chief is a serial killer and I'd just say, 'nope, not gonna deal with that.'" Then Alex's eyes lost focus and his features tightened with apprehension.

I touched his arm. "What?"

He chewed his lip. "There's... my ex. The guy I warned you about on the app? He's..." Alex swallowed. "He noticed I wasn't home when we were in Sevilla. He went by my apartment and saw that my car was gone, so he guessed I was out of town."

My blood turned cold. "Oh. Shit. Is he stalking you or something?"

"No, it's not like that. Not... not really. But he's persistent, and he still comes around looking for a piece of ass sometimes." He sighed. "I still want to do this, but if you don't because he's—"

"Alex." I ran the backs of my fingers along his jaw. "I do want to do this. We'll just have to be careful, that's all."

He searched my eyes, silently begging me to mean that.

I lifted my chin to kiss him softly. "I think we're in the clear as long as we don't get careless."

He hesitated, but then nodded. "Okay. Agreed." His brow furrowed. "Question is, *how* do we do this?"

I chewed the inside of my cheek. "I mean, what we're doing now and what we did in Sevilla—that's probably a good start?" I chanced a cautious smile. "I did want to explore Spain, so..."

"I'm always down to explore more."

"Me too. Though it could turn some heads if we go too far too often." I grimaced. "Since we have to put in out-of-bounds chits."

"There is that," he acknowledged, rolling his eyes.

"Ugh." Sometimes I thought that was a stupid policy—we were grown-ass adults. Why the fuck should we have to tell the military where we were going in our off-time? But truth be told, our commands *did* need to know if we were outside an area where we couldn't be quickly recalled, especially if we weren't on leave. So if we were venturing beyond about four hundred miles from the base—any distance where we couldn't be reasonably expected to report back within a few hours—we had to let someone know.

Madrid was at the very edge of that radius, so I'd put in a chit for this weekend just to be careful. Places like Sevilla, Córdoba, Málaga, and Granada, however, were well within that range. Which meant there were plenty of places we could go without turning in any paperwork.

"We can make this work," I said quietly. "Stay within the out-of-bounds range most of the time—who's gonna know?"

Licking his lips, he nodded. "That's true. And, I mean, we're in different departments. We answer to different superiors. Even if we *are* both putting in out-of-bounds chits for the same area at the same time—hell, if we're going on leave at the same time—no one's going to see both. No one's going to notice. Especially since people go on leave and go out-of-bounds to explore Spain all the damn time." A lot of service members never left overseas bases for some reason, but plenty of them did actually take full advantage of being stationed someplace this amazing.

"Good point. And if we run into someone we know, we just say we bumped into each other."

"Simple enough. So..." He grinned. "We go check out everything Spain has to offer, and we fuck each other senseless while we're there. I'm... not really seeing a downside to this."

I laughed as excitement rippled through me. "Sounds perfect to me."

"Me too." But even as he said it, Alex's grin faded a little. "So do we just meet out of town, then?" He ran his thumb along the back of mine. "That's going to mean weekends only. And only weekends when I'm not on call or on duty."

"There is that. Though... I don't think we'd be pushing our luck too hard by having you at my place."

His forehead creased. "You really think that would be safe? Even with my ex lurking around?"

I did, but I thought about it anyway. My driveway was perfect for hiding his car. There weren't a lot of Americans in Sanlúcar and none at all that I knew of in my neighborhood. As long as the ex didn't tail him right to my doorstep, and we weren't going out to eat or making out on the sidewalk or something... who was going to know?

So I nodded. "Yeah, it's safe. If someone sees you going into my driveway or coming out of it, and someone questions us, we can just say it was a one-time thing. You were helping me with something at the house, or you were dropping something off I'd left in Radiology. We'll—we can come up with a reason why you came by one time."

He pursed his lips, eyes losing focus for a moment. Then, "Okay, so when we're at home, we stick to your place. Keep it behind closed doors." His expression brightened a little. "When we go out of town, there's no reason we can't do touristy shit and eat together. We still have the cover story of 'hey, I ran into someone I know who speaks the language and knows the area' if someone busts us."

I considered that. Then I nodded. "I think that would work. And I mean..." I circled my finger in the air. "We're in Madrid. Feels like a shame to come all this way and not be a tourist."

I liked that wicked little grin a little too much. And I liked the goose bumps that sprang up when he kissed the heel of my hand before he purred, "You really telling me you want to go out and do touristy shit tomorrow?" He slid closer to me. "Or do you want to stay in your hotel room and see how much your ass can handle?"

My tongue stuck to the roof of my mouth. I'd spent part of the train ride up here looking at TripAdvisor to figure out what I wanted to see, and suddenly nothing on that site sounded remotely interesting. Not even the Egyptian temple.

"That's what I thought," Alex said with a devilish laugh. Drawing me back in, he murmured, "We'll come back to Madrid as tourists another time."

Sounded like a damn good plan to me.

CHAPTER 20

ALEX

After Madrid, I was with Connor whenever work schedules allowed, whether at his place or taking off somewhere. That was less than I would've liked, unfortunately. I was on call sometimes, and we both worked at least one day every other weekend (which usually lined up with each other). Plus I had to stay in the barracks once every few days for my duty rotation, so there wasn't much we could do on those nights.

At first, we spent a lot of those nights apart exchanging sporadic texts. Over time, those turned into longer conversations, which didn't take long to evolve into late night sexting. Sometimes, after I went home from his place, we'd end up FaceTiming until we'd both been up way too late.

Neither of us socialized much with our coworkers, so we were hardly missed at after hours gatherings. We liked the people we worked with, and we wanted to keep our workplaces friendly, but it wasn't particularly relaxing outside of work. Plus, most of our coworkers either had families, liked to spend their time drinking themselves stupid, or both.

Connor and I...

Well, I thought the way we spent our time together was *much* more interesting, and he seemed to agree.

It had been a long time since I'd been with someone who was so new to this. Connor had plenty of experience with sex, but sex with a man was still new and novel for him, and I loved letting him explore and experiment. There was something sensual and decadent about lying back and letting someone map out my body with his mouth—from my collarbones to my nipples to my abs to my inner thighs, and then, oh God, the things he did to my dick.

Some guys were intimidated at first by sucking cock, but Connor had dived on in like he'd been hungry for it his whole life. Each night we spent together, he wanted more, and his technique got better and better.

"Holy fuck," I murmured as he trailed kisses down from my hipbone one night. "God, Connor..."

He nipped the inside of my thigh, then looked up to meet my gaze. "I hope this isn't boring for you."

"Boring?" The word burst out of me as a laugh. I gave my very hard dick a pull. "Do I look bored?"

Uncertainty flickered across his expression, but then he grinned, and when the tip of his tongue teased my balls, my whole spine turned to electricity.

"Fuuuck," I murmured, and squeezed my eyes shut. He thought I was bored? Hell, I worried *he'd* get bored once the novelty wore off. I was only the second person he'd ever been intimate with; sooner or later, he was going to want to play the field. In the meantime, anything I could do to keep him interested—to keep him hungry for sex with me—I was in. Gazing down at him, I licked my lips. "You said... You said you wanted to try topping, right?"

Connor looked up at me again, and he nodded. "Yeah. Definitely." One eyebrow rose slightly. "Are you offering?"

I nodded. "Uh-huh."

He grinned and crawled up to kiss me, and oh, yeah, he was in. He might get bored with me eventually, but he wasn't there now—not if his greedy, breathless kiss was anything to go by.

When he broke away, his eyes were on fire. "How do, um..." He swallowed. "How do you like it?"

"Any way I can get it." I ran my palms down his shaking arms. "I really like it from behind. Can't kiss, but it means you can get all kinds of leverage."

The whimper that slipped past his lips made my whole body hot.

"What about prep?" he asked.

I half-shrugged. "I don't need much."

He searched my eyes, then grinned. "All right. Let me get a condom."

As he reached for the nightstand, I sat up. "Did you ever do anal before? Topping, I mean?"

Glancing over his shoulder, he asked, "With my ex?"

I nodded.

So did he. "Yeah, she liked it sometimes. So I've, um, I know how to prep and go slow and all that."

"Okay. Okay, good."

Connor wasn't kidding when he said he knew how to prep and go slow. He did them both, making out with me as I lay on my back while he was on his side, and he took his sweet fucking time. I didn't even know if he was trying to be absolutely sure I was ready for him, or if he just enjoyed winding me up. Maybe that was some payback for the first time I'd topped him. Either way, mission accomplished, because I was a pleading, toe-curling wreck by the time he finally relented.

I was trembling as I got up on my hands and knees. I wasn't even sure I'd be able to hold myself up, but I wasn't worried—the alternative was going all the way down to the mattress and letting him plow me until I couldn't see straight. Win-win.

Though I was more than ready for him, he still pushed in painfully slowly, and I was almost completely sure it was to tease me this time. The dead giveaway was when I tried to rock back and encourage him deeper, and he gripped my hips tightly as he gave a sexy, evil chuckle.

"You are such a bastard," I said through my teeth.

"Uh-huh." He eased in another fraction of a millimeter, because fuck him. "Does that mean you want me to stop?"

"It means I want you to stop fucking around and—"

Connor slammed into me so hard, my breath lodged in my throat. I almost collapsed onto my forearms, and I was genuinely surprised I didn't come.

"Oh my God," I murmured.

"Better?" he asked with a grin in his voice.

I managed something in the ballpark of a yes, and he started pulling out slowly. I closed my eyes, my heart pounding as I waited to find out if I'd be treated to another punishing thrust or glacially slow slide in.

Turned out—both.

He rocked in and out slowly a few times, making me dizzy with need. About the time I'd fallen into that blissfully languid pace, he thrust in so hard it *almost* hurt. Again. Then one more time for good measure. And... he was back to slow and steady. Deep and hard. Slow and steady. Every time I got used to one speed, he'd switch, and all I could do was moan and beg for more.

Connor ran a hand up my back. "So when you say this position means a lot of leverage," he whispered. "Does that mean you like it hard?"

"*Very.*"

The laugh was both soft and wicked, but there was nothing soft about the way he gripped my hips. "Does that mean you want it hard *now?*"

"Yes. Please."

Oh, God. He didn't hold back. At all. One or two hard thrusts was one thing; this was one after the other, relentless, and it was *perfect*. I braced a hand against the headboard to keep me upright, and Connor pounded into me hard enough it was difficult to draw a breath.

"This—is this too much?" he panted.

"N-no." I almost choked on my voice. "It's—Jesus, it's so good."

He moaned as if hearing me say that turned him on like nothing else.

"Fuck," he whispered. "Oh, fuck, this is..." He groaned, digging his fingertips harder into my hips. "Fuck me like this next time?"

The sound I made was somewhere between a moan and a sob. "Anything you want. Yes. I'll—God, yeah, I'll fuck you like this."

He gave it to me even harder, turning my vision white, and I cried out all kinds of things I didn't even understand. I thought he shouted something too. Maybe that was me? Fuck if I knew. All I knew was how good this felt. How perfectly he pounded into me, driving me toward oblivion with every thrust.

"I'm gonna come," I whined. "I'm—"

"No," he gritted out. "Not yet."

I let my head fall forward. "Connor..."

"Not yet," he repeated. "I'm gonna come, and then I'm gonna blow you."

"Fuuuck." I squeezed my eyes shut. "That's... That's not helping me not come."

"You can hold back." He slammed into me harder. "I want you to come down my throat."

I had no idea what I said after that. Something that was a mix of weak protest and white-hot arousal. I needed to come so damn bad, and every time he thrust his dick home, I inched closer and closer, but if he was that eager to suck me off... God, yeah, I wanted that.

"Connor. Please. I'm so damn close. I'm so—"

Right then, he pulled my ass flush against his hips, and he roared as he came inside me. His body jerked as if he were trying to push even deeper, and I had no idea how I wasn't coming too. Self-control, maybe, but I didn't think I had enough brain cells for anything besides getting railed, so who knew?

Connor pulled out, making us both moan. Then he ran a hand over my hip. "You didn't come, did you?"

"N-no. Not yet." I needed to, though. A strong fucking breeze would probably take me over the edge at this point.

"Good. Well, as a wise man has said to me a few times," he murmured, shakily getting to his feet, "let me get rid of this, and then I'm going to suck your brains out your dick."

I blinked as I watched him go. Whatever self-assuredness he'd lacked in the beginning, he'd found it. No more nerves. No more uncertainty.

And oh, fuck, when he came back and started going down on me? Yeah, those nerves and uncertainty were a distant memory. Everything he did with his hands and mouth spoke of confidence, and I was a melting, moaning mess. Then he pushed two slick fingers into my ass and bent them just right, and every time I moved my hips, he'd touch my prostate perfectly to make the whole world spin.

"Oh God," I purred, arching off the bed.

He moaned, which only sent me higher into the stratosphere. Christ, there wasn't a man alive who couldn't learn a thing or two from Connor about how to suck dick. Maybe he didn't have a lot of experience, but his hungry enthusiasm more than made up for it. I'd been with guys who could make me feel good but couldn't get me off like this.

Connor?

Fucking hell, Connor did *not* have that problem.

"D-don't stop," I pleaded. "Don't—baby..." I gasped as he picked up speed, and I couldn't help thrusting into his mouth and fucking myself on his fingers. From the sound he made, he loved it, and he gave me even more. "God, Connor, I'm gonna—I'm coming. Fuck, I'm coming!"

My hips bucked, which only made his fingers drive me on, and he took everything I gave him with a low moan of pleasure.

When he finally relented, I sank back to the bed, gulping in air and shaking all over, my toes still curling from the intensity. "Oh my God..."

Connor was beside me now, his hot body pressed up against mine and his lips curved into a grin. "I don't know if I've mentioned this, but I love sucking you off."

I licked my own lips. "I was, uh... I was getting that impression, yeah." I drew him down to kiss me, my spine tingling as I tasted myself on his talented tongue. After a long, decadent kiss, I met his gaze again. "I've been with some guys who are giving head for the first time, and they're kind of hesitant and nervous. But not you. Not the first time, and definitely not this time."

Connor grinned. "Before I met you, I'd been wanting to

try it for *years*. First time I got your dick in my mouth, I was ready to make up for a lot of lost time." He somehow managed to sound both shy and smug as he added, "Still doing that, I guess."

I squirmed against him. "Well, any time you feel compelled to make up for some of that lost time"—I gestured at my cock—"you know what to do."

His laughter gave me goose bumps. "I'll keep that in mind."

"Please do." I ran my hand up his chest. "So did you not know you were into guys before you got married? Or did you just never get around to experimenting?"

"I..." He furrowed his brow and his eyes lost focus. "I mean, looking back, I think the signs were there. But consciously?" He shook his head. "No, I didn't know. Not until I'd been married... three or four years, I think."

"Does your ex-wife know?"

"Oh, yeah." He waved a hand. "It's kind of funny how it came out, actually. We were out one night with friends—one of those times we actually sprang for a babysitter—and we'd been drinking. She pointed some guy out—one of the bartenders, I think—and said he was hot. That she'd totally do him."

My lips parted. "Really? Was she trying to provoke you or something?"

"No, no. She was just drunk. I can say a lot of things about my ex-wife, but she wasn't like that." He laughed with a note of fondness. "She just hadn't had a drink in a while, kind of forgot her tolerance had come down, and she was just feeling absolutely no pain that night."

I laughed. "Okay, yeah, that sounds about right."

"Exactly. Anyway, so she's all, 'He's hot—I'd blow him.'

And I—also drunker than I'd been in a while—said, 'Fuck, me too.'"

"Really?"

He nodded as some color rose in his cheeks. "Like I said—drunk as hell. The next morning, while we were trying not to die from our hangovers, she gave me this kind of sidelong look and asked, 'Did you mean it when you said you'd blow that bartender?' I said, 'Did you?' She thought about it for a sec, then shrugged and said it would make for a hell of a threesome. Later on, when we were both ourselves again, she came at it a bit more seriously. She asked if it had just been a stupid thing I'd said when I was drunk, or if the alcohol had dissolved my filter enough to let some truth slip out."

I tensed. "What was your answer? And what was her reaction?"

He half-shrugged. "I told her the truth—I'd realized a while ago that I thought guys were attractive, and I was starting to think I was bi. She said if I'd just told her out of the blue, she might've been upset—like she might've thought I'd been hiding it from her or whatever—but the hangover and all that had given her some time to digest it. And by the time we actually talked about it, she'd decided it probably wasn't that big of a deal as long as I wasn't going to cheat on her."

"Which you weren't?"

"Never," he said quickly. "And in fact it was her idea for me to give it a try. Being with a man, I mean."

"Whoa, seriously?"

"Mmhmm. It never really materialized, though. I mean, we tried? We did the open relationship thing at one point. Swinging, actually."

I raised my eyebrows. "No shit?"

"I know, right?" He chuckled softly. "That... didn't last long. We never even got into bed with anyone."

"Never?"

"Nope. The thing is, we found out almost immediately the most couples in that lifestyle are straight men with either bi or straight women. A lot of them are looking for bi women, but if they find out the guy is bi?" He shook his head. "They won't give you the time of day. Not even if the bi guy is totally fine focusing on the women."

I rolled my eyes. "Oh my God. Insecure much?"

"Mmhmm. The straight guys don't feel comfortable getting naked in the same room as a queer guy. And anyway, before we even got to the point of playing with anyone, I started talking to some bi women who really hated unicorn hunters."

I tilted my head. "Those are... people looking for a bi woman for threesomes, right?"

"Yep. And I realized that was kind of what we were doing, just with men. So I didn't want to be that guy, you know? Plus I think the more we dipped our toes in, the more Aimee figured out she's just not wired for that. Especially since it's usually two couples swapping partners and having sex in the same room." He grimaced. "She's really self-conscious about her body after having the kids, especially the emergency C-section with Landon, and I didn't want her to be uncomfortable, you know?"

"Yeah, I don't blame you. So you didn't get into it, then?"

"No. Right around that time, we also talked to someone in the lifestyle who warned us to be careful with swinging or even open relationships and the military."

"What?" I cocked my head. "Why?"

"Adultery."

"The fuck?" I scoffed. "How is it adultery if—wait, it's *still* adultery if everyone's consenting?"

"According to the UCMJ, yes."

"Oh for fuck's sake." I rolled my eyes. "It's stupid that it's a criminal offense to begin with, but if it's consensual? Fuck that noise."

"Right? It's none of the military's goddamned business, but I mean"—he gave a bitter laugh—"when has that ever stopped them?"

I grunted. "No kidding." As I thought about that, my heart sank a little. "That goes for us too, you know. Are you sure you're still onboard with what we're doing? It's not criminal, but the Article 134 isn't fun either."

I instantly hated myself for even bringing it up.

Way to go, Alex. Give him a reason to lock the door behind me when I leave and never do this again.

Connor clasped our hands together and kissed the back of mine. "I'm still onboard. I think Aimee and I were kind of spooked about the whole non-monogamy thing, so potential adultery charges were just a tipping point to make us nix it. What we're doing, though—I'm in."

I had no business being this relieved, but I was.

He must've seen my lingering concern because he slid closer and kissed me softly. "We'll be fine. If you're not comfortable with it, I'll understand, but I know the risk, and I know we're taking every commonsense precaution we can." He brushed his lips over mine again. "I'm still in if you are."

"I'm still in." I gently freed my hand and curved it behind his head. "Especially if you're going to fuck me like that again."

Connor's laugh was a warm gust across my lips. "Any time you want."

"Promise?"

"Promise."

"I'm going to hold you to that."

"Please do."

CHAPTER 21

CONNOR

Though Alex and I couldn't spend as much time together as we would've liked, we did the best we could. We also made good on our decision to explore Spain together. Whenever we had a free weekend, we'd take off somewhere—Málaga, Toledo, some towns I'd never heard of. The day we spent exploring the Alhambra was utterly incredible (and I couldn't complain about how we spent the following night, either).

We also took advantage of the late sunsets to take some short day trips after work. We couldn't risk exploring places like El Puerto, Cádiz, or even Jerez together because not *every* American stayed on-base. There was too much opportunity to be seen by someone we knew.

If we drove a little farther, though? Nobody.

I'd seen photos of Setenil de las Bodegas, the town built under the rocky overhang of a giant cliff, and that turned out to be about ninety minutes away. Nearby was Ronda, which still had an enormous and impressive Roman bridge. There was also the tiny hilltop town of Arcos de la Frontera, and we found some cool churches as well as ruins from the Moorish, Roman, and even Phoenician eras.

I loved the history, the architecture, the scenery, but also the company. We drove separately just to make sure no one saw us together, which was annoying, but as soon as we were together, we talked nonstop. About where we were. About the Navy. About life. And, when we had enough relative privacy, what we'd do once we were alone.

I loved it. I just fucking loved it. Every last minute, even when I was driving back by myself, because I'd spend the whole ride smiling like an idiot and thinking about Alex.

I really wanted to go to Morocco, which was only about three hours away by car and ferry, but that required some clearances from our command. Traveling within Spain was easy, even if we needed to get an out-of-bounds chit for some of the farther places. Those chits were signed off by different people, and nobody really cared. If two people put in requests to visit Morocco at the same time, though, the clearance requests would likely both land on the same person's desk. Maybe that person wouldn't care, or maybe he'd ask questions about why an officer and an enlisted service member wanted to take the same ferry to the same city at the same time. And there were two opportunities for someone to get suspicious—the person who signed off on requests to go to Morocco, and the person who signed off on requests to go to Africa.

So we decided to hold off on Morocco. And anyway, my sons were begging me to take them, so I'd wait until they visited.

"There's also that part about being two dudes traveling to a country where homosexuality is illegal," Alex pointed out one night. "Most people don't really pay enough attention to notice or care one way or the other, and I'm like ninety-nine percent sure my tour guides in Marrakech were a gay couple. But I'd rather not explain things to the Moroccan authorities *or* our commands if someone *does* decide they care."

That was a reasonable point. There were places in the U.S. where I wouldn't be out and proud, and I wasn't going to gamble with my safety in another country either, with or without someone I was already traveling with on the sly.

So... Morocco could wait until September.

We were also making plans to take off to other parts of Europe, especially since we could be reasonably sneaky about the leave chits. We'd probably just blend into the larger stack of people making similar requests. That seemed like a contradiction, given how reluctant Americans were to leave overseas bases, but it was true. For all they didn't explore off-base very much, quite a few *did* go to the big tourist magnets. Especially the seasonal ones. So Dr. Marks and HM1 Barlow were both going to Prague in December to check out the Christmas markets? So was half the base. One of us was heading to Florence, Rome, and Naples while the other was visiting friends in Gaeta (which was between Naples and Rome) before heading to Pompeii (which was right next to Naples)? A lot of people went to Italy after the summer heat died down. And who *wasn't* heading to Munich for Oktoberfest?

Traveling in Europe required a lot less paperwork and scrutiny than going to Africa, and more service members and families stayed within the continent for various reasons, so it didn't really raise eyebrows if people ventured out into the rest of the EU. As long as we weren't on the same flights or staying in the same hotels (on paper, anyway), we could fly under the radar.

Hopefully.

For now, we were sticking to Spain. A lot of coworkers were taking leave, especially those with kids who were enjoying their summer off from school. While everyone we knew spent their off time cooling down at the beach, we met everywhere we could, from Valencia to Sevilla, still being discreet and keeping our heads down.

So far, so good. And the more we did this, the less I was actually concerned about us getting caught. At work, we interacted on a purely professional level, though we might exchange grins now and then when we passed in the hall. Really, unless we did something to brazenly draw attention to ourselves, no one was going to notice and no one was going to care.

As we got into the scorching days of August, I couldn't deny that any thrill I'd gotten out of doing something forbidden—and there hadn't been much—was long gone. The thrill was in being with Alex. The sex, the long conversations, the jaunts to various parts of Spain, the plans for more adventurous trips later in the year—I *lived* for that. After the loneliness of my separation had been compounded with the isolation of overseas orders, I craved his company as much as I craved the orgasms we drew out of each other.

There was only one thing missing, though, and it had nothing to do with wishing we didn't have to keep this a secret. Even on our brief trips out of town, we still stayed in separate hotels, ostensibly in case someone who knew us saw us. And when he came to my house, he was always gone not long after the sun went down.

Lying beside him in my bed, still tingling all over from being ridden into the mattress, I curled closer to him. Sliding a hand over his thigh, I whispered, "It's getting late."

Alex sighed, trailing his knuckles along my chest. "I know."

"You, um..." I swallowed, then pushed myself up on my elbow to look at him. "You don't have to go."

He blinked. "I... But I *should* go."

"You shouldn't be here at all," I said dryly, "but I think that ship has long since sailed."

His laugh was almost soundless. "Okay, fair. But staying..." His humor faded as he chewed his lip.

"You don't have to. Just... You're already here. There's no reason you can't stay all night. If you *want* to stay, I mean."

"I do, but..." Alex's face colored, and he avoided my gaze. "I, um... It's not..." He swallowed hard. "Keeping things on the downlow isn't the only reason I haven't suggested staying over or rooming together when we travel."

"Is that right?"

He nodded but didn't elaborate.

I found his hand and laced our fingers together. "Is everything okay?"

"Yeah. Yeah. It's..." He took a deep breath and finally faced me. "Look, you've been to combat. You know what it does to..." He gestured at his head.

"Of course I do." Then the piece clicked into place. "Nightmares?"

Grimacing, he nodded and dropped his gaze again. "They don't happen all the time. But when they do..."

"It's bad?"

"It can be, yeah."

I squeezed his hand. "Mine too."

He looked in my eyes. "Yeah?"

"Mmhmm. I haven't seen combat in about fifteen years... unless you count what I see at night."

Alex swallowed again. "Still rough?"

"Oh yeah. It can be pretty bad."

"So you get it."

"I do." I squeezed his hand. "If you're worried I'll be annoyed if one of your nightmares wakes us up—I mean, it's just as likely to happen the other way around."

His brow pinched as he studied me. "And you... you want me to stay over?"

I was kind of caught off guard by how vehemently I almost said, *"Yes!"* Because... yes, I really wanted him to stay over. Just the thought of falling asleep and waking up beside him made me ache with a longing I absolutely didn't expect. It was something akin to what I'd felt during those long deployments—that cold, lonely, homesick feeling that was almost as hard to sleep through as all my psychological combat souvenirs.

I tamped down the impulse to plead with him, and I just nodded and quietly said, "Yeah. I do." The uncertainty lingered in his eyes, so I pressed a kiss to the heel of his hand and whispered, "If one of us has a nightmare, we'll deal with it. I, um..." I stared down at our hands. "I don't want to put anyone through that, but I won't lie—it's always easier to go back to sleep when there's someone else there."

I cringed inwardly, sure Alex was going to balk.

Way to go, Connor—make it sound like you just want him here in case you have a fucking nightmare.

I opened my mouth to take it back, but Alex beat me to the punch.

"I wouldn't know," he said softly. "If it's easier with someone else, I mean. I just... I'm always afraid of scaring someone. Or fucking up their sleep. Or..." He sighed and shook his head. "It's... not really an aphrodisiac, either."

"An aphrodisiac?" I looked at him again, not sure how to

read the creases in his forehead or the color that bloomed in his cheeks. I caught on, though. "You think it makes you unattractive?"

The color deepened, and he nodded. With a bitter laugh, he said, "I can't imagine it's a turn-on."

"Do you think it makes *me* unattractive?"

His jaw snapped shut and his eyes widened. "What? No! Of course not!"

I inclined my head and raised my eyebrows.

He held my gaze. Then he huffed a quiet, self-conscious laugh as the tension melted out of his features. "Okay, okay. Point taken." Running his thumb along mine, he said, "I, uh... If you're serious, I have an overnight bag in my car." He paused, then quickly added, "You know, for duty nights."

"I figured that was what it was for. And yes, I'm serious."

His smile made my toes curl. So did the prospect of sharing my bed with him tonight instead of trying to fall asleep alone after he'd gone.

"Okay." He pushed himself up and kissed me lightly. "I'll go get my bag."

I chuckled as I ran my hand over his hip. "You might want to put on some shorts."

He glanced down at himself, then met me with a ridiculously innocent expression. "You want me to cover this up?"

"I mean, if you want to go streaking across my yard while the sun's still up..."

Alex snorted. "Don't threaten me with a good time."

I rolled my eyes and gave his ass a playful slap. "Just go get your shit."

CHAPTER 22

ALEX

Oh, man. We should've done this sooner.
The room was still pitch black thanks to the siesta shades over the window, but my alarm had gone off, indicating it was 0600. I'd hit the snooze button, and now I was lying here, indulging in a few minutes of dozing beside Connor.

It was just as well we'd waited a little while to do this—I wouldn't have been able to sleep because I'd have been so worried about waking him up with a nightmare. Even with his reassurance, the thought of him having a front row seat to me thrashing awake like that was mortifying.

The reassurance did help, though, and I'd slept. There'd been dreams, because there were always dreams, but none of them had been enough to shake me (or Connor) awake. If we kept doing this, there'd be a rough night sooner or later, but I was happy to at least start out smooth and pleasant.

Well-rested and calm, I just lay there and enjoyed this. It had been so long since I'd woken up beside someone, and I basked in it. The warmth, the closeness, the soft sound of his breathing—I hadn't even realized how much I'd missed that until now. It was one of those things I was looking forward to when I started my new life as a civilian—when I could finally be with someone for more than sex, and maybe mornings like these could become a regular thing.

Maybe with Connor.

My eyes flew open, and I banished that thought as quick as it had come. I was not going to get that attached to Connor. Enjoy the sex and the time we spent together, sure. Savor mornings together when we had them, absolutely. But there were a lot of cards stacked against any kind of future with him, and those cards weren't all in the UCMJ.

If, hypothetically, we decided to date for real, it would be a year and a half before we could be out in public. Probably more than that, honestly—we'd need to let a few weeks or months pass between my retirement and us coming out so no one realized we'd been secretly fraternizing. Getting busted after I retired wouldn't affect me, but it could affect him, and I wasn't going to do that to him.

I also didn't have any illusions that being with me was worth gambling with that kind of fallout. Connor was lonely. He was living overseas after his divorce, and he was indulging in the previously unexplored side of his bisexuality.

At best, we'd probably get a couple more months out of this. Then he'd decide what he was getting wasn't worth what he was risking, and he'd move on. I couldn't blame him for that. What the fuck did I bring to the table that would be worth a year and some change of secrecy? I was lucky he hadn't already dropped me.

But who else could he fuck? That's why we're hooking up—because he doesn't have other options.

Sighing, I closed my eyes, cuddled closer to him, and kissed the back of his shoulder. Yeah, I knew that. I was a convenient piece of ass, same as I was for any man. That was all I ever wanted from them or offered them, so it worked out.

It was fun, and it would be fun while it lasted. Then we'd both move on, and I'd just keep counting down the days until I was a civilian.

And maybe once I was out of the Navy, I could actually invest in someone emotionally.

Maybe I could find someone who thought I was worth the price of admission.

The sex, traveling, and texting were fun as hell. Maybe they wouldn't last forever, but I was determined to enjoy them for as long as they did.

I'd had this kind of dynamic with guys before. Great sex, flirty messages in between—it wasn't anything new, though I didn't usually travel with my booty calls. Except Connor and I weren't traveling together as a couple. We were traveling as cover so no one caught on that we were screwing.

What threw me for a loop was the time in *between* all the sex, traveling, and texting. When I had to go through the motions of my job and my daily life, and I caught myself feeling anchorless. Rudderless. Like I was just... drifting along, waiting for a text notification or for the right time to get myself over to Connor's place.

That was weird. I mean, I'd caught myself daydreaming about sex with Isidoro, especially right after a hot night together or when I knew I'd see him that evening. It was distracting, what could I say?

But that hadn't been like this. Yeah, I thought about

everything Connor and I did in the bedroom—none of that was ever far from my mind—but I wasn't used to...

To *missing* someone like this.

God. Yeah. That was what it was, wasn't it? When I wasn't around Connor, I missed him, and not just his body. The long conversations. Chilling beside his pool with cold beers. The crinkles at the corners of his eyes whenever he laughed. Just... being around him.

There was no language barrier, and not just because we were both English speakers. We could talk about the day-to-day bullshit at the hospital because he understood all the idiosyncrasies of that chain of command, the military in general, and everything that came with working in healthcare. I could tell him stories from past commands without having to stop and explain all the acronyms and weird quirks of the military that were alien to civilians.

I liked being around him. I liked *him*. When I wasn't with him...

Hell. Was this what pining felt like? Because I'd never pined for anyone, but now I was somewhere between a lost puppy and a kid trying to sleep on Christmas Eve—acutely aware of his absence and at the same time, almost vibrating with anticipation over seeing him again.

Especially because I would see him again in just a few hours. He'd text me when he was off work, and I'd head over to his place, and we'd—

"Oh, hey, *there* you are."

The voice startled me out of my thoughts. I shook myself and came back to earth, realizing first that I was at the Navy Exchange. How long had I been standing here, staring at trash bags? I needed to get some, didn't I? Christ, I was out of it today.

And the second thing I realized was who had spoken to me.

Tobias.

Fuck me. There went my good mood, deflating like a balloon as I met those irritatingly familiar eyes. I definitely hadn't missed *him* whenever we were separated, not even when things were—well, they were never *good* between us, but they'd been less bad. They'd been okay enough that I'd more or less enjoyed his company.

I schooled my expression. "Hey."

He studied me, and I again wondered how long I'd been standing here like a dumbass. And how long he'd been watching me.

"You haven't been around much lately." The comment was made like an observation, but I'd known him long enough to catch the accusatory edge. The unspoken, *Where the fuck have you been?*

I had to bite back a smile. *Wouldn't you like to know where I've been?*

Keeping my tone and expression bored—not just neutral, but gray-rock-bored, I said, "I've been busy."

"Uh-huh." Tobias inclined his head a little. "So what's his name?"

I tensed before I could tell myself not to. "What's his— what makes you think there's a 'he' involved?"

That condescending laugh made me want to snatch a box of trash bags off the shelf and hurl it at his head. "Oh, Alex. My guy." He stepped closer and put a heavy hand on my shoulder. "I know when you're getting ass."

I jerked out from under his hand and put some more space between us. "You don't know anything except that you're not getting me anymore."

"You say that," he said dismissively. "But we both know

you'll be back at my door once your new piece of ass gets tired of your bullshit."

Anger flared behind my ribs, but I fought to keep it out of his sight. Okay, the gray rock approach wasn't working. Time for the direct one.

"Why do you even want me?" I shrugged as flippantly as I could. "You know I'm not interested and I can't fucking stand you." I looked him dead in the eyes. "What do you want out of this? Hate sex? Or do you have a newly developed humiliation kink and you enjoy listening to me tell you no?"

Tobias worked his jaw and narrowed his eyes. "You can act like you don't want me, but we both know you do." He gave a quiet, ugly laugh. "You know you like what I do to you."

It was a struggle to hold on to my poker face. I hated that he'd been so right for so long. But he *wasn't* right anymore. "I liked it then. I'm not interested now."

"Yeah? So who are you screwing?"

I barked a laugh. "What makes you think it's any of your business?"

"What's making you so secretive about it? Because you happily threw your Spanish Marine fuck buddy in my face."

I shrugged again. "Maybe making you jealous just isn't entertaining anymore."

He rolled his eyes. "Come on. You're hiding something. And you're never at your apartment anymore, so I know you're—"

"What the fuck do you mean, I'm never at my apartment anymore?" I stepped closer, gritting my teeth. "Didn't I tell you to stop coming around? Have you been stalking me?"

"Stalking you?" He gave a condescending laugh and showed his palms. "It's just an observation, Alex. Relax. And I can come to Chipiona any time I want." He half-shrugged. "No reason I can't swing by in case you want to get drilled, but you're never there. You used to be a homebody except when you were off with that Marine." He grinned, and my nails bit into my palms as I balled my fists at my sides. Sounding way too pleased with himself, he whispered, "So what's the deal? Is he married or something? Is he—"

"Who or what I'm doing is none of your fucking business," I hissed.

His laugh made my insides shrivel. Fuck. I'd stepped right into his trap, hadn't I? I'd played his games a million times, and I still fell for it.

"Have fun with him, Alex," he said with a smirk. "Just remember, we both know you'll be crawling back for my dick sooner or later."

And then he was gone, strolling out of the aisle and leaving me there, slack-jawed beside the trash bags, wondering how the hell he'd gotten the best of me again.

I shouldn't have even been surprised by his audacity or his brazen dickishness. I probably wasn't really surprised; just pissed off and ready to punch something.

Swearing under my breath, I snatched a box of trash bags off the shelf, tossed it in my cart, and continued shopping. I didn't know how much hope I had of finding anything else on my list—not even the stuff that had been in the exact same locations the whole time I'd been stationed here—but it was something to do besides stand there fuming.

The worst part was how afraid I was that he was right. That sooner or later, I'd be back in his bed, hating myself but surrendering to the reality that Tobias was the only one who didn't eventually lose interest in me.

I wanted to believe I wouldn't let that happen again. I'd already let him string me along once, to the point that I actually got caught up in things and wanted—for the first time in my adult life—more than sex. It had all been a game for him, though, and it would be again. Even if I inevitably stumbled over his tripwires, I couldn't fall for *that* shit again. I couldn't let myself be drawn back into that snake pit of a relationship, whether we were just screwing or he was gaslighting me into thinking there was more.

God. Why did I ever sleep with him in the first place?

Eh. It wasn't my proudest moment. I hadn't liked him, but he'd been attractive and available, and I'd been horny, so I'd figured if nothing else, he'd shut up once the clothes came off.

Yeah. Not so much.

On the other hand, his bullshit was the reason I'd connected with Connor, so maybe I should be thanking him.

The thought almost made me laugh, which I doubted would've gone over well if Toby the Troglodyte had still been standing here. Though I was getting better at telling him off, I mostly wanted him to just leave, not storm away in a rage and then start aggressively pursuing me again. Though admittedly, the temptation was strong to catch up with him and say, *"By the way, thanks for being a douchecanoe because warning somebody off you led to me getting some of the best sex of my life!"*

I didn't, and I wouldn't. But ooh, boy, did I think about it.

And that *almost* distracted me from how low and awful I felt after our encounter. Almost. As I continued shopping on numb autopilot, my heart sank deeper into my chest, my good mood a distant memory.

What if Tobias was right about me?

What if I did go crawling back to him after Connor got bored with me?

And why did it hurt so much to imagine Connor getting bored with me?

I've never cared this much before.

What happens when that blows up in my face?

CHAPTER 23

CONNOR

Today was yet another one of those days when I envied the people I worked with who still blissfully inhaled energy drinks like they were going out of style. After fooling around with Alex, and then FaceTiming him afterward until *way* too late, I desperately needed the caffeine, and coffee wasn't delivering.

No matter how tired I was, though, I wasn't going to tempt fate. The coffee would just have to do.

And it can kick in any goddamned time now.

In my office, I downed more than I probably should have in one go. Then I headed out to see my first patients of the day.

From 0700 to 1200 was sick call, so I mostly saw service members who needed light duty chits or SIQ, which meant they were sick-in-quarters. I kind of hated that the military required them to show up to sick call in order to get out of work. If they were in bad enough shape that they couldn't go to work, then maybe asking them to drag themselves to medical to prove it was counterproductive?

Buuut I was just a lowly lieutenant commander who didn't make the rules.

This morning, I signed off a light duty chit for a Seabee who'd hurt his back "working on a buddy's car" on his off day. Sure, my dude. That explained the bloodshot eyes and the obvious headache, too. Knowing the Seabees, they'd partied hard the past couple of days, and he'd probably done something stupid while drunk. His back was definitely hurting like crazy, though, and as far as I was concerned, my job was to help him heal, not judge him for how he did it. So I gave him some high-octane Motrin, put him on light duty for the next five days, and told him to come back and see me next week.

After him was a Master at Arms who'd felt like crap for a few days, had been sick all morning, and said her lower back hurt so bad she couldn't even put on her gun belt.

"My section leader kept telling me to just suck it up," she said miserably. "But when I threw up this morning, he got scared because now he thinks I'm pregnant." With a wince, she added, "I'm worried he might be right."

They were both wrong—the UTI she'd been steadfastly ignoring (and he'd been telling her to knuckle through) had spread to her kidneys, which was why her back hurt so bad. I had a corpsman escort her to the emergency room for some IV antibiotics, and I called ahead to make sure they got her in immediately. Then, with the MA's permission, I personally called the security officer to strongly advise him to brief his department about being this reckless with a Sailor's health.

"I just sent one of your MAs to the emergency room, Lieutenant," I snarled at the SECO. "Another day, and she'd have been coming in by ambulance. There is *no excuse* for forcing a Sailor to keep showing up for duty until she's as sick as she is, and this not the first time it's been someone from your department. I see *one more* Master at Arms at sick call with a story like hers, and so help me, I will get my CO, your CO, and the base CO involved. Do I make myself clear?"

"Yes, sir" came the satisfyingly meek response. "I'll talk to my people."

He'd better hope he did, because I wasn't joking.

I was still fuming over that when I headed into the room for my next patient, but I paused outside the door to collect myself. Deep breath. Mental refresh. Whoever was in the room had nothing to do with my lack of sleep, the ineffectiveness of my coffee, or the utter incompetence of the base security department.

I pulled it together and got through that appointment. Then the next. Then the one after that. Little by little, my fury over the MA's treatment died down, but it still set the stage for rest of the day.

God, I can't wait to see Alex tonight.

Every time that thought crossed my mind, my mood brightened a bit and my energy kicked up a notch. The day could be the biggest shitshow in the world, but at the end of it, I'd see Alex. I'd do more than see him, and I couldn't wait.

Not a moment too soon, I was walking out to my car and texting Alex that I was on my way home. All the way from Rota to Sanlúcar, I drummed my fingers on the wheel and fidgeted in the driver seat. I was exhausted from a long day, but just thinking about tumbling into bed with him was like shotgunning a couple of those forbidden energy drinks.

Couldn't. Fucking. *Wait.*

At home, I quickly showered and put on shorts and a T-shirt, mostly so I didn't scandalize my neighbors when I opened the door for Alex. I didn't imagine I'd be wearing any of this for long.

And finally, he was here. My whole body was practically vibrating with excitement as I headed for the door. I always wanted him, but after the long and frustrating day, I *needed* his touch and his warmth.

I opened the door to let him in. Our eyes met, but only for a second before he shifted his gaze away from mine. My good mood and the day's anticipation fled in an instant. As Alex came inside, alarm twisted beneath my ribs.

"Hey." I nudged the door shut. "You okay?"

"Yeah. Yeah." He laughed halfheartedly as he rolled his shoulders. "I'm, uh... I'm good." He stepped closer, his eyes begging me not to notice how weak his smile was.

Something wasn't right.

I touched his waist but didn't move in for a kiss. "What's wrong?"

"Nothing. I'm... I'm good."

"Alex." I ran my fingers along the edge of his jaw. "Talk to me."

He opened his mouth as if to insist that, no, everything was fine. But he held my gaze, and slowly, he deflated. My heart sped up, both with relief that he was dropping the façade and uneasiness over what he was about to tell me.

Breaking eye contact, he raked a hand through his short hair and exhaled hard. "It's... I ran into my ex at the Exchange."

I stiffened. "Your ex? That creepy asshole you warned me about?"

Chafing his arms, he nodded. "Tobias, yeah." He blew out another breath and suddenly radiated bone-deep exhaustion. "God, I am so damn *tired* of him."

My hackles went up. "What happened? What did he—"

"It's fine. Nothing happened." Alex patted the air, then rested his hands on my chest. "I mean, he was kind of a dick, but it wasn't anything I couldn't handle."

I relaxed minutely. "So... what happened?"

As he ran me through the conversation, anger roiled in the pit of my stomach. I'd been wary of Tobias from the beginning because of Alex's warning, but now I knew Alex. I cared about Alex. And the fact that this asshole was harassing Alex made me see red.

And that was before Alex said, "He's been coming by my apartment."

"What? Wait, he's *still* coming around?"

"Yeah. When I'm not there." Alex shuddered. "Thinking—I don't know, I guess he thought if he dropped by, he'd eventually catch me when I was home and horny." With a humorless laugh, he added, "Then I'd let him in and sleep with him."

I didn't know whether to laugh at how pathetic this guy was, or risk my career with a confrontation at the hospital. I wasn't a possessive or jealous man, but anyone who made someone I cared about this nervous—anyone who harassed him this much—deserved a one-way conversation and an attitude adjustment.

Alex continued, "He made some noise about how he thinks I must be seeing someone I shouldn't be. Like asking if you're married and..." He waved a hand. "I don't think he actually knows we're hooking up—that it's you and me, specifically, I mean. I think he's just fishing around for a reason to harass me."

"That fucker," I growled.

Alex's eyebrows jumped.

"Is there anything you can do about him coming to your place?" I asked.

"Not really. He's not trespassing or anything. I doubt the cops would care much, and the MAs can't do anything because he's off-base."

I sighed. He was probably right.

"I'm sorry." Alex's shoulders fell. "I... We were supposed to be having fun this evening, and I—"

"Why are you apologizing?" I caressed his cheek. "You didn't do anything."

"No, but I kinda killed the mood."

I shook my head. "No, you didn't. Your asshole ex fucked up your day."

"Yeah, he did." Alex sighed. "I was really looking forward to tonight, too."

"Me too, but we can take it easy if you want to. We can have dinner by the pool and just relax. There's no pressure from me even when your ex *isn't* being a dick."

"I know. I... You've never pressured me. I just feel bad that we were going to have a fun night together, and then..." He waved his hand. "I'm sorry."

"Don't be." I wrapped my arms around him and let him lean against me. Stroking his short hair, I whispered, "We'll get back to the fun another night. Right now, let's just take the pressure off. I can order delivery from that Italian place around the corner, and we can eat outside. Then maybe put on a movie or something if you want."

He let out a long breath, and his whole body seemed to relax into my embrace. "That sounds really good."

"It does." I pressed a kiss to his temple. "The rest—it'll keep." I paused. "And you're still welcome to stay here tonight even if we're not fooling around."

He drew back and met my gaze. "Yeah?"

"Well, yeah." I smiled. "I like having you here. I'm going to have nights where I don't want to have sex either, but I still want you here."

He studied me for a moment, and little by little, he relaxed even more. Swallowing hard, he nodded. "Okay." He rolled his shoulders. "Okay, yeah, that sounds good." He paused, and when he spoke, he cautiously lifted his eyebrows. "Though, we've been meaning to try that kebab place."

"Ooh, you're right, we have. And I'm pretty sure I can order online."

The smile that broke out was tired but genuine. "Perfect. Let's go have a look at their menu."

I was still angry with Tobias, and I was a little disappointed that Alex and I wouldn't be fooling around tonight. But he was here. As we perused the kebab restaurant's menu, placed our order, waited for our food, and then started eating outside in the evening sun, he relaxed more and more. He came back to life. He smiled and laughed more easily. By the time we'd settled in to watch a movie, he was back to himself enough that I almost wondered if sex might still be on the table after all.

Almost. We'd both eaten enough that we could barely move—holy crap, that kebab place was incredible. But seeing the flirty sparkle return to his eye... feeling him curled against me while we watched the movie... letting those kisses linger as we got ready for bed...

Yeah, he'd be okay.

That, more than anything else, was what mattered.

Nice try, Tobias.

You're not getting that far under his skin again.

The thump against my back startled me out of a sound sleep. For a split second, I thought it was something from the bloody, smoke-scented dream I'd been having, but the movement and the muffled whimper beside me brought me fully back to reality.

I rolled over and caught Alex's flailing arm just before he'd have bumped me again, and I slid up next to him. "Hey. Hey. Alex. Wake up, baby."

His whole body jerked, his heel catching me in the shin, and I gave him a subtle shake as I said his name again.

Then he stilled.

After a second, he released a ragged breath.

"You with me?" I whispered.

"Y-yeah." He relaxed back against me. "Fuck. I'm sorry."

"It's okay." I smoothed his hair, which was damp with sweat. "It happens to me too. Just breathe."

He breathed. "Fucking sucks."

"I know it does." I wrapped my arm around him and kissed the back of his shoulder. "But I'm not upset about it, if that's what you're worried about."

From the way he relaxed minutely—yeah, he'd been worried about it.

"I mean it," I whispered. "It's PTSD. I get it."

He pushed out a ragged breath. "Still. I'm sorry."

I just held him closer and kissed his shoulder again. This didn't surprise me, given how brittle he'd been yesterday. I'd had days like that, too, and the worst nightmares were almost inevitable afterward.

"You okay?" I stroked his hair.

He pushed out a long breath as he relaxed in my arms. "Yeah. I still don't even know what the fuck triggered it, but..." He trailed off into a sigh.

I still wondered if it was the confrontation with his ex yesterday, but I didn't mention that. No point in drawing his attention back to that shitshow when he was already rattled. "It doesn't always *need* a trigger, does it?"

He seemed to think about that. "I guess it doesn't." He scrubbed a hand over his face, skin scuffing over stubble. "I keep thinking it'll get better, but..."

"I know the feeling. Especially when it happens out of nowhere."

"Seriously. And when there *is* a trigger, it's usually the stupidest shit that sets it off, too."

"Right?"

Alex huffed a humorless laugh. "I was a ball of anxiety for a whole damn day once because someone was driving one of those street racer cars, and the NOX system backfired." He groaned. "For fuck's sake. I *knew* what it was, too."

"You knew," I said. "But your subconscious didn't."

"What do you mean?"

"Like, you consciously knew it was a car backfiring. But that lizard brain that's still fucked up from the war heard a bang and didn't know what to make of it."

He sighed again. "Maybe? I guess?"

"It's happened to me too."

"Has it?"

"Mmhmm." I thought for a second. "I took my boys to a sandwich shop once, and you know those big cooking sheets? The ones they use to bake the bread?"

"Yeah?"

"Someone dropped a stack of them." I sighed, my stomach knotting at the memory and my face burning from the past embarrassment. "One of the boys had to text their mom to come get us."

"Really?" Alex breathed.

"Yeah. It was the stupidest thing, you know? Especially since I *knew* what it was. But it hit one of those tripwires in my head, and I just... I didn't trust myself to drive. My hands were shaking so bad I couldn't text Aimee, so..." I cringed. "I had to have Quinn do it."

"How old was he?"

"Fourteen. And they were both pretty rattled from the whole thing. I felt *terrible* about it for a long time."

"But it wasn't something you did," he whispered. "Something triggered your PTSD—that's not... I mean, it's not a character flaw, you know?"

"I know." I kissed his shoulder again. "But in the moment, I felt like it was. Which is probably what you're feeling right now."

He tensed, then relaxed. "Okay, okay. Point taken." He found my hand and clasped it gently in his. "And... thanks."

"Of course."

"Dealing with this shit would be so much easier if we could get some goddamned therapy," he muttered.

"I know, right?"

The military had made some token efforts toward letting us access mental healthcare. The Brandon Act was a good start, but there was still a long, long way to go.

"It's ironic, isn't it?" I said. "The military gives out PTSD like it gives out Good Conduct Medals. We can all name at least a dozen people who very obviously have it, ourselves included. But if we get diagnosed, suddenly we're not fit for duty anymore."

Alex grunted unhappily. "You'd think we'd be better fit for duty after getting diagnosed and treated."

I gave a sharp, humorless laugh, but said nothing. What was there to say?

After a while, he whispered, "One of the things I'm looking forward to the most when I retire is being able to get therapy. Like, without worrying it'll affect my job."

"I'm glad you'll be able to get that. I'm looking forward to it myself."

He released a breath and seemed to relax even more. I wondered if, on some level, he'd been afraid to admit that out loud, and now he was relieved that I'd said the same thing. Or maybe I was projecting.

Either way, I was glad he was starting to calm down now, and that he was going to get help after the military.

I was glad he was feeling better than he'd been when the nightmare had shaken him awake.

And, holding him close and remembering all the nights I'd been in his boots ...

I was glad he wasn't alone tonight.

CHAPTER 24

ALEX

I felt better today. Though last night had sucked, and I was definitely still in dire need of a solid night's sleep, the worst was over. I felt closer to myself. Relieved, too, that Connor hadn't seemed put off by seeing me like that—both after my encounter with Tobias and after that stupid nightmare. He'd reassured me yesterday and comforted me during the night, and this morning, he'd made a few comments about how tonight was *definitely* going to be better.

Just thinking about that made me grin. I couldn't wait to spend some time in bed with him doing something other than shaking and trying to calm myself down. That he was still onboard—talk about a relief.

First, though, I had to get through my day, and while I wasn't sure there was enough coffee to pull that off, I kept pouring it down my throat. Hope sprang eternal, and so did coffeepots in military facilities.

I'd just finished doing some X-rays on a dependent who'd broken her wrist a few months ago. She was in for some good news from her doctor; though I couldn't relay the results to her myself, it was plain as day on the images that the bones had fully healed without issue. I'd been there done that, and there was nothing better than putting all that bullshit in the rearview where it belonged. Broken bones sucked.

After sending her on her way, I went into the office to see if anyone else was coming up. No one was, and I didn't have any pressing paperwork or other tasks, so I passed the time as I often did—texting with Connor.

He wasn't the only one who'd texted me, though. I also had a message from Isidoro, asking if I wanted to hook up this evening or this weekend. That, fortunately, didn't cause nearly the same stir of emotions as Tobias trying to hit me up for sex. When I begged off, Isidoro understood. He also added, *¿Tienes novio?*, accompanying that with a winking emoji.

My face heated as I read the message. No, I didn't have a boyfriend. But I also didn't have the Spanish vocabulary—or the trust in the translator app—to explain my situation. So, I just wrote back that I was seeing someone, and hoped the app conveyed that clearly enough.

It must have, because he responded that he was happy for me.

I felt a little guilty about that. I didn't have a boyfriend, per se. That wasn't what Connor and I were doing. I just wasn't sure how to explain that I had a fuck buddy who blew my mind so fully that I didn't have the time or energy for anyone else.

Though I didn't imagine Isidoro's feelings were hurt. He'd had a relationship recently too, and he was still active on the app last time I looked. And anyway, nine times out of ten, I was the one to reach out to him for a hookup. I doubted he was losing any sleep over when or if he might see me naked again. I doubted any man did. Compared to Tobias's obnoxious persistence, I was more than happy that Isidoro was unbothered that I was unavailable.

The confrontation with Tobias seemed farther and farther away as my day went on, and my mood got better and better. Isidoro's graceful acceptance of my rejection—and his playful teasing—soothed the part of me that had still been on edge after Tobias, and the flirty texts with Connor definitely helped.

And a few hours later, chilling in Connor's pool with a can of beer in my hand after we'd had a quickie, I felt better about... well, everything.

Fuck you, Tobias. My life is so much better than it seems when you're around.

The kitchen door opened, and I looked up to see Connor coming down the steps, barefoot in a pair of swim trunks. He padded across the lawn, sat on the edge of the pool beside me, put his phone down beside my beer, and then slipped into the water. "Okay. Steaks just need to sit at room temperature until my phone goes off, and then I'll put them on the grill."

"Perfect." I put my phone next to his. "Do you need help with anything?"

"I've got all the cooking under control." He grinned. "But I'm pretty sure I can find something for you to do."

"Oh, yeah?" Licking my lips, I took off my sunglasses and added them to the poolside pile. "What do you have in mind?"

He didn't say a word. He just moved around in front of me, curved his hands behind my back, and gently tugged me away from the edge. I let myself be reeled in, and when our lips met, I couldn't help sighing happily. I doubted either of us had another round in us right now, but this? Oh, I could enjoy the hell out of this. Just holding him and kissing lazily while the cool water sloshed gently around us and the Andalusian sun warmed my shoulders.

I loved that Connor enjoyed making out without trying to get anything else started. Most men I'd been with just wanted to get us both turned on so they could get off. Connor—God, he loved kissing, and he always seemed more than happy to do this even when it wasn't likely to end in sex.

In the pool. In the shower. On his couch while we ignored a movie. Lying in bed when we were both too tired for anything more. There were so many times when I found myself just like this, wrapped up in Connor and enjoying his touch and his kiss with no pressure. No expectation to perform.

It was like holding me and kissing me was enough for him.

Isidoro's playful question bounced around in my head. *¿Tienes novio?*

I didn't have a boyfriend.

Did I?

No. No, that wasn't what we were doing.

This was just sex.

And texting.

And talking.

And traveling.

And companionship.

And lazily making out.

And... how was that not a boyfriend?

Except it didn't matter. We *couldn't* be together.

Wasn't that just my luck? I'd finally found a man who seemed to think I was worth a little bit of effort, but the Navy said I couldn't have him. Go figure.

Moaning softly into his kiss, I dragged my fingers through his wet hair. This was all we could have. It was what it was.

I was just grateful that, if only for now, it was enough for Connor.

That *I* was enough for Connor.

CHAPTER 25

CONNOR

I could've stayed in that pool until the sun went down, exploring Alex's mouth like we had all the time in the world.

Naturally, though, the alarm on my phone rudely went off.

I gave a bitchy little groan of protest, reached past him, and silenced the stupid thing. Alex took the opportunity to kiss my neck, and... oh, fuck, maybe the steaks could wait a few more minutes.

I pressed against him, and we both gasped when my hip brushed his thickening erection. I hadn't intended for us to get anything started—hadn't imagined either of us had anything left after earlier—but I didn't mind being wrong.

I rubbed more deliberately against his cock and purred, "Somebody's getting excited."

His breath was a hot, ragged huff, and then he lifted his head to find my lips again. "I'm always excited when you're touching me."

I hummed into his kiss and nudged him toward the edge of the pool.

"We should eat," he murmured, though he didn't sound too insistent. "We can pick this up again after lights out."

I moaned as I slid my hands up his back. "Or you could sit up on the edge of the pool and I could blow you."

Alex swore softly and pressed against me, his hard-on rubbing through the thin fabric of our swim trunks. "Fuck..."

"Like that idea?"

"I always like the idea of one of us blowing the other."

"Then why are you still in the pool with your shorts on?"

He stole another kiss, then slipped off his shorts and tossed them up on the side where they landed with a wet slap. He hoisted himself onto the edge and grinned down at me, stroking his hard dick. "You sure those steaks can wait?"

"They can definitely wait," I growled, and pushed his knees apart. "This, however, can't."

He took a breath as if to say something, but then his cock was in my mouth, and the only sound he made was a low moan. I was pretty sure I did the same. I couldn't help it when I was licking and teasing my way down his thick, hard dick. I tongued everything from the head down to his balls and back, and he murmured encouragement the whole way.

When I closed my hand around his shaft and started stroking, focusing my mouth on the head, he shivered hard.

"God, Connor..." He stroked my hair. "Oh fuck, that is so good."

It was. I loved this. And since I'd already gotten him off once today, it was going to take a while for him to come this time. Perfect—that just meant I could absolutely lose myself in the bliss of sucking him off. I teased him all over. Stroked him. Fluttered my tongue here. Swirled it there. I trailed my fingertips back and forth over his balls, which had him gasping and cursing. I couldn't finger him in this position, but he didn't seem to mind what I was doing.

My jaw ached and even my tongue was getting tired. I didn't care. I couldn't get enough of Alex's whispered curses and sharp gasps. I'd do this until my lips went numb if it meant listening to him egg me on and come unraveled.

After ages, he leaned back, resting a hand on the ground as he kept the other on the back of my head. "Fuck, baby. Your mouth is... oh my God..."

I couldn't help groaning as I took him deep again, and I loved the way that made him gasp as his fingers twitched in my hair.

"Please make me come," he begged. "Please—fucking hell, Connor, I want to come."

I would've licked and sucked him for ages just because I enjoyed giving him head, but I was suddenly eager to give him exactly what he wanted. I suddenly wanted it too. I wanted his cum, and I wanted it now.

Still licking around the head, I tightened my grip and stroked him faster, and I was rewarded with a barrage of curses only a Sailor could muster. His dick got even harder in my mouth. His breathing turned rapid and sharp.

My head spun as I gave him more, stroking him harder and faster as I teased with my lips and tongue. I loved when he was this close, and the anticipation of his orgasm turned me on like I was the one about to come.

Then his thighs clamped against my shoulders as a choked moan escaped his lips, and his hips bucked as his cum spilled onto my tongue. My own voice mingled with his; I fucking loved when he came in my mouth, and I was anything but quiet as I drove him on.

"Jesus fuck," he breathed as he shuddered one last time. "I was... not expecting that."

I let him slide free from my lips, then gazed up at him, loving the sight of his flushed skin and the bliss in his eyes. "Surprise?"

He grinned down at me and stroked my hair. Then, with my help, he eased back into the water, hissing as if it was colder than he expected. I pressed him up against the side and kissed him, and he whimpered as he held on and searched my mouth for every last taste of himself.

His palms slid up my back, and when he broke the kiss, he met my gaze with pure satisfaction in those blue eyes. "Have I mentioned lately how much I love your mouth?" he slurred. "Because I fucking love your mouth."

I laughed softly and kissed him. "Well, good. Because I like having your dick in my mouth."

For a heartbeat, I thought he'd roll his eyes at the admittedly corny comment, but he just slung his arms around my neck and came in for a longer kiss. His hip brushed my hard-on, making me gasp, but it wasn't enough to make me break the kiss.

After a moment, though, I murmured, "I should go make dinner."

"Mmhmm. Maybe." He slid a hand between us. "But maybe I should take care of this first?"

Anything I'd might've said vanished from my brain as he rubbed me through my swim trunks.

His lips curved against mine. "Dinner can wait. Lose the shorts."

I didn't argue.

Somehow, I was still able to walk after Alex worked his magic. Getting me off took a few minutes, sure, but I got there, and we both got out of the pool so I could get dinner started. Neither of us wanted to put our wet swim trunks back on, so we just wrapped sun-warmed towels around our waists.

We ate at the cabana table, then lounged in the sunchairs beside the pool, beers in hand.

I definitely couldn't complain about how this evening had gone. I couldn't complain about any days or evenings I'd spent with Alex, but tonight was definitely in the top five. Blowjobs, a good steak, great company, the Spanish sun—what wasn't to love?

Alex sipped his beer. "You know, we've got a long weekend coming up." He let his head loll toward me, peering at me through his dark lenses. "Maybe we should take off somewhere."

Excitement fluttered in my chest. "That sounds like a great idea. Any thoughts on where?"

Alex pursed his lips. "Depends on what you're in the mood for."

"I think you know what I'm in the mood for."

Even the sunglasses couldn't hide the way he rolled his eyes. "Well, yes, that part's a given. But during the day? Out in public?"

"Ooh, right. That part." I took a swallow of beer. "I'm game for anything, honestly. What about you?"

He seemed to consider it. "Well, if you feel like seeing how much your liver can handle and how little sleep you actually need, we could do Ibiza."

I thought about it, then wrinkled my nose. "The thought of being that hungover in this heat... Yeah, maybe not."

His laugh made my spine tingle; God, this man was gorgeous. "It's not for the faint of heart, that's for sure. Alternatively, we could do our usual and go play tourist somewhere." He met my gaze. "Anything you've been itching to see?"

I considered that. "Well, there was that place up in Córdoba. The mosque that was turned into a cathedral?"

I loved how Alex's face lit up. "The Mezquita? It's really cool."

"Any chance you'd want to hit it again?"

"Absolutely. Córdoba is great in its own right, too. A lot of really good food." He paused. "Do you like Turkish food?"

"Oh my God, yes. I love it."

He grinned. "Well, one of my favorite Turkish restaurants outside of Türkiye is in Córdoba."

"Okay, so amazing food and a cool mosque-slash-cathedral? Sold. Let's do it."

The excitement in his expression had me tempted to whip out my phone and start making reservations right here and now. "Yeah?"

"Fuck yeah."

"Excellent. Do places book up out there? Like do you think we'll have any trouble finding something?"

"Nah. This time of year, a lot of Spaniards are taking their vacations, and they head to the beach. Most people aren't quite masochistic enough to go to Córdoba in August."

"Are *we* that masochistic?"

"Why not?" He flashed me a toothy grin. "Where's your sense of adventure?"

I chuckled and rolled my eyes. "So bring a lot of water and paint on the sunscreen is what you're saying."

"Probably a good idea."
Yeah, it probably was.
Heat be damned, I couldn't wait.

CHAPTER 26

ALEX

On Friday afternoon, I took the 1500 train to Córdoba. Connor followed on the 1800, and he met me at our hotel not far from the city center. We were far enough from Rota that even though we didn't travel together, we didn't bother with separate hotel rooms. No one was going to find us in a tiny place tucked into a hidden corner of this city.

Of course, our activities upon his arrival were predictable. Thanks to duty days, being on call, and staying necessarily discreet, we hadn't had a moment alone since that night in his pool a week ago. What could I say? My hand just didn't get the job done the way Connor did. Judging by the odd looks we got from the older couple across the hall when we left in search of dinner, we'd been... loud.

We both chuckled as we headed downstairs. We tried to be considerate of people around us, but what could I say? Sometimes, especially when I hadn't had him alone for a few nights in a row, we got carried away.

Ah, well. As long as no one from the base had overheard

us or saw us leaving together. I could still be a little paranoid about that sometimes, but I reminded myself that relatively few people went more than twenty or thirty klicks away from the base. I usually thought that was a damn shame—what a waste of an overseas duty assignment to just stay home and never go explore the country!

These days, I was completely fine with Americans sticking close to Rota. The fewer people ventured away from the base, the fewer chances there were for someone who recognized us to see us out *fraternizing* together.

As we walked from our hotel toward the city center where the restaurants were just beginning to open for dinner, I had to fight hard not to put a hand on Connor's back or even slip my hand into his. That wasn't who we were, though, and not just because we had to be discreet. This was friends with benefits—traveling fuck buddies, honestly—not boyfriends.

Are you sure about that, Alex?

I glanced at him in the warm light of the late evening sun, and my insides tumbled in a way they shouldn't have with a man I was just supposed to be screwing on the downlow.

The sex was fun, and there was a certain amount of excitement that came with the clandestine nature of what we were doing. That wasn't what I was feeling right now, though. This wasn't rebelliousness or lust.

I missed you.

The thought almost had me tripping over my own feet. That was it, wasn't it? We lived close together. We worked in the same facility. But the only time we could be Alex and Connor instead of HM1 Barlow and Lieutenant Commander Marks was when we were safely behind his villa's walls or miles away from home.

When we were like this.

No matter how much I liked these moments, they were all we could have as long as we were both on active duty. And no matter how much I liked this man, I was fooling myself if I thought he liked me enough to date me on the downlow for over a year. He may have been enjoying the hell out of the sex, but the novelty of that would wear off long before I'd safely retired from the Navy.

This was all we were, and it was all we ever would be, and I couldn't afford to lose sight of that.

You've known that from the beginning. Why are you suddenly getting all fucked up over it?

Maybe because at the beginning, I didn't know I'd feel like—

"Is that the place?" Connor's question pulled me out of my thoughts.

I shook myself and looked in the direction he was indicating. Sure enough, on the corner across the street, was the restaurant we'd been looking for. I'd been so far up in my own head, I hadn't even noticed their distinctive sign above the familiar patio seating.

"Yeah." I smiled. "That's it."

He eyed me as if he'd caught on that I'd been someplace else, but he didn't question me. He followed me across the street and into the restaurant, and we were seated at the edge of the patio. From here, we had a nice view of a small plaza ringed with orange trees and with a statue at the center. I'd been here for lunch before, and an awning had shielded diners from the brutal sun, but it was nearly 2100 now—still daylight, still hot, but not as blinding or scorching. Like this, it was quite pleasant.

Connor swept his gaze around the plaza. "It's going to

be hard to go back to regular American restaurants after this."

"I know, right?" I chuckled. "Especially now that I'm adjusted to Spanish meal times. You can't just walk into a family restaurant at 2200 in the States and expect a long, sit-down dinner, you know?"

"Ugh, I wish we could do that. When I was stationed in Portsmouth, my shifts would always end late enough that there was no chance in hell of going out." He sipped his drink. "My boys are going to want to move over here the minute they realize their night owl asses can have dinner that late."

"Oh yeah?"

"Yep. I'm a bit of night owl myself, but my kids took after their mom—almost completely nocturnal. I don't know how Quinn's girlfriend deals with it." He wrinkled his nose. "She's one of those... *morning* people."

I made a face. "That's just wrong."

"No kidding." He sighed melodramatically and shook his head. "The things we tolerate in the name of love."

My stomach did a somersault that I didn't want to think too hard about. Yeah, I'd heard of people doing and putting up with all kinds of things in the name of love. Some rogue synapse in my stupid brain even thought there was a chance someone out there might do that for me.

A hypothetical morning person putting up with my night owl tendencies? Maybe.

An actual physician whose entire career would be upended if someone even caught a whiff of us together? Not gonna happen.

But I wasn't going to think about that tonight. We were together for the weekend, and I would enjoy this while I had it.

"So." Connor picked up one of the menus we'd been ignoring. "What do you recommend here?"

"Um." I peered at my own menu, and for a moment, I struggled to even understand the words. Not because they were Spanish, either.

Fuck. What is wrong with me?

Connor turned his menu over, and he sighed with obvious relief. "Oh, fuck yes."

"What?" I turned my own menu over and immediately understood his reaction: the text was in English. "Oh, sweet."

"I thought you knew their menu."

"Not by heart, no." I skimmed over the options. "Last time I was here, I got the steak. That was great. They have really good wine, too."

He nodded as I spoke, furrowing his brow at the menu. "Damn. I must be hungry because *everything* sounds good."

"Yeah, it does."

In the end, we both ordered steak, and the decision wasn't a difficult one. While we'd been hemming and hawing over all the amazing things on offer, the server brought two steaks to the couple at the table next to ours, and the smell was absolutely irresistible.

After she'd taken our order, Connor sat back in his chair, glass in hand. "Okay, so that was easy, but still—thank God for English menus."

"I know, right? My Spanish is decent enough to get by, but an English menu is *always* a relief."

"Seriously." He sipped his drink. "My Spanish is getting better, especially in restaurants. But I'm always afraid I'm going to order something weird by accident. Or just pronounce something the wrong way and insult someone."

"There is that. My first year in Spain, I worked with a

corpsman who couldn't understand why her gardener gave her a weird look when she commented that it was hot out." I laughed, shaking my head. "Our chief had to gently explain to her that in Spain, you don't use 'caliente' to describe the weather. Or the heat of your food."

Connor furrowed his brow. "Wait. How do you *use* it?"

I thought about it, aware there were other people within earshot who might understand English. Lowering my voice, I said, "You'd use it to describe the things we did before we left for dinner."

"Before we—*ooh*." He burst out laughing. "Oh God. Did she basically tell her gardener she was horny?"

I nodded. "Exactly."

"Oh, man. I would *die*."

"She almost did." I laughed. "She couldn't look the poor guy in the eye for the rest of the time she was stationed here."

"I don't blame her. I'm surprised I haven't made some horrible gaffe, but I've only been here a few months, so..." He half-shrugged.

"Give it time. You'll get there. Or you'll end up ordering the fried cuttlefish like I did."

He shuddered and made the most hilariously disgusted face. After another drink, he asked, "So what other things should I try? Spanish food, I mean?"

"You can't go wrong with most of it, honestly, especially if you like seafood."

"So I've noticed." He paused, then wrinkled his nose again. "Though I did try a place out on the beach in Rota that... Ugh. I don't know what they did to those chicken thighs, but..." He shuddered again. "Never again."

"I think I know the place you're talking about. I ate there once, and it didn't taste right. And another corpsman told me she'd seen three different people come in with food poisoning from that place."

"Oh *God*." Connor looked horrified. "And it's still open?"

"We'll see how long it lasts."

"Well, they won't be getting any more of my money, that's for sure."

"Same. As far as things you should try..." I gazed out at the thin crowd and the orange trees in front of the restaurant. "Oh, there's a place out in Cádiz, in the plaza in front of the cathedral where there's a bunch of cafés. One of them —I'll look up the name and text it to you later—they have this dish called patatas aliñadas." I couldn't help groaning. "God, it's *amazing*."

Connor's eyes lit up. "Yeah? What is it?"

"It's kind of a potato salad, I guess? I know, I know, it doesn't sound all that exciting. But it's so good. They make it with olive oil and lemon juice, and then just some onions. That's really all there is to it." I blew out a breath as I reached for my drink. "Any time I go over to Cádiz, I have to put in an extra half hour or so at the gym just to make up for how much I stuff my damn face with potatoes."

Connor snorted. "Okay, now I'm intrigued. It sounds really simple, but hey, some of the best dishes are."

"I know, right? Especially..." I gestured around us. "A lot of Spanish food is pretty simple. I had tapas in Sevilla once, and it was literally just caramelized onions and goat cheese on baguette slices." I chuckled. "I must've ordered like eight plates of them."

"Ooh, I had something like that in Sanlúcar. If I ever get the hang of caramelizing onions at home, I'll never leave the house."

"You don't know how to do it?"

"No, no, I do." He rolled his eyes as he picked up his glass. "It just always ends up FUBAR."

I laughed. "Sounds like me and basmati rice."

"What? You can't cook rice?"

"No, I can. I just... fuck it up. I don't know how or why, but every time I've tried to make it..." I waved a hand.

He chuckled. "Everyone has their Achilles' heel in the kitchen, am I right? My son's girlfriend gets so irritated because he's pretty decent in the kitchen, but any kind of short pasta—like penne or whatever—he just cannot cook it right."

"Well, that balances out her being a weird morning person, doesn't it?"

Connor laughed. "I hadn't thought of that, but I'll tell her that next time she complains about his pasta."

"Fair's fair."

"Exactly."

Shortly after that, our food arrived, and it was exactly as incredible as it smelled. The steak was a perfect medium rare, and the fries were exactly the way I liked them—not overcooked or oversalted. We shared a *very* good bottle of Spanish wine, and this was just... perfect. The warm night. The excellent food and wine. The peaceful surroundings.

And of course, the company.

I tried not to let myself think about how romantic this felt, or how easy and right it was for us to spend yet another relaxed evening as a couple. What that might or might not mean.

I *tried* not to.

But I failed.

"Between dinner, the long-ass day, and everything we did earlier," Connor said as he lay back on one of the two beds in our room, "I don't think there's going to be much happening tonight."

I slid up next to him. "You think *I've* got anything left?" I dipped my head for a soft kiss. "This is perfectly fine with me."

"Good." He wrapped his arms around me. "I like this part anyway."

Sinking into his embrace, I grinned. "Do you?"

"Well, yeah. I like not sleeping alone."

"Me too." I hadn't thought I would—hadn't thought I could relax with someone—but I craved these nights together. I kissed him gently, and we both let it linger for a moment. "Maybe we'll both feel up to more tomorrow. Assuming we don't wear ourselves out walking to and through the Mezquita."

Connor huffed a soft laugh. "I think we'll manage."

We shared another kiss, and then we settled in to go to sleep, his back against my chest and my arm around him. He laced our fingers together, and before long, he was out cold.

I wouldn't be far behind, but my whirling mind kept me awake a few minutes longer. Partly because I was overthinking everything, and partly because I wanted to savor this quiet closeness. I'd done a lot of hooking up over the years, and not every guy was prone to cuddling with hookups. Some did, some didn't.

Connor had, from the start, loved being as close as possible, and I was hooked on it. Even when we weren't going at it, I liked it when we were touching. I couldn't get enough of it, honestly.

Maybe because there were so few opportunities for it.

We had to keep a safely platonic distance between us whenever we were out in public. The only time we could risk a touch, however chaste, was behind closed doors.

Maybe that was blurring the lines of what fuck buddies were supposed to be doing. Whatever. I was too tired to think too hard about it.

I did know that considering our arrangement, it should've been weird that I was so chill about the times we weren't having sex. With other guys, I'd have had my guard up—worried they were subtly trying to steer us toward something that wasn't just physical.

With Connor...

God, I could only hope.

I held him a little tighter and kissed the back of his shoulder.

Is it too much to ask to have this for real?

CHAPTER 27

CONNOR

The Mezquita Catedral de Córdoba was incredible. Huge, too; an enormous wall surrounded the structure, and once we were past the gates, there was a sprawling courtyard full of orange trees and small streams. I hadn't recognized the belltower in Sevilla as being a repurposed minaret from the previous mosque, but this time I knew what I was looking for. There it was—the distinctive rectangular shape of a minaret with the addition of a church's belltower on top.

The security guards only let a few people into the Mezquita at a time, which I appreciated; I hated when places like this were teeming with tourists. The courtyard was crowded enough. When we got inside, it was far quieter, with only a handful of other people wandering the giant structure. It was also a lot cooler thanks to the stone floors and high ceilings, and much darker, too. Such a relief after the oppressive heat and blinding sun outside.

"They really liked archways, didn't they?" I mused as I took a photo on my phone of the seemingly endless series of red-and-white striped archways over our heads.

"No kidding," Alex said. "A guy I used to work with is a photographer, and he said he spent like two hours in here just taking pictures of arches."

"I can believe that."

We weren't going to spend two hours photographing arches, but we did take our sweet time wandering beneath them and between pillars. The place was beautiful, and it was amazingly peaceful. I probably could've spent a couple of hours in here just enjoying the calm inside the immense building.

At the very center of what had once been the mosque, the style and architecture changed dramatically. Instead of the sparse, open space beneath the arches, we were now in the intricately decorated cathedral, complete with two huge pipe organs. It was brighter in here, too, thanks to the soaring white dome overhead and the windows high above either side of the altar.

I looked back at the mosque, then into the cathedral, marveling that two such wildly different worlds had existed beneath the same roof. Not that it had continued as a mosque after the Catholics had taken it over, but the difference between the old design and the new was striking to say the least.

But all the way through both the mosque and the cathedral, my gaze kept drifting away from the archways and pipe organs and paintings to the man walking beside me.

I can't believe you're here.

Do you have any idea how much I miss you when you're not?

That seemed kind of stupid. We saw each other pretty frequently, all things considered. And if this thing continued past when one of us transferred or—more likely—when Alex retired, we'd have an ocean between us.

I'd weathered that kind of separation from Aimee back when our marriage had still been good, and it was hard. Being away from her. Being away from my kids. It was still tough being away from the boys.

What would a long-distance relationship with Alex be like? Because just the thought of being separated by an ocean for weeks or months—God, that made my chest hurt. Only seeing each other once in a while. Navigating time differences and communicating by text and FaceTime more than anything. Savoring every precious minute we could spend in the same place.

Just thinking about that had me missing him already, and he was right here. The need to touch him now had my fingers tingling and curling at my sides. Not here. We were too out in the open, even two hundred and fifty kilometers from anyone who'd care, and also this wasn't really the time or place. I wasn't a religious man myself, but I did try to be respectful when I was in someone else's place of worship.

Still, as we stepped out of the cathedral and back into the mosque, and I chanced sliding my hand over the small of his back.

He glanced at me, surprise raising his eyebrows. Then he smiled, which told me the contact wasn't unwelcome.

I returned the smile. As we kept walking, I took my hand away; disappointing, yes, but we still had to be both cautious and respectful.

When we get back to the room, though...

I shivered, and I had to suppress a grin. We'd be sleeping in the same bed tonight, wouldn't we? Sleeping, and *so* much more. Because even if the future meant living thousands of miles apart, I had him now.

Was it time to go back to the room yet?

No, it wasn't. We were going to be good little tourists

and enjoy everything Córdoba had to offer. *Then* we'd go back to the room and see how much one or both of those almost-queen size beds could handle.

Eventually, we reached the mosque's exit and stepped outside. It was like walking into a wall of heat, and we both squinted against the brutal sunlight even after we'd pulled on sunglasses.

"Ugh," Alex grumbled. "I forgot how hot it was."

"Right? Stupid... August."

He snorted and we continued through the courtyard in search of some refuge from the sun. We found it in the shade of an orange tree, and as we cooled off a little, Alex checked his phone. "Everything's going to be closing for siesta soon. We should grab some water while we can."

Just the thought of drinking something cold right then made my mouth water. "Good idea. Let's go."

We left the Mezquita and stepped out onto one of the narrow surrounding streets. I was a little disoriented, and I wasn't exactly sure which side we were on now, but Alex confidently strode toward some shops across the street. He seemed to know where we were, so I let him take the lead. Worst case, we had GPS on our phones.

I followed him into a small shop full of tourist tchotchkes and souvenirs, and we fished a couple of bottles of water from a refrigerated case. Then we were back outside in the scorching heat, but with the relief that came from those bottles.

"Oh, God," I said after a couple of deep swallows. "I needed that."

"Me too." He tilted the bottle toward a nearby café. "This is also one of those times I love that almost every Spanish café has fresh-squeezed orange juice. Like they literally squeeze it after you order it." He took another swig of water. "It's not super cold, but holy crap, it hits the spot on a day like this."

"I'll keep that in mind." I gestured with my bottle. "This is exactly what I need right now."

"Same," he said, before swallowing some more water. "I will never understand the people who day drink in Spain. The heat gets to me enough when I'm not drinking."

"You and me both. I swear every Monday morning, I've got two or three young guys—because somehow it's *always* the guys—coming in for sick call because they're more hungover than they should be." I rolled my eyes. "No shit, junior. Your blood is half alcohol, half energy drinks, and you've been sweating your balls off in the heat. What do you expect?"

Alex barked a laugh. "They always have to learn the hard way, don't they?"

"Didn't we all?"

"Hey. I resemble that."

I snickered. "I had one kid come in like half a dozen times because his heart was racing and he was sweating like crazy. Thought he was having heatstroke from being out on the flightline." I tsked. "The last time, I finally told him that if he doesn't stop mainlining energy drinks, the next time I see him will probably be for a kidney stone."

Alex grimaced. "Think that got through?"

"Well, let's give it a week or two." I raised my half-empty water bottle. "If he doesn't come back in for 'heat exhaustion', then maybe he got the message?"

"Fingers crossed." He shuddered. "I've seen so many people with those, I'm terrified of getting one."

"Yeah, they're no picnic," I muttered.

His eyes widened. "Speaking from personal or professional experience?"

"Both." It was my turn to shudder. "I thought I was literally dying with the first one."

"Just the first one?"

I shrugged. "Well, the second time, I *wanted* to die, but I knew pretty quickly what it was. That is a pain you *do not* forget."

"Ugh. No, thanks. I swear to God, every time I see a patient with a stone, I go and chug a bottle of water while praying to everyone who might be listening."

Laughing, I said, "Honestly, having been there done that—I don't blame you at all." I toasted with my water bottle before bringing it to my lips. "Bottoms up."

He chuckled and took another drink from his own.

We still had a half hour or so before everything slammed shut for siesta, so we wandered in and out of a few shops. Given the heat—and the conversation about kidney stones—we each grabbed a second bottle of water, too, and we sipped those while we perused souvenirs. I picked up a couple of things my sons might like—a hilariously tacky picture frame and a funny T-shirt for Quinn, a book about the Mezquita for Landon. I wanted to get something for Quinn's girlfriend, too, but I didn't see anything here that would be to her taste.

"She's a tough one to shop for," I explained to Alex. "She doesn't like the kitschy stuff, and I'm not sure what shirts or whatever would be her style." I peered at a display of gorgeous ceramic plates and bowls. "And she's not into really brightly colored stuff like this."

Alex eyed the display. Then he gestured to one at the end of the aisle. "What about some of the unglazed pottery?"

I followed where he'd indicated, and oh, this looked a bit more promising. It was mostly plates and saucers along with some small tagines, and they were more muted colors—plain terra cotta, mostly. "Okay, this is definitely closer to what she likes." I glanced at Alex. "Do you think they'll hold up on the ride home?"

"Sure." He shrugged. "I've bought a few pieces. They're not as fragile as they look, and they're usually packed within an inch of their lives."

There was that—I'd bought a small plate to send to my mother, and the shopkeeper had wrapped it up like it was about to get thrown off a cliff.

I glanced at the time. We had about ten minutes before siesta kicked off, so I quickly picked out a miniature terra cotta tagine and took it up to the counter. As predicted, the shopkeeper packed it meticulously in paper, bubble wrap, and a small box; I'd have to *work* at it to break it on the way home.

Satisfied that Savannah's gift was safely packed, I left the shop with Alex, and the shopkeeper lowered the gate right behind us. All around us, other shops were closing up, too. Tourists were meandering toward cafés or back to the Mezquita (which may or may not have been open during siesta; I hadn't looked).

I followed Alex around a corner off the main drag. Now we were on a street that was probably too narrow for a car and was currently deserted apart from a couple of shopkeepers pulling down their gates.

I was about to ask him where he thought we should go next when he suddenly had his arm around my waist and his lips pressed to mine.

And the whole world came to a gentle stop beneath my feet.

For a few perfect seconds, I was aware of absolutely nothing except Alex and how much I loved the way his mouth moved so perfectly with mine. It wasn't a deep kiss. Not the kind we shared in the bedroom when the doors were closed and the clothes were off. But it was still sexy and hot in its own way.

All too quickly, even though it felt like we'd been lost in that moment for ages, Alex broke the kiss, and he met my gaze.

"Sorry," he whispered. "I've just... been wanting to do that all morning."

I blinked. Then I tugged him in a little closer, and as our lips brushed, I said, "Don't apologize."

I kissed him, and we let it linger for a long, perfect moment before we separated as gently as we'd come together. When he looked in my eyes, I could still see his despite his sunglasses, and they weren't as full of fire as I'd expected. Instead, they were soft and sweet, as was his little smile.

My heart did things it had *never* done before.

Oh my God, I am so stupid for you.

Alex ran his tongue along the inside of his lip, and now I could see the embers of lust in his eyes. "I've, uh... I've got an idea about how we can spend siesta. Since, you know..." He circled his finger in the air. "Everything's closed."

"Oh, yeah?" I grinned. "What did you have in mind?"

As if I needed to ask.

CHAPTER 28

ALEX

The August heat had us both sweaty and disgusting by the time we made it back to the hotel, but a shower—a long, shared shower—took care of that in short order. It also made for some very sexy foreplay; I swear, there was never going to come a time when I got tired of making out with Connor and turning him on until he was trembling and begging.

We stopped kissing and pawing at each other long enough to dry off. Then he led me out of the bathroom and pulled me down onto the bed, and we were off and running again. His hands slid all over my skin as if he were memorizing me. In the beginning, I'd assumed he was simply indulging in the novelty of being with a man. More and more, I thought this was just the way he was—so deliciously tactile.

He didn't just touch and feel me with his hands, either. Every time we landed in bed together, I was treated to this man's eager, explorative mouth. Had I just been with a string of guys who didn't spend enough time kissing my neck? Or was this something Connor in particular loved to do? Either way, he never missed an opportunity to let his lips skate up and down the sides of my throat, pausing to nibble my earlobe or my collarbone, or press a kiss beneath my jaw. Despite his recent inexperience, he was completely confident about giving head, and his ministrations on the way *down* from my neck always had me trembling and gasping before he even touched my dick.

And once he *did* reach my dick...

"God, Connor..." I ran shaky fingers through his damp hair, careful not to push his head down. "Fuck, yeah..."

He groaned low in his throat, the vibration thrumming against my sensitive skin, and I had to bite back a cry that probably would've carried through the whole hotel. Some people did actually nap during siesta, and my few remaining functional brain cells at least tried not to disturb anyone.

It wasn't easy, though. Staying quiet and considerate was a chore and a half with Connor's tongue working that mind-blowing magic from the base all the way to the head of my cock. And then he fluttered his tongue over my balls, and I almost came unglued.

"Fucking hell, baby," I said on a groan. "That is so—Jesus!" I almost levitated off the bed as he did it again. "You are so damn good at that."

He licked his way up to the head again, then swirled his tongue around, driving a whimper out of me. I inadvertently tightened my fingers in his hair, and for a second, I thought he wouldn't like that. Instead, he moaned again, so I experimentally did it a little harder.

Oh, hell. He liked that. He liked it a lot.

And every sound he made reverberated along all my hypersensitive nerve endings, turning me into a mess of bliss and heat, which only made me grip his hair tighter.

This was a feedback loop I could absolutely get used to.

Connor pushed himself up, so I let go of his hair. A second later, about the time I was finding my breath again, he was over me, and that talented mouth was crushing mine. I slid a hand back up into his hair, and I tried that again—the slightest little tug.

"Fuck," he whispered as he broke the kiss. "That is..."

"Like getting your hair pulled?"

"Apparently so." He started on my neck again, kissing along the side of my throat as he rubbed his hard dick alongside mine. "Learn something new every—oh, God, yeah..." He arched like a cat and shivered as I pulled again. I wasn't yanking or anything; at most, I was making his scalp sting just enough for him to notice.

"Should try this while I'm fucking you," I said.

"Holy..." He kissed under my jaw, then found my mouth again, and he broke away just enough to murmur, "Please do."

Duly noted.

I closed my eyes as he kept rocking against me and kissing my throat. I was seriously getting spoiled with this man; I had never in my life been with someone who could make me feel like nothing else existed in his world except turning me on, and it was addictive.

Turning him on was addictive, too, and he'd been doing all the work since we'd gotten into bed. Time to change things up.

I nudged him gently so he'd come up for a kiss. When he did, I rolled him onto his back, and we kept making out like that before I took my chance to explore him the way he had me. I loved the sounds he made. I loved how his ab muscles would contract beneath my lips. How his hips would almost vibrate with the need to thrust, but he'd keep them still while I teased every inch of his cock and balls. I loved how he peppered the air with whispered curses and sharp gasps, and I was tempted to take him all the way because I loved how he sounded and tasted when he came.

I had something else in mind this time, though.

I made myself get up off him, but only for a second so I could reach for the nightstand and the bottle of lube we'd used yesterday.

"Are there still condoms over there?" he asked, sounding as out of breath as I was.

"There are." I returned with just the bottle. "But we don't need them. Not for this."

Interest sparked in his eyes. "Yeah?"

"Mmhmm." I grinned and poured some lube into my hand. "Give me your hand?"

He did, and I gave him some lube too. Then I tossed the bottle aside—still within reach but out of the way—and settled over him again. As I stroked lube onto his dick, he groaned and bit his lip.

He also caught on to what I was doing. That, or he just wanted to touch me. Either way, he closed his slick hand around my cock, and his strokes fell into sync with mine. For the longest time, we made out and slowly, decadently pumped each other, not really trying to get to the climax— just enjoying each other's touch.

After a while, I nudged his hand away, and closed my hand as much as I could around both of us. When I rocked my hips, the underside of my cock slid along his, and that got me exactly the desired effect—Connor's eyelids fluttering closed as he swore and arched under us.

"Holy fuck..." He grabbed on to my shoulder as if he needed something to anchor him. "That... should *not* be that good."

I laughed and moved a little faster, losing myself in this perfect barrage of sensations. "Think you can come like this?"

"Uh-huh." He rocked his hips to complement my strokes, taking everything to a dizzying level of perfect. "God, Alex, you're gonna make me come."

I fucked against him a little harder, driving moans out of both of us. Connor's fingers dug into my arm, and he squeezed his eyes shut as he thrust up for all he was worth.

I let my head fall beside his as I gave in completely, chasing my own orgasm as I tried to drive him toward his. Then his whole body jerked under me, and my strokes turned hotter and slicker in the same instant he cried out, and I was coming too, shouting despite some voice in my head trying to shush me.

I collapsed over him, my supporting arm shaking beneath my weight, and Connor pulled me the rest of the way down. I gave in with a grateful sigh, though I was careful not to rest my *full* weight on his chest.

"That thing you were doing with my hair?" he slurred after a while. "Feel free to do it again. Any time."

I laughed and eased myself up on one arm. "You liked that, huh?"

"More than I thought I would." He arched an eyebrow. "What about you?" He peered at my hair. "Not that there's much to grab on to..."

"Eh. I can take it or leave it. But if it's something you enjoy, I'll definitely remember."

He grinned. "Good." Then he lifted his head off the pillow and kissed me lightly. Glancing down, he chuckled. "We, uh... We might need another shower."

"Mmhmm. We do. But hey, at least the hotel doesn't charge us for water."

My God, I loved how he laughed.

I shouldn't have loved it this much, but I did.

I eased myself up and sat back on my heels. "Shower?"

Connor grinned as he sat up. "Shower."

We hunkered down in our room long past the end of siesta. The heat was intense today—when I touched the siesta shades blocking out the brutal sun, they were hot against my fingers.

So, we just chilled in the room, lounging naked in bed and watching random crap on YouTube. Since we always knew there was a possibility of getting hungry during that window of time when the restaurants were mostly closed—around 1630-2030—we made sure to bring a few munchies with us. That kept the hangry at bay until we could venture out and find dinner.

Now it was getting toward dinnertime, though, so we put on some clothes and ventured back out into polite society.

That was... jarring in a way I didn't expect.

Everything around us felt alien and bizarre, and not because we were in a foreign country. This wasn't culture shock because we were in Spain; it was like we'd just come here from another planet. From someplace where nothing existed except the two of us.

I could still feel everything we'd done and needing to stay a platonic distance apart just felt... wrong. My fingers itched with the desire to be on his skin again, or even resting on his clothed back. After a few hours of cuddling in front of his laptop, I felt strangely untethered now. Keeping this platonic distance between us was perfectly normal when we were out in public, but it felt alien today. Like something was missing in that way that had me checking my pockets to make sure I had, in fact, remembered my wallet and phone.

What the hell is wrong with me?

As if I didn't know.

But I wasn't going to think about that. I was going to enjoy my evening out with Connor, and then we'd go back to the hotel and sleep together one more time before we went back to our normal lives. I wasn't going to dwell on the things we couldn't do and couldn't be, no matter how much I—

My breath hitched.

No matter how much I wanted to.

"Alex?" Connor eyed me. "You okay?"

"Hmm? Oh. Yeah." I shook myself and laughed. "Just thought I forgot my wallet." I tapped my back pocket. "Which I didn't."

He smiled. "Eh. If you had, then I'd buy dinner."

"Oh. Well. In that case." I showed my palms. "I forgot my wallet."

Rolling his eyes, he elbowed me. "Nice try."

I chuckled. "Hey, it was worth a shot."

We continued walking, and before long, we found the Turkish restaurant I'd been to before. In no time, we were seated on the patio, each with a glass of wine as we perused the menus. Connor ordered İskender, which was shaved lamb with yogurt and tomato sauce. I went with the saksuka, a savory vegetarian dish with a lot of cumin mixed in with tomatoes and peppers, topped with a poached egg. Easily one of my favorite meals—one I'd even learned to make at home—and this place always made it perfectly.

As we ate, we fell into conversation like we always did.

Partway through dinner, as we considered ideas for

where and when we should have our next weekend getaway, he said, "My sons will be here next week for ten days." He absently swirled his wine. "So, it'll have to be after that."

"Of course. Are you going to take them around Spain, or just stay around Rota?"

"Oh, we're going to travel, definitely. They've been loving hearing about all the places I've been. Morocco is high on their list, too."

"I don't blame them—Morocco is amazing. In fact, if you're going to Tangier, I can send you the contact info for the tour guide I've used before. He's awesome."

Connor's eyes lit up. "That would be great! Thanks!"

"Have you put in your clearance request yet?" I made a face. "Because it can take those offices a while to approve them."

He nodded. "I already got my clearance for Morocco, and I nudged the person who's handling my theater clearance." He rolled his eyes. "That's so stupid, too. Like, why do I have to get permission to go to Africa when I already have permission to go to an African country?"

"I know, right?" I sipped my wine. "Believe it or not, I actually know someone who got clearance to go to Morocco, but he was denied clearance for Africa."

He snorted. "You know, my first instinct is to say, 'no way, that's bullshit.' But... it's the military." He raised his glass. "Can't say I'm surprised."

I laughed. "I wasn't either. He was sure pissed, though."

"I bet. Was he able to go?"

"Eventually, but he had to reschedule everything. Which sucked because the camel trip he was supposed to take out into the Sahara was booked up on all the dates he was finally able to go. He ended up sending his wife and kids so they could use the plane tickets and go on the camel trip, and then he met them in Marrakech afterward."

"Oh, that blows. I know so many people who've had trips upended because of a clearance or their leave getting jacked up." Connor tsked. "I was on a ship with a guy who had to reschedule his own wedding because his supervisor decided he couldn't take leave."

"Was there a legit reason? Or just a supervisor on a power trip?"

"Little of both, from what I heard. Sea trials had been moved up for our upcoming deployment, and we were suddenly supposed to be out for a week that included his wedding date." Connor rolled his eyes. "I know everyone gets tetchy about people taking leave when the ship is at sea, but come on—it was a weeklong sea trial. Just... let the kid get married, for fuck's sake."

"No kidding." I poked at my food with my fork. "There was a guy in my unit in Iraq who had to reschedule his wedding, too. But I mean, there isn't much you can do about combat deployments, you know?"

"No, there is not," he muttered. "Did they at least do the courthouse thing before he left so they could get all the legal ducks in a row?"

I nodded. "Apparently his mother-in-law was incensed about that, but she got over it."

"They usually do," he grumbled.

Arching an eyebrow, I asked, "Didn't get along with your mother-in-law?"

"Oh, I did. But nothing starts that relationship off on the right foot like saying, 'Hey, we're only seventeen and we're still in high school, but I knocked up your daughter.'"

I barked a laugh that might've turned some heads. "Oh, God. That conversation sounds *painfully* awkward."

"You have no idea." He took another sip of wine. "I was afraid to eat at their house for a long time because I thought she might poison my food or something."

"I can imagine. Did she get over it?"

"Eventually." Connor's smile made the warm evening even warmer. "It's hard to stay mad when you're holding your newborn grandson for the first time."

"Fair enough."

"Though she got mad at both of us years later because she found out said grandson was planning to move in with his girlfriend." Another eyeroll. "They were twenty, for fuck's sake, and they've been together since they were sixteen." He waved a hand. "Savannah was practically living with him at that point anyway, so they might as well put her on the lease."

"Smart kids. How do you like his girlfriend?"

"Oh, she's great. I suspect they'll be getting married before too much longer." He paused to eat some more of the İskender he'd ordered. "So what is there to see in Morocco? We're probably just going to Tangier; I don't think we can swing Marrakech or one of the other cities."

"Tangier's great. The guide I use takes you to basically *everything*, so he's worth the money and then some." I thought about it as I chewed a bite of saksuka. "Oh, if you have time, I'd definitely take a day trip out to Chefchaouen."

Connor blinked. "Chef *what* now?"

"Chefchaouen," I said with a laugh. "It's the blue city. It's just this little town on a hillside where they painted everything blue for some reason, but it's really cool to visit. I swear some of the best Moroccan food I ever ate was there."

"Yeah?" He sat up a little. "Like what?"

"I... don't remember exactly what it's called, but there's

this dish—it's like a pastry with cinnamon and sugar on it, but it's savory on the inside. Chicken and stuff." I groaned just thinking about that meal. "It's so fucking good."

"Sounds like it. I mean, it's not something I'd probably try normally, but if you're giving it a glowing review..." He smiled.

"I am. I definitely am. Oh, and I don't really like tea, but Moroccan mint tea?" I touched my chest. "Holy crap, that shit's good."

We went on like that for a while, me regaling him with everything I could remember from my trips to Morocco. He even wrote a few things down, and I sent him the tour guide's info so I wouldn't forget. I showed him some pictures from my trips, too. Some people's eyes glazed over when others whipped out photo albums, but he was enthralled with everything, from my selfie with a camel to the guy I'd snapped in Chefchaouen delivering cases of soda via donkey.

As we were winding down our dinner with dessert and some more wine, I glanced around, and I was almost startled to realize where we were. I recognized this little street in Córdoba. I'd been here before—the restaurant, the street, the neighborhood, the city. But I'd forgotten we were here because I'd been so lost in conversation with Connor.

Just like I was every time we talked, whether it was over amazing Turkish food in Córdoba, leaning against the side of his pool in Sanlúcar, or curled up together between the sheets.

In bed, I'd realized that no man had ever made me feel like my pleasure was the center of his universe.

Here at this table, it occurred to me that that didn't stop when we put our clothes on. No, he wasn't turning me on or getting me off right now, but the way he looked at me... The way he was completely focused on me and I was completely focused on him…

We were surrounded by stunning scenery in a city that was completely new to him, but we could've been sitting in his own kitchen for all he was engaged with anything around us. It was like nothing and nobody existed for him except for me. Just like nothing and nobody existed for me except for him.

I'd heard of people experiencing that, but it had never happened to me before, and after Tobias, I'd sworn off letting another man get past my emotional defenses.

Until tonight.

I was stupid if I thought this was—or could be—more than sex and friendship. I knew that.

But what could I say?

I couldn't resist enjoying it while it lasted.

CHAPTER 29

CONNOR

I never knew how cold a desert could get. All those stories about trying to stay cool in the sweltering triple-digit heat hadn't prepared me for this. For the kind of cold that makes my jaw ache with fatigue from my teeth chattering for so long.

Everything tastes like sand and copper. My hands shake as I try to keep the Marine on the broken concrete in front of me from bleeding out, but I don't have enough hands for all his wounds. The tourniquet on his thigh is helping the worst of it, but there's still more. Too much blood coming too fast from too many places. The blood soaking through my clothes turns cold against my skin. My teeth want to chatter harder, but I clench them to keep them still.

I want to call out for a bag of blood, but I can't. I can't speak. Can't find the words.

Can't stop the bleeding.

Then the whole world shifts. I can't see. Can't hear. I know someone's screaming but I can't hear them.

It's me.

I'm the one.

There's more blood now, and it's mine. And it's still cold. And it's everywhere. And I can't call out for help. For blood. For—

"Connor." Alex's voice broke through the noise. "You're safe. In Spain. You're safe in bed."

Spain? Bed?

But I was just in...

Everything around me started to disintegrate, fading from a vivid image to near darkness.

"Connor. You're safe." He was stroking my hair. That tightness around me—that was his other arm. "Wherever you were—you're not there anymore. We're in a hotel in Spain."

The darkness...

My closed eyelids in the dark room.

In the dark hotel room.

In Spain.

I pushed out a ragged breath as I opened my eyes. The room was mostly dark, not pitch black like my bedroom would be. Because we were in a hotel room. Our hotel room in Córdoba. Thousands of miles and years removed from the horrors that still haunted me.

The air conditioner alternately rattled and hummed, further separating this place from my bedroom in Sanlúcar, but firmly settling me into this room.

Alex's warmth oriented me. Grounded me. His fingers carded through my hair again, and I shivered as I closed my eyes. My mouth was parched, but I managed, "Sorry."

The arm around me loosened a little. "Don't be sorry. Are you okay?"

I nodded, then remembered he couldn't see me and murmured, "I will be."

"Do you want to talk about it?"

"Not really." I swallowed bile. "I don't know if that's healthy, but... no."

"It's okay." Those fingers through my hair were the most soothing thing ever. "Whatever you need. We don't have to talk about anything."

I closed my eyes and pressed into him. My jaw still ached and my teeth hurt. I must've been clenching them for real while I'd been dreaming; that happened sometimes.

The cold blood I'd felt soaking through my clothes turned out to be sweat making the sheets stick to my skin.

"Ugh." I peeled them away. "I'm sweating like crazy. I need a damn shower."

"Do you want me to join you?"

It wasn't a come-on. If anything, his voice was laced with concern. As if he wasn't sure he should let me out of his sight.

"I'm okay," I whispered as I started to sit up. "I've already woken you up. Go back to sleep; I'll be quiet."

"I'm not worried about that. I'm worried about you." He got up. "And I'm sweaty too."

"Shit. Sorry about—"

He touched my waist in the darkness. "It's okay. Come on." He gently steered me toward the bathroom. "Shower."

The shower helped. Having him in there with me, even though the stall was tight for two people, also helped. Nothing brought me back into the here and now like his affectionate hands soaping up my body while I did the same for him. This stark white bathroom could not be further from anything I ever showered in over there, and there'd never been water this hot or with this much pressure. I didn't have that constant hypervigilance and crippling fatigue. No sand in my boots or under my clothes. I was naked and didn't feel the least bit vulnerable or exposed. I was wrapped up in someone's arms like I never could've been in a warzone.

I was safe. I was here. I was in Spain. In Córdoba. In a hotel. In this shower.

In Alex's arms.

I was safe.

Though the dream had long since dissipated, the metallic tang of blood remained in my mouth.

I drew back a little and touched my lip, and the salt of my finger stung. "Shit. I think I bit my lip."

"You okay?" Alex studied me. "I don't see anything."

"Yeah." I felt around with my tongue. "Yeah, just... It's not bad. It's on the inside, I think. Just stings a little."

He grimaced. "I've done that. It sucks."

I grunted in agreement. "It'll be fine, though."

Alex nodded. "Do you want to go back to bed?"

"Yeah. Might as well not hog all the hot water in the hotel."

He gave a tired but genuine laugh that did more to bring me back to earth than anything else had.

Oh my God, you're beautiful.

Somehow, I didn't let those words come tumbling out or let my stupid face give me away. We got out of the shower and returned to bed, this time taking the other bed since the sheets were sweaty. As soon as we were under the covers in the darkness, Alex gathered me in his arms, and we lay like that for a long time.

He ran his hand up my back. "You okay?"

"Yeah. Sorry I woke you up."

"Don't worry about it."

He stroked a gentle hand over my shoulder and down my arm. "Did something trigger the nightmare? Or was it just random?"

"I think it was just random. I don't..." I thought about it for a moment. "I can't think of anything that might've set it off. We've talked about that—how sometimes it doesn't need a trigger."

"Oh, I know. I had a whole night full of flashbacks after the command's Christmas party one year. Still have no idea why, but that was a rough night."

As much as I didn't want to imagine him going through an ordeal that awful—the original trauma *or* the subsequent nightmares—it eased something in me to be reassured that he understood. Like maybe I wasn't doing this wrong, as if there was any right way to have PTSD.

I hadn't wanted to talk about my dream, but the words came anyway. "During my first tour, we were called out to a convoy that had hit an IED. I remember this one Marine—he was alive, but he was bleeding from everywhere. Just... everywhere."

"Shit," Alex whispered, and he held me a little closer.

I closed my eyes. "I had a tourniquet on him, and I'd gone through every QuikClot in my kit already. One of the other corpsmen had gone to get more, and he was getting some blood because this kid needed a transfusion." I shivered as a chill went through me. "And that's when the mortar hit us."

Alex stiffened beside me.

I swallowed. "I don't remember much after that. I woke up on a Medevac, drugged out of my head and completely disoriented. But... when I dream about it..."

His hand traced over my shoulder. "You remember?"

"I... think so? Like I don't know if it's an actual memory,

or if my mind is just filling in the gaps. It's always a little different, and it's..." Cold water trickled through my veins. "It's fucking terrifying every time."

"I believe that," he whispered, and I thought he might've shuddered. Or maybe he was just getting comfortable.

"What I *do* remember," I went on, "was waking up in the hospital in Germany. I'd... They said I'd been awake a few times on the way back to base and on the flight out, but I was on a lot of drugs and I was concussed, so..." I shrugged.

"Holy shit. How bad were you hurt?"

"I was cut up pretty bad. I think I had almost a hundred stitches, all told?"

Alex whistled. "Wow."

"I also broke my collarbone and fractured three ribs, which was why I was in so damn much pain. Between those and all the bruises..."

"Yeah, that sounds like the aftermath of an explosion." He shuddered and pulled me even closer. "I'm glad you're okay now."

"I'm lucky, in all honesty. The bruises and fractures healed. So did all the lacerations. The concussion was bad, but I haven't had a lot of long-term problems from TBI. I had some balance issues there for a while, and I even had a little trouble speaking for a year or two. Like I'd stumble over or forget a word. But all things considered, I made a full recovery."

"You're very lucky." He kissed my temple. "I know a lot of people who weren't."

"Me too."

"Did you ever—" He tensed. "I... never mind."

"What?"

"I, uh... I don't want to drag up more bad memories."

"Eh, they're already here." I ran my hand up his chest. "What's on your mind?"

"I just wondered, um..." He swallowed. "Did you ever find out what happened to the Marine?"

I exhaled, not at all surprised by the question but still hit in the gut by that particular memory. "He didn't make it. He might've had a chance—I'll never know for sure. What I do know is that the mortar finished him off."

"Jesus," Alex breathed. "Either way, though, it wasn't your fault."

"I know. It took a long time to reconcile with the guilt. I just... I don't know. There was absolutely nothing I could've done to stop the mortar, and I could've died as easily as he did. I might not have been able to save him even if hadn't been hit by that mortar. But I still felt guilty for a long, long time." I paused. "Sometimes I still do."

"I think that comes with the territory," Alex said softly. "Not just of being in a combat situation, but the medical profession. We've all had our hands on patients when they died, and even when there was no earthly chance of them surviving, it's hard not to wonder if we could've done something differently."

I closed my eyes and released a long breath. There was something intensely comforting about hearing my own thoughts rolling off someone else's tongue. Especially when that someone was Alex, even if I was afraid to look too closely at why his feelings mattered that much to me.

"That's exactly it," I said. "It's the 'what ifs' that get to me."

"Me too. I was so glad to come back from deployment and start working toward my radiology designation. I still see some awful shit, but I'm not up to my elbows in it, you know?"

"I get that. My emergency rotation was by far the hardest part of medical school."

"Worse than combat?"

I thought about that. "Not necessarily worse? But it fucked with my head in some of the same ways. And some different ways. In combat, you *kind* of have an idea what you're going to see most of the time. Like there's definitely things you don't expect, but the ways people get hurt in warzones *usually* fall into the same general box, you know?"

Alex nodded.

"Right. But an emergency room in a major city?" I whistled and shook my head. "It's... everything. And every*one*. I wasn't just treating soldiers anymore. It was kids and little old ladies, you know? And it's everything from a new mom who's freaking out because her baby's spiking a fever to parents who are about to hear the worst news of their lives. It was... It was a lot."

"That's what I've heard," he whispered. "I've never envied anyone who works in the ED. I mean, I have to come down sometimes for ultrasounds and X-rays and whatnot, and their patients come up to my department all the time. But it's not the constant barrage."

I nodded. "Seriously. I knew two shifts into that rotation that I would never be an emergency doctor."

"But you've been to combat, haven't you?"

"Only as a corpsman. As a physician, I've only ever been on shipboard deployments."

"Was there ever a possibility? Of going boots-on-the-ground again, I mean?"

"There was," I whispered, that old familiar prickle of fear creeping up my neck. "I got lucky, I guess."

"You did. Me too—I did the three deployments into the desert, but thank God, the last sea duty rotation I did during active combat ops was on a boat. I'll take that over going back to the Sandbox any day."

"You and me both."

"It's funny," Alex said. "My mom told me she was relieved I was going to be a corpsman. She thought that meant I'd be away from the fighting, you know?" He trailed his fingers up and down my arm. "I didn't have the heart to tell her that being a corpsman means being a combat medic, and they're not kidding about the combat part." He paused. "I... really should've told her before I was deployed the first time. I just didn't want her to worry more than she already would, you know?"

"I get that. My dad was in the Army, so my parents both knew exactly what it meant. The whole reason my dad encouraged me to join the Navy instead of the Army was that I'd probably be on a ship. Neither of us thought I'd end up boots on the ground."

"I don't think anyone expected that," Alex said dryly.

Wasn't that the truth.

I sighed. "Well, I made it through. So did you. Now we just have all these psychological souvenirs."

He huffed a soft laugh. "Yeah. The gift that keeps on giving."

"It's like herpes, except in your head with IEDs."

Alex snorted. "Okay, it's probably time to go back to sleep."

"Yeah. Probably."

He stroked my cheek, and his tone was more serious. "You think you'll be able to sleep?"

"I'll be fine."

"You sure?"

"I mean... as sure as I ever am. Go to sleep, baby."

He grunted softly and kissed the top of my head. He

knew what I meant—when the dreams were this bad, there were usually more if I could get back to sleep at all.

"Go to sleep," I said again. "Hopefully I won't wake you up again."

"If you do, it's okay. I know how it goes."

And a moment later, he'd fallen into that slow, steady breathing that meant he was asleep. Typical military—could fall asleep any time, any place, in about thirty seconds flat. I had that same superpower... usually.

Tonight, I just lay there and listened to him breathe over the hum and rattle of the room's air conditioner. I closed my eyes and held on to him, savoring the comfort and the closeness of being in his arms.

The nightmare had been rough, but the rest of it? Showering, cuddling, and talking with Alex? That had *almost* been worth revisiting one of the worst days of my life.

I had never realized before I met him how much I'd needed this. Not just someone who could handle my nightmares, but someone who empathized because he'd been there too. I wouldn't wish PTSD on anyone, but damn if there wasn't something incredibly comforting about the warmth and understanding that came from someone who *knew* what I was seeing and feeling when the demons paid me a visit. Something about being able to tremble and catch my breath beside someone who knew just how horrible those dreams could really get. How *real* they could get and how awful the reality that spawned them had truly been.

My ex-wife had always done the best she could on nights like this. She'd hold me close, stroke my hair, and talk me down until my heartrate was closer to normal and my breathing had slowed. She'd never given me a second of grief the times I'd screamed or cried. For all the problems we had, I'd never stop being grateful for the nights she'd eased me back to earth after my past had visited my dreams.

But the more nights I spent beside Alex, the more I realized there was something to be said for being with someone who *knew*. Who *understood*. Aimee had done the best she could, and I didn't hold anything against her.

But Alex? He was a godsend. It was like the difference between telling a therapist about what I'd seen and talking to a fellow veteran. The therapist might have more ideas about solutions, but the veteran understood on a visceral level what no one who hadn't been there could ever grasp.

I hadn't realized how badly I'd been needing that. How badly I'd needed someone to say, "I get it. It's not just you."

No wonder the nightmares had been harder to deal with by myself recently. The comfort I found in his arms made the nights apart harder than all the ones I'd spent alone between my separation and the first time Alex had slept over.

I sighed as I listened to him breathe. I knew damn well I was getting too close to him. That whatever lines we'd drawn between traveling fuck buddies and boyfriends had blurred beyond recognition.

None of that changed our situation. I *couldn't* have him the way I realized I so, so desperately wanted him.

But tonight, I had him.

Tonight, I let myself feel all the things that were too dangerous to feel for someone I couldn't have.

Tonight, I let myself love him.

CHAPTER 30

ALEX

We slept in that morning. I was awake before Connor, and I very carefully moved as little as possible so I wouldn't disturb him. I had no idea how much sleep he'd managed last night, so I wanted to let him doze as long as he needed to.

As slowly and quietly as I could, I slipped out of bed and into the bathroom to take a leak, then joined him again. He didn't stir once.

While he slept, I lay back on the pillows and scrolled social media on my phone. A few coworkers had started a group chat to plan my chief's upcoming retirement party, and it felt so weird to casually talk to them as if I wasn't lying naked beside Lieutenant Commander Marks. None of us were particularly close, but if they knew where I was and who I was with…

What they don't know won't hurt us.

I paused mid-sentence to drink in the sight of him. He was on his side with his face half-buried in the pillow, his dark hair adorably mussed. I hadn't noticed some of the subtle lines in his skin until now, when his features relaxed and those faint creases smoothed out a little. I probably had my fair share, too; time had that effect on people. It worked on him, too, just like the gray in his hair. Younger guys were still attractive, but now as I got older myself, I liked the signs of age in a good-looking man. It was charming, even if I couldn't articulate quite why.

I also noticed for the first time some scars along his hairline and a couple on his cheek. One had that telltale ragged look of a laceration that had been sutured. Another was short but deep, as if something had lodged into the tissue or even gouged out a small chunk. One was long and fine, only visible because his dark stubble was thick enough to emphasize the thin white line.

Maybe I'd seen them all before and they just hadn't registered, but now that I knew about that mortar that had almost killed him—shit. Were those from shrapnel? His neck was unmarred and the marks stopped where a helmet would've covered, so yeah, it was possible I was seeing where unprotected skin had been hit with metal, glass, stones, or whatever else the explosion had kicked up.

He could've died that day. If the mortar had landed a few feet—even a few inches—closer. If he hadn't had on a helmet and something protecting his neck. If any number of things had happened... Connor could have died beside that Marine, and I never would've known he existed.

Fuck. That was a heavy thought.

Right then, a quiet ping told me that one of my coworkers had responded to the group chat. I shook myself out of my dark thoughts and shifted my attention back to the phone, and several more messages popped up. I really did want to help plan something for Chief Wallace's retirement; I wasn't close to the guy, but he'd worked hard and deserved a good send-off. It just didn't interest me right now. Not on a warm, lazy morning in bed with this gorgeous man.

I muted the chat and switched back to my social media, but nothing kept my interest there either. The news was a mix of boring and terrifying—same shit, different day—and even the games I had on my phone couldn't hold my attention.

Beside me, Connor stirred a little. When I turned to him, his eyes fluttered open. Then they fixed on me, and he offered up a sleepy smile, which brought back all those lines that had smoothed out. Wow, they really were charming, weren't they?

How are you so gorgeous?

"Morning." He scrubbed a hand over his unshaven face. "What time is it?"

I glanced at my phone before putting it on the nightstand, and as I settled on my side to face him, I said, "About 0930."

He wrinkled his nose. "I wonder what teenage me would think if he knew that would one day qualify as sleeping in."

I laughed. "I know, right?"

He chuckled, and he found my hand between us. It was tempting to steal a kiss, but morning breath would probably ruin the moment, so I just settled on enjoying his touch and his adorable smile.

Rubbing his thumb along mine, he said, "We should probably get dressed and get downstairs. I think breakfast stops at like ten."

He was right. On the other hand...

"Counterpoint," I said. "We can be lazy and just get breakfast at the train station."

Connor pursed his lips. "The train stations do all seem to have pretty good pastries and coffee."

"Mmhmm. They usually have some savory things, too. I'm not starving quite yet. What about you?"

He thought about it, then shrugged. "I could eat, but I'm good for a while."

"So... hang out and be lazy?"

"Sounds perfect to me."

That was exactly what we did, too. We took our sweet time getting ready to leave. We showered and dressed. Connor put in his contacts; such a shame since he looked so good in glasses, but he was hot without them too. Then we just lounged in bed with some coffee we'd made in the room. Not the greatest coffee I'd ever had, especially after brushing our teeth, but we'd both endured the "coffee" that flowed on ships, in combat zones, and in hospital staff lounges. I didn't complain and neither did he.

"By the way," I said after we'd hung out on the bed for a while, "I meant to ask—how was the rest of last night?" I touched his stubbled jaw. "I only remember waking up the one time, but..."

"It was fine." Connor smiled sleepily as he pushed up his glasses. "I had a few more, but they weren't as bad as the first." Covering my hand with his, he kissed my palm. "I'm glad I didn't wake you up again."

"You could have if you needed to."

"I was okay." He pressed another kiss to my palm. "But thank you."

I smiled, then leaned in to kiss him for real. It wasn't a long kiss. Nothing deep or hungry that would get us spun up and turned on. Just a gentle taste of those perfect lips.

When I drew back, he held my gaze, and he smiled so sweetly, I was seriously disappointed that we'd have to leave soon. Couldn't we just... stay here and be together in this bed for the rest of the day?

No, we couldn't. Damn it.

And according to the clock on the nightstand, we were getting low on time.

I kissed him again, lightly this time. "I guess we should go. Your train leaves in an hour."

He groaned with theatrical resistance, but he got up out of bed and so did I. After we'd finished making ourselves presentable, we pocketed our wallets and phones, double-checked the room to make sure we had everything, then headed for the door.

As I was reaching for the handle, though, Connor, said, "Wait."

I faced him. "Hmm?"

"Before we're out in public and I can't get away with this anymore..." He cupped the sides of my neck, drew me in, and claimed a soft, spine-melting kiss.

I couldn't help the quiet whimper as I wrapped my arms around him. He slid a hand from my neck up into my hair, raising goose bumps all over my body. I pressed my hardening cock against him, and I was met with a similar ridge beneath his clothes. Oh, fuck yes. Everything he did turned me on, but nothing more than him being turned on himself. I loved having that effect on him—getting him hard, making his breath stutter, making him squirm and shiver beneath my touch.

"We should go," he murmured, but he made no effort to pull away.

"I know." I pulled him closer. "Should get... Don't want to miss our trains."

"Uh-huh." His tongue teased the corner of my lip, then

slipped past to explore my mouth as if this was the first time we'd ever kissed.

What could I do but surrender?

We needed to check out of our room. We needed to get to the train station.

But...

Just a few more minutes.

Because this was what I lived for these days. I went through the motions at work, counting down the days until I retired, all the while looking forward to moments exactly like this one. Connor hit the spot in ways my past hookups and friends with benefits never had. His kiss could reduce my entire universe to that one point of contact between our mouths. His hands could be deliciously rough to the point of bruising, or they could be so gentle they left goose bumps in their wake. His body—every inch of it—was something I could worship for ages with my lips and my hands.

"You know..." I panted. "There's... There's more trains."

"You're right. There are."

"Mmhmm. And we've still got a little time before we need to check out." I nudged him back toward the bed. "Think we can do something in that time?"

"Absolutely," he replied in a hoarse whisper. "We..." He hesitated. "We can fuck when we get back to my place. Not enough time now." He tugged me closer to the bed. "Pretty sure there's still plenty we can do."

"Damn right there is."

Connor pulled me down on top of him, and I sank over him and into a deep, needy kiss. I wanted him to throw on a condom and fuck me into the mattress, but he was right—not enough time. Even a quickie still meant some prep and cleanup, and if he plowed me as hard as I wanted him to, the train ride back to El Puerto might not be very comfortable.

Fine. He could drill me into oblivion tonight.

For now, we made out as we pushed clothes off. Though this had to be a quickie, it wasn't rushed. We still kissed like we had all damned day. We still touched like this was going to be the longest, most drawn-out foreplay of our lives. I was rock hard. So was he. We stroked each other as lazily as we kissed, and when Connor started on my neck—good God, this man loved kissing my neck—I was instantly covered in goose bumps.

"Jesus, baby," I murmured.

He grinned against my throat before kissing beneath my jaw again. "Love it when you're this turned on."

I gave his cock a slow, appreciative stroke. "Likewise."

"We don't have time to fuck," he mumbled against my skin, "but get the lube anyway."

My only objection to that was that I had to let go of him long enough to roll away and reach for my bag.

I only got as far as opening the zipper before Connor was over me, kissing his way down my back. Every brush of his lips blanked my brain—holy fuck, he made me so damn hot.

"If we had the time," he growled, "and you didn't have to sit on the train for a couple of hours, I would be balls deep in you right now."

I moaned, letting my head fall forward and my hand fall away from the bag. "Connor..."

"But that doesn't mean I can't do *anything* to your ass, does it?"

I lifted my head and craned my neck, trying to look back at him. "Oh yeah? What did you have in mind?"

The kiss he dropped on the center of my spine should've been a clue.

The one he planted at the small of my back—that tipped me off.

"Oh God..."

Oh God was right. We'd never discussed rimming aside from me mentioning that I enjoyed it, both giving and receiving. I had no idea if he'd ever done it before. If he hadn't... well, then he was either a very fast learner or a fucking natural, because oh... my... *God*.

"Connor..." I writhed on the bed, my hard-on rubbing against the sheets as he licked and teased me like he'd never been the least bit nervous or self-conscious about sex in his life. His tongue was always magic, and this was no exception. "Oh, fuck, please don't stop."

He didn't. He absolutely went to town on me, and I used what few brain cells were still functioning to make a mental note to return the favor. Bliss like this could not go unreciprocated... even if it had to be later because it was currently turning me into a trembling, moaning mess who could barely think about anything except how bad I wanted to come.

And how bad I wanted to make *him* come.

"Connor, I..." I squeezed my eyes shut and struggled to find my breath. "I'm gonna come if—I want to get you off too."

He relented then, which gave me a chance to suck in some much-needed air. "Anything you want, baby." He sounded breathless and unsteady, as if he were as close to the edge as I was. "Tell me what—"

"Let me get the lube."

His weight lifted up off me, so I fumbled with my bag and grabbed the lube. Then I rolled onto my back, and

Connor was immediately over me. He leaned in to kiss me, but hesitated.

"Are, uh, are you okay with kissing after I've—"

I cut him off with a deep, hard kiss.

He got the message.

We made out for a moment, and then he touched his forehead to mine. "Lube?"

I handed him the bottle. He coated both of our dicks with a generous amount of lube, and then we were back to kissing and lazily stroking each other. I didn't even know who was setting the rhythm, only that our hands and hips had fallen into this perfect cadence, and we made out as we fucked into each other's hands and took each other higher.

"I can't wait till we get home," he murmured, thrusting harder into my hand. "I want to come in you."

The words made all the air rush out of my lungs. "Please? And fuck me hard?"

His eyes fluttered shut as he murmured, "Oh my fucking God..." Then he was kissing my neck, thrusting as if he were doing to my hand exactly what he planned to do to my ass later, and all the while, he was jerking me off like he *needed* my orgasm.

I arched under him, thrusting up into his fist as I pumped him furiously. A throaty groan escaped my lips, and Connor pushed himself up and gazed down at me with fire in his eyes.

"You getting there?" he panted.

All I could do was nod.

A low growl rumbled in the back of his throat. "Come, baby," he pleaded. "That's it. Come for me. God, you're so sexy when you're falling apart."

I was falling apart, and all it took was another brush of his lips across my throat in the same moment he added a twist to his strokes, and I was doing exactly what he'd begged me to do. I cried out, thrusting up into his slick fist, and he egged me on, cursing and moaning against my throat until he also shuddered, swore, and added his cum to mine.

We collapsed against each other, trying to catch our breath.

"Fuck," he whispered. "That was…"

"Uh-huh." I lifted my head to kiss him softly. "I didn't realize you were so into rimming."

He gave a soft, breathless laugh. "Surprise?"

I chuckled, and we sank into another long kiss. We could've stayed like that all damn day, but as the dust settled, reality set in.

We had trains to catch.

Fortunately, we hadn't killed too much time, and we weren't far from the train station. All we had to do was clean up, get dressed, and head out, even if it was a chore to pry ourselves apart.

As we left the room and returned to the real world, I struggled to find my balance. It wasn't just from my orgasm, either; everything felt surreal. The world around us. Everything we'd done just before we left. Just… everything.

It was just a quick and dirty handjob between two guys who were too horny to wait until we got home. Right?

Except… no. It hadn't been like that at all. Yeah, we'd been horny. Yeah, we'd needed to get each other off.

But Connor hadn't kissed me or touched me like he was horny and wanted to get us both off.

He'd touched me like he wanted *me*.

After eating a light lunch in the train station, we decided to board the same train after all. There was no point in one of us loitering around the station for an hour or two, and as always, if someone saw us, we could just say we ran into each other and figured we'd sit together to pass the time.

We settled into a car with our coffee. There were a few people in here with us, but they were mostly clustered toward the other end and no one paid any attention to us.

My head was still light after that orgasm. He always rocked my world, and this morning was no exception.

As the train started moving, though, he seemed to be someplace else. Lost in thought, and not necessarily a good one.

I nudged him gently with my foot. "Hey. What's on your mind?"

"Oh. Um." He met my gaze, but he still hesitated. After a moment, though, he took a breath. "Can I ask you about something personal?"

Now it was my turn to be caught off-guard, but I pretended I wasn't. "Sure. Yeah." I gestured with my coffee cup. "I think we're past the point of 'too personal,' aren't we?"

Connor laughed. "Okay, maybe. But, um..." He sobered a little and searched my eyes. "Out of curiosity... why did you decide to stay closeted all this time?"

Oh.

That.

I took another swallow of coffee. "Like I said before, I was in while DADT was still in effect. After it was lifted, most people I knew who came out were fine, but a few had problems."

Connor scowled. "Me too. I wasn't out myself, but I remember hearing about some people getting grief for it."

"Right? So I just... I decided I didn't want to chance it. I wanted to stay in long enough to retire, and I was afraid it might derail my career."

He nodded as I spoke. "I don't blame you. I remember during that time thinking I was glad I was married to a woman. There was no reason for me to come out, so I didn't have to chance any blowback."

"I was the opposite—I was just hooking up and maybe having a casual relationship here and there. I didn't have anything serious enough to make coming out worthwhile, so..." I half-shrugged. "I kept it to myself."

He watched me silently for a moment. "What changed with Tobias?"

I jumped like he'd kicked me. "What?"

"You dated him, didn't you? Like... an actual relationship?" Connor tilted his head. "I'm just curious what was different with him."

"Oh. Um." I swallowed, the back of my throat acidic just from the thought of that shitshow. "I didn't go into it planning on dating him."

"No?"

I shook my head. "I just wanted sex, but then he was..." I dropped my gaze and shook my head. "In hindsight, it was love-bombing. It's so fucking obvious now. The way he was always telling me how amazing I was, and how hot I was, and how he couldn't stop thinking about me..." I rolled my eyes. "Plus it was just gifts and expensive dinners and... ugh. It really is so obvious now, but at the time, I was just like, wow, someone's actually this interested in me? Because that was part of why I stayed single—it wasn't just that I didn't want to deal with a relationship alongside the military. I never got the impression I was worth the effort."

Connor's lips parted. "Really?"

I nodded, not sure why my cheeks were suddenly hot. "I was always booty call material, not boyfriend material. Then here comes this guy who acts like I *am* boyfriend material, and I thought, fuck it—why not?" I shook my head. "And then it all blew up in my face."

"So he was good in the beginning," Connor said softly. "Then shifted gears."

"Most people like that do. They wait until you're under their thumb, and then the true colors come out slowly." I exhaled. "And like, I was already fucked up from combat. Now I've got issues with men. So... I don't know. I think I just need to finish my career, get some help in the civilian world, and then maybe see if I can pull off a relationship." I laughed bitterly. "If I'm lucky, I might land a boyfriend before I'm fifty."

Connor didn't laugh, and he studied me silently for a moment. Then he put his coffee aside and pressed his elbow into the armrest. "And you'd never had one before? Not even like in high school?"

"Oh God no. In high school, I was just counting down the days until I graduated so I could join the Navy and get the hell out of my hometown."

His eyebrows rose. "So you've just... spent your whole adult life waiting for something to be over?" I very nearly snapped that it worked for me so he could back the fuck off, but before I could say anything, he sighed and added, "Kind of sounds like me for the last half of my marriage."

I blinked, my sudden irritation gone as quickly as it had come. "It... It does?"

He nodded. "I think I knew a *long* time ago that we weren't in it for the long haul. I convinced myself we just needed to get the boys through high school and off to college, and then we could go our separate ways."

Furrowing my brow, I cocked my head. "That's what you did, isn't it?"

He wobbled his hand in the air. "Kind of? We separated before my younger son's senior year." He grimaced. "But we should've done it a long time ago. We thought it would be better for the kids and for ourselves, but..." He shook his head.

I shifted a little in my seat, not sure what to say.

"The thing is, it's hard not to look back and realize how much of my life I wasted being unhappy with someone. Because even before I realized we weren't going to make it... we weren't going to make it. We were just treading water, both of us telling ourselves we'd get through this deployment, or we'd get through this duty station, or we'd get the kids through high school." He sighed, pressing back against his seat. "And then one day I'm forty, *finally* divorced, and wondering how I'm ever going to make up for lost time."

"That's the kind of thing I wanted to avoid," I said. "I see so many people—especially service members—go through that, and..." I shook my head. "The Navy is enough stress on its own, you know? Plus all the therapy I'm not getting."

"I get that." He locked eyes with me. "But it's amazing how easy it is to suddenly realize how much life passed by while you were waiting for the right time to start living." He put up his hand. "I don't want to sound like I'm pressuring you or criticizing you. If this is working for you, then it's the right thing. Obviously." Lowering his hand, he exhaled. "I think I've just been realizing a lot lately how much I could've done differently." He quirked his lips, then rolled his eyes. "But it sounds like I'm trying to tell you how to— I'm sorry. I shouldn't... I'm sorry."

"It's all right," I said. "I've worried about that sometimes, to tell you the truth. That I'm putting things off more than I should. I was never in much of a hurry because I didn't want to have kids, but I probably should've done something about my mental health sooner." I tsked. "Not that the military will let me but... Anyway. It's going to take me a long time to unfuck myself, and... well, like I said, if I'm lucky, I'll land a boyfriend by the time I'm fifty."

Connor studied me again. "Do you have to be through therapy before you can pursue something?"

"Maybe not all the way through it, but I'd rather not be this much of a mess when I put myself out there for something serious, you know?"

He seemed like he might suggest otherwise, but instead, he grunted and nodded. "I get that. It took a toll on my marriage. I don't know if it would've been easier if she'd met me after the wars fucked me up, but at least then she'd have had a better idea of what she was getting into. So... I get it."

"Comes with the territory in this job, doesn't it?"

"Unfortunately."

Thank God, we moved to lighter topics after that. I didn't want to talk about my jacked up mental health or my pathetic romantic life, especially not with him. Not on the heels of such an amazing weekend together.

Not when I was stupidly feeling things for him that I had no business feeling.

I felt good, and I didn't want to think too hard about how there was no point in even entertaining these ridiculous feelings fluttering around in my chest and banging around in my head.

I didn't want to, but I did.

Especially since, about half an hour after our train pulled out of Córdoba, Connor dozed off. I didn't mind, and

I let him sleep. Last night had been hard on him, so he was probably exhausted.

It just gave me time to think, and oh, wow, was I thinking.

I couldn't stop thinking about everything we'd discussed, and about the sex we'd had on this trip. It had been amazing, because sex with him was always amazing, but it had also been... different.

I knew what this was—what we'd set out to do—but nothing we did together felt like the booty calls or hookups they were supposed to be.

And then there were the conversations. Like the one we'd had while we'd settled onto the train. I felt weirdly guilty about not showing him all my cards about coming out and finding a partner. I'd never thought twice about keeping them hidden from fuck buddies in the past, but for some reason, it didn't seem right to keep this close to the vest now.

It felt weird, admitting to things I didn't want him or anyone else to now about me. Like I'd shown him how utterly pathetic I was when it came to men.

Hell, maybe that was why I'd gone ahead and told him—because with as much time as Connor was spending with me, with as much as he was risking for the dubious honor of my company, he deserved to know.

Then again, he probably did know. It just didn't matter because for all I had stupid, ridiculous feelings, this *was* nothing more than sex, traveling, and sometimes hanging out. He wasn't looking at this with any long-term thoughts in mind—just scratching that horny itch and finding his sea legs in bed with a man. He'd probably figured out from the start what other men always did—that I might be worth the effort for orgasms and someone to talk to, but that was about it. I wasn't boyfriend material. I wasn't someone people wanted for anything more than sex or company, and even those only lasted until someone better came along.

He was satisfied with what he was getting from me, but I was kidding myself if I thought I was his Mr. Right. I was Mr. Right Now for a lonely, newly divorced man who was exploring his sexuality and a foreign country. When the time came and he wanted to settle down, Connor could definitely do better.

I shifted my gaze from the passing scenery to the man sleeping across from me.

Yeah, Connor could do *way* better than me.

But the longer we did this, the more I struggled to imagine finding a man who was better than him.

We got off the train in El Puerto and headed to the parking lot. We'd driven in separately, but we'd parked near each other, and we walked down the row of cars gleaming in the blazing sun.

When we reached mine, I stopped, and after I'd put my things in the trunk, I turned to him. "Okay. Well. I guess I'll see you... whenever I see you?"

Why was I so fucking disappointed that we were going our separate ways?

Connor cocked his head. "You're not coming back to my place?"

"I..." Oh. Wait. Was I? "I mean... Do you want me to?"

He raised his eyebrows. "I seem to recall promising to fuck you into the mattress tonight."

Shivering, I bit my lip. "You did, didn't you?"

"Uh-huh." He adjusted his backpack on his shoulder as he glanced around. "You know." He swallowed hard, then met my gaze. "I don't *just* want you to come over to fuck. I've had a good time this weekend, and, I mean, that doesn't have to end right now."

Why was I so relieved by that?

But I just smiled. "Okay. I'll meet you at your place."

I did, and we spent the rest of the day relaxing in his blissfully cool house. He fucked me exactly as hard as he'd promised, nearly driving me to tears with the force of my orgasm. Then we showered and cuddled in bed for a while. Even afterward, he didn't try to herd me toward the door or hint that *now* our weekend was over. When we started getting hungry, he ordered takeout from our favorite kebab restaurant, and we ate outside by his pool. And finally, long after the sun had gone down, we climbed into his bed. No sex. No *expectation* of sex. Nothing more than some lazy kissing, and he seemed just as happy with that as I was.

He fell asleep first, and I lay there for the longest time, just drinking in this comfortable stillness with Connor breathing softly beside me.

How was I going to get used to the next guy? To the usual routine of fooling around and then parting ways for the night? Because I wasn't going to be sleeping over like I did with Connor. It had been hard enough to move on after Tobias. He'd left me feeling worthless, gross, and unlovable. Connor? He'd be a tough act to follow because he'd raised the bar so damn high.

Well, I'd cross that bridge when I got to it. Maybe I'd hit up Isidoro again. He and I had pretty much had sex on demand from the beginning; if one of us was feeling horny or was just bored on a Friday night, the other was usually game. I could go a couple of weeks or even longer without feeling that itch for a man's touch.

I cuddled closer to Connor just because I could.

I hadn't had this with Isidoro. I hadn't had it with Tobias. I hadn't had it with *anyone*.

This thing I had with Connor was different from anything I'd had with anyone else. Maybe because on those nights when I was keenly aware of his absence beside me, there was nothing I could do. We could text. We could FaceTime. But I couldn't have him next to me—not for sex and not for sleeping.

And when I *did* have him beside me, even when neither of us was in the mood for anything *caliente*, the whole world felt right.

Was this what it felt like to fall for someone?

Probably. That would be just my luck, wouldn't it? The first time I let myself catch the feels for someone, it would be someone I absolutely could not have under any circumstances.

I kissed his temple and ran my fingers along his shoulder.

There would come a time when there were no more rules preventing us from being together. Sixteen months and counting, and I'd be retired, no longer beholden to the UCMJ like I was now. It sounded like a long time, but I'd start the retirement process in about four months. A year after that, I'd be a civilian.

I could be with Connor.

I wouldn't be, though, because that wasn't what this was. I was kidding myself if I thought he'd want to do this cloak-and-dagger shit for that long. I could believe I was worth the risk and the effort of dashing off to another city for some sex and sightseeing. I could believe he liked sleeping next to me enough to take the chance of having me stay at his place tonight or any other night.

But was what he got out of this worth over a year of career-threatening secrecy?

Doubtful.

I closed my eyes and just listened to him breathe, savoring his body heat and his soft skin against mine.

More and more, I had to admit to myself that if he wanted to play the long game, I was in. As much as I'd avoided relationships because I just didn't want to balance love and the Navy, I was starting to think that maybe love had found me.

I just wished I could believe the man beside me felt the same.

CHAPTER 31

CONNOR

As I was staring up at the Arrivals screen at the Jerez airport for the hundredth time, the status of Flight IB1091 from Madrid switched to *ARRIVED*.

Excitement surged through me. I hadn't seen my boys in way too long, and now they were *here*. They'd already cleared customs, so all they had to do was get off the plane, get their bags, and come through the double doors.

My phone vibrated, and the text from Quinn had me almost giddy with excitement:

> On the ground. See you in a few!

I had too much nervous energy to stand still, so I paced in the sparsely crowded hallway. I also checked the screen about sixteen more times just to be absolutely sure the flight really had arrived, and that I'd been looking at the right flight, and—

My phone pinged again, and this time it was Landon.

> Is baggage claim always this slow in this airport?

>> LOL It can be, yeah.

> WTF? There's only one plane. How long can it take?

>> Don't ask that question unless you really want to know the answer.

> (skull emoji)

I chuckled and pocketed my phone.

Passengers were starting to trickle out. First, those with only carry-on. A few minutes later, people started leaving with larger luggage. I craned my neck, peering through the doors and searching for three familiar faces. It would be just my luck their bags were the last ones off the plane, or something got lost, or—

There they were. Backpacks on, suitcases rolling behind them, they strode toward the doors. When they caught sight of me, their eyes lit up and they waved.

I waved back, not caring at all if I was grinning like an idiot. I hadn't seen my boys since I'd left Norfolk—hell yeah, I was excited.

Landon got to me first and almost bowled me over with a hug. Quinn was less forceful about it, but he still hugged me tight. When they'd let me go, I shared a gentler embrace with Savannah.

"How was your trip?" I asked all three of them. "Are you hungry? Do you—"

"Dad. Chill. We ate in Madrid." Quinn nodded toward the exit. "Let's just get out of here."

Fine by me. I'd rented a car for their visit, since the

beater I'd bought didn't really accommodate four adults very comfortably. It definitely wouldn't have handled all the luggage.

After I'd paid for parking, we loaded up the car and headed out.

"Wow," Savannah said as we drove through farm country. "It's a lot... drier than I thought it would be?"

"It's a lot like Southern California." I gestured to the left. "Complete with wineries everywhere."

"Ooh, can we tour one of them?" she asked.

Both of my sons groaned.

"If you guys go to a winery," Landon declared, twisting around in the passenger seat to eye her, "I'm just buying a bottle and sitting out in the parking lot getting shitfaced while I wait."

I laughed. "I'll be right there with you."

We shared a fist bump. Savannah grumbled something about us being philistines with no class, but there wasn't any heat behind it.

"Are you guys sure you're not hungry?" I asked. "We're still about forty minutes out from my place."

"I'm good," Quinn said. "I stuffed my face in Madrid."

"Same," Landon said. "Just don't tell Mom we came to Spain and ate at McDonald's."

I snorted. "Secret's safe with me. I think every American I know ends up eating there when they come through Madrid. It's familiar, it's cheap, and you don't have to worry about it disagreeing with your stomach right before you get on another plane."

"See?" Landon twisted around again. "See? Dad gets it!"

There was some tsking and muttering from the backseat. I just chuckled. Quinn and Savannah were definitely proud of their more refined and adventurous palates. Landon was adventurous too, and he'd try damn near anything someone put in front of him, but he was pragmatic about it, too. As far as he was concerned, a layover was not the time to try some wildly new dish.

I couldn't agree more.

"Well, if you're feeling really adventurous," I said, gesturing at some exits coming up, "there's a Taco Bell in Jerez."

All three kids scoffed.

"Taco Bell?" Savannah asked. "In *Spain?*"

"Yep. And it's damn good, too." I paused. "Plus they serve booze."

"No shit?" Quinn sounded interested. "They serve booze at Taco Bell?"

"This is Spain, kid. You can get beer at Burger King."

Landon eyed me. "Okay, now you're just making shit up."

"I swear to God!" I laughed. "McDonald's too! You can order a meal with a beer instead of a soda."

The kids were oddly quiet for a moment.

It was Savannah who finally said, "I can't tell if he's messing with us."

I rolled my eyes and thrust my phone at Landon. "Look it up."

He took the phone. Then, sounding more than a little dubious, he said, "Hey Siri. Does McDonald's serve beer in Spain?"

The phone's robotic voice replied, "Yes, McDonald's serves beer in Spain."

The stunned silence from all three kids made me laugh.

"See?" I said. "I wasn't messing with you."

Landon scoffed. "I can't believe I didn't notice that when we were in Madrid. Unless that one didn't serve beer?"

"You were probably just jetlagged," Quinn said. "I didn't notice it either."

"Trust me," I said. "They serve beer at that one."

Quinn huffed. "Okay, that settles it. We're going to BK or McDonald's while we're here, just so we can order beer."

"Really?" Savannah asked, and I could almost hear her rolling her eyes.

"What? I have to see this!"

"Oh my God," she muttered.

Beside me, Landon laughed. "Guess we're getting fast food while we're in Spain."

"Yep. Guess we are." I shrugged. "Fine by me."

At that point, anything was fine by me.

Quinn, Landon, and Savannah were here.

I couldn't ask for much more.

"Holy shit." Landon gaped at the house. "This place is huge!"

"Did you win the lottery or something?" Quinn asked.

I laughed as I helped them unload their bags. "No, the rent is a lot cheaper here than it is in the States. Come on, let's take all this inside."

There was more "holy shit" and "no, really, this place is freaking huge" as we filed inside. I couldn't blame them—I'd had a similar reaction when the realtor showed it to me. Sometimes I'd thought it was too big. I was the only one here, after all.

But now that my kids had arrived, it seemed just right.

There was plenty of space for them to stay here rather than in a hotel, and we'd all have enough breathing room for four adults in the same house over ten days.

Quinn and Savannah took the guest room downstairs while Landon took the spare bedroom down the hall from mine.

While they settled, I sent their mother a message.

> Kids made it safely. They're all settling in.

Both boys were pretty good about letting me or her know when they'd arrived somewhere, but I knew she'd be worried with them traveling internationally. She was a nervous traveler herself, and she'd almost asked for a Xanax prescription when Quinn and Savannah went to Europe after they graduated high school. So it seemed only right to make sure she knew they were safely here with me.

Landon wanted to take a shower and then FaceTime with his girlfriend back home. Savannah—who couldn't sleep on planes—wanted to grab a nap.

I was in the living room, texting with Alex, when Quinn came upstairs. He'd changed into a pair of shorts and a T-shirt with the name of his university across the front, and he looked pretty well-rested. Knowing him, he'd slept the entire flight to Madrid and the shorter one to Jerez.

I quickly texted Alex.

> Going to hang with the kids. FaceTime later?

> Any time. Have fun with them!

I put my phone aside and got up off the couch. I showed my older son around the upper floor of the house, and then we went outside to enjoy the afternoon beside the pool with a couple of cold beers. The scorching heat of August had relented, and though September was still seriously hot, it felt less like the surface of the sun. Quinn and I took chairs in the cabana, keeping our too-white-for-this-climate skin in the shade.

"So, do you like it here?" Quinn asked.

"The house?" I asked. "Or Spain?"

"The house is fire. I know you like that. But what about Spain? The base?"

"The base..." I waved a hand and made an annoyed sound, which got a laugh out of him; he knew about the politics and bullshit at every command. "Spain is interesting, though. There's been more culture shock than I expected."

"Really?"

I nodded and paused for a pull from my beer bottle. "The language barrier has been tough. Very few people speak English here."

"They don't?"

"Nope." I gestured at my phone. "I have to use WhatsApp and a translator app to talk to my landlord because my Spanish is trash."

"Wow." Quinn laughed. "My landlord speaks perfect English, and communicating with her is a nightmare sometimes. I can't imagine not speaking the same language."

I half-shrugged. "It's tough, but I'm trying to learn as much as I can. It's not his fault I don't speak his language, you know? And he's a good guy. Hell, when I came in to sign the lease, he had his whole family there, offered me wine and food—the works. It's a different world."

"No kidding." Quinn took a drink. "Seems like a nice place, though. The house and what I've seen of Spain."

"It is. I like it here." I put my beer on the table between us. "It's tough being this far from you and your brother, though. Not gonna lie."

"It's hard," he acknowledged. "But it's better with you here than when you were deployed."

I studied him. "Yeah?"

"Well, yeah." He met my gaze. "Mom always told us you were working in a hospital on a base, not out on the front lines, but when you're a kid and your dad is in a warzone... especially after you got hurt..." He trailed off, and I thought he masked a subtle shudder.

Guilt twisted in my chest. I'd never realized Aimee had told them that, and I was suddenly grateful for it. I revisited the truth every night when I tried to sleep. Knowing my boys hadn't known where I'd been and what I'd been doing? That they hadn't thought I was in danger until after the fact? Fuck, yeah, I could live with that. In fact, I felt guilty now for getting hurt; I could've kept them sheltered from that reality. No wonder they'd been so shell-shocked when they'd come to see me at the hospital in Germany. Hell... maybe it hadn't been such a good idea to keep them in the dark. They hadn't worried, but they'd been blindsided, and —was there *any* right way to handle something like that with kids?

"I'm sorry," I finally told him. "I know it stressed you kids out. Your mom too."

"I know. It was your job, though. We got it. But now you're someplace where nothing's really going on, you know? It sucks that you're so far away, but you're just... here. Working at a hospital in a place where nothing's happening."

I nodded. "I am. It's probably one of the most boring duty assignments I've had in my career."

"That's a good thing, right?"

"Ooh, yeah."

He turned his gaze toward the pool and sipped his beer. "Where do you think you'll go after this?"

"Don't know yet. My CO says I can probably extend at the end of my assignment. Or I might go back stateside. Just depends on how things are going when that time comes, I guess."

He was nodding as I spoke. "Are you going to be able to come back? Like for our graduations?"

"Absolutely. I already told my CO I'm taking leave when you and Savannah graduate."

That made him smile. Then he turned a shy look on me. "What about when we get married?"

I smiled too. "Well, you'll have to tell me when that is." Inclining my head, I asked, "Any thoughts on that?"

"Not yet." He absently swirled his beer as he gazed toward the other end of the house where his future wife was napping, a contented smile on his face. "But it probably won't be too much longer."

"Yeah? You thinking of proposing soon?"

"Thinking about it. Maybe her birthday. Maybe Christmas. I was going to wait until after we graduate, but..." He shrugged, still smiling. "I don't know if I want to wait that long."

"Well, if it feels like the right time, then it probably is."

"I know." He turned that smile on me. "Don't be surprised if I forget about the time zones and call you in the middle of the night to tell you she said yes."

I laughed. "I think I can cope with a middle-of-the-night call for something like that."

I could, and right now, I was glad I'd managed to maintain this closeness with my sons despite the long separations and the demands of my career. I was glad they were here now, and that they wanted me to be there for their big events. There'd been times I'd worried they'd resent me too much, but I must've done something right to make up for the places I'd fallen short.

I could live with that.

And today I was quietly grateful to my ex-wife in ways I'd never known I needed to be. I'd had no idea that she'd reassured our sons that I'd *mostly* spent the wars someplace safe and quiet. Whether it was ultimately the best thing to do, I'd never know, but I was glad the boys had only been aware of the danger after I'd been evacuated from the warzone. They'd been shaken up, seeing me stitched and bandaged, but I'd come home after my convalescence and never went back downrange.

Out of twenty-four months, they'd only had to grapple with the dangerous reality for three, and it was all after the fact. Maybe it was for the better, maybe it wasn't, but it eased my conscience more than I'd expected, so I'd take it.

Thank you, Aimee, for sparing our boys the truth.

"I still can't believe Africa is practically in your backyard," Landon said as we waited to board the ferry in Tarifa. "That's just... that's *wild*."

"Is this your first time going?" Savannah asked. "I mean, with as close as you are..."

I nodded. "I wanted to go a few times over the summer, but..." *I couldn't risk going with Alex.* "The heat in Spain was enough—I was afraid I'd melt in Morocco."

"It's still going to be in the eighties this week." Savannah cocked a brow. "That's cooler?"

"Believe it or not? Yes. August is *brutal*."

She made a face.

I glanced up at the screen, which showed our ferry as still leaving on time, but not boarding yet. There wasn't much to do in the terminal, so the kids and I mostly amused ourselves on our phones. Quinn was updating himself on some sports scores while Landon and Savannah leaned over her phone, perusing TripAdvisor for things to do in Tangier.

I, of course, had plenty to keep me occupied on my screen.

> You leaving for Tangier today?
>
> > Yep. At the terminal right now. Thanks for the rec for a tour guide!
>
> Any time. He's really good—he'll show you every inch of the city.
>
> > Would it be cheesy to make a joke about showing you every inch when I get back?
>
> (eyeroll emoji) OMG seriously?
>
> > (grinning emoji)
>
> LOL Have a good time in Morocco.
>
> > Will do.

Still chuckling, I turned my phone over on the table, and when I looked up, I was met with three very curious faces. Glancing between them, I asked, "What?"

They exchanged looks I couldn't read.

I shifted in my chair and asked again, "What?"

It was Quinn who finally spoke. "Okay. I gotta ask." He inclined his head. "Are you dating someone?"

I straightened. "Am I—*what?*"

"Don't play stupid, Dad." Landon rolled his eyes. "You always knew when me or Quinn had a girlfriend because we kept grinning like dorks at our phones." He gestured at my phone. "So... who's texting you and making you grin like a dork?"

The heat in my face had to be a dead giveaway.

Savannah smothered a giggle. "I think you're busted, Connor."

I shot her a playful glare, which earned me an innocent look.

"Come on." Quinn knocked his knuckle against the table between us. "Fess up."

I considered it. There was a part of me that wanted to *explode* with the revelation that, yes, I *was* seeing someone. I was so stupid for Alex that I wanted to change my relationship status on social media, tell my mom, and gush to my kids about this sweet, funny man I'd been seeing.

But I also held back. How would they feel about me moving on from their mom? And though they'd known I was bi for a long time, would it be weird for them to realize I was seeing a man? It was one thing to know in abstract terms that it was a possibility—actually seeing Dad's boyfriend in the flesh might be strange.

Can I call him a boyfriend? And even if I could, it isn't like I can tell anyone about us, so—

"Dad?" Quinn tilted his head, eyeing me uncertainly. "You good?"

"Yeah, yeah, I'm good." I looked from one of them to the next, and finally decided that honesty was the best approach. Exhaling, I rested my forearms on the table and met each of my sons' gazes. "Okay. Yes, I'm seeing someone.

But... there are some circumstances that make it a little... complicated."

All three kids stared at me with wide eyes.

"They're not married, are they?" Landon asked.

"No! Definitely not."

"Good," Quinn said solemnly. "Can't that get you in trouble with the Navy? Like for adultery for something?"

"It can, yes." I drummed my fingers on the table. "And... I can get in trouble for this, too." My stomach somersaulted at the three of them watched me expectantly, probably playing God knew how many worst-case scenarios in their minds. I took a deep breath, then admitted, "He's enlisted."

Both boys seemed to absorb that, and then they took on puzzled expressions that I thought screamed, *"That's it?"*

Savannah cocked her head. "Wait, what does that mean?" She waved a hand. "I mean, I know officers and enlisted are different... somehow. I guess. But I didn't realize you could get in trouble for that."

"You can. And it's the kind of trouble that can end a career." I shot my sons pointed looks. "Which means it does not leave this table. Got it?"

"Got it," they both said.

Savannah nodded too. "Why are they so weird about it? Officers and enlisted, I mean?"

"In theory," I said, "because it can compromise the chain of command. The lowest ranking officer outranks the highest-ranking enlisted service member, so it can cause issues." I rolled my eyes. "The stupid thing is that I can date another officer of a different rank as long as we're not in each other's direct chain of command. And this guy—he isn't in my direct chain of command. We have the same commanding officer, but he doesn't answer to me and neither do his superiors."

Landon furrowed his brow. "So it's like you're the manager of the shipping department, and he answers to the manager of customer service."

I chuckled. "Kind of, yeah?"

Savannah wrinkled her nose. "That sounds kind of stupid."

"It does. But 'it doesn't make sense' unfortunately doesn't hold up in a court-martial."

"Wow," she said.

"Do the military's rules ever make sense?" Quinn asked.

"Some do, some don't." I shrugged. "But they're not up for discussion, so I have to live with them."

Quinn and Savannah made sour faces. I didn't blame them.

"Sooo..." Landon studied me. "Do we get to meet him?"

I cocked a brow. "It doesn't bother you that I'm dating a guy?"

"Pfft. No." Quinn waved a hand. "Don't change the subject. Can we meet him or not?"

Yeah, I should've known it wouldn't be a big deal. My bisexuality wasn't news to them. He was probably right that I was just changing the subject.

Because the thought of introducing my kids to Alex made me nervous... but it also gave me a thrill I couldn't quite explain.

I chewed the inside of my cheek. "Uh. I mean, when I say we have to keep it on the downlow—"

"Dad." Quinn rolled his eyes like he had so many times as a teenager. "Think about it—who are we gonna tell?"

"Okay, it's not like you're going to go tell my command," I said. "But this is the kind of thing that can get back to people. If it slips out on social media, or if someone mentions it to someone who knew one of us at a previous command—it can get messy. Really, really messy."

All three of them nodded solemnly.

"We won't say anything," Landon said. "Not even to Mom."

"Definitely not," Quinn confirmed.

Savannah nodded again.

"All right. I appreciate that." I pushed out a breath. "To answer your question, yes, I met him a couple of months ago. We're not serious or anything, but..." I half-shrugged as renewed heat rose in my face, and I couldn't help smiling.

"Do we get a name?" Landon pressed. "A picture?"

Quinn and Savannah leaned in, their faces echoing his question.

"I..." I chewed the inside of my cheek. "Well, his name is Alex." I picked up my phone and gestured with it as if to indicate how useless it was. "I don't have any photos of him, though."

"None?" Savannah blinked. "Really?"

I swallowed. "We're both a little paranoid about getting caught. So we haven't..."

"Damn," Landon said. "That sounds stressful. Being so secretive that you can't even have a picture on your phone."

"It is," I admitted.

"Can we meet him, then?" Quinn asked. "As long as we don't take pictures or say anything about it?"

"I'll..." I rocked my head back and forth. Then I tapped my knuckle on the table. "I'll talk to him. But don't take it personally if he isn't down to meet. We're... just trying to be cautious."

"Yeah, that's cool," Landon said.

Quinn nodded. "I get it. Let us know what he says, though."

"I will."

And what did it say that I hoped Alex said yes?

Tangier was, as I'd expected and Alex had said, amazing. Our guide took us *everywhere*. We visited Cape Spartel, a beautiful lighthouse perched on the westernmost point of the African continent. There was the Hercules Caves, which were supposedly where the god by the same name lived at one point. The mythology was cool, but I was more fascinated with the centuries-old scars in the limestone from the Romans carving out millstones.

There was a small park where we were given the opportunity to ride camels, which was more fun than I expected. We had to get on them while they were lying down, and Quinn nearly fell off while his camel was getting to its feet. Landon howled with laughter at his brother's near disaster, only to go tumbling off while his own camel was lying down at the end of the ride.

"That's what you get, asshole," Quinn said as Landon dusted himself off.

Landon just rolled his eyes and gave his brother the finger.

Savannah and I both laughed. There was a time when Aimee or I would've scolded them for the language, but they were adults now, and the bickering was good-natured.

I had a small pang of sadness then, remembering the trips we'd taken as a family. The boys and I could still do things together now that they were adults, but it would never include their mother going forward.

Maybe it'll include someone else someday.

Huh. That was a thought. Another partner joining the

family. Savannah was part of the family now, and she'd become a fixture in all our lives. Who was to say I wouldn't find a partner who'd do the same?

What if that partner is Alex?

That thought very nearly made me stumble as I followed my kids and the tour guide back to the van to head to our next stop.

No. That wasn't who Alex and I were.

But...

Why was it so easy to imagine him bantering with my sons and future daughter-in-law? Why was it so easy to imagine him here with us? Or riding a train with us to some destination in Spain? Or hanging out in my pool while I cooked for everyone?

Why did that make so much sense?

But we can't do that.

Not until Alex retired. Which was less than a year and a half away. I'd knuckled through medical school, combat and shipboard deployments, and the three-year-long grind of a separation before Aimee and I were finally divorced. They'd always seemed impossibly long in the beginning, but once they were over, they were *over*.

The last year and a half of Alex's career would be a piece of cake.

Was it too much to hope he'd still want this after he retired?

After we'd visited the lighthouse, the caves, and a few other stops outside the city, our guide drove us back into town. He took us by the summer palace of the Moroccan king and a huge one owned by the Saudi king, as well as several incredible mosques. While he drove us toward the medina to explore the town, I showed my kids some of the photos I'd taken at the Mezquita in Córdoba.

"Do you think we'll have time to check that out?" Landon asked. "Because I want to see that!"

"Probably." I thumbed through some photos. "We could make a day trip out of it. It's only a couple of hours by train, and it doesn't take that long to explore the city or the Mezquita." I looked at each of the boys and Savannah in turn. "I got us tickets for the Alhambra already, and that'll be an overnight trip since they're for the morning. But nothing else is set in stone."

Quinn shrugged. "We can figure out an itinerary when we get back to your place. I really want to see it, though. And the Alhambra."

I nodded, pocketing my phone. "Okay, we'll figure it out. We should have time to do both."

Everyone was in agreement on that, and we shifted our attention back to enjoying Tangier.

Our guide parked just outside the medina, and we continued on foot. He took us through a bustling farmers market and the enormous fish market. We toured an Anglican church, and then a beautiful synagogue. The mosques weren't open to visitors, but they were still cool as hell from the outside.

We wandered shops and stalls in both the Muslim and Jewish sectors, and our guide helped us haggle with shopkeepers. Savannah bought a stunning red-and-gold dress, Quinn found a hardwood carving of a camel, and they picked up a beautiful decorative plate for their apartment. Landon got a straw hat with brightly colored yarn balls around the brim; our guide said it was a traditional hat usually worn by Berber women, but Landon wanted to put it up on his wall. Savannah offered to wear it for the day so he didn't have to carry it, and the shopkeeper clapped her hands and said—according to our guide's translation—that it looked lovely on her.

At one shop, Quinn mentioned to Landon that they should bring a gift back for their mom. "We'll definitely get her something from Spain, but I think she'd really like something from here, too."

"Good idea." Landon scanned the shop's shelves. "What do you think she'd like?"

Quinn pursed his lips. Then he turned to me. "Dad, what do you think?"

It was a little bittersweet, helping the boys pick out something for her. Not in a way that made me long to go back to being married to her, but in a way that made me miss things like this—helping them find a Christmas or birthday present for her, or helping them make breakfast on Mother's Day. They worshipped the ground she walked on, as they should, and I was glad they adored and respected her. That they were always so earnest about finding her a gift she'd really like instead of some tchotchke that would end up in a drawer somewhere.

It made me miss doing things like this with them, which in turn made me miss the everyday things—going to the commissary with them, or having dinner at home, or watching a movie as a family. I'd missed a lot of their lives, and nothing drove that home like only getting to see them when they came to visit me for ten short days. When would I see them again after this? It was hard to say. Quinn and Savannah's graduation, definitely; I wasn't missing that for the world. After that? No idea.

I understood more profoundly than ever why a lot of my colleagues lamented getting toward the end of their careers, being proud of all they'd accomplished, but then realizing to their horror how much they'd missed. No military career advanced without taking a toll at home.

Though if I was honest, the military had probably extended the life of my marriage, for better or worse. We'd done our level best to work together and get through everything the Navy threw at us, and we hadn't had time to focus on all the reasons we were probably doomed from the start. At the end of the day, Aimee and I had gone from a pair of scared, clueless kids leaning on each other to two adults who weren't at all compatible. That had been a tough pill to swallow, but—

"What about this?" Landon's voice pulled me out of my melancholy thoughts and back into the present. He held up a small wooden box with an intricate design inlaid on the lid.

"She might like that," Quinn said. "Can I see it?" Landon gave it to him, and Quinn inspected the inside and the hinges while Savannah looked over his shoulder. They looked at each other and exchanged nods. Then he offered it to me. "What do you think?"

I took it. It was really nice and didn't feel the least bit flimsy. The hinges were strong, and everywhere the wood had been joined felt even and solid. The inlays were smooth as silk—no rough or uneven edges anywhere. Handing it to Landon, I said, "I think she'd love that."

Our guide interjected, "The next shop has lovely Berber and Persian rugs."

The boys glanced at each other, then at him. Grimacing, Quinn said, "We don't have a ton of money."

The guide waved that away. "We'll find your mother a lovely rug. Come, come."

We all exchanged looks, then shrugged. The guide had

been great about helping us haggle prices down until he felt they were reasonable, and Alex had assured me the guy wouldn't let anyone screw us over.

"If he says something is worth the price," he'd told me the other night, "you can take it to the bank." Then he'd shown me a photo of the Persian prayer rug he'd bought on one of his last trips. It was silk and handmade, and he'd bought it for a song.

So... why the hell not?

First things first, the boys needed to pay for the box they were also buying for Aimee. The shopkeeper only spoke Berber, so as he had all day, our guide interpreted for us, and we were able to settle on a price. I counted out a hundred dirham, paid him, and he lovingly wrapped the box in paper before handing it to me in a plastic bag.

"How much was that?" Landon asked under his breath. "Looked like it was like a hundred bucks!"

"It was a hundred dirham," I said. "I think it's about... ten dollars?" I looked to our guide for confirmation.

"About nine euro," he said.

"Okay, so about ten dollars."

"Cool," Quinn said. "I'll Venmo it to you when we've got WiFi again."

I waved his concern away. "Come on. Let's go look at rugs."

With our purchases in hand, we continued to the next shop. A pair of shopkeepers greeted us and led us upstairs, and they offered us mint tea and cookies while they brought out some rugs.

Alex had told me the mint tea was exceptional, and he wasn't wrong; it didn't have that "herby" taste that a lot of teas did. It just tasted like mint. A little sweet, and hotter than I'd usually drink in such a sweltering place, but it tasted amazing, especially with the various cookies.

The rugs were mind-blowing. Savannah immediately fell in love with a Berber prayer rug. It was coarse wool, dyed a bright blue with intricate and colorful patterns, and the price—especially after some haggling and then converting from dirham to euro—was surprisingly low.

"Take my money," she told them as she handed over her card.

While one of the shopkeepers rolled up and bundled her rug, the others continued showing us more. The instant they pulled out a stunning green silk Persian prayer rug, I knew the boys were sold. It was their mother's favorite color, right down to the specific shade of rich emerald dominating the elaborate pattern, which was a mix of gold, white, black, and a couple other shades of green.

After some haggling, our guide pushed the shopkeepers down to a price that he thought was reasonable. When they converted the euro into dollars, though, both boys balked.

"Mom will like it a lot," Quinn said to his brother. "But I'll be almost tapped out on spending money for this trip."

"Me too." Landon frowned. "I mean, I don't know how much I plan to actually buy, but—"

"Guys." I held out my card. "Don't sweat it."

They both blinked. "You're—really?"

"When are you going to have another opportunity to buy your mom a rug like that?" I gestured at the shopkeeper and handed over my card.

They stared at me.

"Are you sure, though?" Quinn asked. "You and Mom are..."

"Yes, we're divorced. But you two are in college and I've

got a paycheck." I smiled. "I don't want you to be pinching pennies for the rest of your trip, okay?"

They still seemed uneasy, but slowly, they relaxed.

The shopkeeper, still holding my card, had hesitated, watching the interplay. I didn't think he understood English, but he had to have picked up on my sons' uncertainty. I gave him a smile and a nod, gesturing at the rug at our feet.

He responded with a big smile, then put my card into the reader he was holding.

Quinn nudged my elbow. "Thanks. We could've made it work, but it'll make the rest of the trip less stressful."

"Don't worry about it." I grinned. "Just means you boys are doing the dishes for the rest of the time you're here."

They both groaned, and Savannah cackled.

"Good luck with that, Connor," she said to me. "I can't get Quinn to—"

"Oh, that is such a lie." He rolled his eyes. "The only dishes I don't do are the glasses you leave all over the apartment."

I chuckled. "I'll believe it when I see it, kid." I clapped his shoulder. "How many times did I have to ask you to load the dishwasher when you were a teenager?"

He just huffed and shook his head.

Landon snickered, and I shot him a look.

"Don't you start," I said. "Or did you finally learn to *empty* the dishwasher without being asked?"

He took on the same playfully petulant expression his brother had.

"That's what I thought."

We all shared a laugh over it, and a moment later, the shopkeepers handed us our rugs, which they'd bundled into tiny packages wrapped in plastic.

After that, our guide announced that we were heading to lunch. He led us out of the shop and up the street, then into a second-floor restaurant with couches and leather stools instead of chairs. We were treated to an amazing meal of b'stilla, which were the puff pastries Alex had told me about that were stuffed with spiced chicken and topped with cinnamon and sugar.

"These should not be this good," Savannah said as she started on her second one. "How is cinnamon and sugar on a chicken dish this awesome?"

"Think we can make them at home?" Quinn peered at his as if he were trying to mentally reverse engineer it.

"There's probably recipes online," she said. "I took a picture of the menu, so we can look it up when we're back online."

Quinn nodded and took another bite.

I'd have to figure out how to make these, too. I was no wizard in the kitchen, but as good as these were, I'd find a way.

"Okay," Landon said, dusting some powdered sugar off his lip, "I am officially in love with Moroccan food."

"Same," we all said, because hell yeah.

They drank more of the mint tea during lunch, and so did I. The boys were forever turning up their noses at the teas that Aimee and Savannah drank, and I'd never been much of a fan either, but this stuff was seriously good.

So was being here with them. Trying new food. Exploring a new country. Just being together as a family.

Still, it felt like someone was missing.

The logical answer was that Aimee was missing. Even though we were divorced, this was our family. It still caught me off-guard sometimes to realize she wasn't there.

Except... her absence wasn't the one that kept prodding at me.

Gazing at my sons and Savannah and our beautiful surroundings, I couldn't help thinking...

Alex should be part of this.

It was too soon for that. We had some professional obstacles we'd need to clear first. Once Alex was retired and we could openly date, then we'd see what happened.

But deep down, I was sure that Alex belonged in this family.

CHAPTER 32

ALEX

"How was Morocco?" I lounged in my bed, phone in hand as I FaceTimed with Connor. "Did your kids like it?"

"We all had a blast. You were right about that guide. He was awesome!"

"He's great. I think I tipped him like a hundred euro last time."

"Okay, so I don't feel so ridiculous for tipping him that much."

"He's worth every penny."

We talked for a while about everything he and his kids had done in Tangier. I'd been to most of the same places, including the shop where they'd bought rugs. It was fun, listening to him talk excitedly about places I'd also been.

But it was also really, really hard not to blurt out, *"We should go there together sometime."*

No. We shouldn't. For a lot of very non-negotiable reasons.

I knew that, but the desire to say fuck it and go anyway

was strong. Probably because in the days since his kids had been here, I'd missed him more than I wanted to think about and definitely more than I wanted to admit out loud.

Unaware of me spinning out over a ridiculous fantasy of him wanting to go to Morocco with me, Connor said, "We also did Gibraltar after we came back. That was a fun trip."

"Oh, yeah? Did you do one of the Rock tours?"

"Of course. Especially once Savannah heard about the monkeys. There was no way she was missing that."

I chuckled. "That's the best part. Especially if you go on a day when there's not a lot of people, so the monkeys just sort of chill. I was there once when it was crowded as hell, and the monkeys were running around and stealing shit. I think some of them were scared, too."

Connor grimaced. "Yeah, I think we got lucky. Our guide said we picked a day when there were no cruise ships in port, so everything was pretty deserted." He laughed. "The guy told Savannah to stand over by one of the railings where there was a monkey so Quinn could take a picture of her. He said, 'Don't worry, it won't jump on you!'"

"Let me guess—it jumped on her."

"Yep. Fortunately, she's pretty chill with animals. It startled her, and it knocked her a little off-balance because it must've weighed like thirty pounds, but she just stood there quietly while it played with her hair."

"That must've made for some great photos. She wasn't scared, was she?"

He shrugged. "A little nervous, but I think that's expected when a wild animal decides to hitch a ride on you. Quinn got scared, though. He kind of froze up, but fortunately, my younger son took a video and I got some pictures."

"Eh, I can't blame him." I shifted a little on the bed, trying to get comfortable. "Good on her for being calm and him being quiet even though it scared him. One of smaller ones jumped on a lady last time I was there, and she started shrieking and flailing." I rolled my eyes. "Like, do you *want* to get bitten? Because that's how you get bitten."

"I know, right?" He shook his head. "Savannah looked at me at one point and very, very quietly asked, 'You can fix me up if it bites me, right?'"

I snorted. "Did she think it would?"

"No, but she knew it would freak Quinn out. Which it did." Connor laughed again. "Those two are forever trolling each other, so it didn't surprise me."

"What did he think of it?"

"Well, once the monkey lost interest and went somewhere else, he was like, 'Really, Savannah? Really?' And she just..." He made an innocent face and batted his eyelashes.

I burst out laughing. "Oh God. Did it work on him?"

"Absolutely not, because he knows her." He smiled. "Anyway, that was the closest thing to a mishap we had. Well, aside from Landon falling off a camel."

My jaw dropped. "He actually fell off?"

"Yeah, while it was lying down at the end of the ride. He didn't have a scratch on him, and he deserved it for trolling his brother for almost falling off while the camel got up."

"Wow." I laughed again. "Never a dull moment with all of you, is there?"

With a fond smile, he said, "Never."

He told me a few more stories about their adventure to Morocco and Gibraltar. "Today, we kind of took it easy and stayed near home. We went to the beach in Sanlúcar this morning before it got too hot, but that's about it." With another laugh, he added, "We had lunch at Burger King today just because the boys wanted to say they've ordered beer at BK."

"Ha! Did they like it?"

"Oh, yeah. Savannah wanted to turn up her nose because she's not a fan of fast food, but even she enjoyed it. We're having dinner at a local café tonight that she picked out, so she'll be happy."

"Good idea. Which one?"

"I can't remember the name, but it's an Italian place somewhere in Sanlúcar. If it's good, I'll let you know." He smiled. "Maybe we can use them for takeout."

"Perfect."

His smile held, but then it faltered, and he dropped his gaze for a moment. When he shifted a bit, he seemed nervous, and I suddenly *was* nervous.

Before I could ask what was up, he said, "So, um..." He cleared his throat. "I told my kids about you."

My stomach flipped. "You... You did?"

"Yeah." He laughed, and I thought he blushed. "I did tell them to keep it quiet. They know how this shit works with the military, so... Anyway, they won't out us."

"That's good. What do they think about it? Did they even know you were into men?"

"They've known I'm bi for a long time, so they weren't surprised. But they, um... They want to meet you."

My spine straightened. "Come again?"

He fidgeted a little on the other end. "They're curious about you, and I don't even have any pictures of us, you know?" He laughed nervously. "So if you're game..."

"Oh." I had no idea what to say. "But we're... they're... I mean, what do they know about us?"

"I obviously didn't tell them we're just hooking up," he

said. "But they caught on that I was seeing someone, and after I swore them to secrecy, I said I'd met you. I didn't tell them much except that we'd been seeing each other and traveling a bit together."

"And they'll keep it on the downlow?"

"Absolutely," he said with a sharp nod. "They know how the military is."

I chewed the inside of my cheek. "And they... They really want to meet me?" That was a lot easier than the question I couldn't quite ask out loud: *Do you really want me to meet your kids?*

"They haven't shut up about it," he said with a laugh. "They've only ever known me with their mom, so they're really curious about me seeing someone else."

"Oh."

But how serious do they think we are? And how serious do you *think we are?*

My heart pounded.

How serious do I want us to be?

I was too much of a coward to ask any of those questions. I was also intrigued by the idea of meeting Connor's sons, and what could I say? I fucking missed him. I'd made peace with not seeing him while he was on leave, but this was my chance to do exactly that. I didn't even care that we wouldn't be having sex. I just wanted to see him.

So, yeah, Alex—how serious do I *want this to be?*

"Sounds great," I said despite my nerves and my racing mind. "I can come by after work tomorrow if you're home."

"We're just doing Cádiz tomorrow morning, so we'll be here by the time you're off work." Connor's sweet, hopeful smile was the best thing in the world. "See you then?"

"Yeah." I returned the smile. "See you then."

My heart thundered as I walked up to Connor's front porch. I was nervous about meeting his sons—I'd been with a few men who had kids, but there'd never been any reason to introduce me to them.

I wasn't just nervous, though. I hadn't seen Connor all week, and I was aching to be in his presence again. Even if we couldn't do anything, I missed him.

Don't get ahead of yourself, Alex. He's just a hookup.

As I cleared the top step, the front door opened.

Oh. Fuck me.

"Just a hookup" never made my pulse kick up like this.

Hopefully I kept that out of my expression as I crossed the porch, and somehow I even kept my feet under me.

I'd decided on the way over to follow his lead on how physical we'd be. He didn't waste any time—as soon as I was close enough, his hands were on my waist as he said, "Hey, you," just before his lips met mine.

It was a quick kiss. A light one. Nothing deep or spicy.

But oh, hell, it was enough to make my head spin and make me wish this wasn't going to be a platonic visit.

When he broke away, he smiled. "Thanks for coming. My sons are looking forward to meeting you, and..." The smile turned to a grin. "What can I say? I like having you here."

Warmth rushed through me. "Even when I won't be—"

He kissed me softly. "Yes. Even then." Fingers laced in mine, he nodded toward the other end of the house. "Come on. Everyone's out by the pool."

"Of course they are," I said as I followed him inside, then out into the backyard.

And oh, wow—there was no mistaking that these two

young men were Connor's sons. One was almost exactly the same height as his father, though he had a lankier build. The other was maybe two inches taller, and I suspected he liked the gym as much as Connor did. The first one's hair tickled his collar, and taller one's was almost as short as mine, but it was the same wavy dark hair as Connor.

"Hey guys." Connor gestured at me. "This is Alex. These are my sons, Quinn and Landon, and Quinn's girlfriend, Savannah."

I shook hands with all three of them. Up close, the resemblance was even more striking, especially with Quinn, the shorter one, who had his dad's dark eyes. Landon's were more hazel; probably from his mom.

As we sat down in the shade of the cabana, I said, "It's nice to meet everyone. Your dad's talked a lot about you."

All three of them shot Connor suspicious looks.

He rolled his eyes. "Oh for God's sake. You know it was all good stuff."

"Bullshit." Landon gestured at his brother. "With as much dirt as you have on him, we know you're—"

"Dude, I will push you into the pool again," Quinn groused. "Do not test me." They exchanged challenging looks, which had Connor and Savannah laughing and shaking their heads.

She looked at me and shrugged. "Brothers. What can you do?"

"Oh, I know. I have a brother and a sister. Trust me—I get it."

"Yeah?" She smiled. "They must love having someone to come visit in Spain."

An uncomfortably melancholy feeling tried to sweep over me, but I kept it out of my expression. "They... don't really have the time or the money to come this far. Kids, jobs

—you know how it goes. So I just bring everyone souvenirs when I come home."

"Damn." Quinn sipped his beer. "I can't imagine missing out on coming over here."

"Good thing Dad's got guest rooms," Landon said, and he fist-bumped his brother.

Connor shot me a curious look, but whatever thought was behind his eyes, he didn't say it. I'd dodged the subject of my family before, but something told me I wouldn't be able to next time we were one-on-one. For now, the conversation moved in a different direction, and I relaxed into my chair. I was in a good mood, happy to be with Connor and his family. We didn't need to get into the complicated stuff with mine.

Fortunately, my comments were forgotten in short order, at least for now, and I listened intently as they all told me about their adventures in Tangier, Gibraltar, and Cádiz. They were still trying to decide what to do with some of their remaining days in Spain, and I offered my suggestions.

"Arcos de la Frontera, Ronda, and Setenil de las Bodegas are all really cool," I said, "but I wouldn't pick those over something like Granada or Córdoba." I paused. "If you're staying in town, there's a little place out past Jerez. It's not super exciting, but it's kind of cool to see—it's an old abandoned sugar factory that's been taken over by storks."

Savannah perked up. "Storks? Really?"

I nodded. "They're everywhere here, but there's a lot at that old factory for some reason. They talk to each other, too, which is interesting to hear, and it's a cool spot to get some pictures."

Quinn smiled fondly. "Well, we have an animal lover with us, so we might have to go."

"Pfft." She elbowed him. "Like you didn't almost lose your mind when we saw those flamingoes today."

"That was Landon!" he insisted.

"Bullshit!" Landon said. "I was just trying to see because I thought you were full of shit."

Connor laughed and rolled his eyes. "Don't let them fool you—they're all animal lovers."

"Ooh, well in that case," I said, "there's a zoo down by Gibraltar you should check out."

All four sat straighter, and I told them about the small zoo populated by animals confiscated from smugglers and illegal collectors. "Most of them can't be released into the wild, and a lot of them are pretty tame, so the zookeepers will actually let you hold them and pet them."

"What?" Savannah sputtered. "No way. That's—you're making that up."

Quinn eyed me. "A zoo that lets you pet the animals?"

Even Connor looked skeptical, so I took out my phone and pulled up an album from the last time I'd visited. Both Savannah and Quinn almost melted when I showed them the baby ocelot batting at my camera strap. As soon as Landon saw me petting the lion cub, he declared, "Okay, I'm going. I will rent a car and take my own ass down there, but I am *going*."

Connor laughed. "I think we're all going, kid."

"You think?" I flipped to another photo and showed it to him. "Or you're definitely going?"

He looked at the screen, and my heart melted as I watched *his* melt. "They let you hold a fox?"

"Uh-huh." I glanced at the image, which was one my friend had taken of me with a tiny Fennec fox lying across my arms. "Softest thing I've ever touched, too."

"Okay. We're going." Connor took out his phone.

"What's the name of the place?" I rattled it off to him, and he pulled it up to check the address and hours.

"It's not a bad place to stop on your way to Granada," I said. "Just means taking the southern route instead of north, and it takes about the same amount of time."

"Perfect," Connor said. "We can go there tomorrow, then stay in Granada tomorrow night. Our Alhambra tickets are for the next day."

"Smart, getting them ahead of time." I groaned. "First time I went, we thought we could get same-day tickets." I rolled my eyes. "Which, yeah, you can—if you're in line at 0500."

"Aww, so you didn't get to see it?" Savannah asked. "That sucks."

"No, we did. We were just up at ass-thirty in the morning to get tickets. Now, I book everything ahead of time if I can." I paused. "If you're going to Barcelona and you want to see the Sagrada Familia, you need to get tickets... two weeks ago."

Connor waved his hand. "Nah. We're mostly sticking with Andalusia for now. Maybe next trip, we'll do Barcelona."

"Smart."

We kept on like that, comparing notes on places they wanted to visit and places I'd been. It was a lot of fun, and I enjoyed seeing them all excited about checking out Spain.

I just pretended not to notice that ache of longing in the middle of my chest. I made the boys promise to get photos of their dad with some of the animals at the zoo tomorrow, but I didn't tell them it was because I wished I could be there with him. I wanted to watch him turn to goo over lemurs and ocelots and whatever other animals the zookeepers let him hold. I wanted to see how he reacted if a snake decided to wrap itself around his camera lens like one had done when I'd visited a few months ago.

It wasn't just the zoo, either. Wherever they went, whatever they were doing, whether it was someplace I'd been to a million times or something I'd never seen before...

I wished I could be there with Connor and his kids.

All too soon, the sun was going down, which meant I needed to get my ass home and into bed. I said goodbye to the boys and Savannah, and while they hung out by the pool, Connor and I retreated inside. At the door, I turned to him.

"Thanks for having me over." I put my hands on his waist. "It was nice to see you. And meet your kids."

"I'm glad I got to see you." He drew me in close. "Ten days is a long time."

I wanted to mention that we were active duty, so we knew more than most that ten days was most certainly *not* a long time for much of anything. But then his lips were on mine, and...

And ten days was a fucking eternity.

Not just because I hadn't been laid, either; just being in the same space as him for a while had satisfied the hunger that had been growing since Córdoba. As much as I couldn't wait to tear off our clothes and make up for lost time in bed, I was perfectly satisfied after just seeing him. Just being here with him.

He broke the kiss. "You know, I realized when the kids asked about you—I don't have any pictures of you on my phone. Or pictures of us."

I tensed. "Do you... I mean, we're trying to be discreet, and..."

Connor shrugged. "No one sees my phone but me." His cheeks colored a little as he softly added, "I'd like one, if you're game."

My heart beat faster, and I tried not to think about why. Or why I was suddenly excited and maybe even a touch emotional that he wanted a photo of me—of us—on his phone. "Okay. Okay, yeah, we can..." I took out my cell. "Selfie, and I'll send it to you?"

His smile made my knees weak, and it was weird to realize how familiar that feeling was becoming.

I clumsily turned on the camera in selfie mode, and Connor put his arm around me as I held up the phone.

Click.

I took a second, just in case, and then sent it to him. When his phone pinged, his eyes lit up.

"Great," he said with a smile. "Now I have something to drool over at work."

I laughed. "Yeah. Me too."

Then he pulled me back in, and... God, I was never going to get tired of his kiss. And I still had to go *how* many days without it? Fuck me.

As the kiss lingered, the desire to stay here tonight and sleep beside Connor was so strong, it was almost a physical ache. I didn't care if we fooled around. I just... wanted him. I wanted to be close to him.

But I had to work tomorrow, and he needed to get back to his family. Reluctantly, I broke the kiss, and we locked eyes for a moment.

I am so stupid for you, Connor, and you don't even know.

Though from the way he was looking at me—assuming I

wasn't imagining my own intense longing mirrored in his eyes—maybe he did know.

Before I could stop myself, I asked, "Is it just me, or does this feel... different?"

He held my gaze, tilting his head. "What do you mean?"

My heart pounded, but to my surprise, the early jitters of a panic attack were nowhere in sight. I was nervous about this—nervous in ways I wasn't used to—but it wasn't hitting those landmines that could send me into a downward spiral.

I cleared my throat. "I mean, we're supposed to be screwing around on the sly. Traveling around, fucking each other senseless in hotel rooms." God, my heart was pounding so hard. "But now I'm meeting your kids. And..."

And missing you so much this week that I can't even put it into words.

Connor dropped his gaze and chewed his lip. For a long moment, he was unnervingly silent. Then, slowly, he nodded, looking at me through his lashes. "I don't think what we're doing is what we set out to do in the beginning."

An impossible mix of relief and apprehension swelled in my chest. We were on the same page, but... now what? Pull back because it was a mistake? Say "fuck it" and keep doing it?

I swallowed hard, my heart thumping even harder than it had when I'd arrived a few hours ago. "Is that... a good thing?"

"I think so?" Connor slid his hands around behind my neck and drew me in. "I won't lie—I have no idea what we're doing anymore." His lips grazed mine. "But I know I don't want to stop."

Then he kissed me full-on, and I couldn't help the soft moan as I sank into it. Wrapping my arms around him, I completely surrendered, wishing like hell I could stay here all night and sleep beside him, but also relieved and satisfied that I was touching and tasting him at all. It had only been a few days since we'd seen each other in person, and I'd missed him more than I had any right to.

No, I still didn't know what we were doing.

I just knew that I also didn't want to stop.

CHAPTER 33

CONNOR

After Alex left, I pressed the button to close the gate to the driveway. Then I stood there in the foyer, just collecting my thoughts as I stared at our selfie.

I loved having my kids here. Being away from them this long sucked, and every minute I got to spend with them was precious.

But still, I needed a moment to myself after that exchange with Alex.

This wasn't just casual anymore, was it? I didn't know how it had changed or when, only that I felt things for him that didn't jive with what we'd set out to be, and I'd felt that way for a while.

Turned out I wasn't the only one.

What was I supposed to do with that?

Well, I could think about it later. Right now, my sons were here, and I wasn't going to waste the very limited time I had with them.

I shook myself, gave the front door another glance as if there might be an afterimage of Alex, and then went back up the hall to join everyone outside.

As I came down the steps into the backyard, three faces watched me curiously. I furrowed my brow as I took my seat. "What?"

"You said you were seeing someone," Quinn said. "You didn't say you were, like, *seeing someone.*"

I picked up my drink. "What does that mean?"

"It means you guys don't seem"—Landon made air quotes—"'not serious.'"

I blinked. "We... We don't?"

"Uh, no?" He shrugged. "I thought you'd kind of just met someone, but you guys looked like you were... I don't know..."

"Really into each other," Quinn said.

"Really happy together," Savannah supplied.

At that, both boys nodded sharply.

I sat back, cradling my beer between my hands. "It's... I mean, we get along great and all, but like I said before—it's nothing serious." Why was the word *"yet"* dangling so precariously from the tip of my tongue?

All three of them watched me skeptically.

"What?" I put up my free hand. "What makes you think it's anything serious? I like him and all, but I did just meet the guy, you know. And we can't be out any time soon."

They all nodded in acknowledgement, but I could tell they weren't budging on this.

"It's just... the way you look at Alex." Quinn gestured toward the house. "You never looked at Mom that way."

My stomach somersaulted. "I didn't?"

"You didn't," Landon chimed in. "I've never seen you look at anyone like that."

I swallowed, glancing back and forth between my sons. "Does that bother you?"

They shook their heads.

"Nah," Landon said. "You and Mom never really seemed happy. Like even when things were good—I don't know."

Quinn nodded. "Yeah. Mom's different now too. And the way she is with her boyfriend—it's kind of like you and Alex. It's... not the way you guys ever were with each other."

It took me a moment to process all of that. Guilt weighed down on me—as perceptive as my sons had always been, it had never occurred to me that they'd noticed the unhappiness between me and Aimee. Maybe because I'd been so far in denial that I hadn't noticed it for a long time.

There was also an oddly empty place where I was sure I should've felt a pang of jealousy at the realization that my ex-wife had a boyfriend. Irrational, of course; she was my ex, and I was seeing someone too. On some level, I was just surprised at how *not* jealous I was to learn she had someone else.

I cleared my throat. "I didn't realize you guys had picked up on that. That things were..." I trailed off, not sure how to finish.

Landon shrugged. "I mean, you weren't having screaming matches or anything. It wasn't like all tension, all the time. You just... didn't seem like you were into each other, I guess?"

I nodded slowly. "We did care about each other, though. We still do. I'm glad she's moving on with someone." I paused. "Do you guys like her new boyfriend?"

"Eh." Landon rocked his head back and forth. "He's okay."

"He is." Quinn smirked. "I think Dad's got better taste in men."

I snorted and rolled my eyes. "I'm telling your mother you said that."

"No, you're not." Landon took out his phone and started typing. "*I'm* telling her."

"Dude, I swear to God," Quinn warned, "I will throw your phone in the pool."

"No, you won't." Landon kept typing. "I have our train tickets, remember?"

Quinn scowled. "You're a dick."

Landon flipped him off.

Savannah giggled, and I just rolled my eyes. Kids. What could you do?

"Just don't tell her any details about Alex, all right?" I said to Landon.

"Nah, I won't." My son pocketed his phone. "I just said that Quinn says you have better taste in men and left it at that."

I laughed, shaking my head, and brought up my beer for a drink.

There was a muffled ping, and Quinn swore. "Goddammit, Landon," he grumbled as he took out his phone.

I almost choked on my beer.

Savannah suddenly looked a little alarmed. "Wait, will your mom be upset? If she knows Connor's with a guy?"

"Nah." Quinn was already typing something out. "She knows Dad's bi."

His girlfriend turned to me for confirmation.

I nodded. "Trust me, it won't be news."

Savannah relaxed. "Okay. Just checking."

Quinn put his phone away without elaborating on what his mom had said or what he'd replied, and he took a drink from his own beer. "To be serious, Dad, I'm glad you and

Mom are meeting people. It's good to see both of you happy."

The absence of "again" at the end of that sentence needled at me. I wanted to ask how long they'd known Aimee and I were unhappy. I was too afraid to, though.

"For the record," I said, "I did have good times while your mom and I were married. It wasn't nonstop misery or anything like that." I paused. "I loved her, and I still do. We're just not compatible for the long haul."

My sons nodded.

"Yeah, we get that," Landon said. "Mom told me more or less the same thing. So... I'm just glad the divorce is over and you guys can live your own lives."

"Yep," Quinn said. "It's all good, Dad. It really is." He tilted his beer bottle toward the house. "How are you and Alex going to do this, anyway?"

"Do what?"

"I mean, if the Navy says you can't date—what happens if you want to get serious with him? Like move in together or something?"

"Oh. Uh." I stared into my drink for a moment. "There isn't much we can do right now. But Alex is retiring in a little over a year."

"Oh, that's not bad," Savannah said. "So just wait it out, and then see each other in public?"

I shrugged. "Basically."

I didn't remind them that we weren't serious. Or that when Alex retired, he'd be sent back stateside. I didn't mention that this was probably a short-term thing, or that I was cool with that because it was all I'd wanted with him from the start.

My silence was partly because no one needed to think about their parent seeing someone casually. No. Just no.

But the other part...

The other part was that all sounded like a lie.

After the way Alex had looked at me in the hallway, and what we'd both said about how we weren't what we'd been when we'd started out—calling us casual or suggesting we'd fizzle out when Alex retired didn't ring true.

My sons and future daughter-in-law could see the way he made me feel.

My heart did ridiculous flippy, fluttery things whenever I saw him, or even when his name appeared on my phone.

My whole world felt a million times better and brighter with Alex in it.

My own words echoed in my head: *"I don't think what we're doing is what we set out to do in the beginning."*

No, we're definitely not.

And my God, Alex—I can't wait to see where this thing with you goes.

CHAPTER 34

ALEX

"*Holy fuck.*" I dropped onto Connor's bed beside him, still vibrating all over from my orgasm.

He was trembling too, and he ran a shaking hand through his sweaty, disheveled hair. "I needed that."

"Me too." I caught my breath for a moment, then levered myself up. "Let me get rid of this. Be right back."

He murmured something in acknowledgment as he reached for the tissues beside the bed. I took care of the condom, and then we shared a shower, which turned out to be something I'd missed almost as much as the sex. His hands all over me. His lips against mine or skating up the side of my neck. Hot water sliding through the tiny sliver of space between our bodies. We were too far past thirty to be getting turned on again this quickly, but that was fine. I loved everything about this, and I didn't care that neither of us was in any danger of getting hard.

I pulled him in close and buried my face against his neck, ostensibly to kiss him in those places I knew he liked. That was part of it, but mostly I just needed to be close to him. I'd missed him, and I'd missed the heat of his body, and now I couldn't get enough.

I want you so much more than you realize, and not just when we're turned on.

That spooked me. It had since the first time it crossed my mind, and it still did even after we'd both admitted this was becoming more than casual. But I couldn't bring myself to pull away. Yes, this scared me, but not enough to make me put any space between us.

"We should get out," Connor murmured. "I think my butano tank is low."

I chuckled and drew back. "Always at the worst possible time, isn't it?"

"Always." He kissed me, then turned off the water.

Houses in this country heated water using butane—which was butano in Spanish—and the tanks had to be changed out whenever they were empty. Of course, they always ran out right in the middle of a blissfully hot shower, either on my own or with this sexy man.

"I'll swap out the tank before I make dinner," he said. "Then we'll have plenty of hot water for later."

I grinned. "Sounds like a deal."

For now, we dried off, left our towels in the bathroom, and retreated to the bed we'd thoroughly rumpled earlier. It was too hot to even pull a sheet up over us if we were touching each other, but that was fine by me; I'd take tangling up with Connor over pulling up the covers any day.

Just like in the shower, we were lazy and affectionate. Touching, kissing, holding on, but not winding each other up. Such a far cry from men I'd been with whose interest in me wilted along with their hard-ons after sex. Even after we'd stopped making out, he still stayed close, running his hand up down my arm as we lay in comfortable silence.

After a while, he spoke. "You said something the other night that I'm curious about."

"I did?" I racked my brain, trying to think what I could've said. "What was it?"

"About your family." He furrowed his brow. "You never talk about them. I don't even know how many siblings you have."

"Oh. I guess... I guess I haven't told you much about them."

He studied me curiously.

I cleared my throat. "I have a brother and a sister. They're three and six years older."

"Are you close to them?"

"Not really. My brother and I keep in touch off and on." I laughed almost soundlessly. "I don't count on him visiting me overseas any time soon. Not with six kids."

"Six?" Connor whistled. "Holy shit. I was overwhelmed with two."

"I know, right?" I chuckled. "But he had two with his first wife, and his current wife already had two, and then they decided to have two together. It's, um... crowded."

"I can imagine." He held my gaze. "And the rest of your family—your parents—they haven't been out here? The whole time you've been in Spain?"

I broke eye contact and swallowed. "No. They didn't come to Japan either. They can afford it—I know they can—but there was always a reason why they couldn't. Then with as excited as my mom was when I got the orders here, I thought for sure they'd visit, but..." I shook my head.

"Really?" When I met his gaze, I could see the confusion. The downright bewilderment. "You've been here for, what, two years?"

"Almost three," I whispered.

He stared at me in horror.

"They love me," I insisted. "I know they do. But even when I was in CONUS, they've... never exactly put a lot of effort into seeing me."

"Because you're so far away?"

I sighed. "My sister did an exchange program in college. Spent a year in London. My parents took my brother and me to see her, and we traveled around the UK a bit." I shrugged. "I don't know if they just aren't into long-distance traveling anymore, or..."

Or if seeing me just isn't high enough on their list.

I didn't say that out loud. It hurt enough to think it. Especially the part where they'd barely put in the effort for semi-regular FaceTime calls.

Clearing my throat, I shifted a little on the mattress. "I sometimes think they might put more effort in if I had a partner, and especially if I had kids."

Connor made a face. "They should want to come see *you.*"

I half-shrugged. What could I say?

"I mean," he went on, "that would be like me going to visit Quinn and Savannah, but blowing off Landon because —well, he has a girlfriend now, but when he didn't have one. Or not bothering to see Quinn and Savannah until they have kids. Quinn and Landon are still *my kids.*" He huffed sharply. "I can't imagine just... thinking it wasn't worth the effort to see them."

I swallowed. That made perfect sense after hearing him talk about his boys and especially after seeing him with them. It was impossible to picture Connor blowing off either of them, never mind because one didn't have a girlfriend or kids.

And holding up my family beside his... fuck. I loved my family, and I knew they loved me, but I didn't much like the unflattering light this conversation was shining on them.

Connor cuddled closer to me and kissed my shoulder. "I'm sorry your family hasn't prioritized you like they should."

My throat tightened, and I closed my eyes as I laced our fingers together. "They *do* love me. I know they do." Why did I sound like I was trying to convince myself, not him?

"I don't doubt they do," he said gently. "But it does sound like things are a bit... imbalanced."

"They are," I admitted. "And I've kind of tried to bring it up in the past, but I get shot down pretty quick."

Connor shifted, and when I opened his eyes, he'd propped him up on his elbow and was gazing down at me, clearly puzzled. "Why's that?"

I licked my lips. "My sister, mostly. Growing up, she always saw things as..." I thought about it. "Well, any time my brother or I asked for something, in her mind, it was always framed as us getting something she didn't, or something being taken away from her. It..." I laughed. "It's just the way she is, I guess. So like when I was home for Christmas and asked my parents if they might come visit me the following year, she started asking why I thought they shouldn't come see her and her kids, and I..." Sighing, I rolled my eyes. "It just wasn't worth fighting over, you know?"

"But they see your brother, don't they? Is it an issue when they see him?"

I shook my head. "He lives closer to them, so they see him pretty often. Plus he has kids, so it would make sense for them to make the effort, even if it cuts into time spent with her kids. I'm just a childless bachelor. Who am I to selfishly take her kids' grandparents away?"

"Good God. Did she also expect a present at other kids' birthday parties?"

I snorted. "If that had been a thing in our generation, I guarantee she would have." I paused. "In fact, I wouldn't be surprised if she does that for her kids."

"Oh my God," he groaned. "Landon had a friend growing up whose parents always made sure he had a present at everyone else's birthday party. My ex-wife came right out and asked how he was going to manage as an adult, and the mom just blew it off as, 'he's a kid, it's not a big deal.'"

"Yeah?" I chuckled. "What's he like now?"

"Probably as much of a hellspawn as he was back then," Connor muttered. "That was when we lived in San Diego, and I don't think Landon or Aimee kept in touch with the family."

"Can't imagine why."

"I know, right?" He chuckled, but then he sobered and squeezed my hand. "Kind of sounds like what your parents did with your sister, honestly. Letting her go unchecked enough that she runs the show now."

"Kind of," I admitted. "And it's just... I guess it's easier to avoid conflict by not bringing it up. Even if I talk to my parents one-on-one, it'll eventually get back to her when they start making plans, so..." I waved my other hand. "It's like pulling teeth just to get them to FaceTime with me."

Connor's eyebrows jumped. "They don't even *FaceTime* with you? When you're this far away?"

I shrugged, not sure why this whole thing made me feel ashamed. "I don't have grandkids for them to fawn over."

Connor stared at me. "I can't imagine not talking to my boys just because they don't have kids. And I still can't imagine your parents prioritizing your sister's tantrums over coming to see their son." He scoffed and shook his head. "If one of my boys took issue with me seeing his brother, we'd have a problem."

That made sense. It made perfect sense. Connor fiercely loved both of his boys, and they quite clearly knew it.

"How did they get along as kids?" I asked, partly out of curiosity and partly to escape this topic.

He eyed me, and I had a feeling he recognized the subject change. Mercifully, he went with it. "Oh, they fought. They're really close now, and Quinn and Savannah even offered to let Landon live with them while he was going to school. As teenagers, though?" He whistled, shaking his head. "Holy shit."

"Yeah? That's hard to picture."

Connor groaned, wiping a hand over his face. "Oh my God. During my last shipboard deployment, I almost dreaded calling home because Aimee would be losing her mind over the boys fighting. She sent me a picture one day of Quinn with a black eye and Landon with a bloody nose, and she captioned it, 'Tell me how your day was—I dare you.'"

"Oh, wow." I laughed. "Okay, that sounds intense."

"Right? But they mellowed, especially after Quinn graduated high school. Now you'd never know they ever had any sibling rivalry."

"Aside from some brotherly shit-talking, right?"

"Well, yeah." He chuckled. "Do brothers ever grow out of that?"

"Absolutely not."

We both laughed, and then we fell quiet for a little while. I was relieved we'd left the topic of my parents behind. No matter how much I tried to tell myself it didn't bother me, the nerve was raw.

Connor watched his thumb trace along mine. "You, um... You said something else the other night. That I've been thinking about a lot."

My stomach tightened. "Yeah?" I knew what he meant this time. Felt it all the way to my core, especially when he met my gaze with those sweet, intense eyes.

"This really isn't just casual anymore, is it?" he whispered.

I gulped. "Is that... Is that okay?" He'd indicated it was the other night, but what if he'd had time to think it through? What if he'd had time to come to his senses?

He let go of my hand and touched my face. "It scared me a little at first, but the more I think about it..." Oh, man, that smile never failed to make my spine tingle. "I like the idea."

"You... You do?"

"Yeah. I mean, we spend all this time together. We talk about everything." He grinned wickedly. "And that's to say nothing about the sex."

I laughed, but quickly sobered. "But keeping it on the DL..."

"It's not forever," he whispered. "We just keep doing what we're doing for now. See what happens between us." The grin broadened. "And then maybe after you retire, we can think about coming out."

My heart was absolutely racing now. "But that's still more than a year away."

"I know." He trailed his fingers along the shaved side of my head. "I can wait."

The hope swelling in my chest was almost painful. "We'd have to do the long-distance thing then. After I get sent back to CONUS."

He nodded and drew me in. "Pretty sure it'll all be worth it in the end."

Then his mouth claimed mine, and I absolutely melted against him.

Was this real? Did he really think we had a future?

And did he really *want* that future?

Or was it just the right thing to say in the moment?

God, please, let him be serious about this...

A few days after Connor's kids left, we were back to our usual routine. He was still bummed out that they were gone, and I didn't blame him, but he seemed to enjoy the time we spent together. If nothing else, it distracted him from their absence.

I could live with that. I just had to remember that was what was happening here. He insisted we could do the post-retirement long-distance thing until logistics allowed us to be in the same place, but that was easy to say. It was easy to imagine it being worthwhile, and it was probably a lot easier to fantasize about that than it was to think about his kids being a few thousand miles away.

I believed Connor liked me. I believed he enjoyed my company. It wasn't that I thought he was lying or being disingenuous; I just couldn't convince myself that when the rubber met the road, he'd still be onboard. When the same ocean between him and his boys was between him and me, we'd see how willing he was to hang on.

In the meantime, I'd enjoy everything we did, and when it was over... well, it would be over.

And it's going to hurt, because I'm getting way too fucking invested in this.

Yeah, probably. But that was a problem for future Alex.

Present Alex, on the other hand, was grinning like an idiot, trying to get comfortable in my office chair with all those telltale aches and twinges bringing back memories of last night. I leaned back in my desk chair and sipped my coffee as every muscle reminded me of last night. Connor and I were both as vers as they came, but lately he'd been topping more often than not. No real reason beyond him wanting to fuck me and me wanting to get dicked down, and good God, did he leave me smiling every time.

I shivered, intensifying all those aches and twinges. We might have to take it easy tonight, if only to give our bodies —or at least *my* body—a break.

That would've been a disappointing thought with anyone else. With Connor? It just meant more hanging out on his couch or in his pool, talking over good food, and/or lazily kissing while a movie played without us. Sign me up.

Right then, the waiting room door opened, and I shook myself back into the present. I was still at work and had work to do.

Pediatric patients could sometimes be challenging because kids struggled to be still even when they *weren't* sick, hurting, or otherwise uncomfortable. Plus some of them were scared of the noise made by the machinery. Then I made it all worse by asking them to get into even more uncomfortable positions. I made a lot of kids cry, and that was definitely not my favorite part of my job.

This little girl today was seven. She'd hurt her foot at the beach, and the pediatrician wanted to rule out any fractures. If I had to guess from the minimal swelling and bruising, she probably had a moderate sprain, but it was always best to check. Unfortunately, that meant she had to lie back with her heel on the table and her toes up, and that wasn't comfortable at all. The lateral view—with her leg and ankle on their side—was even worse. She'd been determinedly stoic and brave when she walked in, but by the time I was finished, her eyes were brimming with tears.

She was still trying to be brave, though, fighting back those tears and working her jaw so hard it had to hurt almost as much as her foot.

After she'd sat up, I said, "You know, I get big tough soldiers in here. Marines. All those guys."

She looked up at me, eyelashes dotted with some of the tears that had escaped.

I smiled. "They cry sometimes. Did you know that?"

Her red eyes widened. "Really?"

"Yep. When it hurts, it hurts. Doesn't matter who you are." I patted her shoulder. "It's okay to cry if it hurts."

Some kids completely fell apart when I said that. Some just sort of exhaled and relaxed, letting the tears fall without shame but not like sobbing or anything. That's what this kid did—her neck and shoulders unwound, and her jaw relaxed. The tears she was fighting back fell, and she released a long, ragged breath.

Her mom, who'd come back into the room once I was done taking the X-rays, met my gaze. *"Thank you,"* she mouthed.

I just offered a smile. I wished I could give her daughter a piece of candy or something. I kept a bowl of fun-size candy bars in the office for exactly that reason, but on the off chance her X-rays came back with a displaced fracture, she could need surgery. Or the doctor might give her pain meds that could upset her stomach. Best not to take the risk.

Her mom and I helped her into the wheelchair she'd come up in, and a moment later, another corpsman came by to take them back down to her pediatrician.

I returned to my office to send her X-rays to the pediatrician. A quick glance confirmed what I'd suspected—no fractures. Good. Poor kid's day had already been shitty; she didn't need a cast, crutches, and an order of *"no getting in the water at the beach for a couple of months"* on top of it.

I sent off the X-rays, and I was just about to check my email when the waiting room door opened again. It was going to be one of *those* days, apparently.

Well, being busy made the day go by faster, so whatever.

It was definitely one of those days. For a solid three hours, there may as well have been a revolving door on Radiology, and I even ended up with a few people in the waiting area. I got called down to the emergency department twice, and for a hot minute I considered calling the other tech or my chief to come in and help.

I kept it under control, though, and I didn't keep anyone waiting too long. My already tired body wasn't thrilled about it, and some of those aches and twinges were getting more uncomfortable than amusing, but... eh. Could've been worse. My job kept that in sharp perspective, too; I really couldn't complain to an aircraft maintainer who'd taken a fall that landed him in the ER with three broken ribs and a concussion. Or the sixteen-year-old whose fractured tibia hadn't healed as well as she'd hoped, and she was going to spend a few more weeks in a cast. Or the XO from one of the ships who'd taken a tumble down a ladder and broken his collarbone.

By about 1530, things had wound down a little. I finished with a civilian contractor who had suspected pneumonia (more than "suspected" from what I saw on that chest X-ray), and my waiting area was empty. There were no summons to the emergency room. HM2 Fox would be arriving soon, too, so there'd be two of us until my shift was over. Nice.

I was just sending off some images to Orthopedics when the door swung open again.

I rose and stepped out of the office, fully expecting another patient (or Fox arriving early), but—

"So you're not answering texts anymore?" Tobias glared at me.

I halted in the doorway. "I—excuse me?"

"I've texted you half a dozen times today, and you haven't even read them."

I blinked, needing a second to process this. Then I shook myself. "I'm sorry, am I obligated to get back to you by a certain—"

"You're ignoring me," he declared.

There was a time when I'd have insisted that, no, I wasn't. I really wasn't! And I'd show him—look! See all these patients today? The summonses to the ER? I hadn't even had time to look at my personal phone, never mind ignore his texts.

But the longer I was away from him—and especially the longer I was with Connor—the less willing I was to be Tobias's doormat.

I affected boredom and sighed. "Well, you've got me now." I spread my arms. "What was so important that I needed to reply to your texts?"

He glared at me. "I just think it's impolite to ignore someone."

I shrugged. "It's impolite to keep texting someone who hasn't answered, so..."

Tobias's jaw worked.

"What is it you want?" I asked, letting the testiness into my voice, something I wouldn't have dared done even a few months ago. "I've got work to do."

"Yeah. Sure you do." He made a big show of looking around the otherwise deserted waiting room. "You're real busy, aren't you?"

I refused to give him the irritated reaction he was digging for. "Oh, you sweet summer child. Have you really been discharged for so long that you've forgotten how much the military loves its paperwork?"

"I do plenty of paperwork," he snapped. "Just because I'm not active duty anymore doesn't mean I don't do the same kind of work."

"Okay, then that means you know why I've been busy and why I have shit to do. So could you please tell me why you're—"

"I just want to know why you've been spending so much time in Sanlúcar."

I froze, realizing a heartbeat too late how conspicuous my reaction was.

A sly grin spread across his lips. "I mean, I know it's not far from Chipiona, but you never seemed to want to go there when we were dating."

I half-shrugged. "I explored it a bit and decided I like it out there."

"Uh-huh. You sure have."

I narrowed my eyes, pretending my blood hadn't turned to ice. "What can I say? It's more fun to explore it on my own than it would've been with you."

"On your own." The grin widened. "Yeah, I bet it's been on your own, hasn't it?"

Oh, *fuck…*

I cocked a brow, still trying to appear unaffected. Then I sighed with theatrical boredom and checked the clock on the wall. "Look, I really do have a ton of work to do. So whatever it is you're trying to dangle over my head—just say it so we can be done with this."

"I think you know exactly what it is."

Fuck, fuck, fuuuck…

"No." I shrugged. "I have no idea what you're getting at, and I—"

"You're screwing Lieutenant Commander Marks, aren't you?"

I choked on nothing, but masked it with a laugh. "What? *That's* your big Sword of Damocles?" I rolled my eyes even as my heart slammed against my ribs. "I'll give you props, Tobias. You're creative, especially when it comes to bullshit."

"It isn't bullshit and we both know it."

"Oh yeah?" I threw him a challenging look even as my insides twisted in on themselves. "How, pray tell, do you know?"

He sniffed indignantly. "You're not nearly as subtle as you think."

I rolled my eyes again because I knew how much that pissed him off. "You're full of shit, Tobias. And I have work to do. So how about…" I gestured at the door.

He glared at me. "We both know I'm right." He stepped closer, farther into my space than I ever wanted him to be again, and he added in a low growl, "Maybe you should've thought twice about dumping me and ignoring me."

And then he was gone, the waiting area door swinging shut behind him before I'd even made sense of everything.

That...

That was not good.

I had no idea how much he'd actually seen. I'd been careful to make sure he didn't follow me, since that had always been a possibility. Had I let my guard down? Been so caught up in seeing Connor that I got complacent? Hell. Maybe. I'd never noticed him behind me, but maybe he *had* tailed me.

Did that mean he'd personally witnessed me coming or going from Connor's house? Had he just seen me in the area? Had he caught a glimpse of us sharing a flirty look as we passed in the halls and decided to fish for a reaction? That was the worst part—without knowing how much he knew, I couldn't shut him down without potentially confirming something he only suspected.

Fuck my life.

I rubbed my eyes and exhaled into the silence of the waiting area. Connor and I were going to have to have a conversation. If it spooked him into ending things with me, then I really couldn't blame him. I'd known from the start he was only going to risk so much just to sleep with me and deal with my nightmares. Even after he'd said this felt like more, even after he'd floated the idea of continuing after I retired—he was going to drop me like the hot mess I was once he knew someone had caught our scent. Especially when he knew *who* had caught our scent.

Some part of me wanted to wait until after we'd fooled around tonight. Just enjoy one last roll in the hay with him before he knew how close we were to being outed.

I couldn't do that to him, though. I couldn't ask him to take a bigger risk than he already knew he was.

My heart sank deeper into the pit of my stomach.
I had to tell him. Tonight.
And just knowing that conversation was coming...
I already missed him.

CHAPTER 35

CONNOR

It didn't matter how long I'd been in the Navy or how far I moved up in the ranks—getting summoned into the boss's office always gave me a panicked butthole clench.

Especially when I wasn't just getting called into my direct supervisor's office. No, today it was the CO who'd summoned me twenty minutes before I was due to leave for the day. I hadn't even had a chance to text Alex and let him know I was on my way home.

"You wanted to see me, ma'am?" I asked.

"Yes, Lieutenant Commander." Captain Tucker gestured at one of her guest chairs. "Have a seat."

I hoped she didn't notice my nervous swallow as I sat down. From her intense frown, my initial instinct had been correct—this wasn't good. She wasn't about to let me know I'd made commander or I was being moved to a supervisory position in the hospital. From the hardness in her eyes, I almost had to wonder if I was getting demoted for some reason.

At least she didn't keep me waiting long.

"To cut right to the chase, Lieutenant Commander," she

said, looking at me over her glasses, "someone has expressed concern about you engaging in fraternization."

My stomach dropped. "Frat-fraternization? With who?" Playing stupid was better than outright denial; if she knew something I couldn't explain away, lying would be a hole I couldn't dig myself out of.

Captain Tucker folded her hands on her desk. "HM1 Barlow has been observed entering and exiting your home in Sanlúcar. On multiple occasions." She inclined her head. "Would you care to explain what he's doing there?"

"Oh." I cleared my throat. "He's, um..." I scratched the back of my neck as some warmth rose in my face. With a nervous laugh, I said, "He's been helping me with my Spanish."

Her eyebrows shot up. "With... your Spanish."

"Yes, ma'am." I sheepishly held her gaze. "I was, um... I was one of those idiots who came here thinking most people would speak at least some English."

She gave a quiet, sympathetic laugh. "Yes, it was eye-opening, wasn't it?"

"It really was. HM1 Barlow heard me complaining about it to someone, and he offered to help." I shook my head. "I can see how it looks inappropriate, but that's all it was."

"I see." She studied me, scrutinizing me as if looking for some kind of tell that I was lying. It was hard not to squirm because, yeah, I was fucking lying. Keeping these cards close to the vest was no easy task; the slightest twitch could tip her off that I was bullshitting her, and then my career would be toast.

By some miracle, though, I must've convinced her.

"All right. Well." She pinned me with a stare. "Given your respective ranks, I would suggest finding someone else to help you with your Spanish, Lieutenant Commander."

I nodded, struggling to keep my relief hidden. "Yes, ma'am. Will do."

She dismissed me.

Out in the hall, I kept the casual façade in place until I was well out of her sight. Near the elevators, I leaned against the wall and finally released a relieved sigh. She'd bought my story. Thank God.

Time to get the fuck out of here.

In theory, I could've stayed and argued with her that there was nothing inappropriate about someone helping me learn the local language. It was pointless, though. The UCMJ was crystal clear, and Alex coming to my house—regardless of why—qualified as a "too familiar" relationship. Especially since we were meeting one-on-one, off-base, and outside of working hours. It didn't matter how ridiculous or outdated it was. It didn't matter that he wasn't my subordinate. The rules said officers and enlisted couldn't fraternize, and that was that.

And if Alex coming to my house to help me with my Spanish was a bridge too far, then the two of us hooking up and traveling together was professional suicide.

I knew that. I'd known it going into this. All along I'd absolutely known what was at stake, and I'd been careful to keep us from getting caught.

Still, someone had seen us. We were on our commanding officer's radar. I'd been warned. Any *"it's not what it looks like"* cards we had were now played.

All the way down to the first floor, my mind reeled, searching for some kind of solution. As I stepped out into the thick Andalusian heat, I was cold all over, too aware that I'd dodged a bullet that I wasn't likely to dodge again.

If someone saw Alex and me again...

If someone saw him entering or leaving my house again...

We were fucked, and not in the fun way.

By the time I reached my car, I'd come to the only conclusion I could think of. I didn't like it, but I was short on options.

Heart pounding, I leaned against my car and texted Alex.

> Change of plans for tonight. Can you meet me in Cádiz instead?

CHAPTER 36
ALEX

The hits just kept coming, didn't they?

First there was the bullshit with Tobias. Now Connor wanted to meet someplace besides his house. Not just someplace else, either—out in Cádiz, at the tiny island fortress that was a long walk down a narrow levee out into the open water. There would be next to no one out there, and even fewer who'd care about us.

I dreaded meeting him, because my gut told me this couldn't be anything good. This wasn't just a case of cabin fever and him wanting us to get out of the house for a bit. I could feel it in my damn bones.

But what else could I do except agree to meet him and hope for the best?

So, a couple of hours after my shift, I walked onto the passenger ferry from Rota to Cádiz. From the pier where we were let off, it would've been about a thirty-minute hike, so I grabbed a taxi to the other side of the small peninsula.

The cab dropped me off by the beach, and I started the fifteen-minute walk along the levee toward the small island fort. The stonework was pale gray and brown, and even with my sunglasses on, I had to squint as the late afternoon sun beat on every surface.

The stone structure at the end of the levee was Castillo de San Sebastián, which if memory served, was three or four hundred years old. I couldn't remember which historical era it was from, and I was too wound up to stop and read any of the placards. And anyway, I had someone waiting for me.

I pushed out a ragged, nervous breath. What was this about? We'd spent the morning flirting via text before my day had gotten chaotic, and then this afternoon, he'd suddenly changed his tune. I'd had a fleeting glimmer of hope that he wanted to get dinner or something. Maybe something touristy? Going out as a couple, even while we could still see Rota in the hazy distance from Cádiz?

But when we'd gone back and forth to figure out where to meet, he'd suggested the Castillo.

My heart sank as I walked along the levee. There was a weird optical illusion that had tripped me up the first time I'd come out here—the farther you walked, the longer the levee seemed to stretch and the farther the island seemed to be in the distance.

Connor was out there. Waiting for me. He'd texted a few minutes ago to say he was there.

But what was going to happen when I got there? When we met up inside the walls of the tiny fortress where almost no one would be able to see us?

That sinking feeling worsened.

This was it, wasn't it? He was ending things. It was over.

Out in public enough that I wouldn't make a scene, but far enough away from Rota and Sanlúcar that no one would care anyway? Well, at least he hadn't waited until we were on one of our trips or something. That would suck ass, taking a train clear out to Toledo or Barcelona or wherever just to get dumped. Just doing the walk of shame out of Cádiz would be humiliating enough, thank you.

Eventually, the optical illusion waned, and the Castillo actually got closer. There was a small walled-in area before another walk would take me to the larger fortress where the lighthouse stood.

I didn't have to go that far, though. I found Connor leaning against the stone wall, gazing out at the Atlantic. He didn't notice me right away, so I paused for a second just to memorize the sight of him. I was tempted to whip out my phone and snap a photo, but that would be a little weird if he turned around just then.

My memory would have to do. As if I could ever forget this gorgeous man, the wind ruffling his dark hair, shorts, and T-shirt.

My throat tightened. I was about to lose him, wasn't I? I was completely, stupidly, irretrievably in love with him, but that didn't matter, did it?

Right then, he turned, and even his sunglasses couldn't mask the apprehension in his expression.

Fuck me.

This is about to be over, and I never even got to tell you I love you.

I called on the same poker face I'd maintained while facing off with Tobias, and I plastered on a smile as I closed the last bit of distance to Connor. I swallowed hard, and when I spoke, I tried to keep my voice casual, as if I hadn't clocked that there was something off about this meeting. "So, uh, why the change in venue?"

The way his face fell made my heart drop. He rested his palms on the stone wall and stared out at the water with unfocused eyes. "I got called into the Captain Tucker's office today."

My stomach flipped. "Oh. Fuck. I... assume it wasn't anything good."

He shook his head slowly. "No." Facing me, he spoke so softly, the wind almost swallowed his voice: "Someone told her you've been seen coming and going from my house."

The panicked feeling I'd had when Tobias had made his accusation had nothing on the *oh shit* that surged through me just then. "They saw... fuck."

"Yeah." He scratched the back of his neck and exhaled. "I told her you were helping me with my Spanish."

"With your—" I blinked. "Whoa. Way to think on your feet."

He gave a quiet, threadbare laugh. "She bought it, too, so... there's that."

"Good. That's good."

"Yeah." He sobered and met my gaze through his dark lenses. "But she also said we couldn't be meeting at my house for Spanish. It's... The UCMJ is..."

"I know," I whispered. "That's one of those excuses we can only use once."

"Exactly." His shoulders sank. "If we got caught again..."

Goddammit. My eyes stung, and I was grateful for my own sunglasses. I didn't want him to see me tearing up. He'd probably decide dumping me was an even better idea once he realized what an emotional tool I was about all this.

I cleared my throat. "So I guess we can't..." I watched my thumb tracing a crack in the stone because I couldn't look at Connor.

"We'll have to be a lot more careful," he said. "Do things a lot differently."

This time I did look at him. "We—what?"

"If we have to start meeting in shady hotels, then... fine. If we have to start burning through leave and traveling all over Europe... fine." He took off his sunglasses and looked right in my eyes. "But I'm not giving this up. Not unless you want to."

I stared at him, disbelieving. "You... Wait, you're still in? Even if—"

"Yes," he whispered. "Yes, I'm in." He must've read my incredulity in my face, because he put his hand over mine on the sun-warmed stone. "It'll be hard. I'm not pretending it won't be. But you're worth it."

"I... really?"

He laughed softly and touched my face. "Yes. Absolutely." And right there, out in public—even if we were far from town with almost no one around—he kissed me. Not just a light peck, either. He wrapped an arm around my waist and kissed me like he fucking *meant* it.

When he finally came up for air, he was as breathless as I was. "I want this. Everything we've been doing. All of it. And not just the sex." He ran his thumb along my cheekbone. "It'll be complicated for a while, but it's worth it."

I had to work to swallow past the lump in my throat. "How long do you think it'll be worth it, though?" I didn't want to talk him out of this, but I also didn't want to set myself up for heartache. Well, *more* heartache.

"You're going to get your retirement rolling soon. In a bit over a year, you'll be done with the Navy." He shrugged. "It isn't like we have to wait very long before we can be out, you know?"

"A... A year isn't very long?"

His smile warmed me more than the Spanish sun. "Baby, I spent a lot of years that I'm never getting back in an unhappy marriage. A year and a half or so is nothing." He sobered a little. "And even if it was more than that, I'm still in. I'm not giving this up."

I couldn't fucking breathe. Since when did anyone not only take risks for me, but face down the possibility of laying low for any length of time? Especially after our CO had caught enough wind that if we got busted again, we were fucked? Anyone else would've taken one look at the situation and said, *"Nah, I can just beat off."*

I finally managed to push out a breath and draw another. "I'm in for as long as you want me. I don't know how we're going to do it, but..." I thought about it, then half-shrugged. "There are seedy motels and stuff around here. We can make it work."

Connor's smile held more relief than I thought anyone could have in the face of realizing they could make it work with me. He drew me in and kissed me again, quickly this time, before murmuring, "We can definitely make it work." As he pulled back, he added with a chuckle, "And there's always FaceTime for those nights we can't be together."

"That's true." I paused, and I cringed as I said, "I, um... I can almost guarantee it was Tobias. The person who ratted us out."

Connor's eyebrows rose. "How do you figure?"

I sighed, then told him about my encounter with Tobias.

"Jesus Christ," Connor muttered, rolling his eyes. "Does this guy have no life at all? No hobbies besides fucking with you?"

I laughed bitterly. "I think he's just not over the fact that I had the audacity to break up with him."

"Ugh, I've met that type. You're supposed to stay until he's done with you, and then he'll dump you. Not the other way around."

"Yeah, exactly."

"One of my ex-wife's friends was married to someone like that. Getting out was not pretty, let me tell you, and her ex-husband still gives her shit. She sort of joked once that she was tempted to take him back, be a horrible partner, and get him to dump her just so he'd finally 'win' and leave her alone."

I grimaced. "I... hate how much sense that approach actually makes."

Connor nodded, squeezing my hand. "Yeah. I figured it would. And with the way he acts, I'm not surprised he found out about us. I also wouldn't be surprised if he's the one who ratted us out."

I groaned. "Fuck. I'm sorry. I should've known he—"

"Alex. Don't." Connor shook his head. "This isn't on you. Your ex is a dickhead. We'll just keep a lower profile so he doesn't have any reason to go tattling to the captain again."

I laughed humorlessly. "I'm sure he'll dream something up."

"Probably, but let's not hand him anything."

I chewed my lip, uneasiness creeping in where relief had set up shop earlier.

"Hey." Connor drew me in close as if we weren't out in public. "It's not on you. And we'll just be careful going forward. It's going to be tough for a while. I know it will be." He touched my face and pressed the softest, gentlest kiss to my lips. "But I'm not giving up on us."

For all I'd told my young patient earlier that there was no shame in crying, I fought like hell to keep my own emotions under the surface. This thing with Connor still felt tenuous, as if he weren't willing to give up on us *now*, but that thread might snap if I showed him what a complete mess I was.

Somehow, I kept my emotions out of my voice. Wrapping my arms around his waist, I whispered, "I'm not giving up on us either."

He kissed me again, and his lips curved into a grin. "Just, um, let me know if you seek treatment for tennis elbow. If we both show up for it at the same time, people might talk."

I burst out laughing, which mercifully chased away the threat of tears. "Okay, duly noted." I brushed my lips across his. "We'll just have to take another trip soon. So our elbows aren't doing all the work."

Connor didn't say anything.

But his kiss said that we were absolutely on the same page.

CHAPTER 37

CONNOR

I was relieved that Alex and I had figured out a strategy, but I couldn't lie—this new arrangement was driving me out of my mind.

I enjoyed the sexting and the hot FaceTiming. When we met up two or three times a week in hotels, that was fun as hell, even if it was stressful. And the secretive glances we exchanged whenever we passed in the hall at work—those were sexy.

But I missed everything else. The lazy afternoons in my pool or lounging in the cabana. Curling up with him on the couch to watch a movie (or make out when we were *supposed* to be watching a movie). Having a beer on the back porch while we watched the sun set over the neighbors' palm and banana trees.

Most of all, I missed having him beside me in bed. Not just the sex, but the affectionate touches and just... having him there. I hated waking up alone in the morning, and even more than that, I hated waking up alone from a nightmare in the middle of the night. It wasn't that I enjoyed interrupting his sleep, but there was so much comfort in having him there with me.

I also knew he was still having nightmares, and every time he mentioned a rough night, I *really* felt the distance between his apartment and my house. I wanted to be there, holding him and stroking his hair until he stopped shaking and we both went back to sleep.

And I couldn't lie—I missed the sex, too. Having him for a couple of hours in a hotel two or three times a week just didn't cut it. All the sexting and fooling around on FaceTime helped, but it also just made me want him more. Every time I watched him onscreen using a toy on himself, I ached to take its place. I wanted to be the one stretching him open and moving inside him. I wanted to come in him —his mouth, his ass, I didn't care—instead of all over my hand and stomach.

Every single time, my need for an orgasm was satisfied, but my need for Alex was even more intense than before. If I didn't get my hands and mouth on him soon—and for more than a hurried rendezvous in a sleazy hotel—I was going to lose my damn mind. Those meetups scratched the itch, but much like watching him play with himself, they only made me want him more. They made me intensely aware of every second we didn't spend together.

Tonight, we were in a hilariously dumpy hotel on the outskirts of Jerez de la Frontera. The décor was decades out of date, there was a weird smell I couldn't put my finger on, and one of the lights buzzed like a pissed-off mosquito.

I didn't care, because I was tangled up with Alex, holding him close and kissing him lazily as we basked in the afterglow of our orgasms. Eyes closed, I ran my palms all over his amazing body, just memorizing all the planes and contours as if I'd never touched him before. I was mesmerized by this closeness and this intimacy with him. Every time his fingertips trailed across my skin or his lower lip dragged across mine, something in me melted. He turned me on, but this went so much deeper than that.

How did I land this incredible man? How did I get so lucky?

No idea, but I had, and I savored every breath and touch as if this was the one and only chance I'd ever had. Just like I had the first time we'd tumbled into bed together, when we'd sworn it would be a one-time thing because we'd known it was a bad idea.

Maybe still being here was stupid. Maybe it didn't make sense. But I loved it, so I didn't question it.

After I had no idea how long, we finally came up for air. Alex drew back and met my gaze, his eyes full of sleepy satisfaction.

I ran my fingers along the shaved edge of his jaw. "Do you have any idea how hard it was to concentrate during the department head meeting this afternoon?"

A sly grin curled his lips. "Hard, eh?"

Rolling my eyes, I nudged him with my foot under the covers. "You know what I mean. And yes, there were a few moments when I was really glad no one asked us to stand up."

Alex chuckled, sliding his palm up my chest. "Well, I'd apologize for being a distraction, but I think we both know I'd be lying."

"Uh-huh. I don't think there's a contrite bone in your body."

He pressed his lips together. "C'mon, now you're just handing me double entendres."

I groaned and touched my forehead to his shoulder. "Yeah. I knew it as soon as I said it."

He just laughed and patted my back.

The conversation fell into a comfortable lull, and we lay there for a while, occasionally kissing but mostly just holding each other. I realized after several minutes that Alex seemed to be lost in thought.

"Hey." I nudged him gently. "You still with me?"

"Yeah, I am." He shifted onto his side and rested his hand on my waist. "I was just, um... I've been thinking, and I didn't want to bring it up in the heat of the moment, but..." He chewed his lip.

My pulse jumped, because I wasn't sure which direction this conversation might go.

I wasn't ready when he whispered, "It's just us, you know? And we've both had physicals since we started sleeping together."

Just us? Physicals?

But then the piece clicked into place. "You want to go raw."

Alex nodded, a hint of shyness in his expression. "Yeah. I do."

I stared at him. "Are you sure? We can wait until you've seen my results. I won't be offended."

He was already shaking his head. "I trust you."

I swallowed, and as my thoughts began to settle, I couldn't help grinning. We had had physicals. I hadn't touched anyone since him, and I believed him when he said he hadn't either. "I'm game if you are."

"I am." He grinned, and then sheepishly added, "Can't promise it'll be a marathon fuck the first time—I've, uh, never done it without a condom before, so I don't imagine I'll last long."

"Never?"

He shook his head. "You're the only one I've..." He hesitated, then barely whispered, "You're the only one I'd ever even consider it with."

My heart fluttered. "So... skip the condoms?"

"Skip the condoms." He drew me in closer and kissed me. "I can't wait."

"Neither can I," I murmured against his lips. I was glad he'd waited until we weren't getting ready to fuck to bring it up. This really was something to talk about when dicks weren't hard and no one was thinking with their little heads.

But goddamn, it made me want him. Probably sooner than my over-forty body was ready, too.

I could live with it, though. Even if we didn't get our first bareback round in tonight, we'd get there.

Eventually.

When we could fucking see each other again.

I forced back an irritated groan. "I really miss doing this all the time."

Scowling, Alex nodded. "Me too. It's fun when we can do it, but... yeah, in between..."

"It sucks." I paused. "We need to go somewhere again. Out of town where no one knows us. So we can actually be together for more than a few hours."

"Yeah, we do." He trailed his fingertips up my abs, the featherlight touch making the muscles contract. "Where haven't we been yet? And do you even have any leave left?"

"I have plenty. Not enough to take a couple of weeks somewhere, but a long weekend? I could swing that."

Alex pursed his lips. "Where do you want to go?"

I thought about it. "What about Ibiza?"

He raised his eyebrows. "You want to go get shitfaced and party?"

"Is that the only thing there is to do there?"

"Well, no. But that's why *most* people go."

I shrugged. "I'm not most people."

His little smile made me warm all over. "You don't have to tell me that."

I chuckled. "Right, and I'm not opposed to partying a bit, just to say I partied on Ibiza. But..." I sobered. "I'd be perfectly happy just renting a nice place and spending the time there with you."

Surprise flickered across his face. "Really?"

"Um, yeah?" I grinned. "Or hadn't you noticed how much of our other trips we spend in our hotel?"

He laughed softly. "Okay, point taken." Humor fading, he said, "I think Ibiza could be fun. Even if we just rent a place on the beach and don't go anywhere."

I slid closer to him, wrapping my arm around him. "I'm all for staying in and seeing how much the furniture can handle."

Alex snorted. "Maybe that should be our bucket list—break a bed in every city we go to."

"Ooh, I can get onboard with that."

"Of course you can." He leaned in closer and brushed his lips across mine. "Guess we don't need to bring condoms, but we better pack a big bottle of lube."

I bit my lip, shivering as my mind filled with pornographic thoughts of our trip to Ibiza. "Guess we better."

He grinned and kissed me again, and hell, maybe this old body could handle another round tonight after all. Maybe not fucking, since neither of us needed to be sore, but we could definitely get each other off.

So we let those pornographic thoughts carry us into another round of trying to break *this* hotel's bed.

Oh, hell yeah. I couldn't wait for Ibiza.

CHAPTER 38
ALEX

I arrived on Ibiza first. Connor would be flying in later this afternoon. He'd originally been expected to land shortly after I did, but his flight to Madrid was delayed. He'd texted to let me know they'd finally taken off, though, so he was on his way. Then he'd have to get on a later flight to Ibiza, and he wasn't entirely sure when that would take off.

In the meantime, I had a few hours to find our rental, check in, grab a shower, and eat some lunch.

We'd found a villa near the town of Puig Manyá, which was about twenty minutes from the airport on the southeastern side of the island. On a rock this tiny, we weren't far from anything, and if we decided to go partying, we only had to go about ten minutes to Ibiza Town or fifteen minutes to Playa d'en Bossa. Assuming we put on clothes long enough to venture out.

And once I arrived at the villa, the odds of us venturing out to party plummeted considerably. Not just because I wanted to spend as much time as possible with Connor, but because this place was incredible.

It was a two-story stucco house with a gorgeous kitchen, a huge living room with a giant flatscreen, and a bed that could comfortably accommodate an orgy. The second-floor terrace wrapped around three sides of the house, offering a beautiful view of the coast and the sparkling Mediterranean. There was also a small pool on the terrace, which looked like an amazing place to sit with some wine and gaze out at the sea.

As fun as it was to party on this island, that lost a lot of appeal when the alternative was holing up in this amazing villa with the man I'd flown here to see.

Might as well enjoy it while it lasts.

I pushed that irritating voice aside. Ever since Captain Tucker had caught our scent, I'd been on edge. Not that we'd get caught, but that Connor would finally get tired of all the cloak and dagger.

Now we were kicking off our four-day trip with his flights getting delayed. He'd sounded *thrilled* about that, and I didn't imagine it would put him in the mood for much besides a beer, a meal, and some sleep.

And it would probably remind him of what a pain in the ass it was to get someplace where he wouldn't get caught with me.

As I leaned against the terrace's stucco railing and gazed out at the Med, I couldn't ignore the knot of dread in my stomach. Sooner or later, he was going to get tired of this. Some airport headache was bound to speed up that process, too; I hated flying even when things went smoothly, and I didn't imagine he was enjoying this shitshow. Especially because he had to get on a different flight, which meant he had to navigate customer service in an airport where most people didn't speak English. His Spanish was getting better, but trying to handle a stressful flight situation in a language you barely knew was *not* fun.

And his only reward is spending a few days with me.

I chewed my lip and thumbed the stucco. Well, I'd known from the beginning this would only last so long. Not much I could do except enjoy the time I had with him and try like hell not to think about the rapidly approaching end.

> Just landed. Be there soon.

>> Awesome! See you when you get here!

I stared at the messages as my heart pounded. What kind of mood would he be in? I had visions of slamming doors and snapping remarks, but I reminded myself that was Tobias, not Connor. He could get irritated just like anyone, but he wasn't like *that*. He'd never taken out his anger on me, and I had no reason to believe he'd start now.

No reason except too much experience with someone else who I'd thought would never do that.

I closed my eyes and wiped a hand over my face. I needed to get a damn grip. Even if Connor was in a bitchy mood when he got here—seriously, who wouldn't be after the day he had?—it would blow over. We could chalk up today as a loss, take it easy, and start our actual vacation tomorrow.

I picked up my phone again.

>> Do you want me to order you some food? I picked up a few things earlier too if you're hungry.

> I'm good. Just ready to be there and not traveling anymore. (skull emoji)

> Yeah I bet. Can't wait to see you.

He didn't respond, and I tried not to read anything into that. I needed to stop being such an insecure jackass and just enjoy this trip, and that included if Connor was in a mood when he got here.

Turned out that Connor was indeed in a mood when he got here... but not the one I was anticipating.

"Fucking finally," he said as he stepped through the door. Closing it behind him, he met my gaze, and though there was fatigue in his eyes, there was even more fire. He took off his glasses, grabbed my belt and pulled me in, and he growled, "God, I missed you," a split second before I was against the door with his mouth on mine. He pinned me there with his hips, and oh, hell, he kissed me like he *meant* it.

All my doubts—all my *thoughts*—scattered. I held on to him and whimpered as he explored my mouth as if he'd never touched me before.

When he went for my neck, I arched off the door, grateful for the support as my knees threatened to drop out from under me.

"You know what I was thinking about the whole way here?" he purred against my throat.

"Gonna... Gonna guess it didn't involve going out partying."

His laugh was a hot breath across my skin. As he rubbed his hard-on across mine, he said, "Not partying. Just... how much I wanted to be balls deep in you."

The whine the escaped my throat didn't even sound like me, but I didn't care. "Y-yes, please?"

"Yeah?" He kissed beneath my jaw, then lifted his head to meet my gaze with eyes full of fire and need. "You want to get fucked?"

I didn't trust myself to speak coherently, so I nodded.

His grin made my spine tingle. Licking his lips, he looked around. "Where's the bedroom?"

It crossed my mind to suggest doing it right here against the door, but the lube was upstairs beside the bed. Without a word, I took his hand and led him to the staircase.

As soon as he saw the bed, he took the lead again, turning me around by my hips and claiming my mouth. We stumbled across the room until my calves hit the bed, but when I started to drag him down with me, he stopped me.

"Wait." He started on his belt. "Let's get all this shit out of the way first."

"Love the way you think," I said, and peeled off my shirt.

With our clothes scattered on the floor, Connor pulled me down on top of him, and... fuck yes. I loved the way this man kissed, but even more than that, I loved the way he touched me. His hands were always all over me, tracing every inch of skin he could reach. His touch was the closest thing to reverent I'd ever felt, and it made me even hotter than our rock-hard dicks rubbing together. Whether he was running his fingertips up my back or gripping handfuls of my ass, I loved it.

And that was before he licked his fingers and slid a hand between us. As soon as his fingertips started teasing my hole, I was shaking with need. We hadn't had a night together since that hotel in Jerez over a week ago, and I needed his dick right the hell now.

For as eager as he'd been when he'd come through the villa's door, though, he took his sweet time. He teased me open with one finger, then two. Then he added some lube and had me ride his hand as if I were riding his cock, and all the while he gazed up at me like I was the hottest thing he'd ever seen.

"Christ, I want to fuck you," he whispered as he kept fingering me. "The other night, I thought about finally doing you raw and blowing my load in you, and I came so hard I almost passed out."

I bit my lip. "Yeah? How did you think about it?" I lifted myself up and came back down on his fingers. "On top like this?"

He shook his head. "No. On your stomach."

I couldn't help moaning. I loved it when he topped me like that. It wasn't the deepest penetration, but something about the angle and the way he'd ride me into the mattress—just thinking about it had me ready to blow my own load.

"You want it like that?" He sounded breathless already. "And you're still good with no condoms? I brought some just in case you changed your mind."

If I'd had any reservations, they were gone in an instant. "No condoms. And I want you any way I can have you." I gazed down into his smoldering eyes. "I fucking love taking you."

It was his turn for a lip bite, and he arched under us. "How about you get on your hands and knees, then?"

Sounded good to me.

I shifted positions, and he settled behind me. He put some more lube on me, then a generous amount on himself. When he guided himself in and teased my hole with the head of his cock, I moaned, my elbows threatening to shake out from under me.

I didn't have to hold myself up for long, though. After

he'd eased himself in a little, Connor whispered, "Down on your stomach."

I sank down to the bed, and he followed, never once pulling out. I closed my eyes as his weight settled over the top of me. I didn't know why that was so sexy, but it was, and I didn't question it.

I especially didn't question it because he started moving inside me again, and most of my thoughts went blank. He kissed the back of my shoulder, then nipped it as he pushed in deeper. I didn't even recognize the sounds I was making, but I hoped they translated to *"yes, please"* and *"give me more."*

He did give me more, but he didn't pick up speed or thrust into me. Though I knew he'd hold back a little so we could still fuck over the rest of the weekend, I still expected him to drill me deep and hard. I expected a frantic quickie.

I did not expect the slow, perfect slide of his cock while he kissed my neck and held me close. I'd been close to coming the instant he'd walked in the door, my orgasm on a hair trigger after too long without him, but somehow he kept that finish just out of my reach. He rode me so painfully slowly that every nerve ending in my body lit up like runway lights, but he didn't make me—didn't *let* me—come.

"Connor..."

"Like that?" he purred in my ear as he eased back in.

"Yes. It's..." I squirmed under him, trying to use my hips to coax him into moving faster. "Harder."

His lips curved against my skin. "We'll get there." He kissed my shoulder. "I don't want to come yet, though." He started to withdraw as slowly as he'd pushed in. "I've been dying to have you. I need to feel you."

"Oh my God..."

He kept at it, his strokes glacially slow, letting me feel every inch of him.

"Does it—how does it feel?" I rasped.

"So good," he groaned. "So fucking hot and tight and..." He shivered hard, and he picked up some speed. I gripped the edge of the mattress and squeezed my eyes shut, overwhelmed and intoxicated by everything he did. None of my toys could ever compare to Connor's dick moving inside me. There was no replacing the heat of his skin or the rush of his breath or just knowing we were as close as two human beings could be. No toy could ever match the low groans or the soft whispers of, "God, you feel amazing" and "I've missed you so damn much."

I was so close to the edge it was painful, but somehow... *somehow* he kept me from going over it. I was in heaven and hell at the same time, utterly blissed out by everything he did, but also on the brink of losing my mind because I needed to come so, *so* bad.

"Please let me come," I finally whimpered. "Connor, baby, I'm—"

I'd go to my grave wondering exactly what he did, but he changed his strokes somehow, and I went careening over the edge with a helpless cry.

Behind me, Connor's whole body jerked. He grunted in my ear, and then he moaned as he tried to push himself deeper. I rocked my hips as much as I could to drive him on, my head spinning as his orgasm forced a helpless cry from his lips.

Bottoming without a condom didn't feel much different, but there was still something so amazingly sexy about him coming in me without one. I didn't care about the mess. The closeness, the intimacy, the trust—it was all on another level with him, and that moment of release turned out to be *mind-blowing*.

He shuddered and sighed, and then he touched his forehead to the back of my shoulder. "Oh my God..."

"Uh-huh." I let my own forehead fall to the pillow. For a moment, we just lay there, both of us trembling and trying to catch our breath.

Then he kissed my shoulder and pulled out. We got up on shaking legs, cleaned up, and returned to the thoroughly rumpled bed.

Connor collapsed onto the mattress and sighed heavily, letting the fatigue really show for the first time.

I lay beside him, propping my head up on my arm. "Long day?"

"Oh my God." He rubbed his eyes with his thumb and forefinger before letting his arm fall beside him. "I should've taken the train to Madrid."

"What the hell happened anyway?"

"Ugh, who knows?" He met my gaze again. "They made some long announcement in Spanish, and then in English, they just said the flight was delayed."

I laughed softly. "That's so helpful, isn't it?"

"Gotta love not speaking the common language."

"I know, right?"

He reached up to touch my face, and a tired smile pulled at his lips. "I'm here, though. It was a long day, but I got here, and now we have the whole weekend."

I smiled back and stole a light kiss. "I don't know how much of the island we're going to see, though. We've got a ton of lube and a swanky-ass place to stay." I half-shrugged. "Don't really need to go out unless we really want to."

Connor seemed to think about that. "Sounds like a plan." He wrapped his arms around me and pulled me all the way to him. "To tell you the truth, it won't hurt my feelings if we stay in this villa until it's time to go to the airport."

"Yeah?" I grinned even as an uncomfortable feeling set up shop in my chest. "You don't think you'll get bored?"

"I've got you. I've got plenty of food and lube." He trailed his fingers along the shaved side of my head. "What else could I possibly need?"

A boyfriend you can see without jumping through all these hoops?

But I just smiled and let myself be drawn into his soft, affectionate kiss.

I wanted to believe this was enough for him, and not just for this weekend.

God, Connor. If you only knew how much I want to believe I really am enough for you.

CHAPTER 39

CONNOR

Being on Ibiza with Alex was amazing. The club scene had been kind of intriguing, but now that we were here, I just had no interest in going, and neither did he. Staying here at the villa was just too perfect.

We lounged on that enormous couch and watched movies on the huge flatscreen. We drank wine in the pool while the sun went down. We walked down to the beach and had an amazing, romantic stroll along the water's edge without worrying that anyone who saw us cared.

There was plenty of sex, too, of course, though we did pace ourselves; neither of us wanted to be sore for our trip *or* for the flights home.

The one drawback was that PTSD didn't take vacations. Our first night together was broken up by several of my nightmares. The second night, his past came to visit. It sucked, but calming down in his arms or holding him while he trembled just drove home how much I wanted to be with him. He was so gentle and supportive on my bad nights, and no matter how much he insisted on apologizing for his, I had no complaints about being there to bring him back down. I wished he didn't have the nightmares, of course, but if they were a part of his reality, then I was grateful that I could do something to help.

The morning after his rough night, he was a little bleary-eyed when he came shuffling into the kitchen, but he seemed okay.

"Hey," I said. "You were finally asleep—I didn't want to leave you alone, but I didn't want to wake you up either."

"You're fine. I think I did finally crash." He rubbed his eyes. "What time is it, anyway?"

"Almost 1100."

He groaned. "Fuck. So much for going anywhere today."

"We still have plenty of time. But we also don't have to do anything. This is a vacation, so we're allowed to relax."

The response to that was a grunt. He gave me a quick peck on the lips, then opened a cabinet to get a coffee cup. "At least I did manage to pass out and actually sleep. I don't think I've slept that well in... hell, I don't know how long."

"I bet." As he poured himself some coffee, I asked, "Any thoughts about what you *do* want to do with today?"

"Not yet," he said over his shoulder. "How about as little as possible?"

"That sounds perfect. We've got a bunch of shows stacked up on Netflix. Want to lounge around on the couch and binge something?"

Alex turned around, steaming coffee in hand and a big grin on his lips. "Hell yeah." He made a face. "I really should go for a run or hit a gym today, but... eh. One more day off won't kill me."

I brought my own coffee up to my lips. "I'm sure we can work in some cardio before the day is over."

He just laughed before taking a careful sip of coffee.

We did in fact spend the entire day alternately indulging in the sins of sloth and lust. Maybe a little gluttony, too, but the pizza we had delivered wasn't *that* big.

It was decadent and lazy, but it was also... quiet. Comfortable. Just the two of us enjoying a chill day together in a beautiful villa with no expectations, no pressure, and no need to put on anything more formal than a pair of gym shorts.

I'd known when I came to Spain how much I needed sex and company, but I hadn't realized how much I needed *this*. How much I'd craved casual affection and just spending time with someone doing little more than being together. This felt so... relaxed. So *domesticated*.

Was this what lazy Saturdays with a partner were supposed to feel like? Because for all the years I'd been married, I didn't fucking know. Relaxed mornings with Aimee were anything but because it always felt like something was about to happen. Like there was this tension between us—a brewing fight, something one of us had forgotten about that the other was stewing over, a reason to think shit was about to go south.

For a long time, I'd thought that was an after effect of combat. Quiet, peaceful moments in a warzone could be more stressful than a firefight. At least in a firefight, you mostly knew where the enemy was and where the bullets and mortars were coming from. After a few bombs dropped out of the clear blue sky, it was easy to start getting paranoid about clear blue skies.

So I'd always figured that was what was happening on those quiet mornings with Aimee.

But here with Alex, I didn't have that nagging, neck-prickling certainty that *something* was going to happen.

I wasn't sure what that said about my marriage.

I definitely wasn't sure what it said about this thing with Alex.

All I knew was that I liked it.

CHAPTER 40
ALEX

By our third night on Ibiza, I was exhausted. Not from the sex or anything else—from being battered internally by my own emotions.

Connor wanted a few minutes for a FaceTime chat with Quinn. I was hardly going to bitch about that; any chance he had to talk to his sons, I was all for it.

While they talked, I slipped out to the second-floor terrace for a breather. Gazing out at the beautiful landscape, I finally stopped fighting all those feelings that had been trying to elbow their way in since I'd landed on this island.

Connor and I had both admitted more than once that we were in this for more than sex, but reality was what it was—we didn't have the staying power I wished we did. Just getting to Ibiza had involved a logistics headache, from him lying to his command about where he was going to dealing with all the fun of air travel. Sure, we didn't have that fear of someone seeing us the way we did when we stepped out of a hotel in El Puerto or Jerez. We didn't have to look over our shoulders here—just enjoy our time together.

But what happened when we were back in Rota? When we were back to that stress and paranoia?

My shoulders slumped and I closed my eyes. I was so ridiculously in love with Connor, but I was torturing myself, and sooner or later, it was going to blow up in my face.

So why wait until later?

A lump rose in my throat as I considered my options. I kind of wanted to wait until tomorrow, right before one of us left for the airport. At least then we wouldn't be stuck in this house. On the other hand, I could say something tonight and be done with it. There was a second bedroom in the house. Or I could go find a hotel if there were any vacancies on the island. Hell, I could go sleep at the damn airport. Anything but staying another night beside the man whose presence was starting to hurt more than his absence probably would.

How do I tell you I don't want this? Because I want it more than anything else, but I can't make myself stick around and wait for it to implode.

Some part of me wanted to cling to the possibility that this wasn't going to fall apart. That Connor really did want me, and that—somehow—I was worth the risk and the effort. He'd been called into the CO's office and confronted about it, and he *still* wanted to see me. That had to mean something, right?

He's fishing in a very, very limited pond.

As soon as he finds a more convenient piece of ass, he won't need me.

Or when he realizes his hand gets the job done without all the risk to his job.

It's only a matter of time, Alex. You know it is.

Your own parents won't even put in the work to visit you. Why would he keep doing this indefinitely?

None of that sounded like Connor, but I still couldn't convince myself that those intrusive thoughts were wrong. I hadn't thought Tobias was that way, either.

I sighed and hung my head, exhausted just from listening to my own mind. The stress of sneaking around was miserable enough. Every moment I spent with Connor was worth it... but there was always that doubt hanging in the back of my mind that he was going to bail. And the more time I spent with him, the deeper I got into this, and the more it was going to hurt when he finally called time.

So why wait around for the inevitable? Why keep walking around with the Sword of Damocles tickling the back of my neck when I could just cut my losses and get a jump on getting over him? Because if breaking up with him hurt today, it was just going to hurt more tomorrow, and the next day, and the one after that.

Behind me, the terrace door slid open. My spine prickled at the sound of Connor's bare feet coming across the stone floor.

When he slid his arms around my waist and kissed the side of my neck, my composure nearly snapped. God, I loved him. And I wanted him. And I didn't want to let him go.

"Hey." He kissed behind my ear. "Sorry it took so long."

I forced a smile as I covered his hands with mine. "Don't apologize for talking to your boys."

"I just didn't want to ditch you."

"You didn't. It's all good." I turned around in his embrace and...

Oh, fuck me.

As soon as I looked in his eyes, my mind was made up. Whether I ended up in the other bedroom, another hotel, or on the airport floor, I had to do this now. I couldn't sleep next to him. Not even one more night. I wanted to—God, I wanted to be with him every hour of every night—but it was only going to make the inevitable hurt even more.

Connor's expression shifted to one of concern, and he tilted his head as he studied me. "You okay?" Hands still on my waist, he said, "You look kind of..." He trailed off as if he couldn't find the words.

I dropped my gaze as all the breath rushed out of me. "Just, um... Just thinking. About... About everything we're doing."

His fingers twitched minutely on my sides. The tension in his body was subtle, but I was too dialed in to him not to notice. "What about it?"

I swallowed hard. It took work, but he deserved to have me look him in the eye, so I did. "I don't think I can keep doing this."

Connor's hands lightened ever so slightly, but they didn't lift away. "You don't... What do you mean?"

I shifted my gaze out to the landscape because I was a fucking coward, and because I was trying like hell not to break down. "Look at everything we have to do just to see each other." I gestured at our surroundings. "It was hard enough when we could sneak off to your place, but now..." I chewed my lip as I struggled to hold myself together.

"You don't think it's worth it?" The hurt in his voice was a gut punch. So was the sudden coolness where his hands had been on my waist.

"It's totally worth it." I forced back all those emotions and faced him again, which dragged all of them right back to the surface. The pain in his eyes was just too damn much. Still, I barreled on. "But sooner or later—I mean, is what we're doing really worth everything you're putting on the line? And all the headache you have to deal with just so you can have a few hours or a few days with me?"

He stared at me in obvious disbelief. "Is it worth—of course it is. That's why I'm here."

Frustration tightened my chest. "And what about a few weeks from now? Or a few months from now? How long—" My voice threatened to break, and I had to clear my throat before trying again. "How long are you going to jump through all these hoops just for..." I gestured at myself.

The disbelief in his expression intensified. "As long as I need to. I wouldn't be here if I didn't want to be." He shook his head. "I know it's tough, and it sucks that we have to deal with the Navy's bullshit, but we can make this work if—"

"We can't, Connor," I snapped unsteadily. "We... Do you realize how *long* we have to keep it quiet like this?"

"Until you retire." He tilted his head. "Is that what this is about? Because you're afraid we'll get caught?"

"I'm *not* afraid of us getting caught," I said. "We're—it's not that hard to be careful, you know? Especially since no one knows either of us is into men. No one except my asshole ex. But in order to keep it that way, we have to jump through hoops and strategize every goddamned thing we do or place we go. All so we can fly under everyone's radar." My voice came out brittle and raw as I whispered, "How much more of that are you going to do before you decide I'm not worth it?"

Connor's lips parted, horror replacing the confusion on his face. "What are you talking about? What makes you think I'm going to decide you're not worth it?"

My shoulders sagged as I pushed out a breath. "I know where I stand with people, okay? My own *family* doesn't think seeing me is worth the hassle of flying halfway around the world or even showing up for a damn FaceTime call. The only man who's ever thought I was worth dating just wanted a plaything." I threw up a hand. "I'm not naïve enough to think someone like you—a goddamned *doctor* who's intelligent and just *amazing*—is going to see me as some kind of fucking prize. Especially not when it takes ten times the work to be with me so you don't throw your whole damn life off the rails."

He stared at me as if I'd spoken in another language. Maybe I had.

As ragged and flayed as I felt, I kept going before I lost what little steam I had. "I know hooking up has been fun. And I know we've gotten closer than we thought we would. But... I mean, I'm the first man you've ever been with. What happens when that novelty wears off? What the fuck is left?"

Connor blinked a couple of times, then shook himself. "Okay. Okay, first of all..." He paused as if he needed to collect his thoughts. "Look, the novelty of being with a man wore off a *long* time ago."

I inclined my head, eyeing him dubiously.

He huffed out a sigh. "Jesus Christ. The first night we went to the club in Sevilla? That was all about being a queer man stepping out for the first time. From the minute you offered me a ride back from the train station, it stopped being about that and started being about how much I wanted you."

My tongue stuck to the roof of my mouth.

He wasn't done yet, either. "You're also the first person who's understood me the way you do. I don't have to be embarrassed when my PTSD flares up. I don't have to feel like I'm alone in it because I'm with someone who *gets* it. I wouldn't wish that experience on anyone, but I can't tell you what a relief it's been to be with someone who really understands why I can't let that trauma go."

"Or why that trauma won't let you go," I murmured.

"Exactly. Yeah, I could be with someone who didn't know firsthand what it was like. I was with someone like that for over twenty years. But it's done me more good than I expected to be with someone who *does* get it."

I avoided his gaze. A bitter remark of *"well, at least I'm useful"* wanted to fall off my tongue, but I held it back. He didn't mean it like that, and he didn't deserve me lashing out at him. Not even if it would speed this process along so I could get on with getting over him.

"Also, I don't know if you've noticed," he said softly, "but I've been having an amazing time with you. Not just in bed, but traveling around. Or when you've been able to come to my place, hanging out in the pool or the cabana. Yeah, I'd love for us to be able to go out publicly without anyone noticing or caring, but there's nothing I can do about that. What we can do in the meantime—that's been more than enough for me. Even since we've had to start being more careful after the captain's warning."

I didn't know how to respond to that. Especially because I really, really wanted to believe him, but deep down... I *didn't* believe him. Or at least, I didn't believe everything we did would be enough a couple of months or a year and a half down the line.

"All the precautions we have to take," I whispered. "It's going to be over a year before we can stop any of that." I made myself look in his beautiful dark eyes. "Probably longer so no one realizes we were involved with each other before I retired. *And* I'll be back in the U.S. while you stay here." I had to fight hard to swallow. "How long do you really want to sign up for this shit?"

"As long as it takes," he said without hesitation. "This isn't a fling for me, Alex."

The words brought me up short.

Him too, apparently, because he tensed a little as some color rose in his face, as if he'd shown a card he hadn't intended. "I... maybe that's what it is for you. Maybe that's what we set out to have in the beginning. But... it isn't like that for me. Not anymore." He squared his shoulders. "I don't want this until we get tired of keeping it a secret. I want this. I want *you*. Full stop.

I dropped my gaze so he wouldn't see me blinking away these sudden stupid tears. "Why, though? That's what I don't get." Fuck it—I swiped at my eyes, then met his and stopped caring if he noticed all the emotions I couldn't hide. "I'm just some almost-forty corpsman who's never had a decent relationship, never been worth anyone's effort, and doesn't know what the hell he's going to do when he retires." I threw up my hands and admittedly sounded a bit pathetic as I whispered, "I don't get the appeal."

Connor laughed softly, though I didn't get the impression he was laughing *at* me. More like I'd said something absurd and he couldn't get his head around it. "Alex. Jesus. I..." He raked a hand through his hair and sighed. "Obviously when you look in the mirror, you see a very different person than I do."

I stated at him. "What?"

He shook his head and stepped a little closer. Then he reached for my hand, and I tried not to choke on my emotions as he laced our fingers together. I should've pulled away—should've kept the lines clear—but his touch felt too damn good to let go.

Connor was quiet for a moment. Then he looked me

right in the eyes. "Listen, I loved my ex-wife. I did. And I tried to make it work with her."

I nodded along, not sure where he was going with this. What did his ex-wife or his marriage have to do with this?

He took a deep breath. "At the end of the day, she and I got married because we had to. If not for our son, I highly doubt we ever would've gotten married. But I still loved her, you know? I was still in love with her, and I still thought what she and I had was what every couple had, even if we sped things along because of the baby."

I swallowed, still confused. "O... kay?"

"The way I felt about her and the relationship we had— I always wondered in the back of my mind, 'that's it? *That's* what people fall all over themselves for?' I felt guilty for that, and I felt like a failure because I'd married my high school sweetheart but wasn't as happy as I should've been. I just always thought there was something missing." He glanced down at our hands, then back up at me, and his voice came out a little shakier. "Turns out I was right to question it all, because I never knew what it meant to be in love with someone until you."

My breath stuttered.

"You're not a placeholder for someone I haven't met yet." He squeezed my hand. "You're not a novelty because you're the first man I've ever touched. You're worth everything I'm risking and all the effort and then some, because I have never felt this way about another human being in my life."

I couldn't speak. I couldn't even breathe, but even if I could, I had no idea what to say. Of all the things he could've told me when we faced off like this, that was the last thing I'd expected.

"My sons figured out I was seeing someone because

they saw the look on my face when I was texting you," he continued. "They told me they were glad to see me happy again because they'd always worried I was unhappy with their mom." His shoulders fell as he looked right in my eyes. "Doesn't that tell you something? When my sons suss out that I've got someone, and they realize I'm happier than I ever was when I was married?"

"They... They really picked up on..."

"Yes," he whispered. "And like, you're worried you're not worth it?" He shook his head. "The thing is, I married my ex-wife because I had to. I loved her, but never like this. With you, there's every reason to stay away and only *one* reason I can't do that—because I love you too damn much to let go."

I closed my eyes, not even caring that I squeezed a couple of tears free.

"I mean it." He let go of my hand, and then I was in his arms, feeling like I couldn't breathe but also that I could *finally* breathe as I leaned into him. Stroking my hair, he whispered, "I don't know why anyone would ever make you think you're not worth the effort." He kissed my cheek. "Because I would keep doing this discreetly for a hell of a lot longer than a year a half if that's what it took to be with you."

"Fuck," I breathed. "Connor..."

"If you don't want this," he went on, still holding me tight, "then say the word, and I'll back off. I won't—"

"I do want you. I..." I drew back a little, and when he released me, I met his eyes. "I've never been in love before. But my God, I am now."

His eyebrows rose. "You are?"

I nodded as I tried to collect my emotions. "Maybe

that's what scares me so bad. Being this... I don't know, feeling this much for someone—it's terrifying."

"Yeah, it is. But it isn't like we have to lock anything down or make any commitments." He caressed my cheek. "All I want is to be with you. The rest can shake out over time."

"That's all I want too." I ran my fingers through his hair, my emotions threatening to break just from my own simple, affectionate gesture. "I love you, Connor."

His smile almost brought me to my damn knees. "I love you, too."

Then he drew me in and...

And...

Oh, my God.

I'd kissed plenty of men in my life. I'd always loved kissing. It was sexy as hell. Sometimes making out was even better than sex; what wasn't to love about it?

But never—not once—had the touch of a man's lips brought me home.

Holding Connor close, losing myself in that perfect, familiar kiss, I couldn't begin to name all the emotions crashing through me. I wanted to cry just as much as I wanted to drop to my knees and make him come right here on this terrace. I wanted to laugh. I wanted to pull him into a crushing hug and just let myself feel all of these amazing and excruciating and perfect and confusing things all at once.

How was any of this *real*? How was it that the man I'd fallen for... had also fallen for me? Men didn't fall for me. They didn't hold me like this. They didn't fight for me. They sure as hell didn't kiss me like the taste of my mouth was everything they wanted in the world.

But Connor... did.

He had every reason not to, but here he was, telling me with his deep, gentle kiss everything he'd already spoken out loud. Assuring me that every word of it had been the God's honest truth.

Connor loved me.

It didn't matter how or why—he did.

"I'm sorry," I whispered. "For freaking out and—"

"Don't be." He cupped my chin and pressed a short, sweet kiss to my lips. "I know why you balked. I'm not angry. I just want to be with you."

My eyes stung. How the hell had I ever believed this man didn't feel something for me? "That's all I want too. It just blows my mind that you think I'm worth it."

"Alex. My God." He kissed me again, letting it linger for a moment. "You're worth that and then some."

Fuck. He was going to make me cry for real.

I curved my hand behind his neck and tried like hell to kiss him like he'd kissed me—deeply, passionately, conveying all the love I'd never imagined feeling or deserving.

When we came up for air, he was as breathless as I was, so maybe I'd succeeded.

Panting as he touched his forehead to mine, he asked, "Any chance you want to move this into the bedroom?"

The arousal that zinged through me was intense, but it was the elation and relief that almost brought me to my knees. "Any chance you want to do more than sleep when we get there?"

Connor's grin melted my spine.

And his kiss was yes, yes, fuck yes.

CHAPTER 41

CONNOR

I meant what I'd said to Alex—the novelty of a man's body against mine had faded away a *long* time ago. It was still sexy, of course, but there was no zing of *"oh, wow, this is a man!"*

Tonight, though, Alex's naked body settling on top of mine gave me a rush I couldn't even describe. Not because he was a man—because he was Alex. Because this man I loved more intensely than I'd ever thought possible was here. Kissing me. Holding me. *Hard* for me.

When he went for my neck, I tilted my head back into the pillow and dragged my nails across his shoulders. "Oh my God..."

He shivered in my arms, then murmured, "I'm so sorry, Connor. About earlier. I'm so—"

"Shh, no." I stroked a hand over the shaved back of his head. "Nothing to apologize for now. We're on the same page again. We're both still here. That's all I care about."

He pushed himself up on his arms and gazed down at me, a mix of heat and tears in his eyes. "I'm probably going to be apologizing for a long time. And... second-guessing us. Everything. It's—"

I lifted my head and kissed him softly. "You can second-guess anything you want. I'll just keep reassuring you that I love you and I'm not going anywhere."

Alex's breath was hot and ragged across my lips, and then he was kissing me again, holding me close as if we were making up for lost time. Though he'd been in my life just a handful of weeks, he was a fixture in it now, and after being sure for a moment that I was losing him, having him back felt like my world was shifting back onto its axis. Everything felt right again.

"I love you," he mumbled against my lips. "So damn much."

"I love you too." I cupped his cheek and let a soft kiss linger. "Every night we have to be apart at home, I miss having you next to me." I brushed our lips together. "Sleeping alone just isn't the same."

"Me too." His voice came out thick. "Didn't realize how much I'd gotten into that."

"I know the feeling."

He lifted himself up again, and a sly but cautious grin spread across his lips. "I don't suppose we can share a shower in the morning before we leave. You know, to save butano."

The elation that rippled through me almost made me gasp. "Absolutely. Gotta save butano."

He laughed, and then we were off and kissing again. We shifted around, and when we settled again, I was on top, straddling his narrow thighs as our hard dicks rubbed together.

This was the best. His mouth against mine. His hands

sliding all over my hips, ass, and back. The sounds he made as we made out.

The first time we'd been together, I remembered thinking, *Wow, if there was any doubt I was into men, those doubts are gone.*

Tonight, all I could think was, *There is no one on this earth I want more than I want you.*

I'd never imagined it was possible to love with someone the way I loved Alex, and every time I saw that love looking back at me, it took my damn breath away. He thought he was unworthy of me? I couldn't even explain how much it blew my mind that I was somehow worthy of all that love and desire and affection.

As we kissed and touched, everything ticked up. My heart pounded. Both of us were breathing sharper and faster, and every time one of us brushed the other's dick, we'd both moan and shiver.

I nipped his lower lip, then pushed myself up so I could look in those stunning blue eyes. "Any chance you're in the mood to fuck me? Because I want to ride you just like this."

His helpless whimper had to be the sexiest damn thing I'd ever heard.

I kissed him one more time, then leaned away to get the lube.

Early on, he'd fingered me for ages before sliding in. I hadn't needed that much—I was, after all, experienced with being penetrated—but he loved teasing me and turning me into a trembling, needy mess who was begging for his dick.

Tonight, he just did enough to make sure I was relaxed and there was enough lube. Then I was lowering myself onto him, my vision blurring as my body yielded to his thick cock.

"Fuuuck," I groaned.

Alex whimpered softly. "That's so hot. Jesus." He slid a hand up my abs and chest. "Feeling you like this, and the view. So... So damn hot."

I gazed down at him. "View's amazing from here, too."

He grinned, but then squeezed his eyes shut and arched, lips parted with a soundless cry. Calling this view amazing was an understatement; I could've stared at him all night, watching him come unraveled as I rode him. The twin ecstasy of watching him and feeling him was almost too much to take, and I wanted more; I loved the way he felt as much as I loved watching the bliss and wonder play out on his face.

Time stopped existing. We just moved together. Felt together. Breathed together. I wanted to come, but mostly I wanted to be here in this moment, consumed by this closeness and the heat in his touch.

We're here, and we're not going anywhere, and I will never take a second with you for granted.

After God only knew how long, Alex shakily breathed, "Holy fuck. That feels..." Squeezing his eyes shut, he gripped my hips tighter and arched under me, pushing himself deeper. "Oh my *God.*" The desire—the *need*—in his voice had goose bumps springing up all over my body. My need for some friction was suddenly too much to ignore, and I started pumping myself.

Alex groaned as I clenched around him, and he stared at my hand on my cock with renewed hunger. "Fuck, that's so hot."

"Yeah?" I licked my lips. "You like that?"

"So much." He grabbed my hips and thrust up into me, moaning almost as if he were in pain. "I need to come, baby. I need—fuck, you feel so good. I need..."

"Come," I gritted out. "Come for me."

As if the words had been an incantation, he jerked beneath me and pulled me down onto him, still thrusting up as if he could get even deeper as he cried out with the force of his orgasm. I kept rocking my hips as much as his grip allowed, trying to drive him on, and I kept pumping myself as my own orgasm barreled toward me.

Beneath me, he relaxed with a heavy sigh. "Holy fuck." He stilled my hips, biting his lip and squeezing his eyes shut as he lay there a moment. I got it—he was probably sensitive as all hell from his orgasm.

"Want me to get up?" I asked.

"No." He opened his eyes, then reached for my neck and drew me down, and his breathless kiss almost had me coming between our bodies. When he broke away, he whispered, "Hand me the lube."

I felt around on the sheets, found the bottle, and pressed it into his hand.

"Stay just like that," he whispered as he opened the bottle. "I want to make you come while I'm still in you."

I bit my lip, genuinely surprised I didn't come right then and there, especially when he started pouring the lube on his hand. "Please."

His grin was wicked and his eyes were on fire as he started stroking me with his slick hand. He was still hard inside me, and he rocked his hips just enough to keep up that amazing stimulation. Along with what he was doing with his hand—Jesus Christ.

I leaned back, putting him at a perfect angle against my prostate, and I released a shuddering breath as I matched the movements of his hips.

"Fuck, you're hot," he whispered. "God, yeah, baby."

I squeezed my eyes shut, fucking into his hand and on

his hard dick as I chased my orgasm, and he murmured encouragement and curses as I started to come unraveled.

"Fuck, Connor," he rasped. "You are *so hot*."

And just like that, I was there, shouting my release as I came between our bodies, and Alex kept right on talking, telling me how sexy I was, how much he loved watching me come. How much he loved me.

When I sank down into his arms, I was trembling and out of breath, and nothing had ever felt more like home than this.

How did you ever think I wanted to live without you?

I didn't say that, though. I understood why he'd pulled away. I was just relieved I'd persuaded him that, yes, I was all in. I wanted him, and this, and everything we could be, and this moment—being as close as two people could possibly be—was so perfect I almost cried.

I pulled myself together, though, and we finally managed to separate. We cleaned up, though we'd still need a shower at some point, and returned to bed. It was too hot for covers, but that was fine—the air was comfortable, and Alex's warm skin against mine was never unwelcome.

After a while, he whispered, "Thank you. For not giving up on us."

"Of course." I pressed a kiss to his forehead. "I wasn't going to twist your arm if you really didn't want to be with me, or if you didn't want to take the risk, but calling it quits just felt... wrong."

Alex relaxed more into my embrace. "It did. I was just afraid..." He trailed off into a sigh. "I'm sorry. About everything. I was—"

"You don't need to be sorry." I kissed his forehead again, then his mouth. "I know other people have convinced you you're not worth the effort, but they're wrong. The way I feel for you—that's worth all the work it takes to be with you."

He held me tighter and sniffed.

I closed my eyes and stroked his hair as we lay in silence. He'd spent so much time believing he wasn't worthy. I had every intention of spending even more time—maybe even the rest of my life—showing him he absolutely was.

"I love you," I murmured. "I'm not going anywhere."

Alex took a deep breath, then drew back enough to meet my gaze. His eyes were a little wet, but he was smiling. "I love you, too. I don't know what I did to deserve you, but I'm glad you're too stubborn to let go without a fight."

"You better believe it." I lifted my chin and kissed him lightly. "All the secrecy—that's temporary. We'll get through that. And then..." I grinned. "Then we won't have anything holding us back anymore."

Disbelief sketched across his face, but after a second, he smiled, and he cupped my cheek as he leaned in for another kiss. "I think I can handle that."

"Me too." I glanced down at our sweaty bodies, then met his eyes again. "We should clean up." I slid my hand along his inner thigh. "Join me for a shower?"

Alex grinned. "To conserve butano?"

"Yes, Alex." I rolled my eyes. "To conserve butano."

His mischievous laugh was the most adorable thing I'd ever seen.

And once we got into the shower, we probably burned through most of that cylinder of butano.

Totally worth it.

CHAPTER 42
ALEX

"Okay, I'm confused." Chief Wallace inclined his head and arched an eyebrow. "Didn't you say you were spending your leave on Ibiza?"

"I did." I grinned. "And that's exactly where I went."

"Okay, but..." He gestured wildly at me. "You don't look like someone who spent an hour, let alone four fucking days, on Ibiza."

I looked down at myself, then back at him. "Well, Chief, I don't know about you, but I don't wear my utilities on vacation, and I don't wear my vacation clothes to work, so..."

He rolled his eyes. "Not your clothes, dumbass." He flailed a hand at my face. "No sunburn. No tan. And no green. How, HM1? *How?*"

A laugh tried to bubble up. No, I hadn't gotten much sun and I hadn't done much drinking. The longest, most romantic weekend of my life had left me feeling amazing instead of sun-scorched or hungover like most Americans who came back from Ibiza.

"I don't know, Chief." I flashed a toothy grin. "Maybe some of us can just hold our liquor better than others."

"Oh, shut up." He rolled his eyes. "Just... get to work."

I snickered and got to work. I was glad I wasn't hungover and sunburned all to hell, too, because the day was a busy one. Especially after Chief left for a meeting, I was slammed with patients, paperwork, and emails. Same shit, different day, but at least it kept the time going by. The more I did and the less I sat around being bored, the less likely I was to get lost in thoughts of the man who had rocked—and then become—my world.

Good God, I am stupid for him.
And it feels amazing.

And I felt amazing... right up until I was coming back from lunch and found exactly one person in my waiting area.

"Well, well." Tobias rose, eyeing me with a sardonic grin on his lips. "Enjoy your weekend away?"

I so did not have time for him. I also wasn't about to let him ruin my good mood, so I just smiled. "I had a great time. Guess I should've taken you up on going to Ibiza when we were together. Except..." I quirked my lips and pretended to give it actual thought. "Nah. Pretty sure I wouldn't have enjoyed it nearly as much."

That barb definitely hit what I was aiming for, judging by the tightness of his jaw. "Did Lieutenant Commander Marks enjoy it as much as you did?"

I ignored the reflexive internal panic and stared blankly at him. "Sorry, what?"

He scoffed. "Oh, please. You were there with him."

"Uh, no? I wasn't?" I shook my head. Then I smirked. "I mean, unless he was one of the very long parade of men in that back alley, but I was pretty drunk and only saw their dicks, so..." I shrugged flippantly.

His cheeks colored as his jaw tightened, but only for a

second. With a caustic laugh, he said, "That does sound like you—enough of a slut to keep sucking dick, but not good enough to make anyone stick around to see your face."

Not long ago, that would've hit me in a tender spot, but not this time. I was far too galvanized by the man who'd not only told me he loved me, he'd shown it by taking massive risks and jumping through all kinds of hoops just to be with me.

Your bullshit can't touch me anymore, Tobias.

I laughed. "So I'm a slut who can't keep anyone around, but you're so hung up on me that you can't let me go." I stepped closer and narrowed my eyes. "What does that say about you, sweetheart? Because I doubt it's anything flattering."

I had about two seconds to be intensely proud of finally —fucking *finally*—standing up to him and throwing his own poison back in his face.

Only about two seconds, though.

Because after that time was up, Tobias backhanded me hard enough to send me stumbling into one of the waiting area's chairs. I cracked my shin against the seat, then grabbed the back of the chair for balance.

Tobias's hand materialized on the back of my neck, gripping painfully tight, and he hissed in my ear, "You might want to watch yourself, you worthless fucking whore."

Then he shoved me away, nearly toppling me into another chair, before he stalked out of Radiology.

I turned around and dropped into the chair, my knees shaking and my heart pounding. Somewhere inside, I could feel the hollow spot where that momentary pride had been. Now there was nothing but confusion and fear.

My face throbbed. A faint itch on my upper lip

suggested my nose was bleeding, and when I touched it—yep. Blood.

Holy shit. My head swam with panic and disbelief and...

And I might've had a concussion. He'd hit me hard, and it didn't take much to concuss someone.

I shakily pushed myself to my feet. Given how dizzy that made me—yeah, a concussion was possible. Or it was just an adrenaline crash. Either or.

Rationally, I thought I should call base security. But mostly, I wanted to go down to medical. I didn't even think I was seriously hurt, though I did take concussions seriously. Truth be told, my health wasn't what was screaming at me to get my ass down to medical.

It was the way I couldn't quite catch my breath. The way my vision started tunneling and my heart started pounding. The way an inkling of *"oh fuck, I'm having a heart attack"* crept into the back of my mind, even though on some level, I knew that wasn't what was happening.

I closed my eyes and took a few slow, deep breaths, but it wasn't helping.

The impact to my face hadn't caused any serious injury, but it had stirred up an all too familiar feeling. In my mind, I already heard myself pleading with a corpsmen to let me see one doctor and one doctor only, ideally before this panic attack completely took hold.

Fuck it.

I grabbed a wad of tissues so I wouldn't get any blood—well, any *more* blood—on my utilities. With shaking hands, I texted both Chief and Fox to let them know I needed to take myself down to medical, and that I would explain later.

Then I slapped the *Be Back Later* sign on Radiology's door and took my ass down to medical.

CHAPTER 43

CONNOR

"Keep it iced and elevated," I told the miserable Seabee. "Motrin is your friend, but so are ice and rest. Got it?"

He grumbled something, but nodded. "Yes, sir." He wiped a hand over his face. "Knew I should've stayed away from the damn fish corrals."

I had to fight back a laugh as I entered my recommendations as well as his light duty chit into the computer.

The Romans had built a system of walls that, when the tide went out, trapped fish in small pools to make them easy to catch. Though the Romans were long gone, the corrals remained, and people still used them to this day.

Apparently one of those uses included drunk Seabees challenging each other to run along the walls without falling in. Having walked on the corrals myself when my sons were here, I was well aware of how uneven and treacherous they were; Quinn and I had both nearly turned our ankles, and Savannah had actually fallen off. Fortunately, it had only been a two-foot drop or so into ankle-deep water.

And fortunately, she'd also been sober, unlike my

patient, who'd been shitfaced, running at full speed, and... well, he'd be regretting it for a few days.

"Make sure you keep the stitches clean, too." I gestured at his forearm, which was wrapped and taped. "If you see any signs of infection, come back in immediately."

He nodded. "Yes, sir."

I released him a few minutes later with a handful of instructions, his light duty chit, and a prescription for antibacterial ointment. Technically he could've bought some Neosporin at the Exchange, but I'd been treating service members long enough to know that if I gave them a prescription and ordered them to fill it, they were more likely to obey.

Maybe I should've prescribed "don't get drunk and run on the fish corrals like a dumbass" too.

I chuckled to myself as I stepped out of the room. Yeah, if I could prescribe that, I would—

"Lieutenant Commander?" HM2 Anderson's voice turned my head, and her serious expression made my humorous thoughts vanish. She gestured over her shoulder. "There's a patient who refuses to talk to anyone but you, sir." The urgency in her eyes made me think this wasn't just someone who was pissed off or throwing a fit and demanding to see the highest-ranking doctor on duty. "I wanted to send him to the ER because I think he's having a panic attack, but—"

"What room?"

"Uh. Room nine."

"Thank you."

She nodded sharply, and we headed in opposite directions. My mind raced as I followed the hallway toward the room in question. It wasn't unusual for a patient to demand to see a specific provider, but demanding to see one in the middle of a panic attack? Not good. Not good at all.

At the door of room nine, I stopped and tapped my tablet to pull up the patient's chart.

As soon as the chart appeared on the screen, my heart dropped because it confirmed what I'd already guessed.

Barlow, Alexander. HM1.

Without another thought, I tapped the door, then pushed it open.

And my heart fell even further.

Alex sat on the exam table with an icepack against one side of his face. He had a wad of bloody tissues in his other hand, and some blood had dried on and under his nose.

And he was shaking all over, sweat gleaming on his forehead as he stared at me with panic in his eyes. The second our eyes met, his posture wavered a little and the shaking got even worse, as if he'd been holding back the panic attack through sheer willpower alone, but he was losing that battle now.

"Jesus," I whispered as I shut the door, and I immediately had my arms around him. "What happened?"

He held me fiercely, and the shaking intensified, making it into his voice as he said, "I stood up to Tobias."

"Shit," I breathed. I wanted to ask for details, but first things first, I needed to help him down from the panic attack that was quickly taking over. For a long, long time, I held him, stroking his hair and letting him come back down. That was the shitty thing about episodes like this—no matter how much he fought them, to a certain extent, they just had to run their course.

After several minutes, his breathing started to slow. The shaking eased a little. Still, neither of us said a word. I just stroked his hair and let him breathe.

Eventually, he sighed. "I'm sorry. I... probably could've ridden this out alone, but I—"

"You shouldn't have to," I whispered, and pressed a kiss to his damp forehead.

Another sigh. Another long silence.

"I've been telling myself all this time that Tobias is just a mouth, you know?" Alex drew back and looked up at me. "He was annoying, and he was intimidating. But I wasn't *scared* of him because he'd never laid a hand on me. And now..." He gestured at his face. "Now he has."

My chest ached. "I'm sorry," I whispered, and pulled him in closer.

He leaned into me. "God, I feel like such an idiot. For... just, everything. Letting him be such an asshole for this long, and today—I mean, I'm fucking combat-trained." He sniffed, then dabbed at his bloody nose. "And what do I do? I just... freeze."

"Because this isn't combat. Even if he's been an insufferable dickhole, he's not the kind of enemy we're trained to fight." I smoothed his hair. "I think most people would've frozen in a situation like that."

Alex's shoulders sagged. He didn't look at me, and he didn't speak.

Fuck, it hurt to see him like this. It didn't take much for Tobias to rattle him, but this time, Alex was... God, he was *broken*.

And Tobias...

That fucker had crossed a line. I'd hated him more and more with every card Alex had shown, but this was a bridge too far.

I took a deep breath. "We need to bring in the MAs."

"What?" His head snapped up, eyes wide with horror.

"Are you insane? The CO will find out for sure that we're—"

"I don't care."

His lips parted.

I touched the uninjured side of his face. "You being safe is the most important thing."

"Connor." Alex shook his head. "We'll both be *done* if we get caught. Our careers will be *over*. Mine more than yours."

"I know. And I... I don't know how to get around that. But he can't get away with laying a hand on you."

Alex swallowed.

"We don't have to tell anyone we're dating," I said, keeping my voice down in case someone was outside. "You were assaulted, you came to medical, and you requested me specifically because you trusted me professionally." I paused. "We can't just let this go, Alex. Not after he's put his hands on you."

"We can't just—" Alex swore, his features crumpling. "Oh my God. You're a mandated reporter. I forgot. I—I'm sorry. I... I didn't even think about that. I didn't want to put you in that position and—"

"Alex." I touched his shoulders. "Look at me."

He did, his eyes full of pain, regret, fear, and shame.

"Listen," I whispered. "I'm not required to report it. You're an adult. If you don't want me to say anything, I won't." I hesitated, then softly added, "But I think we should. Because he can't keep getting away with this. Abusing you or anyone else."

He winced, and the shame intensified.

"This isn't on you," I went on. "None of it is on you. It's on *him*. And you knew he was a terrible person, enough that you warned me about him even though I know that conversation was awkward as hell for you. You didn't want him to be a danger to me, and I don't want him to be a danger to you." I touched his uninjured cheek. "You better believe I'm going to the CO because I love you and I won't stand for someone abusing you. But that doesn't mean the CO has to know that. All she has to know is that a patient came to me after being assaulted, I brought in the police, and we're making an official report of it."

Alex swallowed. "But she's going to put the pieces together. Tobias already put the bug in her ear that we're screwing."

"And that's just going to show a pattern of harassment from him," I said. "Especially since as far as the CO knows, I was only having you over to help me with my Spanish."

"But then when I"—Alex pointed at his face—"I refused to talk to anyone but you. Isn't that going to look suspicious?"

Shaking my head, I wrapped my arms around him again. "It's going to look like someone who was rattled and vulnerable reaching out to someone they could trust. The fraternization rules just mean we can't be friends or date. It doesn't mean we can't trust each other to do the right thing in a crisis."

He slowly released a breath.

"Let me call the cops," I pleaded. "We'll be fine. No one has to know about us. But we can't let Tobias get away with assaulting you."

Alex swallowed hard and lowered his gaze. For a long moment, he stared at his hands. At the bloody tissue he was still holding. I had no idea what was going through his mind in that moment. I just hoped he was coming around to my suggestion. Yeah, I was nervous about the CO catching the scent that we really were fraternizing, but that was a risk I was more than willing to take if it meant Tobias got duly hemmed up.

I needed Alex to be onboard before I said anything, though. And even if my responsibility as a mandated reporter did require me to report this, I *wanted* Alex to be onboard. Tobias had already tap-danced all over his boundaries and consent; this *had* to be on Alex's terms.

Finally, he let his shoulders drop as he lifted his gaze to meet mine. His eyes were full of fatigue and resignation.

"Okay," he whispered. "Call the MAs."

CHAPTER 44

ALEX

It took about twenty minutes for the MAs to show up. Not surprising; the hospital was like three blocks away from the security building, and the cops weren't usually that busy on this base.

And once they walked into the exam room—holy shit. Everything moved fast. A pair of cops took me into an empty office to take my statement. Then they left to take Connor's. I'd texted Chief Wallace to let him know what was going on, and he texted me back to say he'd just watched the MAs escort Tobias out of the building in handcuffs.

A JAG officer took me to her office in the admin building, and the afternoon was a flurry of questions, forms, phone calls, and texts. My cheekbone and nose throbbed as I spoke with the attorney, my boss, Connor's supervisor, the security officer, and even the base CO. Everyone but the hospital CO so far, but I was sure I'd end up in front of her before too long.

"Is this standard protocol?" I asked Commander

Whalen, the JAG officer. "Or is everyone on this base just bored?"

She laughed. "A little of both. The bigwigs are getting involved because they're making sure it's not an international incident." She blew out a breath. "I've already taken two calls from the Spanish admiral about it, so..."

"Wow." I paused. "It, um... There could be others."

Whalen cocked a brow.

I shrugged. "Tobias used the same hookup apps I did. And a lot of the people on those apps are local. I know for a fact he was an asshole to at least one local—I just don't know if it crossed any lines, you know?"

She made an unhappy sound but didn't comment on whether that would be an issue for him or for the base. She did take Isidoro's number, though, after I texted him to see if he'd be willing to talk to her. His response loosely translated to, *Fuck yeah, I'll tell her everything.*

I had no idea what would come of that, but either way, Tobias's career with the DoD and his time in Spain were likely over. Good riddance to bad rubbish.

Commander Whalen was finally done with me around 1600, but my day wasn't over yet.

No, I had a summons to the office of Captain Tucker, the hospital CO. The one member of the brass I *hadn't* seen yet today.

And when I walked in—oh, that wasn't good. Connor was already there.

Heart pounding, I took the empty chair beside him in front of her desk.

She peered at both of us for an uncomfortably long moment. Then, "I understand there was an altercation between you and a civilian contractor, HM1."

I nodded. "Yes, ma'am."

"Mmhmm. And afterward, you specifically requested to see Lieutenant Commander Marks"—she gestured at him as if I'd forgotten he was there—"for medical attention."

My face warmed, which made the bruise throb even harder. "Yes, ma'am. I did."

"I see." She took off her glasses and met me with a hard look. "Lieutenant Commander Marks and I have already had a discussion about the two of you fraternizing." Her eyebrow arched. "The man who assaulted you, HM1, has made multiple accusations about you two having a romantic or sexual relationship. And now, when you're assaulted by this individual, you go straight to him and refuse to speak with anyone else." She inclined her head. "I'm sure you can see how this paints a picture I can't ignore."

I swallowed. "Yes, ma'am."

"Mmhmm." She gestured at Connor while keeping her gaze firmly fixed on me. "So I need you to tell me how I should be interpreting that picture."

Blood pounded in my ears. Connor and I had, fortunately, gotten our story straight before he'd gone to make the call to the MAs.

"I understand the accusations, ma'am," I said. "But he's made similar accusations about any man he's ever seen me with. It's... That's just kind of how he is."

"And why is this?"

I hesitated, my stomach winding itself into knots because I hated showing this card. "The man who assaulted me is my ex-boyfriend."

Her eyebrows shot up. "Is that right?"

"Yes, ma'am. We... had a volatile relationship that ended badly. He's been harassing me ever since. Lieutenant Commander Marks..." I paused for a deep breath. "Very few people at this command know that I'm gay. Lieutenant

Commander Marks is the only one I felt safe going to about this because he's the only one who knows I'm queer."

"I see." Captain Tucker's eyes flicked toward Connor. "Is this true?"

"Yes, ma'am," he said. "HM1 Barlow told me about the issues he had with the man in question. When he realized that I'm also queer, he felt comfortable enough to confide in me."

She glanced back and forth between us. "This doesn't help the allegations of the two of you fraternizing." Her expression hardened. "Especially not after you originally told me it was an arrangement for HM1 to help you with your Spanish."

Oh, fuck...

Connor didn't miss a beat. "He did do that. But there was also what I've just described."

She narrowed her eyes. "Yet you withheld that information when we spoke previously."

"That's correct." He didn't sound the least bit contrite, and he gestured at me. "I withheld it because I was not at liberty to disclose HM1's sexuality without his consent."

That actually seemed to hit its mark, and some of the suspicion in her expression ebbed in favor of surprise. She recovered, though the hostility had eased slightly. "There is still the issue of an unacceptable level of familiarity between the two of you. I can't have heterosexual officers and enlisted meeting outside of working hours for—"

"With all due respect, ma'am," Connor broke in evenly, "people like us have *very* few options for community at commands like this. Very little in the way of support from people who understand some of the unique challenges we face." He gestured at me. "While we've kept our relationship professional and appropriate, I did avail myself to

HM1 as a safe confidante when it came to those challenges."

I almost whistled. He wasn't technically lying, apart from keeping our relationship professional and appropriate, but good God, could he smoothly spin the truth into something the Navy would find palatable.

Captain Tucker shifted a little in her chair and studied us, the scrutiny making me twitchy. After a while, her posture relaxed a bit more. "Well, I suppose that's not something I can understand from personal experience, though I do certainly understand the isolation that comes with overseas assignments." She folded her hands on the desk and looked at each of us in turn. "I know for a fact you're not the only LGBT people on this base, though, so I would strongly recommend finding that community within your own ranks. But given the circumstances—given what happened to you today, HM1—I can't begrudge you for finding appropriate support where it's available."

"Thank you, ma'am," I murmured.

She nodded sharply. "But as much as possible going forward, let's keep our extracurricular interactions within the UCMJ's requirements, shall we?"

"Yes, ma'am," we both said.

After that, she dismissed us. The relief had my knees shaking; she *could've* hemmed us up, and I'd worked for homophobic COs who absolutely *would* have. We were lucky to work for a commanding officer who understood we had limited pools for socializing *and* support, even if she did still warn us to find that support among our own.

Given the things she could've done, I'd take it.

Connor and I didn't say a word or even look at each other in the hall. We walked to the elevator in silence, waited for the doors to open, and stepped inside.

Side by side, we both stared up at the numbers as the elevator took us back down to the hospital's ground floor.

The part of me that Tobias had conditioned to believe I was unworthy of the hassle fully expected Connor to announce that this was it. We were done.

The part of me that had seen, time and again, how much Connor genuinely loved me, was wholly unsurprised when he said, "Meet me at my place?"

Heart thumping, gaze still fixed on the numbers, I smiled.

"See you there."

CHAPTER 45

CONNOR

Though it was risky to so brazenly go back to my house with Alex after a second discussion with Captain Tucker, I couldn't talk myself out of it. We took necessary precautions—he came to Sanlúcar in an Uber, and I left the gate unlocked so he could let himself in. No one in my neighborhood knew or cared why he shouldn't be there, and the only person who'd had any interest in spying on us was still in custody in Rota.

It was worth the risk anyway because Alex was still shaken up, and quite frankly, so was I.

As we settled on my couch with a couple of beers, he said, "I can't promise I'm up for much tonight." He gingerly touched the side of his face and winced.

I took his hand and gently pulled it away. "Don't keep poking it. And I don't care if you're not up for anything. I'm just glad you're okay, and you're here."

He searched my eyes, all those insecurities and uncertainties plain to see in his expression. I fucking hated Tobias for that even more than I did for the mark on Alex's face. It had darkened into an impressive bruise, especially over his cheekbone, but it didn't go nearly as deep as all the psychological damage that asshole had done.

I wrapped my arms around him and let him lean the uninjured side of his face against my chest. Stroking his hair, I kissed his forehead. "I'm glad you're okay."

"He didn't hit me *that* hard."

"He still put his hands on you. Enough that he gave you a concussion."

"Eh. It's a mild one." But Alex still curled closer to me and sighed. "Thank you. For having my back."

"Of course." I kissed his temple. "There's nothing in the UCMJ about advocating for my patient when someone assaults him."

"No, but Captain Tucker was already suspicious of us." He found my hand and laced our fingers together on my chest. "It was a risk. I... wasn't even sure I should come to you because I didn't want to put you in that position." Alex swallowed hard. "I just didn't know what else to do."

I stroked my other hand up and down his back. "You can *always* come to me."

"Thanks," he whispered. We were quiet for a little while, and then he said, "The next year or so is going to be long as hell. I can't wait until we don't have to hide anymore."

"Neither can I. And we'll make it. It's kind of like a deployment—it sounds like a long time, and it'll feel like a long time in the moment, but after it's over, it'll seem like it went by in a blink."

Alex sighed again, relaxing against me. "I sure hope so."

"It will. I promise," I said. "Even if it doesn't go by fast, it'll be worth it."

"From your lips to God's ears." He lifted himself up and pressed a long, soft kiss to my lips. "I love you."

"I love you too." I stroked the unbruised side of his face. "I'm not going anywhere."

"Neither am I. And now I'm counting down to retirement even more than I was before I met you."

I chuckled. "Yeah, I bet you are." I paused. "For tonight, should we find something stupid and funny to watch?"

"Definitely." He took his phone out of his pocket. "Why don't I order something from the kebab place?"

"Sounds perfect."

It did, and it was, and I didn't care if spending tonight with Alex in my arms was a bad idea. I wasn't letting him out of my sight right now, and rules be damned, there was no better place for me to sleep than beside Alex.

We wouldn't be able to do this often. Not until he retired. The next year or so would be tough. There was no way around that.

But I knew it would be worth it.

Because in the end, I'd be with the man I loved.

EPILOGUE
ALEX

T*hree years later.*

"Ready for this?" Connor laced his fingers between mine.

"Shouldn't I be asking you that? I'm not the one who's about to watch his son get married."

He smiled, looking a little overwhelmed at the prospect. "Well, just don't judge me if I cry, okay?"

"I won't. I promise."

"Good. And I meant, are you ready to meet my ex-wife?"

My teeth snapped shut. Oh. Right. I was meeting her today, wasn't I? Probably, like, *now*.

"Uh. Yeah." I cleared my throat. "Yeah. Sure." I laughed self-consciously. "Why am I more nervous about meeting her than I was about meeting your parents?"

"You tell me." He elbowed me gently, then kissed my cheek. "I'm sure it's a little weird. Her boyfriend seemed like a nervous wreck over meeting me, though, so maybe it's normal?"

"Works for me." No, I really couldn't explain my nerves, or the ex-wife's boyfriend's nerves. I was just nervous.

I stuck close to Connor today, not wanting to get overwhelmed by the sea of unfamiliar faces. It also didn't hurt that I loved being close to him, especially when we hadn't seen each other in almost three painfully long months. And what could I say? I kind of wanted to thank Quinn and Savannah for asking everyone to come in civilian attire; as hot as Connor was in his dress whites, he was sexy as hell in that tuxedo. Goddamn.

I was introduced to some other family members, and I got hugs from Quinn, Savannah, and Landon. Connor's parents seemed happy to see me again, so maybe I'd made a good impression when we'd spent last Christmas with them. I'd never met a boyfriend's parents before, so what did I know?

And then... there was the ex-wife.

I'd missed the rehearsal dinner because my flight had been delayed, so I hadn't been able to meet her last night, but I was meeting her now. Even before Connor pointed her out, I'd guessed who she was from across the room. She was a little shorter than Connor with blonde hair, and I could suddenly see where Landon had gotten his hazel eyes.

As we approached, she turned, and she put on what seemed like a genuine smile. She and Connor exchanged a quick hug, and then he turned to me. "This my ex-wife, Aimee, and her boyfriend, Paul." Touching my back, he said to them, "This my boyfriend, Alex."

The three of us shook hands.

Aimee smiled. "We've heard a lot about you. The boys and Savannah have had nothing but good things to say."

I laughed nervously. "Okay, good, because I paid them not to repeat the bad stuff."

She and Paul laughed. Beside me, Connor rolled his eyes and shook his head, but he was smiling.

We sat beside Paul and Aimee during the ceremony. That didn't surprise me; Connor and Aimee had been working hard to keep things friendly, especially while their son was planning his wedding. While they weren't BFFs, they got along like two people who met up at their class reunion after a decade or two—they talked comfortably, and after this was over, they'd go back to living their separate lives until there was a reason to cross paths again.

What *did* surprise me was after the ceremony when Quinn and Savannah wanted Paul and me in some of the family pictures. Of course they did several with just Quinn's parents, and Aimee and Connor were amicable enough that it didn't seem awkward or uncomfortable for anyone. I just hadn't expected the couple to ask his parents' respective boyfriends to join in. They even took a few with just Connor and me, and just Aimee and Paul.

The ceremony and photos were a blur of activity, but then we were finally settling in for dinner. Even the bride and groom seemed happy to have a reprieve; I was overwhelmed by everything, so they must've been worn ragged by now.

As we ate dinner at the reception, I stole the opportunity to just enjoy being near Connor. We didn't get to see each other often these days. Not in person, anyway. I'd long since retired, which had taken a ton of pressure off us. Now if we got caught together—oh fucking well.

The complicated part was that when my active duty

ended, so did my assignment to Rota. Shortly after my retirement, I'd moved back to the States.

We'd known that was coming, and we'd been ready for it. We both had plenty of experience living apart from loved ones for months at a time, but I couldn't lie—it was hard. Turned out living on different continents was orders of magnitude harder than sneaking around in the same town. I jumped on military flights as often as I could. Connor took leave back to the States as often as he could. Still, we could only see each other once in a while. We went weeks or even months at a stretch with only FaceTime for company.

Every chance we had, though, we were in the same place. His command knew about us now. Captain Tucker had apparently side-eyed him after she'd run into us during one of my visits, and she'd asked how long this had been going on. He'd blandly answered that it hadn't started until after I was out of the Navy. We'd finally been able to be friends, we'd stayed in contact after I'd left, and one thing had led to another.

Connor had laughed when he'd told me about her skeptical expression. She probably knew, but there was no proof we'd fraternized before I was discharged, so there was nothing she could do. So far, it hadn't had any noticeable effect on his evaluations, and she hadn't said anything further. Likely because by that point, she'd been starting her own retirement process, so her give-a-damn had probably already bailed. Assuming she'd had any left after dealing with the clusterfuck that was getting rid of Tobias.

With Isidoro's statement alongside mine, not to mention several other American and Spanish guys who'd made statements, Tobias's career as a civilian contractor was *over*. Last I heard, he'd moved back to California and was living with family, relying solely on his Navy pension because no one would hire him. Rumor had it he'd also been banned for life from ever setting foot in Spain again. Possibly even the EU. I wasn't sure if that was true or just wild scuttlebutt, but it was satisfying, so I chose to believe it.

Now Tobias was out of the picture. I was out of the Navy. Connor and I were out of the closet. The Navy couldn't touch us.

Unfortunately, more often than not, *we* couldn't touch us either because of that stupid ocean between Europe and North America.

There were times when I was still sure Connor would get tired of it; the exhausting secrecy had given way to frustrating distance, and how long was he going to put up with that just so he could be with me?

The whole situation was further complicated by him making commander. He wasn't required to stay on active duty, but after a promotion, it was generally expected that he'd put in another three years at his new rank. At this point, he might as well try for captain, and if he made captain, stay in and retire at thirty years for the higher pension.

The Navy wasn't going to be out of the picture any time soon.

Every time I saw him or even talked to him online, there was a knot of worry tucked in the back of my mind. Would this be the trip where he finally decided he'd had enough? Was he coming to see me so he could tell me in person that we were done? Was he planning to have me stay with him for a couple of weeks, and then tell me at the airport that this would be the last time? Would *this* FaceTime call be the one where he shook his head and explained that it was just too much? As the months went on, I thought that would get better, but it had only gotten worse. He said he loved me and this was worthwhile. He was only human, though. Sooner or later...

So just do it yourself and stop stressing over it.

I'd always dismissed that thought as soon as it came. Maybe it made me a masochist, but I wanted to enjoy this ride all the way to the end, even if I did worry the whole way.

That worry was present and accounted for tonight, but I was pretty sure he wouldn't dump me at his son's wedding. So, I was just going to enjoy the wedding. Enjoy my boyfriend's company. Watch him smile with all that love and pride as he watched his son getting married.

This didn't have to be forever. Right now, it was perfect.

He introduced you to his parents, idiot.

And his ex-wife.

At his son's wedding.

Maybe he doesn't really have one foot out the door?

There was that. And maybe eventually I'd stop worrying so much. But even after he'd made it clear what lengths he was willing to go just to be with me, it was hard to let go of that lifelong certainty that I wasn't someone people prioritized.

"He could have anyone he wants," I'd said during a recent televisit with my therapist. "It's just hard to imagine someone like him jumping through all these hoops for..." I'd gestured at myself.

"I think the issue here is less about Connor," she'd replied, "and more about your self-esteem and self-worth. People in your life have convinced you you're not worth the effort. The difficult part is learning to listen to people who say you *are* worth it." With a confident smile, she'd added, "That's something we can work on."

We had, too, and we'd made a lot of progress. But what

could I say? Old habits died hard, especially when it came to being with this amazing man. The worry that *this* would be the visit or *that* would be the call where he'd finally drop the hammer was intense, but it was getting better. I suspected that was the result of therapy as well as Connor still showing up, time after time, as if he really did think I was worth it.

Maybe to him, I was.

I took his hand under the table, and he glanced at me. He'd already been smiling, listening to Savannah's maid of honor giving a speech, but the expression turned to one of affection and fondness that I swore was just for me. I returned it, and we both shifted our focus back to the woman with the microphone.

Though there was still a lot of work left to be done, therapy had done a lot to settle me into this relationship. It had also done wonders for my PTSD. My therapist specialized in trauma for veterans and first responders, and over time, we'd worked through some of mine. She'd started me on a medication to help with anxiety, and the difference had been night and day. It wasn't a magic cure-all, but it helped with the nightmares and the occasional panic attack.

I also hadn't realized just how much anxiety I'd had on a daily basis. I'd always thought I was pretty chill and relaxed, but once the meds took hold—holy shit. I suddenly realized how much low-grade anxiety I'd always had in the background, as if I were constantly on edge, waiting for a panic attack to hit me out of nowhere. Between the prescription and the coping methods, not to mention our sessions digging apart my trauma, I was starting to feel close to normal again. Normal enough that I could function, anyway.

She'd also helped me dig into some of the issues with

my family. That was tricky—we had a pretty good relationship, and I'd been afraid to jostle that by bringing up something that was bothering me. With her help, though, I finally had. I'd gently explained to my parents that it hurt how little they came to see me. My sister had been upset over that, demanding to know why I thought they should give up a visit to their grandkids to come see me, even though that wasn't what I'd suggested at all. In her mind, taking the time and spending the money to visit me meant cutting into time and money that would be spent visiting her and her kids. She and I were low-contact for the time being while we slowly ironed that out.

My parents and brother had been more receptive, fortunately, and we were steadily working on things. They'd come to visit me earlier this year—my parents as well as my brother and his large family—and we'd all had a great time. My dad even admitted he regretted not coming to see me in Spain, both because they'd missed the chance to see Spain, and because they'd missed my retirement ceremony.

It was progress. I'd take it. Maybe my sister and I would someday end up back on the same page too.

For the time being, I was living in Corpus Christi. It hadn't been my first pick, but the cost of living was low enough that I could live off my Navy pension while I worked a civilian job at the naval hospital. I was also using the GI Bill to go to school and get all the certifications necessary to work as a radiology tech in the civilian world. After I graduated next month, I could figure out where to live in the long term.

I stole another glance at Connor.

Is it too much to hope that I'll live with you someday?

Maybe. And all those nagging voices jumped in to tell me all the reasons it would never happen, but a calmer voice chimed in to remind me that Connor was here, I was here, and he'd *wanted* me here. That was a good sign, and I should take it as such.

I had to fight a smile as hope pushed some of that habitual worry aside.

Damn. Therapy's working better than I expected.

Life was good, even if the long-distance thing was tough.

That distance wasn't an issue tonight, though. We were both here, and after the wedding was over, we'd have a week to spend together before we had to return to our respective jobs.

Dinner wrapped up, and then there were the usual trappings: cutting the cake, the bouquet and garter tosses, and the first dance. We all laughed when Savannah's bouquet snagged on a chandelier before tumbling into the outstretched arms of one of her bridesmaids. Landon pretended to be exasperated over his girlfriend's excitement that he'd caught the garter, but we all saw right through him. Everyone but her knew by now that he'd already bought a ring.

Connor was all smiles as he watched Quinn dancing with Savannah, and then sharing a dance with his mother. If there was still any animosity between Connor and his ex-wife—and I didn't think there was much, if any—they kept it well beneath the surface. He even mentioned her in his toast, saying how proud they both were of their son and how thrilled they were to be welcoming Savannah into their family. They may not have been post-divorce besties, but as ex-spouses went, they did all right.

And then...

Then Connor took my hand, smiled, and tipped his

head toward the dancefloor. I froze for a second, disbelieving he really wanted to do this.

He wanted to dance with me. At his son's wedding.

I let him lead me out onto the floor, and suddenly there we were, his cheek against mine as we moved with a song I couldn't hear over my racing heart.

"I'm glad you're here," he said. "I know it was a hassle to get here, but... I'm glad you came."

"Me too." I drew back enough to meet his gaze. "I wouldn't have missed it."

His smile was so damn sweet and cute. "Is it just me, or is it still a novelty that we can do things like this openly now?"

I laughed, my head spinning. "No, it's not just you."

"Okay, good. So I'm not crazy."

"I didn't say that."

Connor rolled his eyes, then kissed me lightly before resting his cheek against mine again. I sighed happily and enjoyed the moment. Holding him. Touching him. Being out in public with him.

Being so ridiculously in love with him.

And just like I had so many times over the past three years, I sent up a little prayer that this really did have some staying power.

Is it too much to ask for this to be forever?

As more guests crowded onto the dancefloor and the music turned to something faster and louder, Connor leaned in and whispered, "I could stand to get away from all this noise for a bit. How about you?"

"Yes. Definitely."

We let the bride and groom know we were stepping out for a few minutes, and then we slipped out of the ballroom and onto the walk along the James River. As soon as we were outside, we both released long breaths. I didn't need to ask if he was as relieved as I was, and I couldn't even say for sure if this was our PTSD or if the noise and activity would've been overwhelming anyway.

Whatever. Being out here was a relief. That was all that mattered.

Across the water, the Norfolk waterfront was lit up and buzzing with Saturday night activity. Here in Portsmouth, things were quieter aside from the wedding reception. My ears were still ringing a little, but this helped. So did the cool breeze; I hadn't even realized how stuffy the reception hall had gotten.

"Oh, man." I exhaled. "It's so nice out here."

"Right? I was having a blast, but..." He waved at the reception hall. "I needed some air."

"Same."

He gently bumped his shoulder against mine. "And a little one-on-one time with you."

I laughed, bumping him back. "So the one-on-one time we had last night and this morning didn't count?"

"I didn't say that." He grinned. "I'm going easy on the champagne tonight because I'm hoping there'll be *more* of that one-on-one time when we get back."

I shivered. Seeing each other as rarely as we did, we were almost insatiable in the bedroom whenever we were in the same place. I loved it. "Guess I should go easy on the champagne, too."

"If you want to get railed in that shower again..."

I bit my lip. "You're such a tease."

"Nah." He drew me closer, and just before he kissed my cheek, murmured, "Teases don't follow through."

"Goddamn..."

He laughed wickedly. Then he found my mouth, and

oh, my God, I was never going to get tired of the way he kissed. I wrapped my arms around him, and we just stole that long, quiet moment for a gentle kiss. It was still novel, being able to do this out in public, just like when we'd danced inside. We still had to be as cautious as any queer men were in public places, but we didn't have to worry any longer about the Navy catching us. In fact, we were in full view of at least two ships in dry dock across the river. I doubted anyone aboard could see us, or would care if they did, but I still enjoyed the lack of worry on our part.

When Connor broke the kiss, he held my gaze for a moment. Then he dropped his and shifted it toward the water, some unspoken thought in his eyes.

"Hey." I put my hands on his waist. "What's wrong?"

"Nothing. Nothing's wrong. I..." He licked his lips. Then he gently took my hand off his waist and laced our fingers together. "I, um... I wanted to ask—are things still going good with your therapist?"

That was what he wanted to talk about right now?

"Um. Yeah. She's..." I pushed out a breath. "She's been amazing."

"Good. Good, I'm glad." He gazed out at the water with a thoughtful expression I couldn't quite read. Then, speaking softly, he asked, "Does she do televisits regularly? Or just when you're out of town?"

"What do you mean?"

"Like if you didn't stay in Corpus Christi, could you still see her?" He turned to me. "Virtually?"

"I... Yeah, I think so? She said she has patients who are fully virtual for various reasons." I tilted my head. "Why?"

He swallowed. "Because I don't want to ask you to give up your therapist. She's obviously been great for you, and I wouldn't want to take that away." He looked in my eyes. "But would televisits with her be enough?"

Puzzled, I half-shrugged. "I don't see why not. But... why?"

"I was just thinking..." He took a deep breath and gripped my hand a little tighter. "It would be a lot harder to see her in person if you came to Spain with me."

I blinked. "If I came to... Like if I *moved* to Spain?"

He nodded. "And wherever the Navy sends me next."

I stared at him. "But... I mean, I can only—I can't get a visa and the Navy won't move me or my stuff unless we're... married."

My own words made my heart stop.

So did the way he smiled. "I know—that was my next question."

"Your..." My jaw went slack. "Are you..."

"Yes. I am. I miss you. And I love you. And I want us to be together—full stop." Still gripping my hand, still holding my gaze, he went to one knee. "Will you marry me, Alex?"

For a couple of heartbeats, I couldn't even breathe. Was this real?

But the earnestness shining those beautiful dark eyes said that, yes, this was real. Connor really was proposing to me.

I managed a quiet laugh as my own eyes welled up, and I nodded. "Are you fucking kidding me? Of course I will."

The way he smiled—oh God. This really *was* real, wasn't it?

Then he was on his feet and his hands were on my neck, and he pressed the softest, most tender kiss to my lips, and I almost cried.

He really wanted this. All that sleep I'd lost, thinking

he'd eventually decide I wasn't worth the effort, and now... this.

He wanted a future. With me. He wanted *forever* with me.

I touched my forehead to his. "I love you, baby."

"I love you too." He brushed his lips across mine. "And I don't care if we do a big shindig like Quinn and Savannah, or if we do it at a courthouse on a Tuesday afternoon." He ran his thumb across my cheekbone. "I just want you as my husband, and I want you on the same side of the ocean as me."

"Me too," I whispered shakily. "And I don't care about the venue either. But... the sooner the better?"

I had a split second to irrationally worry that would put him off, but his eyes lit up and he kissed me again. "How long are you in town?"

"Six days."

"Think that's enough time?"

Holy shit. Were we... Was he...

"You really want to do this?" I drew back and met his sparkling eyes. "Get married like... *now?*"

"I'm in if you are." He sobered a little and glanced toward the reception we'd left. "Or... maybe not quite that soon. I don't want to overshadow the kids."

"No, of course not. But soon?"

"As soon as possible. We can always do something quick —maybe in Gibraltar when you come visit after you graduate?"

My heart fluttered. "Yeah. Yeah, let's do that! Then we can have a reception or something later. So the family can be there."

His smile was the best thing in the world. I didn't give a damn if we did this next week or next year. Connor wanted to marry me. He wanted this for real. That was all I cared about.

"Obviously we'll keep this between us for now." He tilted his head toward the reception. "Since it's their day."

"Of course." I grinned. "We've kept secrets before, so..."

His quiet laugh lit up the whole night. "Yeah, but this one won't be quite such a disaster if it comes out." He half-shrugged. "I just don't want to steal the kids' spotlight."

"No, definitely not."

His laugh turned to a soft smile as he caressed my cheek. "I wasn't even going to do it tonight—I left your ring in the room—but... I don't know." He kissed me gently. "Just didn't want to wait any longer."

Wrapping my arms around his neck. I said, "I think we've both waited long enough."

"Yeah." He pulled me in close. "I think we have."

Then his lips were on mine, and my entire world had never been more perfect than it was in this moment.

Somehow, this man had thought I was worth all the hassle and secrecy of our first year and a half, and the headache of a long-distance relationship ever since. Somehow, we'd weathered all of that, and now he wanted me with him forever.

Maybe it had taken us longer than most to find each other.

But as I held my new fiancé close beside the glittering river, a future laid out in front of us against all odds...

I knew without a doubt that this man had been worth the wait.

For more books by L.A. Witt,

or to subscribe to my newsletter, please visit

http://www.gallagherwitt.com

Newsletter perks:

- Exclusive discounts & giveaways
- Access to ARCs
- All the latest news about pre-orders, collaborations, and more!

Romance * Suspense

Contemporary * Historical * Sports * Military

Romances by L.A. Witt

Rookie Mistake (written with Anna Zabo)

Scoreless Game (written with Anna Zabo)

The Gentlemen of the Emerald City Series

The Anchor Point Series

The Husband Gambit

Name From a Hat Trick

After December

Brick Walls

Interference

Leave

Romantic Suspense by L.A. Witt

The Hitman vs. Hitman Series (written with Cari Z)

The Bad Behavior Series (written with Cari Z)

The Venetian and the Rum Runner

If The Seas Catch Fire

The Truth in My Lies

...and many, *many* more!

L.A. WITT

L.A. Witt is a romance and suspense author who has at last given up the exciting nomadic lifestyle of the military spouse (read: her husband finally retired). She now resides in Pittsburgh, where the potholes are determined to eat her car and her cats are endlessly taunted by a disrespectful squirrel named Moose. In her spare time, she can be found painting in her art room or destroying her voice at a Pittsburgh Penguins game.

Website: www.gallagherwitt.com
  Email: gallagherwitt@gmail.com
  Twitter, Instagram, & Threads: @GallagherWitt

Printed in Great Britain
by Amazon